Brooklyn Roses
a novel

Sequel to *The El* & *The Bells of Brooklyn*
Final Installment in *The El* Trilogy

by Catherine Gigante-Brown

Cover & Interior design by Vinnie Corbo
Author photo by Katy Clements

Published by Volossal Publishing
www.volossal.com

Copyright © 2020
ISBN 978-0-9996916-9-4

TABLE OF CONTENTS

To Peter, who is everything.

CHAPTER ONE

About Roses

There are thousands of different kinds of roses. They are a hardy, forgiving sort of flower and grow in all types of soil: sandy, arid, loamy, wet, and everything in between. Roses seem to flourish anywhere and everywhere, even in the most unlikely of places. From sunny front gardens to shady backyards, up ancient trellises, through wrought iron fences and barbed wire, their stems as thick as saplings. Roses thrive just as well in congested, urban locales as they do in peaceful country lanes.

Their petals are generally a soft velvet no matter the shade and their colors are wildly variant—from snow white to blood red to sky blue and almost black, as well as sunny yellows, explosive corals and more.

All gardeners tend to think that their roses are the finest, the most beautiful, the most fragrant. And this might very well be true because their roses are uniquely theirs, much like their own children are uniquely theirs.

It's been said that the borough of Brooklyn in the city of New York produces the loveliest roses of all, and this might also be true. But it might also be terribly biased. And in Brooklyn, in the neighborhood known as Borough Park, no roses were more stunning than those grown by the Paradiso Family. Margarita "Bridget" Virgilio Musto Paradiso's roses, to be exact. Even after the dear old girl passed away, Bridget's roses continued to thrive. Some might go as far to say that the blossoms were even more brilliant after her death.

Roses had always been a large part of life at the Paradiso place. First, the flowers themselves, which were revered in a type of adulation—for their resilience, their beauty and their otherworldly scent. Then, there were the people in the family who were named for that flower, of which there were several. Namely Bridget's daughter Rosanna, her grandson David Rosario and her granddaughter Chiara Rose.

So spins the circle of Paradiso roses. It has been going strong four generations and it will continue to flourish for years to come, after the last Paradiso has gone. Because Brooklyn Roses are among the very best.

CHAPTER TWO

American Beauty

Tiger called his wife Teresa his "American Beauty," just like the rose. Although they had been married for more than a decade, she still blushed whenever he called her this. The years, and bearing one child, had added a few extra pounds to Teresa's once-slender frame. "But in all the right places," Tiger was quick to remind her, catching his bride around the middle as she ironed or cooked a sauce on the stove. Teresa didn't believe him, which was a shame, for she was still as lovely as ever.

Even when they had first started keeping company, Teresa fit seamlessly into Tiger's family, perhaps because his family was so much like her own. Teresa, known to all as "Terry," felt closer to Tiger's sister Angela than she did to her own sister. But who could blame Terry? For after just a few moments in the presence of Terry's sister Claire's permanently-furrowed brow and razor-sharp tongue, anyone who met her was certain she was one of the most unpleasant people they'd ever met.

"Such a pretty name, such an ugly personality," was a common observation. Terry would smile knowingly and say not a word, even when confronted with a query like: "Are you sure you have the same parents?" Yes, Terry was sure.

A different woman in the Paradiso Family hosted Sunday dinner each week—even Astrid, a self-admitted horrendous cook. To the family's relief, Astrid's husband Al took over in the kitchen whenever Astrid's turn rolled around. His Barese momma had taught him well.

This revolving Sunday supper schedule was an excellent arrangement because someone's turn to host came every six weeks, so no one felt overwhelmed or burdened with cooking for a crowd too often.

This particular Sunday was Terry Martino's turn to make supper. Although Terry was a fine cook plus thoroughly enjoyed having Corsos, O'Learys, Thomases and an assortment of others crowding her table, she was always nervous about making the meal. "What if I overdo the lamb?" or "What if my spaghetti sauce is bitter?" she would worry aloud to Tiger in the dark in bed the night before she made a family feast.

"It never is," he would assure her, a tired amusement in his voice. "Why should it happen this time?"

"Anything is possible," Terry would sigh.

"Yes," Tiger would concede. "Anything *is* possible. But not that."

Lying beside his wife, Tiger had to admit that life was better than he ever could have imagined, emerging a rootless serviceman from the Second World War, not really sure where he belonged. His restaurant, Feel Good Food, had taken off like wildfire, and succeeded in cementing the already-strong friendship between Tiger and his business partner George Thomas. Their culinary cultures blurred, so that George now made steak *pizzaiola* better than the Italians on Forty-Seventh Street did. And not only did Tiger and George's bond grow but their business did also. There was a second outpost of Feel Good Food in George's native Jersey City and talk of opening another somewhere in the tri-state area.

Tiger and Terry would drift off to sleep, he dreamlessly and Terry, to visions of mincing garlic, chopping parsley and marinating pork. The next morning, she would wake raring to go, despite her nocturnal prepping. She would rise with the sun, rested and refreshed, ready to slice and dice. Terry would set the coffee pot on the burner and get to work while Tiger and Chiara Rose were still asleep. Though she adored her husband and daughter, Terry cherished her quiet time alone in the kitchen. While some women deemed cooking a chore, Terry wasn't one of them. She considered feeding the people she loved a privilege.

Terry poured herself a strong cup of coffee, reveling in the nutty scent drifting up from the aluminum pot. She swirled in a dab of cream from the glass Borden's bottle and took a sip. Pure ambrosia. To Terry, there was nothing better than that first swallow of coffee in the morning. Except perhaps the taste of a good-morning kiss on her lips. Terry pushed all thoughts of romance from her mind and addressed the matters at hand, namely making a *marinara* sauce for the eggplant *parmigiana*.

And as she cooked, Terry remembered. This time, she recalled how she and Tiger had announced their engagement less than a year after his grandparents Bridget and Poppa had passed. The family hadn't had the inclination to clear out the elder Paradisos' apartment before then. But when the couple revealed their June wedding date, the family thought it was high time to empty Bridget and Poppa's place so the soon-to-be newlyweds could occupy it. The ground-floor apartment had been closed up for almost a year, since the spring of 1946. The time was ripe to move on and fill the rooms with new life.

Tiger's mother Rose told Terry what had transpired before she and and Tiger arrived, how Rose and her three sisters Astrid, Camille and Jo arranged to meet at the downstairs landing to purge the apartment that bright, early April morning in 1947. Rose made the trek from her apartment directly upstairs and unlocked the door that had never been locked when her parents were alive. The quartet of Paradiso Sisters entered the musty, closed space with trepidation. The railroad rooms were unaltered, just the way each of the siblings remembered them. Yet in another sense, they were oddly changed, drained of life. There was no fragrance of food on the burners, no sounds of The Ink Spots wafting in from the parlor Victrola, singing plaintively, *"If I didn't care..."*

"Let's get some air into this place," Jo suggested. Without waiting for her sisters' response, she began throwing open the parlor windows that faced the wooden-slatted front porch. Her cheeks were slightly flushed, her hair, partially covered with a kerchief, was still a warm chestnut thanks to the bottle of Miss Clairol her hairdresser Lisa LoBue applied liberally monthly.

Jo's sisters followed suit, Rose heading to the kitchen which was situated at the rear of the house, Camille going to the bedroom where her parents had died in their sleep so many months earlier. Astrid, as was her custom, did nothing. She merely stood in the center of the parlor floor, hands on her hips and shouted to Rose from several rooms away, "I can't believe this place has been shut up like a mausoleum for so long."

"What's not to believe?" Camille shot back. "We had no reason to come down here until now."

"I didn't have the heart," Rose admitted, plopping down onto the threadbare sofa.

"Me neither," Jo said, sitting beside Rose and patting her knee in an effort comfort her.

Rose bit her lower lip and sighed deeply. "Every time I thought of airing out the place, I remembered how I found them."

Camille smoothed down Rose's hair, as one might do to a distressed child. "But now we have a reason to be here," Camille smiled sadly. "Getting the apartment spruced up for the kids."

Astrid huffed at her sisters' sentimentality and threw open the china closet doors, setting to work in a rare burst of productivity. The others busied themselves with the carpet cleaner, the feather duster and a selection of rags and mops. They concentrated on one room at a time, conferring on what to keep, what to offer to friends and what to donate to the Sally (their affectionate name for the Salvation Army) or to Saint Vinnie (shorthand for the Saint Vincent de Paul Society).

"Let's split the *chachkas* between us," said Jo, who had quite the *chachka* collection in her own curio cabinet.

"I can't bear the thought of them going to strangers," Camille agreed.

"We bought most of them for Poppa and Momma on our travels," Rose reminded them, "so it makes sense we take them." There was the cast iron Amish couple from Pennsylvania Dutch Country and the blown-glass rose from the little man in Webatuck Craft Village. There was the motherly figurine made from Mississippi mud. There was...

"You mean those dusty old things?" Astrid scoffed.

"Yes, those dusty old things," Rose retorted. "You're a dusty old thing yourself, Maggie."

"It's Astrid!" her sister snapped. "And it's been Astrid for..."

Astrid stopped herself. She didn't want to admit how old she was, though she was aging finely, like a good wine. "At least thirty years, huh, sis?" Jo taunted, finishing the sentence for her. Astrid refused to respond.

Camille said, "You forget that we know exactly how old you are."

"And I you," Astrid blustered. "But I'll always be the youngest."

"But you'll always look the oldest," Jo giggled.

And so, the packing away of two long, full lives progressed, slowly and painfully. It was a morning of concessions, tender memories, soft laughter and yes, even a few tears. As Bridget and Poppa's possessions were cleared, it was as though their lives were being erased, cancelled out somehow. Would all evidence of them disappear within the span of a few hours? Physical evidence, perhaps, but not the indelible mark the pair had made upon so many lives.

After several hours, the Paradiso Sisters' husbands showed up with brushes, drop cloths and buckets of paint. They moved the heavy, old furniture to the center of each room, then rolled up their sleeves and dove in. Astrid's beau Al Dursi proved to be an excellent painter with a steady hand

and a patient nature. This perhaps explained why Al was still keeping company with the sour-tempered Astrid after a handful of years. She was a doozy who poked at her family's last nerve, but Al seemed immune. The poor fool was in love with her.

Where Al was perfect for finessing the detailed work like moldings and wainscoting, Rose's husband Sully was more suited for the grunt work, tackling the ceilings with a stick roller and gusto. Jo's Harry was well-matched for doing the walls with a short roller, just so long as he didn't have to climb a ladder. "On account of my bum wheel," Harry explained, though he didn't have to say this; everyone knew he'd lost part of his left leg in the Second World War. And Camille's hubby John was happy to do anything that was asked of him—and do it cheerfully.

Promptly at noon, Rose's daughter Angela arrived from next door with a satchel full of egg salad sandwiches and the twins in their pram. At just over a year old, they had almost outgrown the big, English-style carriage and would soon be steady enough to walk on their own without assistance. "You didn't have to bring us lunch…your hands are full with those two," Rose laughed, but was inwardly touched by her daughter's kind gesture. "Especially with Augie working at the Loew's 46th today." Rose knew that Saturday was the movie house's busiest day and Augie, who now owned the theatre, always went in on Saturdays, at least for a couple of hours.

"Don't be silly, Ma," Angela said. "I'm glad to finally be done with all of those colored Easter eggs." She placed a waxed-paper wrapped sandwich in front of each chair at Bridget's long dining room table. They all sat and ate while David and Beth slept blissfully in their pram, which two of the men had carried up from the pavement.

Jo took a bite of her egg salad on rye and groaned with delight. "Just like mamma used to make it," she noted. "With a touch of chopped onion and diced pimento olives."

"And a splash of mustard in the mayo to give it some zing," Camille added wistfully.

When the twins awoke, the cleanup crew took rotations at jiggling Beth and David on their knees as they ate, the two wee ones happily gnawing on any knuckle within reach to ease their teethers' gums. The toddlers sampled fingertip portions of egg salad, shuddering first at the sharpness of the onion, then getting accustomed to the taste and clamoring for more.

During the second shift, the bride and groom-to-be arrived. "We had to pick out the menu at Andre's Catering this morning," Tiger explained.

"Then I had a fitting," his bashful partner apologized. There was no doubt that Terry would make a lovely bride and a fine wife, and that Tiger would prove to be a caring husband. Though it had just opened the previous year, his and George's Feel Good Food was already showing a handy profit. For the time being, Terry planned to continue working at Prudential Insurance a few blocks away, until she was expecting, God willing. It would be helpful to have two incomes and Terry was very fond of her boss Helen Pateau and the other girls in the office, Anna and Grace.

To everyone's surprise—and delight—Terry said that she wanted to keep much of Bridget and Poppa's furniture. Without a doubt, the huge, many-leafed dining room table would stay. Its battle scars were mementos of dozens of exuberant family gatherings. The hefty mahogany furniture reminded Terry of her own grandparents' pieces, which had been sent by steamship from Calabria in Southern Italy. "It's good stuff, well made," Terry told them. "We'd be honored to have them, if you'll let us."

"They'll look brand new with some lemon oil and elbow grease," Rose beamed, happy that her parents' prized possessions would be treasured and put to use.

"Antiques are all the rage," Astrid added.

To which Terry shrugged. "I just like the idea of keeping them. Family heirlooms. Carrying on tradition."

Terry and Tiger examined the rooms with careful consideration, not a touch of greed or covetousness, whispering quietly to each other as they went. Together, they decided to keep the sturdy dark wood bedframe but to get a spring mattress to replace Poppa and Bridget's sagging featherbed. The well-worn sofa would go but the marble-topped coffee table and end tables with the intricately-carved wooden legs would stay. The Martinos' new home would be a beautiful blend of old and new, tradition and trendy, and it would be a joyful place.

In Bridget's kitchen, Terry marveled at the gleaming, well-cared-for appliances—the Hotpoint stove, the Waring blender, the Toastmaster toaster, whose sides still shone bright as a mirror. 'I bet hundreds of wonderful meals were made here,' Terry thought, and announced that she wanted to keep all of the appliances. She aimed to preserve what pieces of the Paradiso matriarch remained in the kitchen. "It feels good in this place," Terry told Tiger. "Warm, full of love."

"I know what you mean," he admitted. "But let's upgrade the fridge. It was on its last leg when they were alive." To this, Terry agreed. There was plenty of Bridget that endured in the kitchen, even minus the Frigidaire.

Terry continued to open kitchen counter drawers and pantry doors. She fingered the worn but still sharp Ekco potato peeler, the tent-style cheese grater, the aluminum colander with tiny stars cut into its belly. "I'd like to keep these too," she said. "They're like new."

The handful of times Terry had met Tiger's grandmother Bridget—or "Dear Old Girl" as her husband Michele Archangelo (a.k.a. "Mike") fondly called her—she'd liked the woman immensely. And the feeling was mutual. Bridget had told her grandson that Terry was "good people," a huge compliment in Bridget's book. Indeed, there was also a warm familiarity Terry saw in Bridget, a parallel to the strong, stalwart, loving women in Terry's own family. (Except for her sister Claire!) Bridget, in turn, felt the same kindred spirit in Terry.

There was no need for a bridal shower wishing well filled with kitchen doodads that Terry would hardly use because everything she could possibly need was already in these drawers. Besides, less than two years after the end of the War, many were still struggling. Terry's mother had collected trousseau items—prettily-embroidered sheets and towels—since Terry was a girl. What more did she need than a few things here and there?

When Terry told this to her future mother-in-law and the Aunties, Tiger and Rose exchanged silent smiles. "That one's definitely a keeper," she whispered to her son as Terry went off to change into a housedress and join the others in cleaning. But Tiger's fiancée heard and blushed bright pink as she made her way to the powder room with her work duds.

And now, a dozen years later, Terry still felt Bridget's presence in the kitchen, in the whole apartment, for that matter. Not in an odd, mischievous *The Ghost and Mrs. Muir* way, but in a benevolent watchfulness. It was as though Bridget were silently overseeing the Sunday sauce as it simmered on the stove. As if she were guarding Chiara Rose whenever the girl carefully chopped onions or olives at her mother's side. As if Bridget were keeping a lookout over the girl as she played with her baby dolls on the carpet in the exact spot that had once held "Poppa's chair." Terry sensed his beneficent presence too, but mostly Bridget's. And it felt comforting, protective.

Smiling softly to herself as she minced garlic at the kitchen table, Terry again reflected upon that long-ago afternoon when she rolled up her sleeves and helped prepare the downstairs apartment alongside Tiger's parents, aunts and uncles. It was the first time Terry had felt that she truly belonged to this family, but certainly not the last. In fact, Terry still felt this way, even more so. She was thankful her and Tiger's turn to host Sunday dinner fell just before Sully and Rose's twenty-first wedding anniversary. Yes, Terry would make them all proud—and full.

She felt a presence behind her, then warm breath on her neck. "Did I wake you banging the pots and pans, Chi?" Terry asked her daughter, who took a seat at the table beside her.

Chiara Rose shook her head. "I was already awake."

"Reading?" Terry wondered.

The girl nodded. "I wanted to see what happened to the pony."

Terry slipped the mound of garlic to the side of the cutting board, then began peeling the onion. "And what happened to the pony?" Terry asked, although she already knew its fate.

Chiara Rose shrugged. Her hair, black as shoe polish, was worn in a bowl cut and jostled like ebony fringe when she moved her head. She eased herself onto Terry's lap and found the spot beneath her mother's chin where her head fit perfectly, like it belonged there. "I don't want to ruin it for you but it wasn't a good book for horses," the girl told her.

"I know what happens," Terry said, massaging her daughter's head with her cheek. "I read *The Red Pony* when I was your age. It's a sad story but a first-rate one."

Chiara Rose looked at Terry. Her eyes were like big, brown buttons. "Why are the best ones always so sad?" she asked.

Now it was Terry's turn to shrug. "Maybe because that's the way life is—a good life is also a little sad." Terry glanced at the stove. Her gravy was bubbling away. "Feel like giving it a stir?" she asked her daughter. "We don't want it to stick, do we? Then it gets bitter."

"Bitter like life, Poppa Sully says," Chiara told her mother sagely. The girl stepped up and grabbed the wooden spoon from the canister. It was a vintage utensil carved by either Tiger or his brother Stan in shop class years earlier but no one could remember who the artisan was. Chiara Rose stirred.

Terry laughed. "That's one way of looking at it," she conceded. "But I prefer to focus on the sweet." Terry kissed the side of her daughter's head, which smelled of Johnson's Baby Shampoo. "Besides, it's a special dinner."

Standing beside her daughter, Terry slipped the now-chopped onion into the warmed cast iron frying pan then added a touch more olive oil. The strong aroma of the oil and onions filled Terry with a wave of nausea which soon passed. Could it be that she was in the family way? Terry's cycle had never been regular and she couldn't remember the last time she'd had her "friend." For a moment, she thought of how she couldn't tolerate the smell of olive oil when she was expecting Chiara Rose but immediately pushed the thought from her mind. There was too much to be done.

"So, why is this supper so special?" the girl wondered.

"We're celebrating Nana Rose and Poppa Sully's anniversary, remember?"

"And what else?" Chiara Rose pressed.

"Nothing else, not yet. You'll have to wait until Friday for your party, until your actual birthday." Terry nudged her daughter with her hip. She knew how the girl hated waiting, for anything.

"That's not fair," Chiara Rose moaned in mock drama. "Nana and Poppa don't have to wait…"

"Because they don't want to steal your sunshine," Terry explained patiently. "Even though you stole theirs. I mean, being born on their anniversary and all."

"I couldn't think of a nicer present," said Rose. Terry smiled at her mother-in-law while Chiara ran into Rose's arms, careful to set the stirring spoon down on the pineapple-shaped spoon rest first.

The doors in the Sullivan/Martino House were always open so they could come and go freely between apartments, just as they had done when Poppa and Bridget were alive. "Can I help?" Rose asked her daughter-in-law, even though she knew the answer.

"Not this week," Terry told her. "It's your party. But please, help yourself to a cup of tea. The pot's still warm."

On the kitchen table waited Pip's Pot, with its two gossiping hens painted on the front. Terry had already prepared the tea, knowing Rose would soon arrive. Rose poured a cup for herself as well as for her daughter-in-law. Though Terry preferred coffee, she also enjoyed sharing a cupper with Rose, so she switched beverages whenever her mother-in-law came downstairs.

Next, Rose took her granddaughter's mug from the shelf above the sink, the one with Peter Rabbit on its side. This time, Chiara Rose didn't complain that it was a "baby's cup," for she relished the way her grandmother made her tea—with a splash of cream and a drizzle of honey. Plus, Chiara would be ten in a few days and no one would dare dispute the fact that she was practically grown up and not a baby anymore.

Tiger emerged from the bedroom already dressed. "Here are my three American Beauty roses, all in the same place," he said. Tiger kissed each of them on the cheek and poured himself a cup of tea from Pip's seemingly endless pot. It did Tiger's heart good to see all three of "his gals" together, his mother enjoying a generous square of Ebinger's crumb cake while his wife and daughter worked side by side at the Hotpoint, Terry sautéing the escarole in onions and garlic and Chiara Rose methodically stirring the gravy as though it might explode if she didn't.

"Can you spare my American Beauty for a few minutes," he asked. "I need her for a special chore."

Tiger and his daughter, still in her plaid pajamas and bedroom slippers, padded down the front steps, hand in hand. He took a small pair of pruning shears from his jacket's breast pocket. "I'd like you to pick the flowers for the table," he told Chiara. "You always pick the best ones."

She nodded seriously. "Maybe it's because of my name." Chiara approached Bridget's rosebush, which scaled an eight-foot trellis and wrapped itself around the nearest porch pillar. Although it was early October, the last of the summer roses brazenly bloomed. A large bouquet of the flowers would be the perfect addition to the anniversary dinner table.

"It will bring a piece of the Dear Old Girl from the outside to the inside," Tiger explained.

"I wish I had known her," Chiara Rose said as she snipped.

"Mind the thorns," Tiger warned; she did. "I wish Grandma Bridget had known you, too. She would have loved you to pieces. And vice versa. Poppa also. He would have gobbled you up."

This particular rose bush held American Beauties, with downy, vivid red petals. Planted in front of the American Beauty was a smaller shrub of cream-colored Vendelas. The girl clipped those next. "There's another thing I wish," Chiara told her father.

Tiger raised his eyebrows. "Which is?"

"That you wouldn't call me that," she said in a pinched voice.

"What?" he wondered.

"Your American Beauty," she told him. "I'm not beautiful." Her eyes filled with tears and she bit the inside of her cheek.

It was true that at nine, Chiara Rose was an awkward creature: skinny, spindle-armed and legged. Then there was her stammer, which sometimes visited when she was in groups larger than three or four, though not generally when she was with her family, with whom she felt especially safe. However, the stutter occasionally reared its ugly head in Aunt Astrid's presence. But Astrid made everyone nervous.

Chiara Rose's eyes, as well as several of her other features, were almost too big for her face. They were too harsh for bones so fine and delicate, like one of the porcelain figures in Aunt Jo's china closet. 'She'll grow into her nose, her mouth,' Tiger told himself. But it didn't help the child now, when most of the other girls were more petite, curvier, more classically pretty. Tiger had no doubt that his daughter would be stunning, just as soon as she grew into herself. Chiara was a late bloomer, just like her mother. And then, watch out, world.

But instead of telling his graceless daughter this, Tiger said, "The most beautiful things about you can't be seen with the eyes, Chiara Rose."

She knew exactly what he meant and it seemed to please her. "Thanks, Daddy," she told him, clipping a blossom of sunny yellow from Bridget's third rosebush in the front yard.

Chiara cradled the armload of her great grandmother's flowers and went inside with her father.

CHAPTER THREE

Golden Celebration

T he autumn sun streamed in through the parlor windows facing Forty-Seventh Street, painting the walls, the floors, the people and everything within reach shades of gold. The streaks of sunlight even stretched as far as the Martino dining room, where the family joined to ring in Rose and Sully's twenty-first wedding anniversary. The couple had married late in life, and more than two decades later, their deep, quiet love was still going strong. Now, that was something to celebrate, wasn't it? The meal had begun at two and here it was, several hours and several courses later, and much like Rose and Sully's ardor, still chugging happily away.

Extra leaves had been toted up from the cellar for Bridget Paradiso's ever-expanding dining room table, which was now Terry's ever-expanding dining room table. 'It has to be at least fifty years old,' Angela thought, handing her sister-in-law a platter dusted with the remnants of the stuffed artichokes she'd brought. Angela grabbed another plate, which had recently held the gravy meat to accompany Aunt Jo's *lasagna*. Although Terry had done the bulk of the cooking, none of the clan could come without toting a home-made dish—except for Astrid, who usually purchased a confection which met with everyone's approval—like Ebinger's famed blackout cake or hand-dipped chocolates from Li-Lac.

All of the women, even Astrid, cleared the table to make

space for Terry's pork roast, which was prepared Cuban-style, marinated the way her friend Zarela had taught her. Between courses, the men smoked cigars (also Cuban) on the porch. Just as they'd helped set up the dining room earlier, the gentleman would help break down the feast later, after dark, toting chairs and table extensions to the depths of the basement. The work was distributed more or less evenly between the men and the women. (More less than more.) This was simply the way things were done in 1959.

"Can't we take a break to digest a little bit?" Wendy pleaded, putting the two gravy boats onto the crowded kitchen table. "I'm stuffed. The *antipasto*, the *lasagna*...I barely fit into my new skirt." Then, after a beat, she added, "I don't know how you people eat like this."

Wendy's mother Jo did her best to stifle a laugh. "You people? You're part of us people! You're going to look like *us people* one of these days." At twenty-two, Wendy was lithe and slender just as Jo had been at the same age. With her generous curves, Jo couldn't be considered heavy, but pleasingly plump, with a bit of succulent meat clinging to her frame.

"You know what I mean, Ma," Wendy sighed.

Rose caught her willowy niece around the waist. "What is it Elaine Thomas always says?"

"'Ain't nobody want a bone but a dog,'" Jo finished for her sister.

Wendy shook her head. "Honestly, you two are like a comedy team."

"Martin and Lewis, that's us," Rose said.

The girl rolled her eyes dramatically. Wendy was quite sensitive to the fact that at her advanced age, she didn't have a steady beau. However, this wasn't for lack of suitors. Wendy was clever, sassy and pretty, with flashing emerald eyes and mounds of chestnut curls. All the boys loved her. But Wendy didn't seem to have patience for the antics of any male companion for longer than a few weeks.

Except perhaps her cousin Stanley. Born just a day apart in separate parts of Brooklyn, Wendy and Stan were raised like twins. In fact, sometimes they seemed more twin-like than David and Beth, actual twins who their neighbor Ann, a London native, said were as different as cheese and chalk.

"Aunt Rose, you know what I mean too!" Wendy said, exasperated.

"Your skirt's so tight I can see what you had for breakfast," Rose remarked. "And supper."

"Pencil skirts are all the rage," Astrid noted in her niece's defense, sneaking a peek at the pork roast, which was resting on the range top. "I think the roast is a tad overdone," Astrid whispered loudly to Rose. Everyone, including Terry, who withered slightly at Astrid's remark, heard.

"Since when did you become Betty Crocker?" Rose asked her sister. "That roast is done to perfection."

"And when was the last time you made a roast?" Jo offered. "Pork or otherwise?"

Astrid was visibly flustered. She adjusted her chic suit's Peter Pan collar, then straightened the already-straight lines of her peplum skirt. It was the shade of a rotting pumpkin, which was the "in" color that autumn. "Well, I never," Astrid managed to stammer.

"Then maybe you should," Camille said, taking the squash soufflé out of the oven. Then, to her niece Terry, Camille commented, "This looks perfect too, dear." As she often did when complimented, Terry blushed.

Dressed simply in a sleeveless knit top and flared skirt, her face lightly flushed and slightly damp from the heat of the busy kitchen, Terry was lovely. Her scallop-edged half apron was carefully chosen to flatter her outfit and depicted the falling autumn leaves outside.

As Terry opened the oven to check the doneness of the scalloped potatoes in the dependable Hotpoint, she glanced at her daughter Chiara Rose who was writing in a corner she'd procured in the crowded kitchen. Writing, that girl was always writing in that little bound book her cousin Wendy had given

Chiara on her previous birthday. "What are you writing?" Terry wondered aloud.

"Stuff," the girl said. "Just stuff."

Astrid puffed through her renovated nostrils, the only one of the Paradiso Girls "blessed" with a button nose instead of a proud, Roman one. (She'd had a nose job years earlier and thought no one remembered.) "Writing? You should be helping!" Astrid, the least helpful of all, noted to her grandniece. This fact wasn't lost on Astrid's sisters, who chirped like chicks, cackling at her outrageous remark. Their voices swirled in the kitchen air, like heat:

"You? You of all people…"

"Astrid, really. Terry has been slaving away all morning and Chiara has been quite the helper. Why, I saw…"

"And where were you when it was time to make the antipasto?"

"Basta! Basta! *No arguing at my anniversary supper."*

"We're not arguing, Rosie, we're just talking."

A few feet away, Chiara Rose sat, diligently scribbling, capturing every word. Out of the corner of her eye, she saw her mother poke the golden-brown scalloped potatoes with a scallop-edged knife, then gauge the warmth of the knife against her wrist. "They're done to perfection," Chiara proclaimed, without looking up. All the women laughed, even Astrid.

Meanwhile, on the front porch, it was warm enough for the men to be outside this October afternoon in just their shirtsleeves. An Indian Summer… a stretch of unseasonably warm, calm, dry weather in the autumn. The fellows gently debated the phrase while puffing on cigars Poppa's old pal Manny Ortez Vega managed to ferret out of his homeland before Batista was finally ousted on New Year's Day earlier that year.

"Why is it called 'Indian Summer?'" Stan wondered. "The Indians never get credit for anything. Well, nothing good, anyways." Trying not to cough, he pulled on the cigar, which tickled the tip of his tongue with its peppery tang. Somehow, Stan managed not to choke on the smoke. He was a man after all, twenty-two on his last birthday that past February.

"Beats me," Sully admitted. He took a deep draw on the Cohiba. Robustos were his favorite. To Sully, they were as distinctly flavored as a spicy Italian sausage or a delightful Brooklyn lager, like Schaeffer.

Sully was still a loyal Schaeffer drinker, which had been the official beer sponsor of the Brooklyn Dodgers before they hightailed it to Los Angeles two years earlier. He liked the idea of a beer brewed in his hometown, even though he was a die-hard Yankees fan. Patrick Sullivan never had much of a taste for the Yanks' Ballantine's ale, although they sponsored his favorite team. Whereas, George Thomas, a Jersey Boy, preferred Newark's brew, Ballantine. Go figure. Sully concluded that life held something for everyone, even beer.

Recently, the policeman found his mind wandering often. Whether it was the weight of Sully's job, his worries about retiring too early (what would he do with all that free time anyhow?) or general concern about his children and grandchildren's wellbeing, Sully hadn't a clue. But if truth be told, he'd been having trouble sleeping lately—and Sully normally slept like a log. He took another puff on the Cohiba and pondered some more.

While Sully considered cigars, beer and life, Tiger waxed philosophic about Indian Summers. "Funny you should ask," he began. "I remember reading that the term was first used in the 1770s, around the Revolutionary War, by some French-American guy."

Harry gawped at his nephew. "How do you know such things?"

Tiger shrugged. "Blame it on Poppa. He was always telling me stuff like that. Besides, I always liked history."

John let out a steady stream of blueish cigar smoke. "I wish I could. Blame Poppa, I mean." John shook his head. "I still miss the old coot after… how long has it been?"

Stan recalled, "Wendy and me had just turned nine a few months before they died. So, it's been thirteen years. But who's counting?"

"We are," Sully, Tiger, John and Harry said in unison. Al, who was a relative newcomer to the group even after so many years, bowed his head in remembrance of the kind gentleman he'd met only a few times before Poppa and Bridget passed. After keeping company with Astrid for a few years, Al had inexplicably married her. No one could understand why. But the jovial, plain-looking man seemed content, even though Astrid was so ornery and nitpicky. But that was just her way and he'd made peace with it.

"Anyways, Indian Summer," Tiger continued. "That French farmer in the 1700s used the term in a book of letters. Then it popped up in a poem…something about an Indian Summer of the heart. And Oliver Wendell Holmes…"

"The guy who wrote Sherlock Holmes?" Sully asked.

"No, that's Arthur Conan Doyle," Tiger corrected.

"The Supreme Court guy?" Harry offered.

"No, that's his son," Tiger sighed, frustrated. "Don't you Neanderthals know anything about the arts?"

Harry nudged Tiger with his elbow. "Will you get a load of this fellow? A glorified short order cook and he's putting on airs."

Tiger smirked. "A restauranteur," he corrected. "With two fine dining establishments and counting. But who's counting?"

"Obviously you are," Sully joked his stepson. "So, who was this Holmes character?"

"A doctor and a poet is all."

"Overachiever," Harry nodded to Sully.

Tiger ignored them. "In a story, he once wrote, '…an Indian Summer of serene widowhood.'"

"What the heck's that supposed to mean?" Stan wondered.

Bright as a shiny, new dime, Stan was never one for schooling and book knowledge. Like his father, Stan was a child of the streets in some aspects, yet miraculously unjaded, and a little rough around the edges in others. Although Stan hadn't found his passion or his path in life, he was still a hard worker, helping his half-brother Tiger and George manage Feel Good Food, stepping in when his brother-in-law Augie needed an extra set of hands at the Loew's 46th. Stanley Sullivan was what was known as a step-up sort of fellow.

Stan examined the sidewalk in front of 1128 Forty-Seventh Street. His niece and nephew Beth and David were embroiled in an intense game of "Hit the Penny"—and Beth was winning, much to her twin brother's displeasure. The two had been newborns when their grandparents passed away and had never known them. Stan (and Wendy) had been fortunate enough to live almost a decade in the light of Poppa and Grandma Bridget's benevolence and love; it didn't seem nearly enough.

Though it was thirteen years earlier, Stan remembered his grandparents' funeral like it was yesterday. Brizzi's largest room wasn't large enough to contain the outpouring of sympathy at the dual loss of Michele Archangelo and Margarita Paradiso, who the neighbors affectionately referred to as "Poppa" (or "Mike") and "Bridget." It seemed that all of Borough Park mourned their loss. Plus, there was nothing sadder than a funeral parlor with two caskets on display.

At the wake, everyone had their own stories of Poppa and Bridget's compassion and shared these tales readily with the Paradiso children. Julius and Lettie were in attendance, as well as their sons Matthew—fresh from the military and resembling a Roman centurion in his well-pressed uniform—and Carlo, who was just as dashing but with a craftsman's calloused hands. All of the Paradisos listened patiently to stories they had heard many times before. It was as though the tellers of the tales needed to retell them in order to feel more a part of Poppa and Bridget's lives, to prove that they had held their place and made their mark in the legends of these great people.

For example, Mr. and Mrs. Wong of the Chop Suey Palace under the El spoke of how Poppa was the first one on the block to befriend them and how all the rest of their neighbors followed suit.

Antoinette Dario (née DePalma) recalled how Bridget had helped her when her oldest, Concetta, was born. Anne was sure the baby was dying from a horrific skin condition; Bridget managed to convince Anne that it was only diaper rash and prescribed liberal amounts of cornstarch in Connie's nappy. It worked like magic.

Janet Farrelli mentioned how Poppa had interrupted his Thanksgiving dinner one year when a pipe burst in her newly-purchased home down the street, flooding water from the kitchen into the basement. Poppa not only replaced the pipe but helped Janet mop up the ocean of water without hesitation or complaint before going back to Thanksgiving supper.

Through tears he didn't try to hide, Tiger's childhood friend Jimmy Burns remembered how Bridget was always trying to feed him (and hug him) when he was growing up, a scrappy street urchin with parents too far into the cups to care about their brood of unruly hellions.

At nine, Stan had been deeply moved hearing all of these stories. He never forgot them. When Poppa and Grandma Bridget were alive, the boy mistakenly thought his grandparents were his and his alone. (Well, his and his cousins'.) But not an hour into their wake at Brizzi's, Stan realized that Poppa and Bridget were everyone's grandparents, that they belonged to the whole wide world, not just him.

Another thing Stan never forgot was the roses. The roses that made up the fiery heart-shaped wreath between his grandparents' caskets were called Golden Celebration— yellow with a red center. And yellow roses signified remembrance, Stan was told by his mother. The funeral parlor had been filled with floral arrangements, each one roses, for everyone knew how Bridget cherished her roses. Along with Nunzi DeMeo's blossoms, Bridget's roses were the pride of Forty-Seventh Street. (Bridget's secret was that she cultivated hers with coffee grounds as well as with love.)

'Roses are part of the garlic family,' Poppa would often remind his wife. 'Maybe that's why you have a way with them. You sure know your way around a head of garlic.'

'I thank you very kindly, Michele Archangelo,' Bridget would customarily respond. 'But that's not exactly true about garlic and roses. They're actually a member of the lily family.'

'Then why is garlic called the Stinking Rose?' Poppa would propose. Bridget would shrug. It was a dance of words that they danced often.

Recalling his grandparents' conversation made Stan pensive among the uncomfortable upholstered chairs of Brizzi's funeral parlor. As he sat by himself, remembering, Mrs. Lewis remarked to Mrs. DeMeo that Stan looked so alone, even in a room full of people. One could go so far as to speculate that perhaps on this day, Stan's life once again changed, but this time, not for the better. This day, he lost something instead of gaining something like he did when the Paradiso Family took him into their lives as a foundling.

Green-Wood Cemetery was especially beautiful that spring, all ablaze with the flowers of the season. The azalea bushes, some as big as small trees, popped with bright purples and fuchsias. The pink magnolias were as full as human lips. The buttery daffodils and wild ginger shared the stage with the delicate blossoms of the Callery pear tree. But it was the cherry blossoms, the magnificence of the cherry blossoms, that had everyone talking.

Some ventured that it was the warmth of an early spring that caused the cherry blossoms to bloom before their time. Others said it was God's way of marking the passage of a truly remarkable pair of human beings. But whatever the reason, the cherry blossoms were spectacular the spring of 1946. A carpet of pristine white and blush petals coated the ground under the funeralgoers' polished shoes like confetti leftover from a parade, a sad, silent procession to celebrate these two simple yet extraordinary people's lives.

So, the cherry blossoms cried down their blossoms, as did one rosebush near the gravesite. It bloomed brazenly nearby, with thick, silky petals as dark as spilled blood. But it was far too early for roses, everyone said. In Brooklyn, roses usually didn't bloom until June.

At his grandparents' funeral, Stan saw people he never thought he'd see cry sobbing openly and without shame. From Herb the Pickle Man to Moe the Greengrocer, and Mr. and Mrs. Wong. From Stan's flint-skinned Aunt Astrid to his Uncle Harry, an ex-cop and a decorated World War II veteran. Seeing his own parents weep made Stan's heart ache.

There were perhaps a hundred people circling the double grave. Some stood on distant hillocks, hats in hand, unknown to anyone except the two who were gone. Perhaps it was a vagrant who'd been treated to a hot meal at Bridget's back door, an act of kindness which made all the difference and turned their life around. Perhaps it was a boozing Brooklyn Navy Yard worker who was given a second chance by Poppa, the bloke's foreman, which made the fellow vow to never touch the sauce again. No one ever knew for sure.

People came from down the block, from across the Queens border and from distant Long Island, too. Folks like Sam, who wasn't technically Stan's uncle anymore since Sam and Astrid's divorce, as well as Stan's cousins Maria and Joyce from the wilds of Valley Stream.

The family understood completely that Kelly's widow Sophie Veronica and their children couldn't make the pilgrimage for the elder Paradisos' funeral. It wasn't just the expense but the time it would take to travel from Arizona to Brooklyn. Sophie Veronica had a business to run—a catering company called "Brooklyn Made"—and a family to support. Even though Kelly had been gone for more than ten years when his parents died, Sophie Veronica still phoned during Sunday supper at least once a month.

More than a dozen years after the Paradiso funeral, the cloud of Cuban cigar smoke on what would always be considered his grandparents' front porch made Stan's stomach lurch. Or maybe it was the "bat and a ball" (a beer and a shot)

Stan'd had at the Stumble Inn before supper. He couldn't be sure which.

Stan's brother Tiger elbowed him gently in the side. "Where did you run off to?" he asked.

"I'm right here," Stan told him.

"Sure, you are," Tiger said knowingly.

Down the block, Stan saw his brother-in-law Augie rounding the corner of Forty-Seventh Street and New Utrecht Avenue. Even at a distance, his identity was clear, for Augie had a distinct, loose-limbed, loping walk. Although his trademark shiny pate was covered by a felt fedora, the other fellows knew it was Augie as well. With a nod from their uncles, Beth and David bolted down the block to greet their father, the girl winning by a sidewalk square or two.

"The Loew's still standing?" Tiger wondered as Augie approached. After the former owner, Mr. Acerno, had passed, his family sold the movie house to Augie, who'd been working there since he was a teenager.

"It is," Augie conceded, taking off his fedora and mopping his head with a monogramed hankie. "So's my new assistant manager, although I had my doubts. Figured I'd check on him between courses."

Stan shared Augie's doubts about the new assistant manager. Larry wasn't a bad guy but a bit of a drinker. This wasn't sour grapes on Stan's part since Augie had offered Stan the position first. Augie believed that his brother-in-law was a good egg, had a fair head for numbers and possessed solid people skills. But Stan politely turned down Augie's generous offer. Why? Because Stan didn't want to get stuck. He didn't want to get tied down, which was one reason he didn't have a steady beau. 'I have a nice girl every night,' Stan was known to tell anyone who asked why he didn't have a nice girl.

Before Augie could light his cigar, Chiara Rose came out to the porch, announcing that the roast was on the table and that it was getting cold. As the men and children filed inside, the telephone rang, no doubt, long distance from Sophie Veronica in Tucson, Arizona. Still.

CHAPTER FOUR

Temptation

I t was something Stan asked himself all the time: the nature of good and evil. Why certain people always took the sure and solid path, the "straight and narrow," the high road, putting others' needs ahead of their own, even though that road was often more difficult. And why other people always chose the easy way out, consistently shirking responsibility and trying to pull one over on everyone else.

Where did Stan lie in this good/evil equation?

The trouble was that he didn't know. Someplace in the middle, he figured. And being middle of the road, being wishy-washy, was a lot like being nowhere at all, Stan reckoned.

"Make a decision, then live by it!" his father Sully often told his son in frustration. "Do *something*, even if it's wrong."

A bit more diplomatically, Stan's mother would offer, "Find what makes you happy, then do it." But Stan could tell that even Rose was getting frustrated with his moping about, with his indecision. Only she was too kindhearted to say so.

But that was the trouble with Stan: not being able to make up his mind. He truly *didn't* know what made him happy. Stan tried drinking his confusion away but this only made him more melancholy, more indecisive. Alcohol numbed him, which was the point—feeling nothing as opposed to feeling blue—until he drank too much. Then he ended up feeling worse.

"Young men need a war," his Uncle Harry would mutter time and time again. Whenever Harry said this, Stan's Aunt Jo and cousin Wendy looked at Harry incredulously. Because of his combat injury, they couldn't believe he would say such a callous thing. Although false limbs had come a long way in the decade and a half since then, Harry still walked with a limp and experienced intermittent pain. But even this didn't temper his peculiar thoughts about wartime being beneficial to fledgling men. In a feeble attempt to right himself, Harry would add, "I know it sounds crazy but war gives young bucks a sense of purpose."

To this, Aunt Jo would just shake her head, flabbergasted. But Wendy, who had a fire within her and sometimes simply could not keep her pretty mouth shut, would respond, "Pop! Really? How can you say that? With all you've been through?"

Then Aunt Jo would add, "The only positive thing about war is the peace that comes after. The peace war brings. Only it's never long enough."

The first day of 1959 had brought a revolution in Cuba, that long, slender island in the Caribbean situated just ninety miles from the shores of Key West, Florida. Too close for comfort. Nobody trusted that greasy soldier Fidel Castro as far as they could throw him, what with his grisly beard, Army fatigues and all of that yelling. And across the globe in Russia, Khrushchev was even worse.

Whenever Stan considered the tenuousness of all that was happening in the world, he felt shaky inside and wanted a drink. Only it didn't take much for Stan to want to drink. Maybe drinking was part of him, part of his D.N.A., that newfangled substance which supposedly made up who and what you were.

This could have been the root of Stan's problem: he wasn't exactly sure who he was. Ever since the age of eight, Stan knew Sully and Rose weren't his real parents, that his "family" wasn't his real family. Yet, they felt more real to him than his actual folks—a man named Tony who had been married to Rose and a woman named Denise who had been

Tony's paramour. This Tony fellow had died a few months before Stan was born, some sort of mysterious accident in the basement's coal cellar, and Denise had passed away many years later of tuberculosis. Stan officially met his birth mother on her death bed, for one of her last wishes was to see the son she had abandoned. Stan remembered Denise vividly: hair the color of straw, pale almost translucent skin with blue veins just beneath its surface. Like rivers and tributaries on a map, Stan had noted. He could never forget the infinite sadness in Denise's eyes.

His adoptive family was so loving to Stan that he never once felt like he didn't belong, but Stan also knew that he wasn't like any of them. This was despite the fact that he was the spitting image of his older, half-brother Tiger, whose given name was "Anthony," just like their mutual father.

Whenever Stan asked about Denise or Tony, the answers were always truthful, charitable. "Oh, she had a hard row to hoe," Rose would say sweetly. Or, "Tony had a tough childhood…he wasn't lucky like you and me," she would offer. And Sully's, "Deep down, your mom was good; she just got a raw deal. She loved you, though. She loved you something fierce."

"That lady might've had me but Rose is my mom. My true mom," Stan would say quietly in response.

Sully couldn't argue with Stan's reasoning. "Practically any woman can have a kid but it takes someone special to be a mother," Sully conceded. Maybe that was what troubled Stan so—he was trying to find the "special," the decent within himself and he wasn't sure it existed.

So, Stan drank. None of the men in his family drank, not really. Oh, sometimes Sully had a glass or two of Budweiser in Farrell's after a funeral. Sometimes Tiger and Augie had a tumbler of wine at Sunday supper but that was it. His Uncle Al was a teetotaler while Harry and John had given up the sauce entirely, explaining, "One was too many and ten wasn't nearly enough." Stan knew exactly what they were referring to.

Tiger's business partner George's wife Elaine was from the South and had a number of sayings to fit practically every situation. One of her favorites went: "Trouble will find you." Elaine went on to explain to a tableful of perplexed Northerners that this meant no matter how hard you tried to behave, no matter where you went, trouble would be on your backside, chasing you down like a bloodhound.

For Stan, "trouble" meant temptation. He was awful at resisting...anything. If temptation was an extra piece of butter sunshine cake, he would eat himself sick. If temptation was self-pleasure, he would partake in the sin of Onan until nothing but sawdust came out, as his friend Jerry so delicately phrased it. If temptation was drinking, Stan would indulge until he was overserved and practically incoherent.

And if there were an easy way to make a buck, legal or not, Stan was always game. Never mind that his stepdad Sully was a cop. Stan took not getting caught as more of a challenge when he dealt in merchandise that had "fallen off the truck" under his Pop's very nose. It wasn't that Tiger and Augie didn't pay Stan well for his work; they did. But Stan reveled in the allure of being bad, in the pure adrenaline surge of almost being nabbed. Almost, but not quite. It was that simple. The enticement of *almost* made Stan feel like he was alive.

Several other things in Stan's life were more complicated but equally as confusing as his dance with temptation. Like his relationship with his cousin Wendy, for instance.

Although they had been raised like brother and sister, the attraction between Stan and Wendy was undeniable, despite the fact that they were mirror opposites. Wendy was bookish and had fancied everything about school; Stan did everything he could to avoid reading and couldn't wait to finish New Utrecht High. Post-graduation, Wendy took a correspondence course in reporting and recently started talking about enrolling in a Saturday-morning class at The New School for Social Research. Stan couldn't imagine doing anything that smacked of being the least bit educational or that cut into his weekends. Wendy's scholarly activities were in addition to working full-time as a bank teller and writing the occasional article for Poppa's favorite newspaper, *The Brooklyn Daily Eagle*.

Stan and Wendy couldn't be more different and each thought the other was nuts. And yet. And yet. There was an indisputable allure between them. Something that kept them craving each other's company. Something that made the opposite sex's companionship seem shallow, silly and empty in comparison. "Maybe it's because we grew up together," Wendy would tell her friend Maureen when Wendy fretted about her feelings for Stan.

"Maybe it's because Stan is so dreamy," Maureen would respond with a toss of her honey-blonde curls.

"Stan? Dreamy?" Wendy would sputter back.

"Why, sure," Maureen would say "And he's not technically your cousin. So, why not?"

"Ieeew, he feels like a brother," Wendy would respond, a bit too quickly. "Besides, he's not my type."

"And what exactly is your type?" Maureen would pose.

And yet, why was Wendy having those odd dreams about Stan? Dreams from which she woke with a start, breathless and twitching and throbbing between her legs. Wendy had no idea that Stan was having dreams like this about her, too. Dreams that left him sweaty and stiff and sometimes sticky. Dreams neither of them could remember the details of but felt wicked and guilty nonetheless.

After these nocturnal oddities, Wendy and Stan would avoid each other for as long as they could, then reluctantly meet to go to a picture show, a mutual friend's house or a dance at the Lyceum, growing comfortable in each other's presence once again, only to have another disconcerting dream soon after.

And yet…there was that time when they were kids. In the cool of the summer cellar, escaping the shattering heat, it had started innocently enough: a wrestling match to determine who was stronger. Wrestling led to a tickling contest to see who could withstand the delightful arm-tickles longer. But wrestling and tickling led to touching, exploring. Damp, probing fingertips in the dimness of the concrete basement. A fleshy worm that grew hard as a twig. The delicious tingling between her legs. Then Grandma Bridget's footsteps on the floorboards above, creaking hard and heavy. "What on earth are you two doing down there?" their grandmother asked.

In unison, Stan and Wendy gasped, "Nothing!"

But it wasn't nothing. They were definitely up to something but what it was, neither of them knew. What they did know was that this "nothing" felt good and bad at once. They also knew that they wouldn't mention it to Father Dunn in the confessional booth that Saturday or on any Saturday to come. In that guilt-ridden basement, the two children covered up, went out the cellar door and into the blinding August sunshine. They never spoke of it—or did it—again.

But more than a decade later, neither Stan or Wendy had forgotten their carnal fumblings in the cellar. Whenever they thought of "the basement incident," it was difficult to sleep or think of anything else. Stan would have no choice but to relieve his hardness into a handkerchief (which he surreptitiously rinsed out afterwards then hung to dry). Wendy found release by pressing her thighs together and rocking on her belly in bed. Sometimes she fell asleep, but others, she felt a strange, wonderful sea change within her: a relentless trilling, a beating like the heart of a small creature held captive in a cage then suddenly let go. After a while, Wendy figured out that slipping her fingers between her legs might hasten the throbbing, first outside, then, when she grew bolder, inside the elastic band of her bloomers.

Stan hoped he wouldn't think about "the basement incident" when he and Wendy went to see *Ben Hur* when it opened at the Loew's 46th the week before Thanksgiving. Wendy was crazy for Charlton Heston, who she said was "real boss," and she made Stan promise he'd take her to see *Ben Hur*. As for Stan, he could take Charlton or leave him. Although he had to admit that Charlie was pretty okay in last year's *Touch of Evil*. But what kind of name was Charlton anyhow? To listen to Wendy, you'd think the actor could walk on water. Well, in *The Ten Commandments*, Charlton Heston actually *had* parted the Red Sea, but still…

Stan longed to be calm, cool and collected as he sat in the velvet theatre seat beside his cousin. But sometimes, the feel of Wendy's breath in his ear when she commented on Rosalind Russell's gold lamé gown in *Auntie Mame* or the touch of Wendy's arm on his shoulder when she whispered about how gorgeous Grace Kelly was in *High Society* made him lose his composure. Stan would find himself stiffening at the most inopportune moments and convinced himself that Wendy didn't notice, grateful for the forgiving blackness of the Loew's 46th.

Sometimes, when they were little, Wendy would dig her fingernails into Stan's arm as they were watching a *Dracula* movie at the theatre. Once, Wendy, Stan, Grandma Bridget and Poppa actually held hands during an especially scary part in *Phantom of the Opera*—when they showed the Phantom's acid-burned face. Though Stan was only six, this horror combined with the delight of Susanna Foster's heaving bosoms spilling out of her satiny gowns threw him into a state of perpetual bafflement.

And just the other day, Wendy grabbed Stan's hand as they were watching *The Blob*. She'd held it throughout the whole second half of the picture until their palms got sweaty. "Why'd you do that?" Stan had asked Wendy on the walk home. "Hold my hand, I mean."

"That picture was creepy," she'd explained. "The Blob was so gross. Especially when it swallowed up that old man. It just kept eating everyone!"

"But still…" Stan prodded.

She rolled her eyes. "Steve McQueen is kind of cute," she said, trying to change the subject.

Stan bumped into Wendy's shoulder, like he used to when they were kids. "And me?" he pushed. "What about me? Am I kind of cute?"

"Maureen thinks so," Wendy admitted.

"But how about you?" he pushed.

Wendy stopped and considered her cousin. Stan wasn't bad looking. He was no Steve McQueen or Charlton Heston but he was all right: bottle-green eyes, slight dusting of freckles across the bridge of his nose, a swirl of unruly brown hair which was cropped short at the sides, strong, straight nose, welcoming smile, especially with that slightly-chipped front tooth. Stan waited expectantly for Wendy's response, holding his breath. "You? Oh, you're all right, I guess," she conceded.

They continued down Forty-Seventh Street, Stan feeling hot about the ears and neck. He wondered if his face was coloring. "You're my cousin, though," Wendy reminded him. "I don't see you like that."

'But then how do you explain those dreams?' Wendy asked herself silently. There was no answer to this question.

Continuing past Nunzi and Violetta DeMeo's place, the fragrance of roses hanging in the thick autumn air, Wendy repeated, "But Maureen McMahon thinks you're dreamy. She has a crush on you."

Stan blushed a deeper crimson. "I like Maureen fine. She's nice enough," he said, "but she's not my type."

"Then who is your type?" Wendy asked.

Stan bit his tongue. He resisted saying, 'You.' Instead, he responded, "I haven't met her yet."

When the brick house on Forty-Seventh Street came into view, Stan and Wendy noticed a uniformed beat cop on the sagging wooden porch. He was speaking to Sully, who stood in the house's doorway, jacketless, in his undershirt and slacks, as though he'd dressed hastily. Stan's heart dropped. "Isn't that Izzy?" Wendy gasped, alarmed. "Is someone sick?"

"I don't think so," Stan told her. He insisted on walking Wendy home that night, both of them nodding a silent hello to Sully and Izzy as they passed them on the porch. Like a gentleman, Stan escorted his cousin to her limestone row house on Fort Hamilton Parkway a few blocks away. He hoped Izzy would be gone when he returned. Maybe Stan would take a detour until he was sure the officer had left.

Stan knew exactly why Izzy was talking to his dad. The boy had long been running with a bad crowd (namely a thug named Big Paulie Morrongiello). This had recently evolved into more than just hanging out on street corners or in rough-and-tumble bars in the wrong neighborhoods. Lately, more and more items had been "falling off the truck." (Big Paulie, damn his fat ass, swore that no one would miss them.) Lately, Stan had been helping his friend "move" those things: a rackful of winter jackets from the garment center, a crate of radios, a pallet of *Encyclopedia Britannicas*. Parts of shipments that Little Petey at the Red Hook docks turned a blind eye to when they were being off-loaded. Little Petey didn't have to lift a finger; Big Paulie's crew did the rest.

The light was burning in the parlor of the O'Leary apartment on the first floor of the handsome limestone building. The dermatologist's office on the ground floor was shuttered and dark. Stan could see the shadow of his Uncle Harry just beyond the first-floor window frame, his bad leg propped up on the ottoman.

"You in trouble again?" Wendy asked when she and Stan stopped at the bottom of the stairs.

"Probably," Stan admitted.

"That Big Paulie is a bad seed," she told him.

"Who said anything about Big Paulie?"

"Nobody had to. I have eyes. I see who you hang around with."

Stan shrugged. "I known him since third grade."

"I have, too, but I still steer clear of him."

"It's different for boys," Stan said.

"Is it?" Wendy challenged. "Bad is bad."

"Well, maybe I look good in bad."

Wendy arched her eyebrows and shook her head. "Maybe you'll look good in pinstripes."

"I don't get you."

"Prison pinstripes," Wendy spelled out. "Don't play dumb."

"I ain't playing," he insisted.

"You're a lot of things, Stanley Sullivan, but dumb isn't one of them. I'm serious. Keep your nose clean. Just because your dad's a sergeant, doesn't mean you can break the law."

Stan toed a sheet of newspaper that had blown to his feet. *The Eagle*'s headline said something about the President Eisenhower/Nikita Khrushchev meeting a few weeks earlier. "I'm not exactly breaking the law," Stan pointed out. "More like bending it."

To this, Wendy shook her head. "Well, thanks for coming with me to see *The Blob*. I couldn't have watched it alone."

"It took forever for Augie to get it at the Loew's," Stan complained. "I mean, it was last year's model."

"But still, it was nice of you to come," Wendy told him.

"It was nothing," Stan said. The newspaper blew away. "Besides, I like going to the movies with you."

"Why?"

"It reminds me of when we were little, when we'd go with Poppa and Grandma Bridget."

When Wendy smiled, the night sky seemed to glow brighter. "Except Grandma would have fallen asleep," she told him.

Wendy stood on her tippy-toes to kiss her cousin's cheek, lost her balance and brushed his lips by mistake. A sharp, sudden electric shock shot through each of them. Stan steadied Wendy with his hands on her forearms. His grip was strong. "Sorry," she said.

"It's all right," he told his cousin, releasing her.

Wendy trotted up the steps. The light in the parlor went out. "And go straight home," she called to Stan.

He had already begun walking. "I will," he assured her.

But instead, Stan headed to the Stumble Inn. Big Paulie didn't like to be kept waiting.

CHAPTER FIVE

Dark Engagement

Most days, Big Paulie Morrongiello could be found in his usual seat at the far end of the Stumble Inn. He liked to prop himself on the last stool way in the back, near the bathroom with its putrid aroma of ammonia barely masking the stench of drunken, badly-aimed piss. There was a none-too-clean aura about Big Paulie himself. Stan's friend Rich joked that the rotund, wanna-be gangster was too portly to reach around and give his butt a good wipe. It might very well have been true.

When Stan entered the bar, Big Paulie's legendary posterior was set precariously on the Stumble Inn's rickety barstool. Like the pub itself, the chair had seen better days. Stan recalled his brother telling him how their Dad had brought Tiger there on several occasions when he was a tyke. Instead of taking Tiger to Owl's Head Park as he'd told Rose he would, Tony stole off to the Stumble Inn to get sloshed on a Saturday afternoon with his toddler in tow. Stan figured that the pickled eggs in the oversized jar displayed on the bar top were the same ovum from decades earlier when Tiger had visited with their Pop.

Big Paulie was glaring at Stan. He couldn't avoid the brute's ire any longer so Stan sauntered toward the rear of the pub to join him. "What's shaking?" Stan asked.

While Stan awaited Big Paulie's response, the barkeep slid Stan a pint of Budweiser without him asking for it. Ted Jr. was the owner's son and had a second sense for this sort of thing. "Chaser?" Ted Jr. inquired. To which Stan shook his head 'no.' He wanted to keep his wits about him for this meeting.

"What's shaking?" Big Paulie mocked, his voice sounding out of breath with the mere strain of speaking. "This and that. Mostly that."

Stan pulled up a barstool beside the enormous man. Big Paulie was reminiscent of a toad in a cheap suit, the younger man noted. In fact, that's how Sully and most of the cops at the Sixty-Sixth Precinct referred to Big Paulie: the Frog Prince. But for some reason, Stan felt an allegiance to the brute, perhaps because Morrongiello had stood up for the skinny kid in the schoolyard of P.S. 131 when the other guys were picking on him. They knew better than to pick on Big Paulie, who was already known by that moniker at the tender age of ten.

"I guess that's what you wanted to talk to me about," Stan said, then took a gulp of his beer.

"You guessed right, my friend," Big Paulie responded dryly. When he smiled, the gigantic man was more imposing, showing off his widely-spaced teeth which were tinted with an odd greenish cast. "Let me tell you about my little plan," he continued.

A few blocks away on Forty-Seventh Street, Sully and Rose couldn't sleep. Usually it was Rose who lay awake until she heard her son's key in the door, but this night Sully tossed and turned until Rose switched on the fringed-topped nightstand lamp. "What's on your mind, Paddy?" she asked.

"Who says anything's on my mind?" he asked in return.

"You're flipping around like a pancake," Rose told him. She sat up and leaned against the headboard, crossing her arms over the front of her nightgown, expectant.

From past experience, Sully knew that Rose wouldn't let up until he talked. Sully told her that his old beat partner Izzy Novie had stopped by that evening while Rose was next door at Angela's.

"Izzy came by again?" Rose gasped.

Next, Sully told Rose how Izzy had shared his fears with Sully—that Stan's friend Paolo Morrongiello was suspected of being involved in the rash of pickpocketing during the blackout in Manhattan that past August.

Rose shook her head. "That pudding head's too lazy to go all the way to the City to pick pockets."

"Not Big Paulie himself," Sully corrected. "Too recognizable. But his crew." After a sigh, Sully added, "That Big Paulie is bad news."

"I think you're a worrywart," Rose told her husband, rubbing his arm. "Paul's just a lazy *schlub*."

"A lazy *schlub* with a criminal record," Sully pointed out. He covered Rose's small hand with his bear paw, squeezed it. "You ever look into his eyes?" Sully continued.

"Can't say that I have," Rose admitted. "But Paolo Morrongiello is nothing but polite to me when I pass him on the street."

"Yeah, they say the Boston Strangler was a charmer, too," Sully told her. Rose burst out laughing but Sully was dead serious. "Do me a favor and look in his eyes the next time you see him. They're black holes. Nothing inside. No heart. No compassion."

Rose lay her head on Sully's shoulder. "Please try to get some rest."

"I'll get shut-eye when Morrongiello is behind bars," Sully said. "And in the short term, when Stan gets home."

There was silence for a few moments which permeated the night's blackness and made it seem even deeper. "I'm too old for this," Sully finally admitted. "To be a father, I mean."

He felt Rose smile, her cheek resting against his flannel-clad chest. "No matter how old your child is, you never stop worrying," she told him softly. "It's part of the job, Paddy."

Sully cupped Rose's head, palming it like a skull cap. Gently stroking her bobbed hair always relaxed him. Even in the dark, Sully could feel the difference between the silver strands and the brown ones; the silver hairs were more coarse, more wiry. "I've got a bad feeling about Morrongiello," Sully whispered. "I'm telling you, he's got no soul." This time, Rose didn't respond. She let her husband speak. "Remember the Capeman?" Sully continued. "Salvador Agron?"

Rose shuddered. "How could I forget? That boy was a monster."

"He stabbed two innocent people in the chest. Thought they were gang members. Meanwhile, they were just kids in a playground."

"At midnight," Rose added.

"True, but that doesn't mean they should have gotten stabbed. They were just hanging around a Hell's Kitchen park on a hot, summer night."

"Nothing good happens after midnight," Rose said dreamily.

"Do you remember the *Daily News* headline?" Sully asked.

"No but I remember his cocky attitude. That boy needed a beating," Rose snapped.

"That boy needs the electric chair," Sully told her emphatically. "The headline read: *Slew 2 because 'I felt like it' says Cape Man*. Can you imagine, Rose? Sixteen years old and no regard for human life."

"Plus, he did it all wearing a cape. Unbelievable," she added. "But what does the Capeman have to do with Big Paulie?"

Sully took a deep breath. "Same dull, dead eyes. Same lack of remorse. He scares me. And I don't scare easy."

Rose lifted her head, craned her neck, reached up and kissed her husband on the mouth. She didn't know what else to do.

At the Stumble Inn, Big Paulie Morrongiello shifted his weight on the barstool. It creaked in protest beneath his expansive buttocks. "So, what do you think?" he asked Stan when he finished his proposition.

Stan shrugged and drained his beer. "I think I'm busy enough working for my brother at the restaurant and working for my brother-in-law at the movie house. I'm thinking I don't need the extra dough that bad. I mean, moving a few blenders that fell off the truck is one thing but stealing a crate from Idlewild Airport, that's another. That's grand larceny."

Big Paulie mopped his brow with a handkerchief the size of a small tablecloth. Even the strain of talking made him perspire. "Don't have a cow, Stan the Man. Remember, your Daddy-O's a cop."

"Yeah, but he doesn't have no pull in the ass-end of Queens where Idlewild is."

"Who are you kidding? Sully knows everybody everywhere. And everyone likes your Pop."

Ted Jr. refilled Stan's pint glass with more Bud. Big Paulie gave the server a sign. "A bat and a ball?" the barkeep confirmed then clanked a shot glass next to the pint.

"No," Stan said, pushing away the empty glass. "I'm opening the restaurant tomorrow morning. Early."

"Well, I say 'yes'," Big Paulie countered, pushing the shot glass back toward Stan. "Besides, it ain't late." Ted Jr. filled Stan's short glass with Seagram's 7 then refilled Big Paulie's squat whiskey tumbler with the same. "And don't be stingy," the hoodlum told the barkeep. "Fill it to the top." Ted Jr. did as he was told.

Then to Stan, Big Paulie offered, "Don't you ever get tired?"

"Of what?" Stan wondered.

"Of doing everything for everybody and having nothing to show for it?" Big Paulie waited a beat so his words could sink in, sink deep. The he continued, "Getting up at the crack of dawn, peeling potatoes while everyone else is snoring away in bed. Scraping gum off the floors of the Loew's 46th while the boss man is counting all the dough."

"It ain't like that," Stan told him.

"Sure, it is." Big Paulie leaned in closer. Stan could smell the staleness of his breath: beer and Pall Malls and halitosis. Stan's stomach did a flip-flop. Ted Jr. moved to the other end of the establishment; he didn't want to hear what couldn't be unheard. "Little Petey got the scoop," Big Paulie pressed on. "His brother Johnny is night watchman at Idlewild. They're moving in a shitload of diamonds from South America..."

Stan downed his Seagram's. "Wait a minute, I thought diamonds were from South Africa."

"South America, South Africa. What's the diff?" Big Paulie said.

"A few thousand miles," Stan suggested.

Big Paulie's face mottled with anger. He poked his finger into Stan's chest. "Don't correct me and don't nitpick," he spat. "The point is that Johnny Russo is willing to look the other way for a small piece. So, are you with me?"

"Let me think about it," Stan told him.

"Just don't think too long. I got plenty of guys who will do it in a heartbeat," Big Paulie assured him.

Stan nursed his beer, staring straight ahead into the smeared mirror behind the bar. In the reflection, he noticed Betsy Mulaney, one of the neighborhood girls. She was sitting alone at a table, applying blood-red lipstick with the help of a plastic compact. Betsy's eye caught Stan's in the mirror. He thought he saw the brief flick of her tongue as she touched up her face with a fluffy powder puff.

"Besides," Big Paulie continued. "I can use a fellow with your smarts. And you're a good driver. The picture of grace under pressure."

"Plus, there's my Pop," Stan added.

"Yeah, that too," Big Paulie admitted.

"I'm heading out," Stan told him.

Big Paulie grabbed the front of Stan's jacket to stop him. "Just remember, when you're getting up with the birds, I'll still be catching some extra z's," Big Paulie taunted. "You'll make a pretty penny for a couple hours work. Enough to put a down payment on a nice house or buy a cool set of wheels. Think about it."

"I will," Stan said.

"You don't want to be a sucker all your life, do you?" the ruffian posed rhetorically.

When Big Paulie let go of Stan's jacket and slid his girth from the barstool, Stan swore he heard the chair groan in relief. "Catch you later. I gotta go drain the dragon," Big Paulie said. With that, he disappeared through the double doors that led to the can. Stan slipped Ted Jr. a few bucks and thanked him. As Stan left the Stumble Inn, Betsy snapped her compact shut and followed him out the door.

Rose's kiss led to a cuddle which led to more. As Sully let nature take its course, Rose tried to listen with one ear for the sound of her youngest son unfastening the front door's lock but she soon lost herself in the rhythm of lovemaking, in the gentle thrusts, in the urgency, the intensity. Her short fingernails dug into Sully's shoulders as her toes curled. She bit softly into his flesh to stifle her cry. His gasps followed hers seconds later.

By the time Rose came back from the bathroom with a warm washrag, she could tell that Sully was fast asleep. She cleaned his body anyhow. He barely stirred but groaned with pleasure as he slumbered. Rose gave her own body a quick wipe then settled down uneasily beside her husband, her ear still cocked for the click of her son's key in the door.

"Hey, wait up!"

Stan stopped, turned. It was Betsy Mulaney, chasing after him, her white poodle skirt glowing in the streetlight, the crinolines she wore underneath rustling with every step. Her ample chest heaved when she stopped a few feet away from Stan. "I, uh, I just wanted to say hi," Betsy explained. "I didn't get a chance to say hello inside."

Stan smiled politely. "Well, hi. And bye. I was heading home. It's getting late."

"Mind if I walk with you?" Betsy's expression was hopeful. She held her breath.

"It's a free country," Stan said. They started moving along Thirteenth Avenue toward Forty-Seventh Street. As they strolled, Stan noticed the pancake makeup piled onto Betsy's skin like a fine layer of plaster. Beneath it, he could make out the craters of acne scars. Her makeup was starting to wear off in spots, despite her powder-puff primping.

"It's nice to have company," Betsy told Stan. "Sometimes a girl just doesn't feel safe." She slid her arm through his without invitation. "But I feel safe with you," Betsy added.

"I'm glad," Stan told her. They walked a few steps in silence. "I thought you were Big Paulie's girl," he ventured.

"Oh, I'm nobody's girl," she said.

"That's not what I heard," Stan responded and immediately regretted it. Quite to the contrary, Stan's pal Rich had said that Betsy was "everybody's girl." With liquor loosening his tongue, Stan almost told Betsy so but stopped himself. Since grade school, Stan had been warned about the Mulaney kids, who, like Big Paulie, were "bad news." It was also said that the sole Mulaney sister, Betsy, was "loose." Stan wasn't exactly sure what that had meant when he was younger but it didn't sound good. These days, he was more than familiar with the term and he knew that "loose" was not an entirely bad thing.

"Why? What have you heard, Stanley?" Betsy wondered. She hugged his captive arm closer to her body. Stan could feel the warmth of her flesh through her fuzzy angora sweater. He could feel the swell of her left breast and the outline of her brassiere against his skin. That sensation alone made him harden. Stan hoped Betsy couldn't see this in the streetlight.

"Nothing," he stammered in belated response.

"Much ado about nothing," Betsy teased.

'She knows!' Stan thought. 'She knows!'

To make matters worse, Betsy made like her purse had slipped from her grasp. To catch it, her hand grazed the front of Stan's slacks. She looked him straight in the eye. "That don't feel like nothing to me," she said. "It definitely feels like something."

"I...uh..." Stan choked.

"I...uh..." Betsy mimicked. "I...uh...been eyeballing you since fifth grade," she told Stan and steered him into the alley between the greengrocer's and the pickleman's. The stone corridor smelled like vinegar and dirty potatoes.

"Who? Me?" he stuttered.

"Yeah, you," Betsy told him.

It was almost too dark to see in the alleyway but sight wasn't necessary. Here, sensation was sufficient. The blackness almost heightened Stan's sense of touch. The softness of angora. The scratch of rough dishpan hands against Stan's fly. His own hands trying to stop the action, then relinquishing. Betsy's fingers squeezing, then pulling. The brush of her cheek against his thigh. The warm wetness of her mouth surrounding him, engulfing him, then swallowing him to the root. Once. Twice. Then more.

A million thoughts coursed through Stan's head at once. The notion of good and evil. A quick image of Lucifer (before the angel fell from grace) wrestling with Michael the Archangel. The flash of Wendy's lips, curled up in a grin, her tiny pink tongue darting through her teeth. A peek behind a Coney Island curtain at Tirza, the wine-bath girl. A ripe, dripping peach. Pamela Thomas's long, lean, cinnamon-colored legs. A crimson rose. The moist crease between Wendy's breasts.

Suddenly, an explosion started in Stan's toes, unfurled up his legs, zoomed through his torso, tingled up his fingers then simultaneously blasted out the top of his head and the tip of his cock. It took his breath away.

Stan's knees buckled. He gasped, steadying himself by grasping Betsy's shoulders. By now, Stan's eyes had gotten used to the darkness. He could make out Betsy's strawberry-blonde head, the glint of her blue eyes. She peered up at him and smirked, wiping her mouth on the back of her palm. "Your first time?" she wondered.

"No," he lied. "Of course not."

CHAPTER SIX

Home Run

Stan felt so ashamed about what had happened with Betsy Mulaney in the alleyway that he couldn't look his mother in the eye the next day. Rose kept trying to serve him a proper breakfast but Stan kept refusing. It was a silly dance of words they did practically every morning. "Only a cup of tea?" Rose asked in disbelief.

"Yeah, Ma," Stan told her. "George will be in before you know it and he make us a mess of eggs to get us going." Stan gulped a mouthful of Lipton; it bubbled down to his stomach like lava. "Besides, I've got a lot of prepping and chopping to do." He convinced Rose to return to bed because it was before six, too early for even she to rise. Sully didn't have to work that day so Rose padded back to bed in her worn slippers without much complaint. Stan heard the creak of the old mattress and whispers in the bedroom before he left.

Borough Park early in the morning was a true thing of beauty. It woke slowly and gently like a baby did: stretching its soft limbs, blinking its blurry eyes, uncurling its fists and toes, yawning widely and profusely. When Rose used to take Stan's infant niece Chiara upstairs for the night to give Tiger and Terry a break, the child would sleep in Stan's room, in the second single bed, walled in by a fortress of pillows. And each morning, Stan would marvel at the baby's transition between slumber and wakefulness like a time-lapse photography progression of the birth of a flower. That's exactly what the awakening Avenue was like.

All along Thirteenth, deliveries were being made from panel vehicles and wood-sided wagons. The bright yellow Coca Cola truck waited by the curb as Joey D provided musical accompaniment, rolling a stack of clanking, crated glass bottles into Bohack's on his dolly. The idling engine of the white Wonder Bread truck, with its spray of primary-colored balloons and Twinkies advertisement on the side, sang in harmony with Joey's rig. Cosmo, the ruddy-faced driver from Shannon's, with his bucketful of roses and carnations always whistled "Don't Sit Under the Apple Tree" while he worked. These sounds, and many more, made up the neighborhood's early morning tapestry of which Stanley Martino Sullivan was a part.

Not a word was exchanged between the players or else the spell would be broken. Instead, they swapped polite nods and half-smiles. This was their quiet time, their silent moments of solace which they shared yet did not discuss. If ever these men ran into each other at Farrell's or in the Lucky Buck, drinks would be bought and they would greet each other like old friends, for they shared the hushed stillness of early mornings.

Stan continued along the Avenue, avoiding a glance down "Betsy's Alley." He half-expected to see the two of them huddled there. Steps away, Herb's son was rolling out the pickle barrels with a helper. All three men nodded wordless hellos. The girls at Mickey's Bakery, their dusky, Italian hair pulled into white kerchiefs, stacked golden loaves of Italian bread in the front window which would be empty by day's end. There was the scent of warm yeast and sugar which masked the essence of dill and vinegar emanating from Herb's. Yes, life was good, Stan thought, especially in Borough Park at six in the morning.

He unlocked the restaurant's front door but kept the lights dim because they would be closed until just before noon. Although the place had been spruced up with several coats of paint since Tiger and George opened it thirteen years earlier, they kept the same soothing shade of yellow on the walls, had the same type of gingham curtains, the same sort of colorful tablecloths with fabric culled from a Bridge Street shop. The linoleum had been replaced and still gleamed, though it was a few years old. Stan saw to it that it shone and took great pride in this.

On Saturdays, Feel Good Food didn't offer breakfast and lunch, but instead, lunch and supper. That Saturday, the specials were roasted chicken and meat loaf. This required a mountain of both chopped and minced vegetables, which is where Stan began.

After years of being George's prep man, Stan knew the portions by heart. He gladly took this scepter from his brother Tiger who now dedicated himself more to the business aspects of the eatery than to the culinary details. Though he spent much of his time overseeing the Jersey City outpost, George spent two mornings a week in Brooklyn. His brother-in-law Tyrone, a part-time trucker with a flair for cooking, took over the duties across the river whenever George was in Kings County. Feel Good Food was indeed a family affair and it all worked out swell. They had a small, dedicated staff they could trust. Both places were packed from the minute they opened their doors until closing time.

The lights at the front of the house remained low while Stan peeled and chopped in the open kitchen. Methodically, he first did the carrots, then the potatoes, then the onions and garlic, and placed them each into their own bowls. He carefully selected the spices George would need and lined them up on the counter. When Stan set out the butter to soften, he heard the front door open and knew it was George.

"Howdy, partner," said the barrel-chested, coffee-skinned man. It was a greeting that Stan looked forward to hearing each and every morning he shared with George. He never tired of seeing George's pleasant, wide face break into a gap-toothed grin.

"Howdy, partner," Stan said back. They had been sharing this greeting for the decade or so Stan had been pitching in at Feel Good Food.

Helping Grandma Bridget at a young age had made him an adept *sous chef*. Stan had learned how to mix and whip and fold before he was trusted to handle a knife. 'A sharp blade is safer than a dull one,' Bridget was known to say. 'You just have to learn how to respect it.' Stan's cousin Wendy, who'd also been taught at their grandmother's elbow, didn't share Stan's fondness of cookery. She thought of kitchen work as a chore. But to Stan, as it was to most of the Paradiso women, feeding someone you cared for was another way of saying "I love you."

The two men, one with silvery wires creeping through his short military crop and the other with a dusty brown side part and impressive quaff, caught up on the past few days. George talked with pride about the way Feel Good Food's Jersey City eatery had grown as he added Stan's chopped onions, garlic and carrots to the fragrantly-spiced mixture of ground beef, pork and veal which Stan had pressed through the grinder earlier. Cut paper-thin, George contended that carrots added sweetness to a meatloaf and it was his secret ingredient.

Stan mentioned how busy both the restaurant and the theatre had been recently. Signs of an improving economy, George agreed. But Stan neglected to remark on his encounters with Big Paulie and Betsy. He thought that somehow, perhaps through George's New Orleans voodoo powers, that George already knew.

When he'd molded the fourth portion of meatloaf with his catcher's mitt-sized paws, George effortlessly moved from small talk to what he called "big talk." "You keeping your distance from that *boeuf gras* Morrongiello?" George asked as he put the finishing touches on the loaves with his thick fingers. The term was a favorite of George's and literally translated to "fat beef" in French Creole. It was his polite way of calling Big Paulie a fat ass.

Unable to lie to George, who was like another burly uncle to him, Stan countered with, "Why do you ask?"

"No reason," George said, lifting the aluminum tray with both hands. (It held about ten pounds of meat.) Stan opened one of the O'Keeffe & Merritt's oven doors, which still gleamed firetruck red. George slid in the tray. "I just got a feeling," George added.

Stan was all too familiar with George's "feelings." He had supposedly awakened with a "feeling" the morning of Pearl Harbor. Likewise, in January of this year, when Castro overthrew the Batista government in Cuba, George had warned, "Mark my words, Old Beardo will be ten times worse than Old Fulgencia ever was." Just twelve days later, Castro had ordered more than seventy Batista supporters shot and buried in a mass grave. And that was just the beginning.

Due to George's premonitions, Stan knew he had to tread lightly, so he tried to shift gears. "How's Pamela doing? And your new grandkid?" Stan wondered.

"Pam is just fine," George said, palming a large chicken. Stan grabbed another whole poultry, but unlike George, needed two hands. They placed the plucked birds onto the gleaming counter. "And so is Little Quentin, thank you very much," George added. "Hey, stop trying to create a diversion, boo. I know what you're up to."

Stan just shrugged and silently stuffed the chicken carcass with hunks of onion, celery, bread and peeled cloves of garlic. George did the same and worried aloud, "I seen that troublemaker hanging around here. Trust me, that boy's up to no good."

"Oh, Paulie's all right," Stan told him.

"From where I see it, that boy's nothing but a skeeter hawk. A predator. Hanging around just to see how many skeeters he can eat."

Stan salted and peppered the chicken then added a generous pinch of George's mystery spice mix and spread it across the bird's skin. Lastly, he drizzled on peanut oil and rubbed it in. "Can you blame a guy for Jonesing for your fried chicken?" Stan offered.

"And my meatloaf. And my pork chops," George admitted. He put both chickens into a roasting pan and set to work on the third while Stan prepped the fourth. If there were any leftovers—which there probably wouldn't be—chicken salad would be on the "Specials" menu the next day. "Can't fault a fellow for that," George added. "But I can fault him for not paying. Or for not tipping Crystal."

"Paulie's my friend," Stan smiled. "I known him since I was ten. I take care of Crystal for bussing his table, don't you worry. And I can give a buddy a free meal every once in a while, can't I?"

"You mean, every once a week. Oh, you might have known him since you were knee high to a tadpole," George agreed. "But he's not your friend. His kind don't have no friends. Only people who can give him something for nothing. He's a user."

George slammed the last two chickens into the pan with more force than was necessary. Stan opened the oven's second door. "The Jews have a word for what he is," George continued. "Sadie Lieberwitz taught me. It's a *schnorrer*. Your Big Paulie is a *schnorrer*. A user. A grabber."

Although George shut the oven door, he didn't close the conversation. "You watch your back with that one, Stanley. He gives me a bad feeling. And you know about my feelings."

"Yes, sir," Stan told George. But in truth, Stan was certain that Big Paulie would continue to wangle his way into his life. Especially on Meat Loaf Day.

Tiger and Chiara Rose were on their way home from seeing *Pillow Talk* at the Loew's 46th. They had given Terry a much-deserved night off, though she said she didn't need one. It didn't take a great effort to convince Terry to attend her friend Margie's Tupperware Party.

Although his daughter loved George's roasted chicken and meat loaf equally, Chiara said that she wanted a square, a corner piece, to be precise, at Mario's for supper. Tiger easily gave in and as they ate, he told his daughter the story of how he'd once chomped his way through Borough Park with his friend Jimmy Burns, starting with Mario's Pizzeria. His and Chiara's father-daughter date began with giggles and

Dr. Pepper from a waxed cup going up through Chiara's nose when Tiger got to the part where he puked an orange volcano of vomit into the street before Uncle Harry rescued him from himself.

"You mean you ate pizza, a pickle, an egg cream and a Charla Russe?" Chiara gasped in wonder.

"And an onion bagel," Tiger told her.

"That's so gross," she laughed.

Before he and Chiara left the apartment, Terry had complained that *Pillow Talk* was too grown up a movie for a ten-year-old. "I read in *Silver Screen* that Rock Hudson turned down the film three times because the script was risqué," Terry pointed out.

"But it's Rock Hudson's first comedy," Chiara whined. "And they're talking about an Oscar nomination for Doris Day."

"Even the picture's title is indecent," Terry sighed.

But Chiara Rose begged so heartily, expounding so convincingly on the handsomeness of Hudson, the pristineness of Miss Day and the combined comedic flair of Thelma Ritter and Tony Randall that Terry finally relented. "She's going to be a lawyer," Tiger whispered, patting his wife's round belly. Terry smiled tiredly. Although her second pregnancy was taking its toll on her, his wife seemed even more beautiful in her plump contentedness, watching her family leave for the evening to give her a few hours with her girlfriends.

After squares at Mario's, Chiara practically skipped to the Loew's 46th, dragging her father by the hand. He let her secure the best seats—tenth row, center—after carefully selecting their movie-time snacks—Chocolate Babies and a large popcorn with extra butter (and extra napkins). Tiger's brother-in-law Augie never let him pay, just as Tiger never let Augie pay at Feel Good Food. Family doing for family, they liked to say.

Stan usually worked Saturday nights at the theatre, after putting in a full day at Feel Good Food. But this night, Stan was nowhere to be found, although the eatery was long closed. Tiger was sure his brother would show up since Stan'd had a serious crush on Doris Day ever since her record "Che Sera Sera" came out a few years earlier. He never missed one of Doris's flicks, especially when he knew Tiger and Chiara Rose were going. It wasn't like Stan to ditch them.

Tiger had to admit that *Pillow Talk* was an entertaining picture. A playboy, a career girl, a party line, a case of mistaken identity, a romantic triangle…hilarity ensued. But he cringed at the part where Rock dragged a pajama-clad Doris out of bed and carried her through the streets of Manhattan to his apartment. In his mind, it catapulted Miss Day from girl next door to sex symbol. Tiger's enjoyment of the film was compounded when he glanced over to see his daughter's exuberant face illuminated in the dark theatre.

"It's what goes on when the lights go out," *Pillow Talk*'s movie poster boasted. Tiger was sure there would be a sea of questions, which is why they would take the long way back.

Before they even left the Loew's 46th, Chiara had queries like "What's a hangover?" and "What's a stripper?" and "Why did he slap her?" and "I don't understand why she said, 'I'm yours tonight. My darling, possess me.'" These questions were deftly fielded by Tiger.

The Queen of Non Sequiturs, Chiara's conversation quickly shifted onto the child's favorite subject: how her parents met.

"Was it like that with you and Mommy?" the girl wondered.

"Not at all," Tiger said. "I didn't have to woo her. We liked each other straight off."

They made their way out of the theatre lobby, past couples lined up for the late show. "Good picture?" Augie asked from the office.

"The best!" Chiara gushed.

Out on New Utrecht Avenue, the girl continued her barrage of questions. Her father handled them as best he could. "What's 'wooing'?" then "How did you and Mommy know you liked each other?"

Tiger shrugged. "We just knew. The first time I met your mother…"

"…you told Uncle Jimmy that you didn't want to go out with her again because you knew you'd end up marrying her."

Tiger squeezed his daughter's hand. "If you know the answer, then why do you ask?"

"I like the way you tell it," Chiara confessed. "By Christmas that year you were engaged and you got married the next June."

Tiger nodded. "Your mom looked like a queen in her wedding gown…"

"…a queen with a broken crown because the limousine got into an accident on the way to the church," Chiara said. "She kept trying to fix her tiara but it was crooked."

As they turned down Forty-Seventh Street, Tiger saw a man with a familiar gait coming toward them, head down, fists in his pockets. Without seeing his face, Tiger knew it was his brother. When Stan had a few drinks, he often dug his fists deep into his pants pockets in an attempt to steady himself. (Their father had done the same thing.) It never worked.

Stan weaved his way up the pavement until they met on the sidewalk in front of 1128 Forty-Seventh Street. "Uncle Stannie!" Chiara Rose shouted and jumped into his arms, almost knocking him over. He quickly regained his balance and held her tight. She hugged him fast around the neck.

"You smell funny," Chiara whispered to him.

"New cologne," he whispered back, fibbing. "You like it?"

"No," she told him.

Tiger wondered why they were in this clinch for so long but Stan soon released her. "Down, girl!" Stan joked and set the girl onto the pavement. "What's shaking, Chi?" he asked.

Stan was one of the few people who could get away with calling her "Chi." Depending on her mood, the precocious child was known to correct anyone who tried, but her Uncle Stannie was different. They had a rapport, a connection, that few in this close-knit family shared. The child babbled about *Pillow Talk*, about how Doris Day looked with her new hairdo and fancy wardrobe and her décolletage showing. "That means boobies," Chiara explained, then added, "She even looked great in a bubble bath."

"Speaking of which, time to go inside and have yours," Tiger said.

"Aw, nuts," she complained but went in anyway. Both Tiger and Stan watched her go, as did Terry from the window.

Tiger took the opportunity to study his brother, who seemed worse for the wear. Stan's hair fell into his eyes and his shirt was half untucked. There was the fragrance of whiskey and beer about him, just like their father had exuded. "Cop-a-squat," Tiger said, purposely mangling the French phrase. Stan sat on one of the cement ledges at the left side of the stairs; his brother sat on the right. "How's it going?" Tiger asked.

"It's going fine," Stan told him, avoiding his brother's gaze. "How's it going with you?"

"Busy," Tiger admitted. "We couldn't do it without you. Run the joint, I mean. And now with us thinking about opening a third place, we'll need you even more."

"I ain't going nowhere," Stan assured him.

"I'm glad," Tiger smiled. "Me and George, we want to give you a raise. A hefty one."

"Thanks. That's swell."

"But with more dough comes more responsibility. You up for it?"

"Sure, I am," Stan said. He struggled to sit up straight because suddenly, the world seemed slightly off kilter.

"'Cause I hear you coming in late lots of nights and Ma says…"

"Ma's a worrier."

"Maybe she's got something to worry about."

"Me? Nah. I'm on the straight and narrow," Stan lied.

"You sure about that?"

"Never been more sure about anything in my life."

"I'm happy to hear it," Tiger said. The moon was only half full and with the autumn came a chill in the air. "Well, it's getting late. I guess I'd better get some shut eye. You?"

"I think I'll sit out here a while," Stan mused. "It's a nice night." Tiger briefly rested his palm on his brother's shoulder. Stan squeezed it, then let go. Tiger was almost in the vestibule when he heard Stan call his name.

Tiger turned. "Yeah, Stanley?"

"Do you ever wonder...do you ever wonder if you're like him?"

Tiger stepped toward his brother. "You mean Tony?" Stan nodded. "I used to. But not anymore. We come from good people. More good than bad."

"But my mom, my real mom. She wasn't..."

"There was a lot of good in Denise," Tiger assured him. "She had a kindness in her eyes. She just made bad choices. But you...you were the best thing she ever did. She said so herself and I believe it."

Stan bit his lip. "Okay," he said. "Okay."

Tiger sat on the steps beside his brother, who was still on the cement block. Their knees touched. "There's a lot of good in you too," Tiger said. "The way you are with Chiara. The way you are with customers. You're really something." Tiger ruffled Stan's hair just like he used to when his brother was little.

After Tiger left, Stan thought he saw a pair of shadows in the vestibule. Two old, familiar folks seemed to have been watching the two brothers through the front door. Stan could have sworn the shadows belonged to their grandparents. He thought of calling after Tiger but his brother hadn't seemed to notice anything awry when he'd left.

Stan blinked and tried to refocus. But when he opened his eyes again, the wraithlike shapes had disappeared like smoke. Maybe it was the drink; maybe not.

CHAPTER SEVEN

Grandma's Blessing

When the twins were babies, sometimes Angela found her mother standing over their crib. (Yes, crib singular. Early on, as preemies, the babies made it clear that they preferred sleeping together.) But Angela knew that Rose was doing more than simply watching them sleep. She knew that her mother was appealing silently for blessings, perhaps quietly speaking the Overlook Prayer, which Angela had taught her mother soon after Bridget and Poppa passed. Rose finally agreed to learn the Prayer because she felt that someone besides Angela should know its powerful words to protect the family from the evil eye. Though some scoffed at the Overlook Prayer as Italian voodoo and an Old-World Guinea superstition, Angela (and Rose) had seen its might firsthand. Angela knew that the Overlook Prayer helped keep her children—and the rest of them—safe from harm.

Where other prematurely-born twins were sickly and frail, Beth and David grew stronger and more solid with each passing day. They were born one month early but you would never know it. Thirteen on their last birthday, they were hale, hardy, sharp and sturdy. Beth's dark eyes flashed with intelligence. Her hair was as windswept and unrestrained as her personality. Beth's mirror opposite physically, David's eyes were green-gray like his mother's, his hair bone-straight and a shade lighter than Angela's. The boy was thoughtful and tread lightly where his sister just dove right into situations. The children were constantly keeping each other in check.

Now that the twins were older, Angela still felt her mother's watchful eye on her offspring, plus something more. In times of trouble, Angela liked to recall her grandparents cradling the children in their arms at their baptism, then proudly gazing up at her and Augie. Angela had this beautiful picture of Bridget and Poppa stuck in her head and she called upon its memory often to ferry her through difficulties.

For example, when the twins were colicky or refused to go to sleep. Or more recently, when Beth was sent home with a note from school that they'd found a copy of *Lady Chatterley's Lover* in her bookbag. To shield his sister, David said the paperback was his but their teacher—and Angela—knew the truth. David wasn't much of a reader—especially of a thick tome like this. But Beth had an appetite for books as voracious as her mother's.

Instead of chiding Beth or punishing her, Angela and Augie sat down with their daughter at the kitchen table, *Lady Chatterley's Lover* on the Formica between them. Beth nervously fingered the kitchenette's blue turquoise Naugahyde seat. "Am I in trouble?" she wondered, staring hard at the tabletop's gray swirls. David was within earshot yet not within sight, hovering near the doorway.

"Not with us," Augie assured her.

"But maybe it's best not to bring the book to school," Angela added.

"What's so bad about it?" Beth asked.

"I don't know," Angela admitted. "I haven't read it."

"Would you like to?"

"Sure. I'm curious what all the hoopla is about," Angela told her. "Banned in all fifty States."

Beth glanced at the cover. "Plus, Canada, Australia, India and Japan."

"Do you like it?" Angela wondered.

Beth shrugged. "It's interesting. Lots of it I don't understand. But I like how the woman is the most important part of the story."

"I want to read it too," Augie said, "But I don't have time right now. Your mom will take a crack at it and fill me in." Angela nodded in assent. Because Augie was expected at the Loew's 46th (the afternoon ticket taker was a no-show), Angela would finish things up with Beth. He kissed them both, Beth on the forehead and his wife on the mouth.

After her father left, Beth slid the book toward her mother. Angela picked up the well-thumbed paperback. It appeared so harmless with its simple white cover. A provocative red circle announced: "This and only this is the uncensored edition making today's headlines!" "Complete and Unabridged" and "This is the Grove Press edition, the only unexpurgated version ever published in America!" *Lady Chatterley's Lover* cost fifty cents, which Beth must have saved up from babysitting money.

Angela turned the pages. Some were dog-eared and folded down as placeholders. Particular words stood out, words like: *sex-thrill* and *demi-vierge*. Phrases popped out at her:

> *"What a frail, easily hurt, rather pathetic thing a human body is, naked."*
> *"'Why don't men and women really like one another nowadays?'"*
> *"But it seems to me you might leave the labels off sex."*
> *"We could be chaste together just as we can fuck together."*

Angela closed the book. "What's your favorite thing about it?" she wondered.

Beth thought for a moment. "Well, it's sort of old-timey, but I like that it tells you what people are thinking in their heads."

"Who's your favorite character?" Angela wondered.

"That's easy. Connie."

"Lady Chatterley?"

Beth nodded. "She seems very real. Especially what she thinks about her body. She doesn't like it much. At first."

"Your body is just fine," Angela assured her daughter. "Everything works. Everything is perfect."

"I know," Beth said. "But I wish my chest was bigger. Boys like girls with big chests."

"Those kinds of boys have small brains," Angela told her.

"Maybe," the girl admitted. "But those kinds of boys are usually kind of cute." Mother and daughter smiled quietly together. David, still lingering on the periphery, breathed a sigh of relief that his sister wasn't in trouble. He left the two to discuss the book which didn't interest him in the least.

"I'll start reading it tonight and we'll talk about it more in the morning," Angela said.

As promised, that night in bed, Angela Corso, who had been intimate with only one man in her life, began reading *Lady Chatterley's Lover*. Words stuck with her, like:

> *"Ours is essentially a tragic age, so we refuse to take it tragically..."*

The story of Constance, Clifford and Oliver immediately gripped Angela. The war Clifford had fought was not so different than the war Angela remembered, the war her brother had fought in and the war that had taken her Uncle Harry's leg.

And old D.H. wasted no time getting into the sex (by page three!) It was gripping, fascinating. Angela simply could not put the book down, even after Augie arrived late after closing the theatre, changed into his pajamas and slid into the warm cotton sheets beside her. "It's so beautiful and true," Angela said without looking up from the page.

Augie eyed the book splayed open in his wife's lap and read silently to himself:

"He was the trembling excited sort of lover, whose crisis soon came, and was finished..."

"All of this crisis," Augie said. Then, reading aloud:

"But then she soon learnt to hold him, to keep him there inside her when his crisis was over. And there he was generous and curiously potent; he stayed firm inside her, given to her while she was active...wildly, passionately active, coming to her own crisis..."

Augie closed the book. "Lady Angela..." he said, holding out his hand to his wife. He didn't have to say anything more. Angela was in his arms, swiftly moving toward her own crisis.

The next morning, Angela was up earlier than usual. Although it was cool in their autumn bedroom, she awoke sweaty and sticky. *Lady Chatterley's Lover* sat on her nightstand just where Augie had placed it. Angela picked it up and read for at least a half-hour before she crept out of bed to begin breakfast and wake the twins for school.

The Maxwell House was perking when Beth came into the kitchen, fully dressed. She grabbed the box of Corn Flakes from the counter as well as the Cheerios (her brother's favorite). Then she took two bowls from the cupboard. Angela set the teaspoons on the table then fetched the bottle of milk from the Frigidaire. Beth smooshed the Corn Flakes into a soggy, mushy mess, just the way she liked them. "So," she said, mouth half full. "What did you think?"

"About what?" Angela asked, dimming the burner's flame under the percolator.

"About the book," Beth pushed.

"What makes you think I started it?" Angela teased.

"You said you would."

Her mother smiled. "It pulls you right in," she conceded. "Even though it's old as anything."

"It's not that old," Angela said. "Just a few years older than me."

"My point exactly," Beth laughed through the milk.

David showed up at the table, dragging his feet. Unlike his sister, he was not an early riser and he preferred his cereal crisp and crunchy. This is why he ate it quickly, similar to a hungry puppy, as though he were afraid the bowl might be taken from him. "Come up for air," his sister teased. Impervious, David went right on scooping the circles of oats into his mouth while reading the latest issue of *Tales of Suspense*, which featured Captain America, a kid from Brooklyn just like him.

With the children off to school and Augie off to the Loew's 46th, Angela divided her time between housework and reading. After she mopped the speckled kitchen linoleum and waited for it to dry, she read Chapter Seven of *Lady Chatterley's Lover*. Satisfied that the bathroom tiles sparkled, she sat to take in Chapter Eight. After she picked up the odds and ends on the Avenue needed to make supper, Angela tackled Chapter Nine. Before she knew it, she was halfway through the book.

In less than a week, Constance Reid and her randy gamekeeper made their way to all the Paradiso women, who read it fervently, feverishly, and their husbands were glad for it. Astrid had already read it, she being so cosmopolitan and ahead of the curve. Wendy had also read the once-banned book, and she had done so breathlessly, usually late at night, taking several breaks to calm herself before picking up the tale again.

Rose was the last to take on Lady Chatterley, though she quibbled that she didn't have time to read books anymore. "Oh, you'll find the time to read this one," Jo assured her, and she did. Though Rose blushed and flushed with practically every page, she read it quickly, with a lusty appetite which surprised her. It took her mind off the troubles with Stan, for Connie's life was more complicated than her own.

Before she drifted off to sleep, Rose wondered if her dear mother, God rest her soul, who had been an avid reader, would have tackled the book with the same appetite as her daughters, granddaughter and great granddaughter had. Would Bridget have given it her blessing? Or would she have been taken aback at their boldness. It was a question for the ages.

CHAPTER EIGHT

Little Mischief

S tan hoped Big Paulie had forgotten all about his proposition. But no such luck because the creep never forgot anything. He was worse than an elephant in that regard. And not only didn't Big Paulie forget about things but he harped on them like a record that kept jumping on the same scratch. It was grating, like hearing Connie Francis singing the line: "Lipstick on your collar" over and over and over again.

"You're in, right" or "You're gonna do this, right?" or "I can count on you, right?" Big Paulie had the irritating habit of saying the same thing in a slightly different way *ad infinitum*.

"Yeah," "Sure" and "You got my word" were Stan's typical responses. But Stan didn't mean it and Big Paulie didn't seem to believe him either. Which is probably why he kept questioning Stan like an insecure suitor. And why Stan kept answering Big Paulie's queries like a guilty swain with noncommittal statements like: "Of course" and "I told you so, didn't I?" and "Uh-huh." These retorts would spark another round of insecurities from the rotund man.

Betsy Mulaney always seemed to be hanging about on the sidelines of the Stumble Inn, lurking in the shadows, as if hoping for another go at Stan. Had Big Paulie put her up to seducing Stan to get on his good side? To secure his hold on Stan? Offering his would-be henchman, the charms of this mildly pretty, moderately tarty girl as a reward for Stan's fidelity to Big Paulie and his half-baked schemes? Stan sure hoped not.

Still, Betsy seemed overly keen to be Stan's steady beau but he didn't have his sights set on any gal in particular. Except maybe one he considered to be unattainable.

Perhaps this was the reason for Stan's floundering, for his being unable to find his niche in life, his place. Rose felt certain that Stan would eventually find it; Sully was not so sure. From his years walking the beat and more recently, as sergeant, Sully had seen far too many decent kids who went astray by hanging around with the wrong crowd, only to take the wrong path—which led straight to Rikers Island. That prison was filled with good guys gone bad, otherwise sweet kids whose "little mischief" led to "big mischief." 'There but for the grace of God…' prayed Sully under his breath.

It had been years since Sully had visited The Stumble Inn, which is why Stan was so shocked to see his teetotaler father there. But Stan didn't let the shock register on his face and he didn't approach Sully immediately. He just sat with Big Paulie, hoping his father wouldn't notice him. But Sully and his cop sensibilities noticed everything.

Sully reckoned that the last time he had been at that particular pub was when he'd spotted his brother-in-law Harry through the bar's filthy front windowpane, slumped over an empty whiskey glass and a pint full of beer, drowning in his own postwar sorrow. Just as Harry had made it through that tough patch, Sully hoped his own son would too.

Patrick Sullivan sidled up to the bar, relieved Teddy Long was behind it that night. "What'll it be, stranger?" Teddy wondered.

Sully contemplated the taps for his choices. "A Budweiser," he said. "A short one."

"If I were you, I'd go for the Rheingold," the barkeep advised. He leaned in closer to Sully. "I ain't saying the Bud is bad but if it were meat, you wouldn't eat it."

"Rheingold it is," Sully agreed. "You don't have to tell me twice."

"I only carry Bud for the kids who don't know any better," Teddy said as he drew from the Rheingold tap. "They wouldn't know a fine Brooklyn brew if it hit them over the head." He slid the beer in front of Sully. "How are things?" he wondered.

"Things are good," Sully admitted.

"If I didn't see you at St. Catherine's fundraisers, I wouldn't see you at all," Teddy grumbled.

"Although I enjoy your company, Theodore, I doubt my one beer a week would make or break you." Both men laughed. "How are things with you?" Sully ventured.

"Can't complain," Teddy said. "And if I did, who would listen?"

"I'd pretend to listen," Sully told Teddy, taking a sip of the frothy amber liquid. He winced. He never did acquire a taste for the stuff.

"Life is all right," the barkeep continued. "I got Junior picking up the slack when I'm not behind the bar. I have a chance to spend more time with the Missus." Then after a beat, Teddy added, "Then again, that might be the end of us." Sully shook his head and gave a chuckle as Teddy explained, "Either the end of our marriage or Junior running us into the ground."

"Drinking away the profits, is he?" Sully asked.

"Not him. His friends. Gives away too many on the house. Especially to that shit-for-brains chooch who holds court here." With his head, Teddy gestured to the joker at the end of the saloon.

"Big Paulie?"

"That's the one. He never pays a cent when Junior's on the stick. But his friends do and they tip well, which is why I don't run him out of Dodge."

"Well, if you ever get tired of him and his shenanigans, just say the word. I know some people who could set that mook straight."

Teddy smirked. "I appreciate that, Paddy." He ran a damp rag across the mahogany bar top. "How about you? You thinking of kicking back and taking it easy?"

"Thinking, yeah. Doing, no. Don't get me wrong, my Roe is a saint but I don't know how much Sully she can take."

"I get ya," Teddy said. "But you're not getting any younger. And you must be sick of dealing with skells like that clown all these years."

"Sick isn't the word for it. And it would be nice to spend more time with the grandkids."

"I hear there's another one on the way. Congrats."

Sully raised his glass. "Thank you. Terry just told the family. Boy, news travels fast around this neighborhood."

"Faster and cheaper than Western Union. Tiger comes in now and then for a drink. Turned out to be first-rate, that fella. Not like his Pa."

"The only other one I know like his Pa is Satan himself," Sully growled. Instead of refilling Sully's beer glass, Teddy took it away and replaced it with a tumbler of ginger ale. "You still remember," Sully remarked. "I'm impressed."

"Remember what? That you drink like a toddler? How can I forget?" Teddy added a couple of maraschino cherries to the soda. "And Tony's other son…" he continued, pointing his chin toward Stan at the opposite end of the bar where he conferred with Big Paulie. It was almost as though Stan sensed they were talking about him because he glanced at his stepfather and finally acknowledged Sully with a nod. "That one, he's not so bad either," Teddy told his friend. "A little knockabout but I think he'll do all right."

"Despite the company he keeps?"

"In spite of himself, yeah. He comes from good people. That's got to count for something."

"I hope so, Teddy. I sure hope so."

The barkeep intuitively walked away when he saw Stan coming toward Sully. Stan didn't smile until his father did. "What's shaking, Pop?"

"Oh, not much," Sully admitted. "Just felt like getting some fresh air. Your ma's over at Angie's with the other hens. Some sort of book club. It was getting lonely back at the ranch."

"Sure you're not checking up on me?" Stan pushed.

"Why? Do you need checking up on?"

"I don't think so." Although he didn't have a drink in hand, Stan's voice was slightly fuzzy, his tongue thick. Sully had dealt with many a drunk with the same vocal intonation who had crashed a car into a tree but swore he was fine. "Do you think I do?" Stan added, almost defiantly.

"You're a grown man, free to make your own decisions. Right or wrong," Sully said. Without meaning to, he glared toward where Big Paulie had planted himself at the bar. Then Sully looked his son dead in the eye. "Buy you a drink?"

"Thanks, but no. I got work in the morning."

"Yeah, me, too. Your Ma left you a plate of macaroni if you're hungry when you get in."

"I had something to eat before I left the shop."

"All right," Stan's father said. Just as Sully got up to leave, Big Paulie stood as well. Stan hoped it was to use the can and "drain the dragon," but instead, the rotund man waddled to where Stan and Sully were chatting. Stan cringed. Sometimes the mini-mobster had no common sense. Why couldn't he just leave well enough alone?

Stan watched his father's face stiffen into the mask he knew well: it was the same mask he donned when Stan was a kid and wove a little white lie that Sully knew was a falsehood, the same mask he wore when a perp swore he didn't do it. Sully steeled himself for the storm of horseshit that would descend from the thug's lips.

"Mr. Sullivan," Big Paulie began, extending his hand. He grinned so broadly it must have hurt. Stan couldn't get over how much the guy resembled an overweight weasel when he grinned.

Reluctantly, Sully took Big Paulie's outstretched paw, swallowing it with his own and purposely squeezing it too hard. A major league pissing contest was about to begin.

Big Paulie grimaced slightly when Sully corrected, "It's Sargent Sullivan."

"How could I forget?" Big Paulie said, peeling his hand out from Sully's granite grip. "You've got quite a son here," he added.

"I know it," Sully told him. "Hard worker, a good man."

"We been friends forever, since we were kids."

"I know that, too," Sully said. "I remember you. I remember picking you up for vandalism. More than once. And another time for what you done to that stray cat."

Stan hung his head, studying the tile pattern on the floor. Alternating black and white hexagons, pretty clean considering it was a well-trafficked bar. When Stan heard Big Paulie's voice, he looked up again. Still cool as a cuke, the ruffian tugged at his necktie and shrugged, "People change."

"Mostly, they don't," Sully told him. "Mostly, they're still the same snot-nosed kids they were growing up, only bigger."

Undaunted, Big Paulie gave it one more try. "How's the family? Your niece Wendy…"

With this, Sully stepped closer to Big Paulie, towering over the sharkskin-suited hoodlum. He lay his hand on Big Paulie's shoulder, and not affectionately. Sully leaned in and whispered into his ear, "You go anywhere near my niece and I'll snap your geek neck like a toothpick. You got me?"

Big Paulie reeled. "Yeah, I got you."

Sully pulled the ne'er-do-well closer, grabbing his wide lapel onehanded. "And while you're at it, stay away from my son. Okay?"

"Okay! Okay!" said Big Paulie, smoothing down his suit.

"Okay what?" Stan asked.

"It's between me and Mr. Morrongiello right?"

"Right," the crook agreed. This time, Big Paulie did disappear into the bathroom. 'Maybe he shit himself,' Sully thought hopefully.

"You keep your distance from him," Sully warned his son. Stan didn't respond because he knew he wouldn't do as his father ordered. "See you at home." Sully drew Stan close and kissed his forehead. "Don't be too late."

"I won't." But it was already past ten.

Teddy Long was clearing away empty pint glasses from the front window's ledge. "Everything all right?" he asked Sully.

"Ah, Teddy," Sully sighed. "Little kids, little problems. Big kids, big problems."

Teddy nodded meaningfully. "Don't I know it."

CHAPTER NINE

Happenstance

Although Tiger's grandparents had taken him all over New York State and to New Jersey when he was a kid, he had rarely been to Connecticut. Despite the fact that the Constitution State skirted his own, Tiger had been overseas courtesy of World War II before he crossed Connecticut's border near Wingdale, New York.

Having made a wrong turn off Route 22, Tiger was in pursuit of the scenic route to Waterbury, Connecticut—to visit Terry's Aunt Beatrice and Uncle Nello—and boy did he get it! Quaker Hill's museum of oddities and its quaint cemetery led to a pretty hamlet called Sherman. That's when Tiger finally admitted to his wife that he was hopelessly lost and pulled into Rizzo's Gas Station at the intersection where Route 39 kisses Route 37.

As luck would have it, a helpful fellow named Bill was at the pump, filling another customer's Impala. Bill gladly provided excellent directions which he promised would get the Martino Family to the Suscella's doorstep in less than an hour. "You'll be eating macaroni in no time," Bill smiled.

While Terry and Chiara Rose used the restroom—the former holding the latter over the bowl to perform her duties midair—Tiger and Bill chatted politely. Bill Karpi had recently moved his family to Sherman from Queens, tired of the stench from the Elmhurst gas tanks and the noise.

Between "real" jobs, Bill wasn't too proud to pump gas to support his family and he wasn't embarrassed about his choice or his predicament. "You've got to do what's best for you and yours," Bill said, cleaning off the windshield of Tiger's two-tone Bel Air with a squeegee after filling its tank. "Something better's bound to come along. I can feel it in my bones," Bill added.

On the way out of Sherman, Tiger noticed a row of stores. A card shop, a liquor store and a vacant space. He pulled in and stopped the car. "Aunt Bea's going to think we're dead on the highway," Terry sighed. She had become less patient than usual during her second pregnancy. Everything seemed to make Terry nauseous or irritated, especially the winding country roads of Connecticut.

"It'll only take a minute," Tiger assured her, squeezing her hand.

"I'm timing you," Terry warned him. She and Chiara got out with Tiger, the spirited child already jumping out of her skin from being cooped up in the car for so long. Chiara immediately started climbing a small Japanese maple with blazing red leaves, promising not to scuff her Mary Janes or muss her Sunday dress while she did so.

As Terry stood beside her husband, she could feel the electricity sparking from his skin, the excitement of possibility oozing from his pores. Where she saw a ruined, empty shell of a store, Tiger saw potential. Terry both loved and hated this about her husband—she treasured his vision, his enthusiasm but she also loathed that it would consume him and take him away from her, just when she needed him most, when the family was growing. Was this the best time to expand the business? Sometimes Terry felt she could hardly manage one lively child. How could she handle two?

Back on the road, Terry struggled to keep down her breakfast as they swerved down Route 37 to Route 7 to Route 67. 'Do all of Connecticut roads have sevens in them?' she asked herself, stifling an acidic belch. They passed all sorts of "burys"—Roxbury, Woodbury, Southbury, Middlebury until the "bury" they sought eventually came into view.

Along the way, Tiger bubbled on about what a swell guy Bill Karpi seemed to be and what potential the humble Sherman storefront held. "There's even space behind it to put out tables and chairs in the nice weather," Tiger told Aunt Bea and Uncle Nello as they enjoyed one of Elaine Thomas's sweet potato pies, which was a novelty in Waterbury, just as Connecticut apple-picking was a novelty to tried-and-true Brooklynites like the Martinos.

Uncle Nello, whose girth attested to the fact that he appreciated a good meal, thought an outpost of Feel Good Food in Sherman was a fine idea. He, for one, would travel an hour for delicacies like sweet potato pie and Southern fried chicken. Aunt Bea agreed, cheered by the thought of not having to cook an elaborate supper once in a while. Coupled with a trip to nearby Kent Falls, spending an afternoon in Sherman sounded like a pleasant way to pass the day.

On the return drive to Brooklyn, with Chiara Rose curled up, fast asleep in the back seat, Tiger continued his plans out loud, ironing them out in the air with Terry listening closely and offering a suggestion or two. Opening shop in Sherman was the last thing Tiger spoke of before he floated off to Dreamland that night. "I can reach Bill at Rizzo's where he works," was the last thing Tiger said. Terry rested one palm on his shoulder, the other on her belly, wondering if the twinge she felt in her side was another miscarriage or simply indigestion. Then she slipped off to sleep too.

Tiger couldn't wait to discuss the possibility of Feel Good Food expanding into the Nutmeg State with George. As a rule, he was a touch more cynical than Tiger but he could usually win George over. Tiger decided to take it slow until the time was right to unveil the Connecticut proposal to his business partner.

The Monday following Tiger's family jaunt to Waterbury and Aunt Bea's, he broached the subject. Tiger was prepping corned beef with all the fixings (potatoes, cabbage and carrots) and George was running the cabbage through the mandolin for Ma's Coleslaw. "Save me a couple of carrots for this, would you?" George requested.

Tiger put two aside. "Need some red cabbage?" he wondered.

"Just a touch. For color." Tiger pushed it through the box grater for he knew George preferred the red cabbage finer than the white. George glanced over at Tiger's pile of shredded vegetables and nodded approvingly. "Perfect," he conceded. "You know just how I like it."

"After all these years, I should," Tiger said. Both men smiled slightly, enjoying the proximity of working side by side. Tiger next began shaving the carrots with the box grater. George measured out the apple cider vinegar, mayonnaise, sugar and a touch of water by eye and added them all to a Mason jar. He capped the jar and shook it vigorously.

As George poured the creamy mixture over the dark and light cabbage, Tiger slid the carrot bits into the huge bowl. "How's Uncle Nello doing?" George wondered.

"Terrific," Tiger told him. "Still driving Aunt Bea crazy. Flipped for Elaine's sweet potato pie. Told me to tell you that he misses your fried chicken and to say 'hey.'"

"Hope you told him I said 'hey' back."

"I did." Tiger had meant to slowly ease into the details of his Connecticut visit but the words just tumbled out of him. "Perfect location…hell of a guy…good feeling about… nothing like it out there…Uncle Nello says…"

As Tiger bubbled on about this possible new venture, he found that he was out of breath. George watched him with a grin on his face, the gap between his two front teeth unhidden. "What?" Tiger asked, exasperated.

"Oh, nothing," George teased. "It's just that you remind me of a kid fresh out of the Service who came to my house in Jersey City and told me about this great idea he had for an eatery."

"Whatever happened to that kid?" Tiger pushed.

"Even though he's way past thirty, he never grew up. He's still excited about life, about possibilities," George said.

"And how about his partner?"

George gave the coleslaw a toss with the spatula, mixing the dressing through evenly. "His partner's still excited," he conceded. "Just tired. Anthony, seems I been in the kitchen my whole life. I'm likely to die here."

"Don't say that."

"Why not? It's true. But I wouldn't want it any other way. The kitchen's where I want to be. I don't like the planning and budgeting and figuring out part like you do. That's why I leave that all up to you."

"Which is why it works so well," Tiger said. "The only reason I like prepping is so you and me can jaw. Just like the old days." Tiger took a forkful of the slaw and nodded. "Damn, that's good."

"Sure, it's good. It's mine." They laughed quietly together. George eased the coleslaw into a plastic tub, fastened the lid and put it into the stainless-steel Frigidaire. He took out a cooled-down bowl of boiled potatoes and set it on the counter.

"So, what do you think?" Tiger asked.

"I'm not sure what the market can bear. Is that the saying?"

"The market has never seen the likes of Feel Good Food, not out in Connecticut, anyways."

"In white picket fence country? What if they don't like Eye-talian and Southern cooking?"

"Don't forget Jewish soul food," Tiger added. "Vot's not to like?" he said, perfectly capturing Sadie Liberwitz's Yiddish accent." This drew a tiny smile from George but only for a moment.

"What I mean is, won't we be spreading ourselves too thin?" George worried. "There's only two of us. Three locations might be too much for us to manage. It's like my buddy Grizzly Grimes used to say about having kids: 'More than two and they outnumber you.'"

"That might very well be true," Tiger admitted. "But you see, that's where this fellow Bill Karpi comes in."

"Only you don't know him from a hole in the ground."

"I got a feeling..." Tiger began. "A good feeling." George knew all about Italians and their feelings, superstitions, signs and signals from beyond. Italians weren't much different than colored folk in that regard, so George didn't dismiss his business partner's premonitions entirely.

Undeterred, Tiger continued, "Something about Bill reminded me of Poppa..." He paused, overcome with emotion, then started up again, "And something inside me says to give it a shot, to give this Bill fellow a shot."

George flashed Tiger "that look," a weighty gaze of doubt. He didn't suck his teeth at Tiger as his wife Elaine might have done but the implication was there. Tiger plowed on, impervious, "Listen, Tyrone is helping out in the Jersey City kitchen. Say the word and I think he'll quit trucking and work for us full time. Plus, we got Stan and me and..."

"Slow down, cowboy," George told Tiger.

"Listen, alls I'm asking is that you meet Bill. Tell me what you think. But don't make your decision about opening up a place in Sherman until then. Deal?"

George considered it. "Deal." They shook on it.

Without being asked, Tiger began peeling the potatoes, using the back end of a butter knife, just like Aunt Sophie Veronica had taught him when he was a boy, before she, Kelly and their brood had set off to Tucson. Tiger was surprised that George denuded potatoes the same way, no peeler. "Less waste, more potato," he'd explained, exactly as Sophie Veronica had decades earlier.

For the dressing, George used Rose's recipe, which incorporated sweet pickle juice instead of the vinegar many people added, plus a healthy dollop of strong mustard. Kosciusko was George's personal preference, and not just because he liked the way Mrs. Lieberwitz pronounced it, like a sneeze—"Ko-chusco!" George mixed the dressing until it was a uniform light-yellow paste. He sighed heavily. "What gives, old man?" Tiger asked.

George sliced the peeled potatoes directly into the dressing bowl. "I, for one, can't wait for this year to be over and done with, dead and buried. A year that starts with a revolution isn't a good start."

"Yeah, but that was in Cuba," Tiger said. "Has nothing to do with us."

"Cuba's only ninety miles away from Florida," George reminded him. "It's practically in our own backyard." He sliced the last potato into the bowl. "And a few days after that, the Lovings pleaded guilty."

"Yeah," Tiger agreed. "But that was in Virginia."

"Virginia ain't so far away." All of the potatoes sliced, George added chopped onion then mixed the salad with a wooden spoon. "Mmm-mmm-mmm," he clucked disapprovingly. "Richard and Mildred Loving, guilty of a criminal offense just by sheer virtue of marrying each other. The Racial Integrity Act. I don't see no integrity in that."

Tiger took the spoon from George, who was crushing the delicate spuds beneath it, so fervent was his displeasure of the Lovings' plight. "How about you get the paprika?" Tiger suggested.

George returned with the brilliant red ground spice, which Sadie Lieberwitz had brought from Budapest, as well as the salt and pepper. As George added all three to the potato salad, Tiger recalled George's rage when he'd caught his daughter Pamela and Stan kissing in the eatery's pantry as teenagers. "Don't you know that people get killed for doing things like that!" the normally-tranquil man had ranted, slapping his daughter and yanking Stan across the room.

Tiger had said nothing. He let it go because the incident had happened so soon after a boy named Emmett Till was found murdered in Mississippi. Tortured, beaten with a pistol, stripped, shot and thrown into a river, a heavy cotton gin fan strung around his neck. All for whistling at a white woman. Emmett Till was only fourteen, a child.

No, Tiger could never forget the expression on George's face when he saw the photograph of poor Emmett in *Jet Magazine*: the boy's bloated, mutilated, distorted body. He was missing an eye and didn't appear to be quite human.

Emmett's mother insisted on an open casket because "the whole nation had to bear witness to this." Raw grief painted Mrs. Till's normally-lovely features as she looked at her son, who rested uneasily on a pillow in his coffin, his face melted like a cruel candle. Mrs. Till clutched her purse to her chest as any distressed mother would, weeping.

Tiger had quietly closed *Jet Magazine* and slipped it from George's clenched fists. He didn't know what else to say so he said, "I'm sorry."

"You didn't do anything," George told his friend softly, and focused his attention on the pot of greens on the stove.

And four years later, in that very same kitchen, not much in the world had changed.

George added more paprika to the potato salad. (Sadie Lieberwitz insisted that Hungarian paprika was "the best" just like George's potato salad; and it was.) "No," George continued, "1959 was not a good year for negroes. Back in April, Mack Charles Parker was lynched in Mississippi. They haven't prosecuted anyone for his murder yet, and it's been seven months. *Brown v. Board of Education* was five years ago yet they're still closing schools in the South so they don't have to desegregate."

"But that's in Virginia too."

"Don't you see, Anthony, what happens there happens here," George said plaintively. Tiger grabbed the tube of plastic wrap. Together, he and George covered the bowl tight. "For Emmett Till, an all-white, all-male jury came back with a not-guilty verdict after only an hour. And for Parker, they ain't gonna pin it on nobody, mark my words."

"I hope you're wrong," Tiger told him.

"I hope so too but I won't be. You wait and see."

A bushel of apples from Tiger's trek to the Land of Steady Habits (did Connecticut have more nicknames than any other U.S. State?) waited to be cored and peeled. The men began the prep work for Miss Addie's Apple Crisp, a tray of Apple Brown Betty and a few containers of applesauce. They worked silently side by side for a few minutes, preparing the apples. "Look, I know you and your people aren't like that but plenty of whites are," George said. "Plenty of folks in this neighborhood don't eat here because a negro is cooking."

"Coloreds do the cooking in some of the best restaurants in New York City," Tiger began. "People don't know it because they don't see it." Tiger gestured to the dining room in full view of the prep area. "No open kitchen."

"But that don't make it right," George told him. "Just because they don't know don't make it any less wrong."

"To hell with them," Tiger barked. "We don't want their kind in here. And besides, those racist S.O.B.s don't deserve your cooking."

George shook his head. He diced apples while Tiger continued peeling them. "It all just makes me feel so tired," the cook admitted. "Weary to the bone. Tired of fighting, tired of hearing about it, tired of seeing the pictures. Rosa Parks, Mamie Till, her child Emmett, Martin Luther King's house bombed. What's going to be next?"

"I don't know," Tiger said. He slid the pile of green apple peelings into the trash. After washing his hands, he grabbed the canisters of sugar and the cinnamon.

George took the butter out of the Frigidaire so it would soften enough for him to work with. "I know you don't see color but the rest of the world does. I fear for my wife. I fear for my kids."

"I hate to admit it but I do too," Tiger said. "And I fear for my kids living in a world where we have to be afraid for the safety of people we care about." Tiger took a portion of the diced apples and put them in a pot, covered them with water. When they were cooked soft enough, they would be drained, seasoned with brown sugar, cinnamon and other spices, mashed fine then cooked again to meld the flavors. "What's the answer, then?" Tiger wondered after he'd lit the burner beneath the pot.

"It beats me," George said. "We just keep doing what we're doing? Stiff upper lip? Keep on keeping on, the hell with anybody else?"

"It's worked this far," Tiger smiled.

"For some," George pointed out. Not for all." He tested the butter with his fingertip. It was still too hard to work with. "And prayer. Lots of prayer," George added thoughtfully. "Miss Addie likes to say, 'Life ain't nothing but a whole string of prayers.'"

"Amen to that."

They were silent for a few moments. George's great hands molded the flour, oatmeal, butter, salt and brown sugar into a crumbly paste. While many preferred using a pastry blender or an electric mixer, George liked using his bare hands— just as the women in Tiger's family used their hands to mix meatballs and such. George said the flavor of life, both the sweetness and the bitter, made its way into the food this way, made it taste better, more personal, more real. The Paradiso women believed this, too.

"But living in fear…" George said suddenly, "living fearful slowly eats away at you."

Tiger nodded. "What did F.D.R. say? 'The only thing we have to fear is fear itself.' But he borrowed it from a crusty English guy named Sir Francis Bacon, who said, 'Nothing is terrible except fear itself.'"

George shook his head in disbelief. "You're a fountain of useless knowledge, yes you are."

Tiger shrugged. He peered into the pot of gently boiling apples then gave them a stir. "Just stuff Poppa told me. Sticks with me, after all these years."

"No disrespect to your Grand…you know I loved the man," George began. "But those quotes are just pretty words from old white men. They never had to sit in the back of a bus in Alabama. They never felt the cold dread of being stopped by a state trooper on a dark road in the South. They never had to hear their kid called a 'pickaninny' or their wife called…"

George stopped, unable to continue. Tiger was relieved, for it was too painful a subject for them to discuss any further. The quiet grew in the warm kitchen air between them, blossoming like a yeasty bread rising in the oven, but it wasn't uncomfortable, it just was. The only sound was of George mixing the apples, cinnamon and nutmeg with the wooden spoon. He was ready to pour the apple bowl into the baking pan when Tiger stopped him. "You forgot something," he said, grabbing the box of brown sugar.

George measured out a quarter cup of white sugar by eye and added it to the bowl while Tiger added the brown. They'd made the recipe so many times together Tiger knew it by heart. "Let's do it," George said suddenly.

"Do what?" Tiger wondered.

"Let's meet with that fellow Bill. I don't believe in happenstance. I believe things happen for a reason. Maybe he's our reason to grow. Maybe not. But let's see," George said.

CHAPTER TEN

Prosperity

In the throes of Thanksgiving preparation, Terry's kitchen was bustling and happily cramped. It reminded Tiger of his grandmother Bridget's kitchen when he was a child. True, it technically *was* the same kitchen but so much had changed since the dear old girl had passed—and not just the linoleum and the wallpaper.

Terry looked content instead of overwhelmed with his mother, sister and a couple of aunts helping her prep for the festive meal. To date, this would mark the largest crowd they would host for what was undeniably Tiger's favorite holiday. Twenty-one guests and counting, depending on who might pop by unannounced. Everyone was welcome at the Martino table, expected or unexpected.

To ensure that there was enough space, Tiger and Sully put both leaves into the massive dining room table. "Glad you kept it," Sully remarked, fitting Leaf A into Leaf B, which had been thoughtfully marked by Poppa in grease pen. It gave Tiger comfort to see his grandfather's neat, squared-off handwriting on the leaves' undersides, Poppa's no-nonsense foreman's script.

"They don't make tables like this anymore," Tiger agreed.

"Well, they do but they cost a fortune," Sully said, running his finger across the polished mahogany. The table had to be at least five decades old but it shone like new. "Terry takes good care of it," Sully noted.

"Terry takes good care of everyone and everything," Tiger told him with pride. "Besides, she loves this table. She actually smiles when she polishes it."

Back in the kitchen, Tiger glanced at his wife, beaming. As if Terry knew she had been spoken of kindly, she looked up at her husband and returned his smile. Her growing belly strained against the fabric of her apron and beneath it, her dress puffed out slightly at the waist. Well into her pregnancy, Terry positively glowed.

But being superstitious Italians (and a family who had lost several babies), Terry and Tiger decided not to tell anyone about this pregnancy until she was past the danger zone. However, most of the female relatives had already suspected it when Terry's pregnancy had been officially announced a month earlier. Now, practically the whole of Borough Park knew.

Everyone was ecstatic for Terry and Tiger because they'd wanted a second child for so long. Besides, a new baby brought blessings and prosperity along with it. Rose, in particular, was over the moon at the thought of having another grandchild to pamper. Chiara was excited about the prospect of being a big sister but it seemed so far away right now. However, in the immediate future, she was thrilled about Thanksgiving.

For Chiara, the lead-up to Thanksgiving was almost better than the actual holiday itself, which always passed too quickly for her liking. She adored going grocery shopping on Thirteenth Avenue with her grandmother, her hand lightly gripping Rose's or else helping her push the aluminum shopping cart. (Now that Terry was "in the family way," she relented and let Rose do the heavy lifting—and shopping.) Rose would wait for the girl to get out of school so that together, they could go out on a quest for the best sweet potatoes or the freshest acorn squash.

Chiara also loved watching the women work together in the kitchen, sometimes hardly talking yet without words, knowing exactly what each needed. Items like salt, pepper, oregano, butter and spatulas were passed from one to the other silently, perceptively. Similarly, the child loved observing the men prepare the dining room, wiping down basement chairs with wet rags, fitting together the table's leaves like jigsaw pieces, talking constantly, telling stories and laughing, always laughing about something Poppa had said or done. Sometimes they even let her help.

In recent years, the women let Chiara lend a hand in the kitchen, and whenever she did, she felt as though she were part of a secret society which operated in plain sight. Grandma Rose taught her how to create the pinwheel pattern of *antipasto* that the family favored. Her mother showed her how to measure the perfect amount of olive oil for the marinated cauliflower salad just the way Anne Daurio made it. Aunt Angela demonstrated the perfect cheese-grating technique so that bits of your knuckles (and blood!) didn't end up in the box grater or in the crystal serving bowl.

Believe it or not, Great Auntie Astrid (which she often insisted on being called, depending on her mood) had something to teach Chiara as well: she showed the girl how to effortlessly fold napkins into graceful swans—fancy cloth napkins that Great Auntie Astrid had made herself on her portable sewing machine. There was a lot to learn in an industrious kitchen...and not just about cooking and mending: about life.

"All I'm saying is that baby is the spitting image of Judgie's father," Camille piped.

"And Judgie himself looks nothing like his father," Jo agreed. "He favors his mother Butchie."

Chiara clutched the wedge of Pecorino Romano in her fist. "Why do they call her 'Butchie'?" she wondered.

Great Auntie Astrid huffed, flustered. "Well, just look at her, she's... positively butchie!"

"What's 'butchie?'" the girl asked innocently as a snowy mound of cheese grew in the bowl before her. Chiara was careful to do this chore just as Aunt Ang had taught her, remembering to use the medium-sized holes on the grater so that the cheese looked like shredded coconut, not snowflakes.

The women considered each other quizzically as Chiara diligently grated. Of staunch Scandinavian stock, their neighbor Butchie more resembled a man in a housedress than a woman: she was big and broad and could lift a baby buggy onto the porch by herself without the help of a passing gentleman. Yet she wore lipstick and perfume and painted her nails. Terry quickly offered a response to her daughter's query. "You remember 'Butch' from *The Little Rascals*, don't you?" she suggested. Chiara nodded vigorously. "Well, Butchie looks a lot like him, don't you think?"

Chiara pondered for a moment. "No," she said emphatically.

"I think she does," Angela countered, slipping the grated cheese into the fancy dish.

"I do, too," Rose agreed. At the sink, she drained a pot of ziti into Bridget's battered colander, careful not to let the steam scald her face.

"Nicknames are funny things," added Camille." Who knows where they come from."

Offered Angela, "I used to be called 'Kewpie' when I was a kid. Can you believe it? Poppa said I reminded him of a Kewpie doll when they took me home from United Israel Zion."

Chiara only half believed her.

Into a large bowl, Jo had already placed cubed mozzarella. Rose emptied the hot ziti into the dish and gave it a mix with a wooden spoon, evenly distributing the melting cheese. Camille had a saucepan of *marinara* sauce waiting, which she added to the mootz and pasta. Then came the container of ricotta. "But why…" Chiara Rose continued.

"Hon, I'm going to need more grated cheese for the baked ziti. About a handful," Rose told her granddaughter, hoping this would change the topic from the origin of their manly female neighbor's nickname. "The size of my hand, not yours." Chiara grated more. She caught the edge of a knuckle, saw blood begin to blossom, sucked it away and continued grating.

When the Thomas Family arrived, Elaine went directly into the kitchen with Liora Rose (all the roses!) while George helped the men wrestle with the creaky folding chairs. Elaine looked splendid in a dress of burnt orange with a poufy skirt and a pattern of rust-colored falling leaves across it. The frock beautifully complimented the bronze of Elaine's skin. Liora was Elaine's twin facially, but insisted on dressing differently than her mother, wearing a plaid skirt and romper.

When Liora, who was nearing fifteen, put two pies on the kitchen windowsill, the women oohed and aahed at how "the baby" had grown. Then they shifted to how pretty Elaine's dress was. "Why, this old thing?" Elaine bubbled. "Ma whipped it up in one afternoon. Saw a picture of Lizzie Tish wearing something like it in *Photoplay* and made one for me."

Part of the family for so long, Elaine knew where Terry kept the aprons—and everything else. She opened the correct drawer and took out a turkey-embossed bib affair with a ruffled top. "Elaine, you'll muss your smart dress," Jo told her. Elaine clucked her tongue at Jo and continued fastening the apron around her waist.

"Besides, you're a guest," Camille added.

"Oh, am I?" Elaine snapped. "I thought I was family."

"You got me there," Camille admitted, laughing.

The talk circled to Elizabeth Taylor as Elaine washed, then cut celery stalks to be stuffed with Roquefort spread. "I bet that dress looks better on you than it does on Liz, that hussy," Rose commented, pouring the ziti mixture into a well-oiled baking dish, then topping it with more sauce. "Imagine, going from Mike Todd…"

"…she was only married to him for a year before he died in that plane crash!" Camille interjected. "Give Liz a break!"

"…to Eddie Fisher…" Rose continued, undeterred. "Stealing Eddie away from that sweet-as-pie Debbie Reynolds."

"How many kids do he and Debbie have?" Jo wondered.

"Two," Angela said without hesitation. "There's Carrie and little Todd, who's barely a year old."

"Imagine, snatching away your best friend's husband," Elaine tutted, now slicing a variety of cheeses into cubes for the *antipasto*.

Astrid shook her head. "But still, Liz is quite the dresser. Plus, she's got some figure."

"What's a 'hussy?'" Chiara asked innocently.

"Never you mind," Terry stammered.

"That's more than enough grated cheese," Rose said to her granddaughter, slipping the baked ziti into the oven after she dusted it with Pecorino Romano. "Thank you, dear."

"But what's a…" Chiara continued.

"Chiara, why don't you wash your hands so you can help me set the table?" Liora suggested. Chiara worshipped the ground the older girl walked on, this lovely teenager who treated her like a pal instead of like a child. When Chiara ran into the bathroom to scrub up, the other ladies breathed a collective sigh of relief.

Elaine kissed the side of her daughter's head. "That was slick."

Liora kissed her back. "I learned from the best. You and Gram."

"Where's your mom today?" Terry wondered. "Why didn't Miss Addie come along?"

"Oh, she's with my brother Tyrone and his brood," Elaine said. "You know they live right next door to us in Jersey City now. Mama's not much for long car rides these days."

"How's Miss Addie's rheumatism?" Rose checked.

"Still paining her, thanks for asking," Elaine said, moving on to dicing squares of yellow cheddar. "And she's still paining me, God bless her," Elaine added, chuckling softly.

Chiara bolted into the kitchen, her fingertips still dripping. She dried them on her party dress, leaving a streak. Terry winced. "Come on, Rosie," Liora said to the child.

"Okay, Rosie," Chiara replied. Since the girls shared the same middle name, they often called each other by some form of it. Liora and Chiara headed for the dining room to set out the tablecloth, napkins, good dishes, utensils and tumblers.

Elaine moved on to rolling circles of provolone into narrow tubes. "Before you know it, you'll have another one to make a mess," Elaine told Terry with a knowing glance. "How are you keeping?"

"Better now, thank you," Terry said. "But I'm tired all the time. Although Chiara helps around the house. Tiger, too."

Elaine studied Terry up and down. "You're not carrying the same way you did with Chiara Rose. I'd say this one's a boy. Momma says so, too."

"We did that needle and thread thing," Angela told her. "It went back and forth instead of around, so yep, it's a boy."

"Needle and thread? My people tie the momma's wedding ring to a string and hold it over her belly," Elaine said.

"Same difference," Angela agreed.

Wendy came in through the back door carrying an armful of Italian bread. In that short space of time, she'd heard enough of the chatter to know what they were discussing. "Old wives' tales," she sighed. "But then again, you're old wives."

"They're not old wives' tales; they work!" Rose stressed. "The needle and the ring. And who are you calling 'old wives'?" Rose took the bread from her niece, looking for the loaf with one heel gnawed away. Rose smiled to herself when she found it. She'd never sent Wendy to fetch Italian bread without having it come back with the heel eaten.

"Slice up two of those, will you?" Terry asked her cousin, handing Wendy the serrated knife that was older than the two of them put together.

"Sure," Wendy said.

The main dining room table set, the men (including George) were now negotiating with the card table in the parlor. Six "kids," three of whom were technically not children anymore, were relegated to the kids' table. "When do we grow out of sitting here?" Wendy wondered, setting down the baskets of Italian bread.

"Sweetie, it's not a question of age," her father told her, "It's a question of space."

"The youngest have to sit there," Sully said. "You know the drill."

Wendy tugged on one of Chiara's chin-length braids. "He means the best," she whispered to her cousin. "The kids' table is the better table."

"Just so long as I don't get the leg," Chiara bellyached. "I always get the leg."

"But you're the smallest," Stan told her, snapping a card table limb into place.

"Not for long, Uncle Stannie," Chiara winked. Where and when had the child learned to wink, Wendy wondered.

Wendy located the square linen tablecloth in the breakfront drawer. Liora grabbed two edges and fanned it open with her. "Plus, we get the best dishes," Liora told Chiara.

The child already knew which plates to take out of the cupboard—the plain, white Dish Night dishes. Chiara treated each one like they were spun from gold. She loved hearing her father tell of how these plates were collected during Wednesday Night Dish Nights at the Loew's 46th, which he attended religiously with his grandparents when he was young. How Uncle Augie would give them each one, though it was against the rules—you were only entitled to a dish with each adult ticket, not a child's. Even then, Uncle Augie was sweet on Aunt Ang, so he would do anything for her, even risk losing his job over a sugar bowl.

But Chiara knew not to ask her father to retell the Dish Night saga, though she knew it by rote and could repeat it herself, word by word. Especially the part where someone would always fall asleep during the newsreel, drop and shatter a plate. Her father was too busy right now.

How Chiara Rose treasured these stories! Perhaps she would ask her dad to tell the *Singin' in the Rain* anecdote again at bedtime. It went like this: her parents had gone to see that movie when Chiara was three while Grandma Rose babysat her. After the picture, it had started to rain but instead of using an umbrella, Chiara's parents danced in the downpour all the way home along Forty-Seventh Street.

At one point, Chiara's father jumped up onto a light post just like Gene Kelly had done in the movie and he stomped in puddles, too. Tiger and Terry ran into Grandpa Sully's old beat partner Izzy the same way Gene Kelly ran into that policeman in the film. But Izzy laughed instead of wagging his finger at them. Yes, Chiara's pop would probably agree to tell her that story again that night, guaranteeing that she would have sweet dreams about Gene Kelly, fresh, clean rain and love.

By now, the baked ziti was done and resting on the stove to set. The gravy meat was simmering on the burner, ready to be spooned into a huge bowl. It was now proclaimed "time to eat." The Thanksgiving procession of food began, starting with the first course. The women carried in platters of *antipasto*, olives, cheeses, dishes of salads, tubs of butter and other condiments, roasted peppers on a bed of arugula, endives and more. Both tables were covered with food.

Everyone took their places, which were not officially assigned but had somehow become their usual spots. Chiara was, of course, wedged beside one of the table legs but she didn't care for she was sitting between her cousins David and Beth, which was all that mattered. To Chiara, this was the best seat in the house, table leg and all.

Toting a tumbler of dark wine, Tiger stood and raised his glass. "I thank God that we're together, and I hope that we can all be together again next year," he said, voice cracking with emotion. It was a simple salutation, the same one Poppa would say at the start of each family meal, and it always choked up the grownups. Even Wendy and Stan, who said they still remembered Poppa's version of Grace from when they were kids.

The Martino living room (or parlor) and dining room were right beside one another with a wide archway joining them. The tables were arranged the same way they'd been when Poppa and Grandma Bridget were alive. This way, no one felt isolated at the small table. In fact, the setups were so close that they could—and did!— pass platters between them. However, there were two *antipastos* because one was never enough.

Back and forth went the dish of stuffed artichokes, the plate of lard bread, still warm from the oven, the bowl of *burrata*, oozing its milky goodness. The two loaves of Italian bread quickly disappeared. Angela got up to slice the third and fourth so Terry didn't have to. She'd noticed her sister-in-law's swollen ankles and the delicate way she stepped about the kitchen, as if walking on eggshells. They encouraged Terry to sit and relax while they quickly cleared the dishes for the next course.

To make things easier for her daughter-in-law, Rose asked if it would be all right if she served the ziti. (So weighty and vast was the baked macaroni that the server had to stand while doling out portions.) In deference to her puffy ankles, Terry relented. Angela and Camille brought in the bowls of gravy meat and tureens of extra sauce.

Though not by design, someone always ended up "holding court" over family dinners, and this Thanksgiving was no different. As Rose stood in her place cutting and serving squares of ziti onto plates, Astrid's husband Al regaled diners with stories of his boss, the illustrious Fred Trump. "Nothing but a crook with bad hair and a greasy grin, if you ask me," Harry said.

"Nobody asked you," Sully told him, dousing his macaroni with sauce, "but I think you're right."

"And don't forget his cheesy mustache," added George. "Speaking of which, would someone please pass the grated cheese?"

Al handed it over and continued. "All of the above are true but a paycheck is a paycheck."

Elaine shook her head and tutted. "I heard that Trump was arrested once while marching in a K.K.K. rally."

"In the South?" Rose wondered.

"No, in Queens," Elaine qualified, taking the dish of grated cheese from her husband.

"I hate Queens," Wendy muttered, eyeing her father mischievously, knowing full well that Harry hailed from the borough.

"Hey, watch it, toots," Harry warned her.

"Who are you calling 'toots'?" Jo asked her husband. "I thought I was your only 'toots.'"

Elaine observed the easygoing exchanges as one might take in a tennis match, not that she was partial to tennis matches. Holiday dinners at the Martino compound were so unlike any family supper or church social Elaine had ever attended. Initially, George had tried to warn her about Eye-talians, and she had certainly been to plenty of buffet dinners and potlucks at the Martino clan's various abodes, but nothing quite prepared Elaine for the jovial to and fro of a holiday supper. It was like verbal badminton.

Even their version of Grace was different. Not bad or wrong, just different. She liked the way Tiger had stood at the head of the table, just as his grandfather had stood before him, and praised the Lord for their togetherness as well as for the meal itself. The sentiment was so sweet and homey, decided Elaine. She might work Tiger and Poppa's Grace into her own family celebrations. After so many years, the same old "God is great…," "Bless us O Lord…" and "Good food, good meat, good God let's eat…" was wearing thin. At least a Grace like the Martinos' kept the Lord on His toes.

George nudged his wife and smiled. She tapped her knee into his and smiled back. Liora glanced at her parents from across the table, Chiara chattering happily nearby. Around them, the Trump talk continued. "Wasn't he under investigation a few years ago?" Wendy asked.

"Yep," Sully confirmed. "For profiteering from public contracts. In 1954, I think it was."

Stan laughed. "If it's a crime, you never forget it, do you, Pop?"

"Not likely," Harry said.

Elaine joined in. "Why, Woody Guthrie even wrote a song about that Trump. And not no praise song either. No, sir."

"'This Land is Your Land?'" Liora asked.

"Not hardly," her mother told her.

"A little ditty called 'Old Man Trump,'" Tiger said, helping himself to another meatball.

"Save room for the turkey and all the fixings," Terry warned.

"Don't worry, I've got plenty of room," Tiger said, patting his belly.

"I think I remember that song," Terry added. "Maybe about 10 years ago. It talked about racism at Beach Haven."

Rose asked, "That's a building complex in Brighton Beach, isn't it?"

"Closer to Coney Island," Angela said. "Woody accused Trump of stirring up racial hatred."

"...*in the bloodpot of human hearts*," quoted Elaine. "Or something like that. And another part was about *where no black folks come to roam*." The entire table looked at this quiet, reserved woman in disbelief; Elaine was more often silent than not, except when faced with instances of social injustice. "It's a catchy tune," Elaine said in her defense.

"What's he like, this Trump?" Wendy asked her uncle.

Al thought for a second. "He's a pretty decent fellow," Al conceded.

"Oh, please!" Astrid snapped. "He works you like a dog."

"The hours are long, it's true," Al admitted. "But any respectable businessman gets the most he can out of his people. The pay's fair, though."

"For selling your soul!" Astrid bleated. "It should be!" She stabbed a sausage, dropped it onto her plate and tucked into it with relish. Everyone knew that Astrid was perturbed because her husband routinely worked extra hours. But whether this could be blamed on Fred Trump or on Astrid's constant nagging was up for debate.

Elaine sucked her teeth and tutted, "*For what shall it profit a man if he shall gain the whole world, and lose his own soul?*"

To avoid hearing another of Astrid's tirades against her poor husband, the other women took this as their cue to begin clearing the table for the main course: turkey and all the trimmings, including the Cuban-style stuffing, courtesy of Lydia Martinez's mother Rachel's recipe. It incorporated ground sausage, chopped ham and pimento olives. The ladies heard bits and pieces of the Trump talk as they went to and from the kitchen. "What are your coworkers like?" Tiger asked.

"They're nice enough, I suppose," Al said, toying with an anthill of grated cheese that had fallen onto the tablecloth. "His sons are always hanging about when they're in town, though. Fred Jr. is still in college in Pennsylvania but I doubt he'll follow in his father's footsteps. He doesn't have the same killer instinct. I think Freddy has a passion for flying."

"Planes?" David wondered.

"No, flying around the room like a ghost," his dad Augie joked. David blushed as his father ruffled his hair. Beth rolled her eyes; her brother was constantly saying ridiculous things like that.

"And then there's little Donny," Al continued. "He's an ass, even at thirteen. So annoying, his folks sent him off to a military academy. A cushy one, I admit, but who does that?"

"Rich folks," offered Elaine, retreating from the dining room with the half-empty platter of gravy meat. "They're partial to sending their kids away for other people to raise."

Al smiled, then finished with, "But it's easy to see that little Donny is the favorite. I bet he'll take over the family business, not Freddy."

Elaine was back again, this time taking the grated cheese in one hand and a gravy boat in the other. "Sounds like this Freddy belongs up in the clouds, not among brick and mortar," she commented. The men at the table stared at this humble cafeteria worker in disbelief for proposing such a lofty notion. "But who am I to say?" Elaine added and shrugged. "I'll leave the judging up to the good Lord." Then Elaine was gone again, a one-person, honey-skinned Greek chorus.

CHAPTER ELEVEN

New Dawn

It took a fair amount of time to get the Thanksgiving turkey carved, all the side dishes reheated and into serving bowls. This gave everyone a chance to digest the first two courses and whet their appetites for the next. While the men chatted in the dining room, a few loosening their belt buckles to make space for the succulent bird and its accoutrements, the women scraped and washed and stirred and arranged in the kitchen. It hardly seemed like work because the conversation was merry and good-natured, filled with chuckles, prods and double-entendres which would succeed in shocking anyone who overheard the crew of faithful, churchgoing wives dishing dirt.

Terry helmed her kitchen while seated at the table, gently asking her helpers if they wouldn't mind mashing the potatoes or if they could be so kind as to take the candied yams out of the oven or lower the burner beneath the gravy. At thirteen, much of the conversation floated above Beth's head like elusive smoke but she was glad to be considered grown up enough to pitch in. Some of the words made no sense to Beth yet caused the other ladies to laugh and sigh, scold and grow teary-eyed:

> "Then Groucho asked the contestant why he had twelve children and he said, 'Because I like my

wife.' That's when Groucho told him, 'I like my cigar too but I take it out of my mouth every once in a while.'"

"Camille, shush, the kids…"

And…

"Did you hear about Ann Elvin? Passed away suddenly just like that. At 37! She had five kids, was the picture of health. I don't know what Kevin is going to do without her. I mean, Little Roy isn't yet three. Imagine, growing up without a mother…"

"Do you think she could have…taken her own life."

"Bite your tongue! Ann was a God-fearing Catholic woman, always so happy, so bubbly. She never would have…"

"You never know what goes on in a person's head, Camille."

And…

"Those poor Clancy children look so raggedy. Last time I was in Moe's, I saw him give a satchel of fruits and vegetables to Kylie, the oldest one. No questions asked, no money changed hands. He just gave it to the girl and sent her on her way."

"God bless Moe."

"I ask you, would Waldbaum's do such a thing?"

"Maybe. I hear Julia Waldbaum has a good heart… not like that S.O.B. Trump."

"I doubt he has a heart. You know…"

And…

"Augie said he saw that strumpet Susie McKenna with a man who was not her husband. They were pitching woo in the balcony at the Loew's 46th."

"No!"

"Yes! You would have thought she'd have enough sense not to dirty up her own backyard."

And…

"Beth, please get the flour to thicken up the gravy. It's right on the windowsill."

The gravy was thickened and poured into the fluted server Anne Daurio had brought from Portugal. The fresh-made cranberry sauce gleamed like garnets on its platter. Rachel Martinez's savory sausage stuffing sat in its bowl. The candied yams steamed in their deep pan while tureens of green beans, yellow corn and sweet peas dotted with caramelized onions waited. The turkey, expertly carved by Rose and enticingly arranged on a serving platter by Astrid, dark meat separated from white, was ready to be presented.

The parade began and the wonderful meal was set onto the table, then happily devoured, amid much jocularity and private heart-to-hearts. The talk went from Trump ("the rat bastard") to *Ben Hur* ("that Charlton Heston is the dreamiest… those legs…those muscles…") to everyone's new favorite television program, *The Twilight Zone* ("I almost cried when Burgess Meredith's eyeglasses broke!") and the blue record "The Sick Humor of Lenny Bruce," which John had managed to get a copy of and was making the rounds from house to house, like Lady Chatterley had.

Ever since Terry and Tiger had married a dozen years earlier, the new bride had earned the honor of hosting Thanksgiving dinner. A solid but relatively new cook, Terry was relieved when Rose sheepishly asked if her daughter-in-law wouldn't mind Rose making the turkey that first holiday. The wound of losing her parents less than two years earlier still stung, Rose explained, and she thought the ache might ease if she could roast the Thanksgiving turkey just one last time. But only if it was all right with the new Mrs. Martino. (Which it was.) Every year thereafter, Rose formally asked Terry for permission to make the turkey. The answer was always yes. Especially this year, in Terry's delicate condition, she doubted she could even lift the twenty-pound bird herself.

Every single dish was perfect, prepared with skill, love and the freshest ingredients Thirteenth Avenue had to offer. To take the pressure from Terry's aching feet and legs, every woman brought her best side dish, proudly and willingly, grateful to be more a part of this special supper, to feed the people they cherished.

Later in the meal, when practically every person claimed they couldn't eat another bite, the women began to again clear the table. As the females divided and stowed away the leftovers, Beth took the opportunity to ask her cousin Wendy what "pitching woo" meant, what a "strumpet" was and why a dear, sweet woman like Mrs. Elvin might take her own life. Perhaps Wendy would tell Beth; perhaps not. But Beth decided to ask Wendy anyhow. For what was the harm in asking?

Quite diplomatically and cryptically, Wendy responded, "Kissing," "A very friendly girl" and "I honestly don't know, sweet pea." Her cousin's candid yet curious answers satisfied Beth for the time being.

While the women were washing up and putting the finishing touches on the desserts, the men snacked on fruit and nuts, passing several nutcrackers between them and making small piles of shells. Who didn't have room for a grape or two, a single walnut or a sliver of rose-petal coated Turkish Delight Camille's friend Suzan had brought from Istanbul? The gooey sweet dusted with saffron was especially delicious.

Over the din of football talk, there was a light knock on the front door, then another. "I'll get it," Tiger announced. Although it could have been any of the neighbors, Tiger had a vague idea (a hope?) who might be on the other side. Soon, he returned with a man of medium height and build, nicely dressed in a suit of nubby brown fabric. The man held a cake box from Piccolo's by the string. "Everybody, this is Bill. Bill Karpi," Tiger introduced. "I met Bill a few weeks back, in Connecticut."

"Just happened to be in the neighborhood..." Bill explained. "Visiting the wife Joanie's family in Sunset Park."

For Bill's benefit, Tiger named his friends and family one by one. One by one, they rose and shook hands with the visitor. Even David, the youngest male, knew how to behave when introduced to a gentleman, his father Augie noted. "We should all have name tags," George joked.

"Lots of folks to remember," Bill conceded, "but I'm not half bad with names."

"That's a decent trait to have," George told him.

"Been in the hospitality business a while," Bill said. "It's kind of a tool of the trade."

"Front of house?" George wondered, though he knew the answer. Bill nodded. "People like to be remembered. Makes them feel special," he said.

"Well, I think they are special, every last one of them," Bill agreed. "By feeding them, they help feed me and my family and I'm grateful for that. Now, that's pretty special, wouldn't you say?"

George decided right then and there that this Bill fellow was an okay sort and that Connecticut, though a pale, mysterious place, might be a suitable location for Feel Good Food to spread its wings.

Tiger brought the Piccolo's box into the kitchen. He untied the candy-striped twine which held it closed (cutting string was thought to be bad luck by superstitious Italians— the act was said to sever relationships). Inside, were *pignoli* cookies and seven-layer cookies, Tiger's grandparents' and his favorite bakery treats, respectively. How could Bill have known?

"That's a good omen," Terry remarked, handing Tiger a plate.

He arranged the sweets on the china dish in two circles, one within the other. He placed the sugar-coated almonds included in the box in the center of his arrangement. "I'd say it's a good omen too," Tiger admitted. "No need for you to do the Overlook Prayer later tonight to bless this business venture," he added.

At first, Terry gave her husband a surprised glance. How did he know that she often did the Overlook Prayer when something worried her? But somehow, Tiger knew everything. Rose said he'd possessed a keen intuition even when he was a child. He just *knew*. Tiger often felt things, both good and bad, before they happened. Similar to George's, Tiger's premonitions were typically spot on.

But perhaps, just for assured luck, Terry would do the Overlook Prayer anyhow. Just as the sun was setting, when the Prayer's power was strongest. Her sister-in-law Angela had taught Terry how to do it—Angie had learned from her grandmother Bridget. The Overlook Prayer was a secret invocation, passed down in a family from woman to woman. The Prayer asked for safety. It asked for health. It asked for protection against life's evils, of which there were so many.

Sometimes, though not always, the Overlook Prayer involved water, salt and a dash of olive oil. But it always involved, faith, fervor and love. Yes, Terry might just do the Overlook Prayer this Thanksgiving evening to bless Tiger's new business venture, this new dawn for Feel Good Food. For everyone could use a blessing every once in a while.

Tiger carried out the platter of cookies. Other desserts followed: Anne Daurio's crunchy almond *biscotti* (which she once sent to Rose through the mail from Long Island, along with the recipe), pumpkin pie made with fresh pumpkins which John and Camille had brought down from Davenport Farm upstate and Elaine's duet of pies (shoofly and chess), both of which this Brooklyn crew had never seen but immediately became fans of. Also in attendance was their former next-door-neighbor Ti-Tu's apple kuchen. Although Ti-Tu had sold the house to Augie and Angela and moved to Port Washington with his new bride Lily, he visited regularly around holidays and brought one of these whenever he did.

To wash down dessert were two types of coffee, American and Cuban, thanks to a tradition begun by their friend Consuelo Ortez Vega, and a never-ending pot of tea in Pip's chicken-embossed teapot which Rose let Terry borrow for the occasion.

As they enjoyed their sweets, Rose asked Bill, "Karpi, is that Italian?"

"Ma…" Tiger started to complain. He swore that Rose liked people better if they were Italian, which she vehemently denied.

But Bill just smiled. "I wish," he said. "Used to be 'Karpinski' but they chopped it off at Ellis Island. Polish nobility, if you believe my dad." Everyone laughed.

Amid all of this syrupy decadence, they'd forgotten to set out the lead crystal sugar bowl, so Stan dashed into the kitchen to fetch it. On the way to the dining room, he caught a glimpse of a thick-shouldered, blue-suited body that filled the width of the window by the porch, then disappeared. It was Big Paulie Morrongiello. Stan almost dropped the sugar. The lid rattled against the bowl like chattering teeth.

Stan wondered if anyone else noticed the looming shadow in the front window. When Tiger's and Sully's eyes sharply met his, Stan at once knew that they had seen the thug as well. "Why don't you invite your friend inside, Stanley?" Rose said. (She didn't miss a trick, did she?) Stan passed the sugar bowl to his brother.

"Yes, Stan," Terry insisted. "Any friend of yours…"

Reluctantly, Stan went to the porch but he knew Big Paulie wouldn't come in. Imagine him sitting between John and Harry, making small talk while his uncles gave Big Paulie the stink eye? More than anyone, the hoodlum knew where he wasn't welcome and Paolo Morrongiello certainly knew the *malocchio* when he saw it. "They want you to come in for dessert," Stan whispered loudly to the large man.

In response, Big Paulie shook his head and walked down the front steps. "Meet me at Farrell's, pronto," he said. "McBears if Houlie's tending bar." Farrell's owner Kevin Houlihan had barred Big Paulie from the pub merely because he "looked like he was trouble," which, of course, he was.

"Okay," Stan told Big Paulie. He went back inside and shut the door behind him as a dark car drove off down Forty-Seventh Street.

Stan managed a mouthful of Eileen Fiori's cheesecake for he knew Rose would remark that he should try it. When Stan grabbed his overcoat from the rack, it was his niece Chiara who complained, not his mother. "But you can't go now, Uncle Stannie," she whined. "Dessert's the best part!"

When the women glared at the girl for slighting the lavish meal they'd slaved over, Chiara corrected herself, "I mean, the second-best part."

Stan kissed the top of his niece's head, smelling Ivory Soap and all things clean and right. "I've got to, Chi," then to his mother, he said, "Don't worry, I won't be late."

"I always worry," Rose shot back. "It's a mother's job to worry."

Stan quickly worked his way around the table, kissing the women and shaking hands with the men. It's wasn't quite an Irish Goodbye—where you sneak out without saying anything to anyone—but it was close. Sully and Tiger glanced at each other and shook their heads. When Stan bid them each farewell, he didn't make eye contact with either of them.

"Take your scarf," Rose called when Stan was at the front door. "And your cap. It feels like snow."

But Stan didn't hear his mother and was gone before he could heed her prudent advice. In his haste, he hadn't taken either.

CHAPTER TWELVE

Firecracker

"Stan's always been a firecracker," Sully said to Tiger. "Even when he was a babe in arms."

The two men watched the bruised pink and purple Thanksgiving sunset fade and darken from the front porch. They each leaned against a post and silently considered the fleeting beauty, puffing on a peppery Cuban cigar which had been given to them by Bill Karpi. Neither were smokers but the opportunity to enjoy the gentle bite of a Bolivar was too generous an offer to refuse. Bolivars were rarities in the States since Castro overtook the island nation earlier that year.

"You get your pleasures where you can," Harry had told Bill earlier that evening when he accepted the gift of tobacco from him. George promised he would give his cigar to his brother-in-law Tyrone, who appreciated a fine cheroot now and again. "A good cigar would be lost on me," George assured Bill, who understood completely that cigars weren't everyone's cup of Java.

By now, Harry, George and the rest were hopefully safe in their warm homes. Sully wasn't sure Tiger had heard him but then the young man finally responded, "You're right, firecrackers seem to run in the family," Tiger conceded. "Myself included."

"Yeah, but you're more a quiet firecracker, a slow burn," Sully nodded. "You never gave us much trouble, whereas Stan…"

"Stan's another story," Tiger agreed. "Where do you suppose he ran off to?"

"Where do you think? You saw that S.O.B. Big Paulie lurking about, didn't you?"

"He's kind of hard to miss," conceded Tiger. "Big as he is."

"Hence the name," Sully smirked.

"I sure hope Stan stays out of trouble."

"Me, too. I might not be able to get him out of this one. I have a feeling that whatever this is, it's a doozie. My old cop instinct says that Big Paulie's hatching a crazy plan of some sort."

"I tried talking to Stan about steering clear of him," Tiger began.

"I appreciate that," Sully said. "I did as well. Don't think it made a dent, though." Sully and Tiger smoked their cigars in silence, relishing the November chill and the twang of the Bolivar in the air. There wasn't anything more to say.

With the Thanksgiving guests gone, the women were sitting in their respective parlors with their feet propped up, their bellies full and their children tucked away in bed. Tiger suspected that his wife and his sister Angela were comparing notes, chatting on the telephone in houses next door to each other. It wasn't enough that they'd spent the past few days in each other's company, contently working side by side preparing the feast. They generally felt the need to recap the events of the day at its close, too. It made Tiger smile, knowing that his sister and his wife got on so well.

When Terry was through chatting with Angela, Tiger could bet his wife would make a quick call to his mom upstairs to thank Rose for all of her help, then a bit of gossip about who said what to whom. Although Rose lived in the same house, long flights of stairs were Terry's nemesis this far into her pregnancy. So, perhaps Rose would pop downstairs briefly, make a pot of tea and share a cupper with her daughter-in-law, who would probably be perched in the ottoman with her tender feet raised on the cushion by now.

These thoughts gave Tiger solace as he finished smoking his cigar with his stepfather on the front porch. Since Sully wore a bemused expression on his pleasantly-doughy face, Tiger suspected he was thinking similar thoughts, reliving the agreeable day: the food, the drink, the laughter, and most importantly, the company.

Sully doused the cigar stub on a brick step, raining down fiery red sparks that soon expired. Then he opened the cigar's tobacco wrapping and scattered its contents into the garden below. Tiger did the same. Bits of tobacco were supposedly beneficial for a garden. "I can go for a little snack," Sully admitted. "Maybe a stuffing sandwich on a couple of slabs of Italian bread."

"Sounds good," Tiger agreed. They went inside in search of leftovers.

A few miles away on Prospect Avenue, Stan peered through McBears' picture window. It was easy to spot Big Paulie at the end of the bar. As instructed, first Stan had gone to Farrell's just a few blocks away. When Houlie nodded to Stan through the glass, he knew Big Paulie wouldn't dare venture inside, so Stan rounded Sixteenth Street and headed toward Tenth Avenue and Prospect, where McBears stood on the corner. Stan took a deep breath and entered. "What the hell took you so long?" Big Paulie growled instead of "hello."

"I had to wolf down a slice of cheesecake before I could go," Stan told him. "Just to make it look good. You're not exactly Tiny Tim, you know. My whole family saw you. Even my pop."

Big Paulie flashed Stan an annoyed glance then thought better of it. You catch more flies with honey than with vinegar, he remembered. Big Paulie clapped Stan on the back, which propelled the smaller man forward a few inches. "I'll tell ya, those Italian mothers," he offered with a guffaw. When Big Paulie laughed, it was full of phlegm and foreboding, not a jovial sound in the least. "I got me an Italian mother myself,"

Big Paulie added. It was hard for Stan to imagine the massive goon as any mother's son.

A tall, lanky man stepped out of the shadows and chucked his chin toward Stan in greeting. "Meet Morty, my…" Big Paulie began.

"Accomplice?" the stringbeany fellow suggested.

Big Paulie made a face. "Associate. Associate has nicer ring to it. Morty, this is Stan. The best driver in Borough Park."

Morty nodded knowingly. "Our getaway driver."

Big Paulie rolled his eyes at Morty. "Don't be so *déclassé*. I prefer 'chauffeur,' don't you?"

"Whatever you say," Morty agreed. He offered Stan his hand to shake. "Pleased to meet you."

"Likewise," Stan said.

As Morty and Big Paulie went over the finer details of the Idlewild heist, Stan studied the new man in their trio. Morty was indeed an odd bird. He was well over six-foot tall and slim, with taupe-shaded skin. His hair was close-cropped on the sides with a nest of dark curls on top. Morty appeared to be of an exotic mixed heritage, hinting at ancestors from the Caribbean or at least from Sicily. Incongruous with his swarthy complexion, Morty's eyes were a light aqua, reminiscent of a sea far away from Brooklyn.

For a moment, Stan wondered if his and Pamela Thomas's children might have looked something like this, then shook the thought away. Despite Pam's generous thighs, her welcoming laugh and her full lips, Stan knew that she was off limits. Even when they were young, George made it clear that Stan could break bread at their table but not take Pam to the altar. Besides, now she was married and had a kid of her own.

But still, this Morty fellow was living proof that people indeed did things like this—fell in love with, fell into bed with and made babies with people outside their race. People somewhere but not anyplace like here.

Excessive thoughts of Pamela Thomas might prove to be troublesome, both to Stan's spirit and to his body, so he forced them from his head. Only to be replaced by visions of Wendy:

her wild chestnut hair with a mind of its own, her cherubic face, her long, coltish legs that seemed to go on forever. But it was Wendy's wonderful brain, the way she challenged Stan to think, even of things he didn't want to consider, the way she exploded into a room like a comely firecracker, demanding your attention and always getting it. The way Wendy...

"Earth to Stanley...earth to Stanley..." Big Paulie boomed. He and Morty laughed at Stan's expense. "This is important," the thug emphasized, his tone turning sharp as a knife. "You better be listening."

"I am," Stan said. "You don't have to tell me how important it is."

"What was the last thing I said?" Big Paulie challenged.

"'Two weeks away' and 'Cargo Area D, right off the Conduit,'" Stan repeated. "Am I right?"

"You're right," Morty nodded, pushing a beer in front of Stan, who took a sip. "When he's right, he's right, Paulie."

"December 11, just in time for Christmas," the enormous man added.

"But one thing I don't get," Stan confessed, "is why they're keeping something as important as a shipment of diamonds in a vault overnight."

Big Paulie shrugged. "I don't know. Something about the Sabbath and not being able to move them until Saturday after sundown. From the airport, they're supposed go to that Jew diamond exchange on Forty-Seventh Street in the City. At least that's what Little Petey said. But we're going to nab the hot rocks before they get to the vault, see?"

"Beautiful," Morty said. "It's foolproof. Practically."

Stan shook his head. "But I don't get why we need a panel truck."

"You never drove a truck before?" Big Paulie challenged.

"Sure, I have. But how big are diamonds? I mean, why do we need a truck at all? A car's easier to handle. And easier to hide."

"Little Petey said they'll be in a crate. How big's a crate? Small crate? Large crate? I don't know," Big Paulie said, exasperated. "It's better to have a truck that's too big than a car that's too small, right? Better than to get there and find out the box don't fit in the trunk of a Studebaker. Am I right or am I right?"

"He's right," Morty agreed. "When he's right, he's right." Whenever Stan thought about the Idlewild heist, he got a sharp stabbing in the pit of his stomach. He knew the theft was wrong and he had strong doubts they could pull it off, but Stan couldn't find his way out of it, not now. December 11 was so close and he was in too deep. Stan tried to convince himself that it would just be this once but he knew that when it was over, Big Paulie would drag him into another and then another scheme until it got so bad that Stan wouldn't be able to look at himself in the mirror. That is, if he didn't end up in prison.

Things were so simple when Stan was a boy, when Poppa and Grandma Bridget were still alive. The choices were more cut and dry, more black and white. Then Stan reminded himself that this wasn't exactly true—he had found out about his birth mother, a broken woman named Denise and he had also found out about his father, an evil man named Tony, when Poppa and Grandma Bridget were alive. Stan had watched Denise die in the hospital's charity ward when he was only eight. He had stood at Tony's grave at that same tender, young age. No, life was never easy, just the memory of it was.

"Where do you drift off to, Sullivan?" Big Paulie's voice bellowed.

"I want a paid vacation to wherever he goes," Morty sneered.

As Stan willed himself to snap out of his own head, Big Paulie grabbed his arm and squeezed his bicep. "I'm starting to think you ain't the right guy for the job," he said, spewing Budweiser spittle into Stan's face.

"Maybe I'm not," Stan told him, shaking off the meaty fingers. "Listen, Paulie, I…"

Big Paulie stabbed his fleshy pointer into Stan's chest. "Oh, no. You ain't backing out now. It's only a couple of weeks away and besides, you know too much."

"I won't tell anyone. I swear. It's just…"

"What part of 'no' don't you understand?" Big Paulie snapped. "I got a hell of a lot riding on this and I ain't about to let no Momma's boy guttersnipe screw it up." Stan started as though he'd been slapped but didn't say a word. Neither did Morty. "Gotta hit the head," Big Paulie added, then made his way toward the back of McBears.

Morty shook his head. "Never met a man who peed as often as this guy," he sighed when Big Paulie was out of sight.

"I'd see a doctor if I were him," Stan agreed.

They drank their beers in quietude. "Don't let the Big Man get to you," Morty offered.

"Who says I am?"

Morty shrugged. "He sort of ropes you in, then traps you in a corner…like a rat."

"You can say that again," Stan sighed. "Why are you here? You seem like a decent fellow."

"Thanks. You too," Morty told him. "Whereas Big Paulie seems dumb as a stump. Or is it me?"

"It's not you, it's him." Stan admitted. "Just this once, I keep telling myself. Then I'm out."

"I keep telling myself that too," Morty said. "If Paulie doesn't get us caught. Or killed."

"But we won't be carrying guns, will we?"

"I won't and you won't but who knows what he has under all that blubber? You get me?"

"Yeah, I get you," Stan said. "Why are you doing this, if you don't mind my asking?"

"There's not much else for someone like me to do," Morty confessed. Stan looked him up and down. "You know, a fellow caught in between. A zebra. A halfie. A mulatto. Whatever you want to call me."

"I don't want to call you anything," Stan told him. "You seem like an okay kind of guy."

"I am. But all my life I've been stuck. Never sure where I belonged."

"I hear you. Been there myself."

"For real?"

Stan nodded. "Different reasons but same feelings, I guess."

Big Paulie barreled out of the men's room, waving his arms to chase away the stench that followed him. "Phew! I'd let it air out if I were you," he warned. "Ming, I feel ten pounds lighter. I just launched two logs and a woodchuck."

Both Stan and Morty grimaced. "What? Like you guys don't crap?" Big Paulie taunted.

They assured him that indeed they did crap. "But if it smelled like that, I'd check myself into Maimonides," Morty said under his breath. Stan disguised his laugh as a cough.

"What?" Big Paulie asked.

"Nothing," Morty told him.

"Just like I thought," the large man said. "Now, we'll reconnoiter next week. Same time, same place. And don't make yourself disappear. No matter what, I'll find you. And I won't be happy when I do. Trust me, you won't like me when I'm unhappy." Big Paulie left them to contemplate their fates and waddled out of the pub.

Morty finished his beer and said goodbye. Stan guzzled his pint and followed Morty onto the pebbled pavement outside of McBears. "Hey," Stan called after him. "What you said about not having much choice…"

"Yeah, what about it?" Morty challenged.

"I think we always have a choice. It might not be a great choice but it's a choice all the same."

Morty smiled. "You got a choice for me, Sullivan?"

"I just might," Stan told him. "Let me talk to my brother."

CHAPTER THIRTEEN

Patience

Tiger, George and Bill stood inside the empty store on Route 37 in Sherman, Connecticut. The real estate agent waited outside on the pavement, as though he didn't want to dirty his shoes on the unkempt plank floor. Stefan Abol was Swiss and neat as a pin, with leather tassels on his loafers. In all his thirty-three years, Tiger didn't recall ever wearing shoes like that. Or wanting to. "Never trust a man with tassels on his feet," Tiger whispered to his business partners.

"I was thinking the exact same thing," George admitted.

"But still," Bill told them. "The place has potential, never mind the tassels."

"I recall someone telling me that another place had potential many moons ago," Tiger laughed quietly.

"Was I wrong?" George asked. "That place has taken us here. And to Jersey City."

Bill added, "Great location, this is. Right near the intersection of Routes 37 and 39. Heavy traffic area, for a town like Sherman, anyway."

"And you know what Baron Sammy says the three most important things about real estate are," Tiger told him.

"Location, location, location," George responded.

"Well, at least it's got that going for it," Bill said. "There's steady foot traffic too." Bill gestured past the door. A smartly-dressed woman holding a young boy's hand walked by, peered inside and smiled. "The post office is nearby and so's the hardware store."

"What did this place used to be?" Tiger asked Stefan through the propped-open door.

Before Stefan could answer, Bill said, "A florist. This was Old Man Wicks' shop for years. He passed a few months ago. The store's been shuttered ever since."

"It's in pretty good shape, clean. We could get this up and running in no time," George figured. "Couple of months, if we pushed it."

"Maybe we should hold off till spring," Bill told George sagely. "Winters can be long and harsh in these parts. Not many people walking about. In my humble opinion, winter's not the best time to open."

George and Tiger agreed. "Point well taken. We'll wait till spring, then," George nodded.

Bill took a few steps through the vacant space littered with a dried-out ferns, the occasional sprig of brownish baby's breath and a stray rose petal or two. "There's lots of natural sunlight streaming in," Bill said. "Plus, it's got good bones. Lots to build on."

Tiger dove right into planning mode. "I see a prep station going in the back," he said, gesturing. "And a setup like the other two places: open kitchen, nice-sized dining area, a few tables outside in the warm months and maybe flower garden."

"Why not grow fresh herbs, too?" George suggested. "They look and smell great when they blossom. Mint for tea, basil…"

"That would definitely work," Bill nodded, having visited both Feel Good Food establishments in New York and New Jersey. "If it ain't broke, don't fix it. Your places have a certain comfortable, welcoming air that make folks feel at home. We should build on it. I like the garden idea, too. My Joani's got quite the green thumb. I bet she can put in a first-rate garden."

"I bet she could," George smiled.

Tiger nodded. "We can make this happen," he said. "All it takes is a little work, a lot of dough and patience. We could do this."

"And we will," George told him. "Three's a charm."

They called Stefan inside to go over the particulars of the lease. The realtor reluctantly came into the shop, stepping gingerly on the dusty floorboards as though they were alive. Stefan promised to have the paperwork delivered to them within the week.

It was a mild December day. After the realtor left, Bill suggested they take a stroll down to Candlewood Lake along Sawmill Road, and they did. He knew the way with his eyes closed. They passed the sort of white clapboard houses encased by white picket fences that Tiger and George had only seen in books and movies but were common sights for Bill. "You sure this storybook village is ready for shrimp and grits?" George asked.

"Or escarole and beans?" Tiger tagged on.

"Are you kidding? They're starved for it," Bill laughed, pushing his porkpie hat back on his head. "I can tell you one thing—they're sick of navy bean soup and Presbyterian pies."

"My Elaine's got a buttermilk pecan pie that'll knock your socks off," said George.

"Tastes so good, makes you wanna slap your momma," Tiger agreed. "Did I say it right?" he asked George.

"As right as a white boy can say it," George conceded. He had to explain the Southern vernacular to Bill because George could tell he had no clue. "Means it's so delicious, you wonder why your mother don't serve you up a pie like that...so you smack her." Bill's face registered shock just as Tiger's had when he first heard the expression. "It's a joke, son," George added. "Relax. No one's going to hit their mother."

Bill shook his head, smiling. "I see I got some learning to do. And some pie-tasting."

"Elaine's got her recipes all written down on index cards," George said proudly. "I'm sure your Joan can make my wife's pies just like her. From what I can tell, Joan's an excellent cook." He indicated Bill's slight paunch for emphasis.

"She is," Bill told him. "And she makes a hell of a pie crust."

"Before my Grandma Bridget passed, she was making Elaine's peanut butter pie like nobody's business," Tiger boasted.

"God rest her soul," George whispered, bowing his head slightly. "Your grands were good people. I do miss them."

"I do, too," Tiger said. "I think you would have liked them," he told Bill, who nodded thoughtfully as they kept walking down the country lane, three abreast.

"This town sure looks old," George said, taking in the wooden capes, bungalows and well-worn fences surrounding carefully-planted yards. Most sported late autumn mums in a variety of fiery shades. The paths were swept clear of fallen leaves, the trees mostly bare but still majestic. Although some of the more adventurous homeowners had painted their abodes a pale Federalist blue or a hint of yellow, the fences were still white picket posts.

"It is old," Bill detailed. "But not as old as Brooklyn."

"Our fine borough was first settled in 1643, by a Lady Deborah Moody, an Englishwoman fleeing religious persecution," Tiger recalled.

"Now, don't get him started," George sighed in mock frustration.

"I'm something of a history buff," Tiger conceded.

"I am too, but west of the Housatonic is my area of expertise," Bill told them. "Sherman was founded in 1802 by a fellow named Roger Sherman who was a shoemaker, a land surveyor, a lawyer and a Statesman."

"Couldn't he make up his mind?" George joked.

Bill ignored him. "Candlewood Lake down there," he pointed out, "is our crown jewel." They caught glimpses of blue water glittering through the trees as the men continued down Sawmill. Bill continued, "Candlewood's not a natural lake, though. It was created back in 1926, when Connecticut

Light and Power needed a place to store water. They said they'd use it for power during times of high demand."

"Go on," Tiger said, interested.

"Well, C.L.&P. got permission to flood the valley," Bill explained.

"How'd they manage that?" Tiger asked.

"Easy," Bill told them. "They had the power of eminent domain."

"Meaning the government can take public property for the good of the people," George said.

"Right. Farmers like my grandfather sold off thirty acres for three-thousand dollars, a small fortune then."

"What happened to the people?" Tiger wondered.

"Oh, they were all relocated. But lots of the buildings were left standing and farm equipment was left behind. Even the roads stayed in place when C.L.&P. poured water into the valley from the Housatonic. Swimmers and boaters swear you can see houses under the water, still intact."

"Well, I'll be," George sighed.

"It was beneficial in the long run, I think," Bill admitted. "Created lots of jobs. Five hundred men came in from Maine and Canada to fell something like 4,500 acres of trees. The bonfires were massive. They built a bunch of dams and the valley filled quickly. In the fall of 1928, Candlewood Lake was complete."

By this time, the three men had reached the lake's shore. Candlewood was vast, its surface placid and calm. Tall trees ringed a beachy area which was speckled with a few geese. Cabins dotted the periphery. Several docks jutted into the water and a rowboat or two were still tethered to posts, so mild was the autumn. Bill waved to a man fishing on the near shore and the man waved back. "Seems to go on forever," Tiger noted.

"It's only about eight square miles," Bill told him. "About sixty miles of shoreline all the way around."

"It sure is pretty," George said. "How deep is it?"

Bill thought for a moment. "Oh, about forty feet most places, eighty feet at its deepest. People love to swim at Candlewood in the summer."

"Like you and your family?" Tiger asked.

"Sure. My Karen learned to swim right here. My cousin Bobby lost his front tooth swinging on that rope at Chicken Rock," Bill remembered, gesturing off into the distance. "Bobby got 'chicken' and wouldn't let go of the rope. Slammed into the rock." He indicated a ledge with a rope tethered to a nearby oak.

Bill continued telling the story of the lake. "I hear there's the remains of a Model T Ford and covered bridges down below the surface. Divers like to explore the lake and follow the underwater roads. The town was called Jerusalem before they flooded it. Now nothing's left."

The men were silent for a short while, gazing out upon the still waters. "Well, I think this Sherman is a good place to branch out, the perfect spot to open our third shop," Tiger said. "Different than Brooklyn and Jersey City but it feels right, doesn't it?"

George agreed. "It does. And the space is perfect. We'll be up and running and feeding these Yankees by spring."

"They won't know what hit them," Bill smiled. "Their bellies will be full and their pockets won't be empty."

"And hopefully, neither will ours," Tiger said.

They started the walk back to town, to where their cars were parked in the lot in front of their future shop. A woman raking up brilliant yellow sugar maple leaves in her front yard wished them a good afternoon as her son gleefully jumped into the pile she'd just made, scattering them. Somewhere, a dog barked. A young girl shakily riding her red Schwinn two-wheeler in the middle of Sawmill dinged her handlebar bell at them.

"How'd the lake get its name?" George asked Bill as they strolled.

"A Candlewood's a tree," Bill said. "The early settlers sometimes used the sapling branches as candles. Also, there's a mountain in New Milford named Candlewood."

"Candlewood has a nice ring to it," Tiger nodded.

The talk turned from pleasure to business: the logistics of running Feel Good Food's Sherman outpost, how often Tiger and George would visit to check on the progress, who Bill would get to do the carpentry work, who would help him run it. Bill's brother Ron might be coaxed into the last role. Together, they'd operated the family establishment in Queens, and Karpi's Luncheonette became one of the best-known candy and ice cream parlors in Elmhurst at the time. Their father's decision to retire and their longing for a quiet country life sent Bill and his brother to Connecticut. Ron had found work as a short order cook in a nearby town.

"I was thinking that maybe my brother Stan could use a change of scenery," Tiger suggested. "This might be the perfect chance for him to make a clean start. But he might need some convincing."

To catch Bill up, George explained, "You see, Stan's been hanging out with the wrong crowd lately."

"I have a brother like that myself," Bill admitted.

"Doesn't everybody?" George said.

"Plus, Stan says he has a friend who's looking for work as well," Tiger added. "Between the four of you, if Ron will go for it, I think we'll have a great team."

"*If* we can convince Stan," George pointed out. "That boy's a solid worker. And he can cook. But he's a city kid at heart."

"Well, this Queens boy loves it here," Bill told them. "I spent my summers on my grandad's farm and I loved every minute of it. I have a feeling your little brother will take to Sherman, too."

Tiger smiled. "Thank you, Bill. That means a lot."

They were already approaching Route 37, which was essentially Sherman's Main Street. In someone's garden, there was a burst of creamy lushness amid the early December landscape: a late-blooming rosebush. Tiger pointed it out to the others. "Would you look at these end-of-season roses," he said. "They keep on going, despite the cold, despite the wind."

"I'll bet that shrub is older than you and me both," Bill told him. "That's the Patience rose. It reminds you of ivory lace, doesn't it? Might take a while to bloom but when it does, watch out."

"Sounds like someone I know," George grinned at Tiger. This was a polite nod to the difficulty Tiger had finding his way when he came home after the War. But once Tiger found his path, he never lost sight of it.

The men paused, giving each other a turn to lean forward and breathe in the scent of the Patience rose. "Looks like buttermilk, smells lemony, doesn't it?" Tiger said.

"Some say lilacs or myrrh, but yep, to me, it does smell like lemons," Bill agreed. After a beat, he added, "And I like the name of that flower, too. Reminds me that with patience just about everything is possible."

Back in Brooklyn, Terry hobbled about the parlor, suffering through her weekly dusting. The swelling in her ankles hadn't subsided. Dr. Lewis said not to worry, that it was common. He had been the Paradiso family doctor for as long as anyone could remember and Dr. Lewis was to be trusted. He was very old now (no one knew exactly how old) and experienced hand tremors. For this reason, he didn't perform surgery anymore. Many surmised that he was still in practice because he didn't know what else to do with himself. For moral support, to relieve fevers and to assure pregnant ladies that they were fine, Dr. Lewis was perfect.

Terry lovingly polished the mahogany breakfront as gently as she had sponged Chiara Rose when she was a baby, as softly as she would wash the new baby when it arrived. Once a month, Terry dusted the china closet's knickknacks (or *chachkas* as Aunt Jo liked to call them), taking them one by one into her palm to clean them. The blown-glass rose from Webatuck Village near the Connecticut border, the Syrian doll in full costume that Goomada Serani had brought from her latest visit, the angel fashioned from dried banana leaves from the Caribbean, and all the rest. They each held memories and stories that Chiara Rose demanded to hear from time to time, so often that she could probably tell those stories herself.

Terry limped through her chores. "Six months is long enough to be pregnant," she'd sighed to Angela earlier that week as they sat and kibitzed.

"Trust me, it's not," her sister-in-law had responded wisely. She'd delivered the twins a month early, which almost killed her—and them. "Tough as it is on you, it's easier having your baby finish growing on the inside than on the outside."

Both women were sitting on the sofa, sharing a final cup of tea, for it was growing late. Despite Terry's protests, Angela convinced her sister-in-law to kick off her slippers and let Angela massage her tired feet. Angela managed to cull a tube of Johnson's Baby Lotion from Chiara's room, careful not to wake the child, who slept like a sweaty cherub atop her ballerina bedsheets. "You need this," Angela had said. "You deserve this."

Terry sat back and let her sister-in-law take care of her. The selfless act of kindness practically moved the pregnant woman to tears and brought to mind Jesus washing the Apostles' dusty feet. When Tiger massaged Terry's feet, it felt different, and one thing led to another—usually to bed. But with Angela, it was something else entirely: a pure expression of empathy and love.

Dusting her parlor days later, Terry remembered this exchange with Angela and hummed to herself as she cleaned, moving gingerly from one foot to the other.

"All it takes is patience," Angela had assured her. "Patience until this child is ready to be born."

Terry sunk further into the sofa cushions. "What if it's a Leap Year Baby?" she mused aloud.

"Wouldn't that be a pip?"

"But what if it comes earlier? Like on Wendy's birthday? Or Stan's?"

Angela reached for more pink cream, then warmed it between her hands. "Elaine Thomas always says there's nothing sweeter than a Valentine's Day Baby," Angela offered.

"I think that would be nice." She cradled Terry's heel in her palm. "Do you feel better?" Terry nodded.

Rubbing more lemon oil into the rag, Terry fell deeper into her memory of the conversation. "It feels different," she'd admitted to Angela. "This pregnancy."

"You look different," Angela agreed. "You're carrying lower with this one. More in your hips. And you're positively glowing." Terry smiled upon hearing this. "You're even more beautiful," Angela said. Terry blushed. "I'm serious." The two women knew the Jewish belief well—that carrying a girl drained the mother of her beauty but carrying a boy made a woman appear even lovelier. Mrs. Lieberwitz had said it many times.

"And don't forget the needle and thread test," Angela reminded her sister-in-law. When the Paradiso women convinced Terry to let them do that silly test on her, the needle moved back and forth like a pendulum, signifying a son. They tried not to get too excited but couldn't help it. After a daughter, a son would be a blessing.

"What name would you pick if it's a boy?" Angela wondered as she massaged Terry's toes.

Terry didn't have to think long. "I'm partial to your grandfather's name. But Tiger says it's a mouthful."

"Michele Archangelo," Angela said slowly. "It doesn't exactly roll of the tongue."

"In Italian, no. But Michael Archangel has a nice ring to it. Michael Archangel Martino," Terry mused.

"That it does."

"But we could just call him 'Mike.'"

Angela had to laugh. "You should know by now that this family isn't one for simple nicknames. Tiger for Anthony, Kewpie for Angela, Kelly for Carmine, Bridget for Margarita."

"But still…I like it," Terry said. For the first time in many months, she was free of pain and felt light as air, though she was certain she resembled a manatee.

"Just be patient," Angela told her. "The baby will be here soon enough. Wait and see."

Patience for Camille meant something else completely. She didn't know how it felt to wait for a baby to be born because she and John hadn't been that fortunate. They saw no need to know which one of them was to blame because it made no sense to blame anyone—together they couldn't bear a child and that was what mattered. When Dr. Lewis suggested each of them be tested, they politely declined. No one in the family or in the neighborhood ever asked questions regarding their childlessness to embarrass them. Just like no one asked the Slavins why they had eight children, no one asked the Palumbos why they hadn't any. It simply was.

As the years passed, Camille came to realize that for some, their fate was to be a beloved godmother, auntie or grand aunt, which was fine with her. Being chosen to cherish many children instead of just a handful wasn't such a bad thing. Plus, this left Camille and John free to travel, to visit his buddies on the other side of the country, to see Broadway shows whenever they pleased. Although John was no longer a private detective, he still worked as a part-time projectionist, often at the Loew's 46th a few blocks away. And Camille herself was a secretary for Mr. Sunshine, a realtor who had an office on the Avenue. She and John were as busy as they wanted to be and there was always enough of everything, more than enough.

Was it patience, or more closely, acceptance, coming to terms with what was instead of pining away for what wasn't? Camille didn't feel the need to name it. She looked forward to having Chiara Rose for sleepovers, treating her to a doll or a toy at Wonderland, setting up a pallet on the sofa, feeling the child's head grow heavy on her shoulder as she read *Goodnight Moon* to her for the umpteenth time, then making French toast on Wonder Bread with the girl for breakfast.

But sometimes, late at night, Camille longed to have her own child, to have produced another human being made from the two of them, John and herself. Only it simply wasn't to be and Camille had made peace with it. "You can make peace with almost anything with time and patience," John liked to say, which is one of the reasons she loved him so dearly.

Although Wendy told herself that she didn't need a man to be happy, and that it didn't matter, she couldn't figure out why she was alone. She kept herself as busy as possible and her world expanded far beyond the narrow frontiers of Borough Park. In addition to working at the Dime Savings Bank on Thirteenth Avenue, there were her Saturday morning classes at the New School and writing articles for *The Brooklyn Daily Eagle*. But no one Wendy met in the newsroom or in the classroom, and certainly not at the Dime, turned her head or set her heart racing. Young men (and a few old ones!) were constantly trying to convince Wendy to go on a date. But she couldn't imagine sharing a peanut, let alone dinner or a movie, with them.

Wendy's parents told her to be patient, that the right man was waiting for her, waiting to be found. "He might be under your very pretty nose," her mother was known to say. But Wendy was sure Jo only told her this because she treasured her daughter more than anything in the world and that she didn't want Wendy to lose hope.

"If it can be solved with money or time then it's not a problem," her father would say in a knowing tone. "Patience, my girl." But Wendy was sure Harry only said this because he loved her best, too.

At twenty-two, Wendy positively felt like a spinster. Many of the girls she'd gone to New Utrecht High School with were married, mothers, some working on their second child. Not that Wendy was sure she wanted children. Her cousin Chiara Rose was fine but some of the brats who came into the Dime with their parents, screaming for lollipops, then shrieking again when the lollies weren't the right color, well, she could easily cram them into a safe deposit box and throw away the key.

Many nights, Wendy drifted off to sleep with a lonely hollow in the pit of her chest, longing for someone special to hold her close, to brush the hair away from the side of her face and kiss her neck. Did that man exist? Was he pining away somewhere for her? Sometimes Wendy cried herself to sleep for the loss of this man not yet found.

Why couldn't she find someone like her cousin Stan? Stan, who Wendy could tell anything—except those strange dreams she had about him. Stan, who could make her laugh and cry and rage, all in the same breath. Stan, who could make her think and question and defend her convictions, all over a cup of tea before nine in the morning. Stan, who was foolish and wise and wonderful and terrible simultaneously. Stan.

Once, Wendy happened upon her aunts having a heated discussion in Aunt Rose's kitchen. The girl had stood in the doorway listening until she was spotted. "Why doesn't someone just tell them?" Aunt Astrid had hissed.

"Surely they must know," Aunt Camille said.

"Shush!" Aunt Rose snapped.

"Why, it's so clear a blind man could see it," Aunt Astrid continued, undaunted.

"Astrid, if you don't shut that big trap..." Aunt Rose warned. "I'll shut it for you." Then Aunt Astrid saw Wendy out of the corner of her eye and the conversation abruptly ended.

"Tell who what?" Wendy asked, but no one would respond. All Aunt Astrid muttered was. "The truth shall set you free."

At the time, Wendy had looked at her aunts suspiciously, but no one would speak. She picked up a potato peeler to help them prepare the meal.

"Patience, child. Patience," Aunt Rose had told her but Wendy didn't know what this meant. She still didn't.

Confused, Wendy began to pare a carrot and wondered how long she would have to wait.

CHAPTER FOURTEEN

Paint the Town

Stan greeted each day with a sense of dread, for every new dawn brought him closer to Big Paulie's nightmare. The young man knew he had to worm his way out of the Idlewild heist but he didn't know how. Stan couldn't speak to anyone about it, not even Wendy, and he told his cousin practically everything. Except about Betsy Mulaney. Stan told no one about his encounters with Betsy and intended to keep it that way.

Sully greeted each day with a sense of uncertainty. True, he was glad to be alive, especially considering the alternative, but he wasn't sure where he fit into the scheme of things. He was too tired to continue working and too antsy not to. "You'll know when the time is right," Rose kept telling him. "Trust me, you'll know." But Sully wasn't so sure he would; he saw himself as kind of thick-headed.

Wendy greeted each day like a panther. That's what her folks told her, anyhow. Every morning, Wendy tore the covers from her bed and practically sprung from it, planting her feet firmly on the ground. She'd done so ever since she was a toddler. It was Harry who came up with that nickname for his daughter and "The Panther" was perfect.

Rose greeted each day as she always did: with a prayer. Sometimes it was a prayer of thanks, others it was a prayer for protection. Every morning, she was grateful for another day and she was happy she got to spend that day with her family, even if it just meant prepping vegetables for stew, taking Chiara to the playground or watching *Dennis the Menace* on the sofa with Sully at night. ("Compared to Dennis, Stan was an angel growing up," her husband invariably commented.) Every day was a gift. Especially with her granddaughter downstairs and a new grandchild on the way.

Chiara Rose greeted each day with the hope of a child. Each dawn held a sense of wonder—you never knew exactly what might happen. For instance, you could go upstairs to Grandma Rose's one day and smell the essence of cigar smoke as soon as you hit the hallway. This meant Uncle Sam was visiting. Which meant a quarter pressed into one palm, a Werther's pressed into the other and a hard pinch on the cheek. But suffering through the last one was well worth the first two.

Another day, like today, for example, Chiara might wake up and stumble into the kitchen to find her mother and grandmother making spaghetti sauce and frying meatballs. They waited for Chiara to assemble the *antipasto* because it was now her job to roll up the cold cuts into little tubes and pile them onto a plate beside Grandma Rose, who would then arrange them into the most exquisite pinwheel shape alongside the wedges of cheese, artichoke hearts, marinated mushrooms and such. Terry knew to buy an extra can of black olives because Chiara liked to place several on her fingers and eat them off the tips. Sometimes she would feed them to her mother and grandma that way.

"Your father used to do the same thing," Rose would remark, smiling. "When he was your age, he used to help Grandma Bridget make the *antipasto*. Once, he ate so many black olives he had a bellyache."

"How many is too many?" Chiara wondered.

"You'll know," her mother told her.

Chiara was starting to feel queasy. She hated tummy aches and the Pepto Bismol that followed so she pushed away the olive can. "That's a good girl," Rose said. "Now, please pass me the *prosciutto*." Chiara did.

During the day, the Martino door was propped wide open, as was the Sullivan door upstairs. The families came and went easily between the two apartments. Stan knocked on the doorjamb, politely announcing his arrival. Chiara leapt from her seat at the kitchen table, dripping black olive juice. "What's shaking, Chi?" her uncle asked, kissing her on the forehead, ending with a noisy raspberry.

"Oh, nothing," Chiara said, stifling her laughter. "Just making the *antipasto*. You staying for supper?"

"I might be late," Stan said, swiping a piece of stuffed celery. "I've got business to attend to."

"Monkey business?" wondered Chiara. All three adults stared at her in surprise.

"Chiara Rose! That's not polite!" Terry scolded.

"But that's what Poppa Sully says. All the time." The women gasped audibly. Stan chuckled.

"Well, then I guess Poppa Sully is right," Stan told her. "Always is, isn't he?"

"A man with a gun is always right," Chiara remarked thoughtfully. "Isn't he?" This brought more gasps from the women and a belly laugh from Stan. "That's what Daddy says when we watch *Bonanza*," the girl explained. "Right, Mom?" Terry was too stunned to respond.

Stan kissed his sister-in-law on the side of her head and gave his mother a squeeze. "Out of the mouths of babes, huh?" he said amicably. For his niece, he left a wet, sloppy kiss on her forehead like an overly-affectionate Saint Bernard. Chiara quickly wiped off the drippy kiss and didn't care who saw. "They're both right...Poppa Sully and your pop," Stan told them. "I am caught up in a little monkey business but I aim to fix it. Don't you worry. Then I'm going to paint the town, just you wait and see."

"What color?" Chiara asked.

"Red, green, any color you like." He grabbed a tube of salami from the platter and left.

When they heard Stan's footsteps creaking on the stairs, Terry whispered to Rose, "I know he said not to worry but I'm still worried."

Rose countered, "Me too, dear. Me too."

Ignoring them, Chiara Rose popped shiny black olives onto her pointer and middle fingers, hoping no one would notice she was eating so many. She galloped onto the next subject. "Tell me about my name," the child demanded, her mouth full of the patent-leather colored fruit.

"Again?" Terry sighed.

"Again," Chiara smiled.

"You were the prettiest baby any of us had ever seen," Rose began as she pushed a waxed paper sheet piled high with dry-cured pork toward her granddaughter. Instinctively, Chiara began to roll the slices one by one.

"Prettier than Wendy?" she asked.

"Yes," Rose admitted, "but don't tell her."

"Prettier than Beth?"

"Beth was so tiny, she looked like a plucked chicken but don't tell her either," Rose said. "You were prettier than both of them put together."

"And your eyes..." Terry began, opening a jar of artichoke hearts.

"What about my eyes?" Chiara asked.

"They were the brightest eyes I'd ever seen," Terry told her child. "They shone like...like black diamonds."

Chiara turned to her grandmother, who was inspecting her pile of rolled *capocollo*. "They were," Rose concurred. "Just like black diamonds. Your mom and dad, they didn't know what to call you."

"We liked so many names but we couldn't decide on any of them because none of them seemed exactly right," Terry added.

"But then I told your mom what 'Chiara' meant," Rose said. The girl held her breath in anticipation to hear the meaning of her name, although she already knew. "It means 'bright' or 'clear,'" her grandmother continued.

Terry pushed the cheeses she had just cubed toward her daughter so Chiara could place them onto the *antipasto* platter beside the other delicacies the girl had helped her grandmother arrange into the trademark swirling pattern practically patented by the Paradisos. "Well, when I heard what 'Chiara' meant, I knew it was the perfect name for you," Terry said.

Tiger entered the kitchen silently, surprising all three of them. He grabbed his wife around her thickening waist. "With Rose as your middle name, of course," he told his daughter. "I couldn't think of a better middle name." Rose wiped a tear from her eye under the pretenses of cutting an onion for the cauliflower salad but she hadn't pierced its skin yet.

Meanwhile, less than one hundred miles away, in Sherman, Connecticut, Bill Karpi was contemplating colors. As the Martinos and their in-laws enjoyed Sunday supper, Bill considered going bold. He dipped a brush into a pail of deep red paint and streaked it across the primed white wall. Yes, it was a daring move but sometimes, things, such as venturing into a new business, called for boldness. Fire-engine red walls with white trim and window frames, accented by real cloth tablecloths. Bill was going to paint the sleepy town of Sherman red, with a little help from Tiger and George. They had given him free rein and he was indeed taking it.

Bill considered himself lucky to have this new employment opportunity and also fortunate that his wife Joan was one hundred percent behind him giving it a shot. Other wives might fret that they needed a sure thing, a stable job with Connecticut Light & Power like his brother Stew, for example, but not Joanie. She saw the potential in Feel Good Food and was glad to see the spark of excitement in her husband's eyes when Bill did something he believed in. It didn't matter that they had a wee one to feed ("Karen will get fed," Joan said) or that they had another child on the way ("He'll get fed too," Joan smiled, convinced this one was a boy.) All that mattered was that they were together and happy and working toward a dream, side by side.

Joan marveled at how her and Bill's lives mirrored the Martinos in Brooklyn—both had a daughter and both were expecting their second child in February. As she contemplated curtain patterns from the Butterick catalog—café or tab top?—she discussed with Bill the merits of the color red. "It makes people feel cheerful," she said. "Not only is red a strong shade but the Chinese think of it as a lucky color." So, red it was.

As Bill painted the walls, Joan sat at a card table, looking at fabric swatches for the curtains while Karen busily scribbled beside her. They had finally decided on café style window dressings to complement the tablecloths of red and white checkerboard. Joan held up a length of sheer white material embroidered with the tiniest flowers of blue, yellow, red and purple. "I like this one best," she told Bill emphatically.

"And I like what you like," Bill said, careful not to get the darker shade on the white baseboard as he painted.

Karen, who was only three said, "I like…I like…"

At her folding table perch, Joan announced hopefully, "I have a feeling 1960 is going to be a good year."

"1959 wasn't so bad," Bill told her.

Several months earlier, Joan had suffered a miscarriage, Bill had lost his mom plus he'd lost his job when his dad decided to close and sell the luncheonette. But still, Bill's spirits were high and he was able to remain positive amid all the sadness and worry. "Part of 1959 was challenging, but you're right, it wasn't so bad," Joan conceded.

Out of nowhere, Bill began to sing an old song from his childhood, from before his childhood, that his mother (God rest her soul!) had fancied. *"I'll get by…"* he began, in a voice that was unwavering, *"as long as I have…"*

"YOU!" Karen shouted. She'd heard her father warble the tune so often that she knew it by rote.

The Karpis all laughed and continued their important work.

Back in Brooklyn, Stanley Sullivan was treating himself to a glass of Brioschi. But his *mal di stomaco* wasn't due to his sister-in-law Terry's cooking, which was as fine as ever. It was because of his trepidation and guilt. December 11 was less than a week away and he still had no clue how to get out of the Big Paulie fiasco. He'd discussed it with Morty at length and neither could think of an escape route. Simply saying "no" to a small-time thug like Big Paulie could only lead to more trouble. Morty was seriously considering running off to relatives in Maryland to avoid the dreaded heist.

But not even the Brioschi gave Stan relief. Often, just the name Brioschi alone brought comfort because it reminded him of his grandfather. Poppa swore Brioschi was superior to all other antacids, even Grandma Bridget's sacred Pepto Bismol. Why? Because Brioschi was invented by an Italian. Achille Brioschi, to be exact. But this evening, all Brioschi brought Stan was painful gas. He held off as long as possible but when Stan couldn't take it any longer, he retreated into the black-and-white tiled bathroom and vomited up the contents of his stomach as quietly as he could manage.

But nothing was a secret in a railroad apartment. Wendy was helping Rose bring wrapped leftovers upstairs when she heard Stan's purge, followed by running water and a vigorous brushing of teeth. "You okay?" Wendy asked her cousin when he came out of the bathroom. Stan visibly startled at the sound of Wendy's voice. "You're awfully jumpy," she noted. "And you hardly said a thing during dinner. Plus, you were late."

"I had something to take care of," Stan told her. He could see that Wendy wasn't buying it, so he added, "I'm all right. I just ate too much."

"You barely ate," Wendy pointed out. "That's why there are so many leftovers." But even this remark didn't bring a grin to Stan's face. Born a day apart in different hospitals, Wendy and Stan were as close as twins sometimes, but not this time, not this day.

"Maybe it was a bad mussel," Stan suggested.

"There wasn't a bad mussel in the bunch," Wendy told him. Her uncle Sully had been given a few bags of the mollusks, fresh from Sheepshead Bay, by a grateful neighbor (and commercial fisherman) whose daughter had just secured a job as a secretary at Sully's precinct. All he had done was put in a kind word for Daria, but that was all it took for the qualified, amiable girl to be selected for the position.

To Wendy's inquiry, Stan merely shrugged. She pushed, "Maybe a guilty conscience?"

"About what?"

This time, Wendy shrugged. "You tell me."

"Maybe I drank too much last night," Stan said. Wendy gave him a sidelong glance. They stared into each other's eyes. Stan had never seen eyes so unbearably green. Wendy had never seen eyes so stubborn. "I wish I could tell you. But I can't," he told her.

"But you tell me everything."

"Almost everything," Stan corrected. "Not this, though. I don't want to…what does my dad always say?" Then he remembered. "I don't want to implicate you."

"I'm telling," Wendy said, sounding like she did when she was a child. But Wendy never told. Ever.

Stan moved closer, so close he could feel Wendy's sweet breath on his face. It smelled like the *anisette* she'd slipped into her coffee at dessert. "What's to tell? You don't know anything."

"I know you're in trouble, though."

Stan shook his head. "Not yet." He moved closer to his cousin, who had instinctively surmised everything about him since they were little: when he had failed a test, when he had broken something he was trying to hide. Wendy always knew.

"Be careful," she whispered. "He doesn't care anything about you or about anyone but himself. Stanley, Big Paulie would just as soon throw you under the bus as…"

Stan didn't know why but he kissed her. Wendy didn't know why but she didn't pull away. She accepted Stan's kiss, leaned into it, pressed her body into his. They stood there kissing in Rose's scrupulously-scrubbed kitchen, leftovers spoiling on the countertop, and did not pull apart until they heard heavy footsteps on the stairs.

CHAPTER FIFTEEN

Night Owl

"Y ou're a real night owl," Rose remarked to Stan as she and Sully were sitting down for their evening mug of tea and their son was getting ready to go out. "We're in our pajamas and you're…"

Sully looked at Stan and admitted, "Boys will be boys." But he was afraid it was more than that.

It was December 11 and the kitchen clock said it was ten minutes till ten. Stan was supposed to meet Big Paulie and Morty on the corner of Forty-Seventh Street and Thirteenth Avenue at ten sharp. It was only a block away but he didn't want to be late.

Stan hoped his parents didn't detect his hands shaking as he straightened his necktie in the vestibule mirror. He could see his father watching him in the glass's reflection. Briefly, their eyes met. Stan's gaze flickered away; Sully's held fast. The jaded cop knew something was brewing, something bad, but he tried to let it go. Although it pained him, Sully also knew that his son had to work things out on his own.

When Rose kissed Stan goodbye, her arms seemed to linger around his neck a little too long. Did she know? Did she sense he was going to do something stupid with someone stupid? Stan nabbed a *pignoli* cookie from the dish on the table. His grandparents' favorite treat, he'd never understood it when he was a kid. But the older Stan grew, the more he liked *pignolis*: the sublime sweetness of the almond paste, the woody texture of the nuts. As Stan dashed out the apartment door, he wondered what his grandparents would think of him now. Would they still be proud or horrified?

Rose stopped him in his tracks with an urgent, "Stanley!" When he turned, Stan saw that she had his tartan muffler in hand. She wrapped it tightly around his neck, twice, and eased his tweed newsboy cap onto his head, her fingers fussing with the brim. "The weatherman says the temperature's supposed to drop tonight," Rose said in explanation. He nodded and hurried down the stairs.

It was snowing lightly and the moon was almost full, limping toward its gibbous phase. Already well below freezing, Stan flipped up his collar and squared his shoulders against the weather. As he did most often when he had a moment alone, Stan considered his kiss with Wendy five days prior. No other woman moved him that way. He should have felt guilty or embarrassed, yet these emotions did not come into play. Was it possible to marry your cousin? Creaky old British royals used to do it, he recalled, so why couldn't he? And technically, Wendy wasn't a blood relative; she was so much more than that.

Most importantly, did Wendy feel the same about Stan as he did about her? She hadn't pulled away, after all. In fact, Wendy didn't seem repulsed by the kiss in the least. Afterwards, she stared him dead in the eye and gave Stan a small smile. "Just be careful, you knucklehead," she told him, then left the apartment as his mother came in.

At the fire hydrant near the corner of Forty-Seventh and Thirteenth, Stan spotted a black panel truck idling. Somehow, he knew it was the vehicle Big Paulie had procured. Morty sat in the driver's seat and slid over once Stan tapped on the window. "Cold enough for you?" Morty asked.

"And how," Stan told him. "It's supposed to get even colder."

"Enough with the chitchat," Big Paulie barked from the benchlike seat behind them. "I'm freezing my balls off here. Let's go!"

Stan shifted the truck into gear, passing his childhood along the Avenue. Herb's Pickle Place. Moe the Greengrocer's. Piccolo's Bakery. He almost cried when he rolled by the darkened picture window of Feel Good Food. "I spoke to my brother about a spot for you," Stan said low to Morty so Big Paulie couldn't hear. "Tiger wants to meet you."

"Thanks," Morty told him. "Thanks a lot. I want to meet him, too. If we live through this."

Big Paulie was in especially poor spirits. When Stan headed toward the Gowanus Expressway, he complained. "Take the streets!" he wheezed.

"It'll take longer," Stan told him. "Besides there are more cops on …"

"Hey, who's running this shindig?" Big Paulie snapped.

Stan was silent.

"Yeah, I thought so," Big Paulie sneered. "Do me a favor and just do what you're told." Stan and Morty shared curious glances but no more words passed between them.

Grand Army Plaza's Arch, modeled after the *Arc de Triomphe* in Paris, looked swell with its spotlights illuminating the snow. Prospect Park was a huge, black patch beyond it. Poppa used to take Stan and Wendy there for walks in the nice weather, Stan remembered, and if they were lucky, he let them rent a rowboat, but only if they promised not to tip it. (P.S., they never tipped it.) Stan wanted to tell Morty about Poppa, Wendy and walking through the Vale of Cashmere. He thought Morty might appreciate a sweet recollection or two, but Stan was sure that Big Paulie wouldn't, so he kept his lip zipped.

After Prospect Park came the central branch of the Brooklyn Public Library with its graceful curved façade, gilded accents and lots of fancy words over the front, right and center of the entrance doors. Stan's favorite phrase was: *"The world for men with all it may contain is only what is encompassed by the mind."* Wendy always scoffed, 'The world for men! What about women?' Stan would have liked to discuss the library's inscriptions with Morty to see what he made of them but Big Paulie would have hatched a turtle, so Stan kept quiet.

After the library was the Brooklyn Museum, where, as a child, his Uncle Julius would sit on the floor of the Egyptian Rooms and sketch. It was the very same museum Poppa would take Stan and Wendy to as youngsters. Each time, he would ask them what their favorite piece was. For Wendy, it was the oil painting of Niagara Falls and for Stan, it was the cat mummy in the Egyptian Collection, possibly because of how Uncle Julius used to love to draw it. (Uncle Jul had even given Stan one of his sketches for his room.) If he were permitted to tell Morty the story, Stan knew his companion would probably ask what Poppa's favorite piece was. For the record, it was a portrait by a man named Thayer because Poppa said the woman in it reminded him of Grandma Bridget when she was young. But Stan didn't say anything so Morty didn't ask.

As they sailed down Eastern Parkway, Big Paulie wanted to rehash the details of the heist, particulars they'd gone over many, many times before. "Cargo Area D…right off North Conduit…" Morty droned before Big Paulie could say it again himself.

"Large crate…from South America…" Stan picked up.

Morty shook his head. "I don't know, it doesn't sound Kosher."

"What?" Big Paulie barked. "Diamonds ain't Kosher to begin with."

Stan didn't want to tell Big Paulie that the term "Kosher" usually referred to food, not precious gems. He knew all about the notion of Kosher from Mrs. Lieberwitz.

Impervious to Big Paulie, Morty tried again. "I mean, Stan is right, what he said a while back. Aren't diamonds mostly from South Africa? I mean, I looked it up in the *Encyclopedia Britannica* and…"

"Trust me," Big Paulie said. "It all checks out. I heard it from John Russo who heard it from Little Petey. Everything is copacetic. Trust me."

Morty leaned over and whispered to Stan. "Whenever someone says, 'Trust me,' I immediately don't."

"What's that, moolie?" Big Paulie asked.

Stan almost went through a red light at Saratoga. He jammed on the brakes. "Hey, please don't call him that," Stan said to Big Paulie. "Moolie" was short for *melanzana*, (Pronounced "moolenan.") which meant "eggplant" in Italian. It was a derogatory term for colored folks and wasn't permitted in Stan's home or in his presence. Stan wondered if Morty knew what "moolie" meant but by the wounded expression on his face, Morty did. He'd probably been called that terrible name before, more than once.

For a split-second, Big Paulie looked like he could have throttled Stan if the kid hadn't been driving. But when Morty commented good-naturedly, "Besides, I'm only half a moolie," the large man couldn't help but laugh. His whole body shook and all three of Big Paulie's chins jiggled.

After a brief silence, Morty told Stan, "I heard that if you drive at a solid twenty-three on Eastern Parkway, you make all the lights."

"I never heard that," Stan told Morty. "But it makes sense. Let's see for ourselves." When Stan slowed down to twenty-three, he sailed through every green traffic light.

Soon, Atlantic Avenue came into view with its distinct overpass rising above the street below. Stan made a right and kept going. The streets were wide open here. After Atlantic veered onto Conduit, a firehouse stood out among the factories, warehouses and commercial buildings. Engine 236 catty-cornered on Liberty Avenue, standing alone, tall and true with pride. The three-story light brick building had B.F.D. emblazoned on the front, a throwback to the days when the Brooklyn Fire Department was a separate entity from New York City's. Stan thought Morty might find this fact interesting, but not Big Paulie, who didn't find anything that didn't have to do with dinner or dames or the heist interesting.

Around the next curve, Idlewild Airport came into view. Big Paulie shifted nervously on the bench, moving the van noticeably with his considerable girth. He took a gulp from a metal flask and didn't offer the other men any, just slipped the silver flagon into his coat pocket. "It's coming up," Big Paulie said.

On North Conduit, Stan stopped outside a large, open area that was closed off by a chain-link fence. Inside were a series of warehouses. Without Big Paulie's bidding, Morty hopped out of the truck. Just as John Russo had promised, the gate was unlocked. Morty pulled it open wide enough for the truck to pass. Stan eased the van through the fence's opening and paused long enough for Morty to get back into the truck. "See? Easy peasy," Big Paulie told them.

"So far, so good," Morty sighed nervously.

"Move it," Big Paulie warned Stan. "The night watchman takes his break between eleven and eleven-thirty. We only got fifteen minutes."

Stan nodded silently then guided the truck forward toward the warehouses. Each could accommodate a small aircraft. "It's that first one on the right, Johnny told me," Big Paulie reminded them, although neither man needed to be reminded; both Stan and Morty remembered every last detail down to the fact that the crate would be standing alone within the hangar. Johnny had placed it there with the aid of a forklift before his shift had ended that evening. He was confident the night watchman, Jake, wouldn't notice the lone crate. 'Jake ain't the brightest bulb in the box,' John Russo had told Big Paulie.

In front of them was an entrance through which a man could pass. It resembled a garage door except it was built into the front of the hangar. In addition to the man-sized opening, another part of the door could also extend all the way open so a plane could roll through and cargo could be loaded and unloaded easily. This would necessitate operating a mechanism with noisy gears that would draw attention to them, so they were warned not to use it.

As arranged, Johnny Russo had left the hangar door unlatched. Morty went inside through the smaller opening then reappeared and signaled to Stan to join him. Stan shifted the truck's gears into park and left the engine running just outside the hangar. It had started to snow again.

When Big Paulie shifted his weight to stand, the entire truck moved. Stan offered his arm to help his boss get out of the truck, which Big Paulie waved away. He grunted as he took the deep step down to the asphalt and toddled toward the hangar. Stan followed, noticing that the thug was almost as wide as the door itself.

Just inside the hangar was a wooden crate that measured about three-foot square. Nails held the lid in place and there were spaces between each slat. Words in a language they didn't understand—probably Spanish—were burnished into the wood. "J.R. said he couldn't leave the forklift because it might look fishy," said Big Paulie. "Even to a dimwit like Jake. So you guys are gonna have to carry the crate to the truck."

Morty lifted one corner of the chest, just to test its weight. "Doesn't seem heavy. Just bulky," he concluded.

"We can handle it, no problem," Stan told his boss, slipping on his gloves. "No fingerprints," Stan whispered. Morty donned his gloves as well. Outside the hangar, he noticed that it was starting to snow harder.

"You better be able to handle it!" Big Paulie snapped. "That's why you're here."

Morty and Stan each took a side of the box. "Be sure to bend your knees," Stan reminded Morty. Although the carton wasn't heavy, the weight inside seemed to shift as they lifted it, as though it were liquid, alive. Stan could have sworn he heard a fluttery sound, a flapping. It was low, almost nonexistent but it was still there. "You hear that?" he asked Morty.

"Nah," Morty told him. "I didn't hear nothing. But I'm half deaf from getting whacked around by the nuns at Our Lady of Sorrow, man." They had to turn the crate on an angle to fit it through the doorway. It barely cleared the jambs. That's when Stan heard it again, a fluttering like a…

Suddenly, the crate seemed to move violently from within, pulling it from Stan and Morty's grip. One side of the box crashed to the ground, badly crushing a corner. Big Paulie cursed his helpers under his breath, struggling to keep his voice low in case anyone else was lingering in Cargo Area D. His foul-mouthed litany against Stan and Morty, their mothers and grandmothers would have made Rose and Mrs. Morton blush. "You sorry sons of bitches!" the rotund criminal snarled in a harsh whisper. "Pick it up and get it in the truck."

Despite the mobster's accusations of incompetence, Stan and Morty had the foresight to open the rig's double doors before they initially set out to retrieve the crate. It was all part of the plan.

"We're trying…we're trying," Morty sighed.

"Well, try harder," Big Paulie snapped, his hands balled up into fists which reminded him of raw mutton, tortured into redness by the cold.

Stan ignored him. "On three," he told Morty, who nodded. On the count of three, both men dipped their knees and heaved the crate off the ground. Again, its weight pitched unevenly as if the box were a living thing. "This is weird," Morty said. "Almost like there's a haint inside."

The crate visibly jerked and hurled itself to the ground once more. This time, it cracked open like an egg. There was a bright flash of green against the night sky, which suddenly filled with flapping wings. The air was flooded with the bodies of birds, monk parakeets transported all the way from Buenos Aires, startled out of sleep in their dark prison and confronted with the reality of a frigid December evening in Jamaica, New York. There were dozens of them.

Morty, Stan and Big Paulie gawked at the sky, their mouths wide. "What the freak?" the whopping man shrieked. "What the…"

Big Paulie's underlings gazed up at the beautiful South American birds disappearing into the wilderness of Queens County and laughed. They guffawed loudly into the blackness and cackled into Big Paulie's face. They laughed until tears streaked down their faces, holding onto each other so they wouldn't fall down. When he regained his breath, Stan said to Big Paulie, "A thousand diamonds, eh?"

"More like a shitload of parrots," Morty qualified.

"Let's get out of here," Stan said to him. Morty buttoned his jacket to the collar.

Big Paulie grabbed Stan's arm. "You can't leave me like this."

"Says who?" Stan wrenched his arm away from Big Paulie's ham hock grip.

"Why, I'll…" Big Paulie stammered.

"You'll what? Who you gonna tell?" Stan challenged. Big Paulie thought for a moment but said nothing. "You ain't gonna tell nobody," Stan assured him. "Why? Because you'll be the laughing stock of Borough Park, that's why. They'll hear about this in Babylon, in Jersey, even. You'll be nothing but a joke."

Morty picked up where Stan left off. "That's right. You're gonna let us go. You're not gonna threaten us. You're not even gonna talk to us when you see us on the street. Ever. Or else…"

"Or else what?" Big Paulie growled.

"Or else we're going tell everybody everything," Stan said. Big Paulie's face reddened, then purpled. He said nothing because there was nothing to say. "Let's go," Stan told Morty. They both started walking out the open gate, toward North Conduit Avenue.

Helplessly, Big Paulie watched them leave. Stan glanced back once to see the mobster stamping his feet in anger. He was a husky Rumpelstiltskin in a cheap sharkskin suit, fedora and overcoat. Several green birds fluttered around him. A couple perched on the lampposts nearby. One large parrot settled itself on Big Paulie's shoulder then let loose with a white streak of shit when the man shooed it away. Big Paulie shouted and cursed into the night. The monk parakeets screeched and chirped along with him. Stan and Morty quickened their pace.

"Come on," Morty said. "I know a place."

CHAPTER SIXTEEN

Friend for Life

Stan and Morty walked together in a comfortable silence, their shoes making tracks in the snow as they went. The Idlewild Diner wasn't far, Morty had said, and he wasn't wrong. After only ten minutes, its lights came into view, the identical appearance all diners seem to have, no matter where they are across the States. The orange (or green or red) Naugahyde cushions, the mushroom-like stools, the cozy booths, the soothing aroma of slightly-charred coffee emanating from the stainless-steel Bunn machines, their Pyrex pots gently stained from years of caddying strong brew. The Idlewild Diner was no different.

Workers at the twenty-four-hour eatery were accustomed to a steady influx of pilots, baggage handlers, stewardesses and maintenance workers so no one gave a second glance to the two young men of distinctly dissimilar shades who shuffled in past midnight, half-frozen. The waitress, a brassy blonde whose nametag read "Shirley" told them to sit anywhere. They chose a spot by the front window near Conduit so they could watch the snowflakes swirl in the streetlight's glow. "You guys sure look like you can use a cup of something hot," Shirley decided, toting a coffee pot. She turned over their cups without waiting for their response.

"Sounds good," Stan smiled at her.

Something about Shirley made Stan feel at ease and homey. Something was strangely familiar about her bleached-blonde hair, her generous body stuffed into a too-tight uniform. Shirley was battle-worn yet cheerful. She wore thick, flesh-colored stockings that didn't do a decent job of masking the varicose veins that had sprouted on her legs from years of working on her feet. Stan felt sorry for Shirley yet admired her spunk, her tenacity. He decided to give her a nice tip when they left.

Stan and Morty sipped their coffee without saying a word. It was hot, so hot that it blistered the roof of Stan's mouth, his throat. But Stan didn't mind; it reminded him that he was alive. If something had gone wrong—or right—during Big Paulie's thwarted heist, he and Morty could be dead or on their way to jail, all because they were afraid to stand up to a bully. Stan counted his blessings, even if the first blessing was just a burned palate.

Out of nowhere, Morty said, "You know, they used to call my pop 'The Bird Man.' Liked him some birds, he did. Before he flew the coop, pun intended, Old Walt taught me a thing or two about them."

"That so?" Stan remarked.

Morty nodded. "Those green beauties? The ones we just saw?" Now it was Stan's turn to nod. "Monk parakeets," Morty continued. "Also known as Quaker parrots. Though some call them 'monk parrots,' because they resemble parrots more than parakeets, their true name is monk parakeet. It's the only member of the genus *Myiopsitta*."

"Where the heck do they come from, these monk parakeets?" Stan wondered.

Without missing a beat, Morty said, "From the temperate to the subtropical areas of Argentina and the surrounding countries."

"Well, now they're New Yorkers," Stan told him. "They'll have to learn to muddle through, just like the rest of us. What else do you know about those guys?"

Morty sipped his coffee, winced. "They build these big, ugly nests that look like a holy mess from the outside but on the inside, they're like apartment houses. They can be three foot across, almost, with a separate entrance for each pair of parakeets."

Stan studied the menu Shirley had soundlessly slipped in front of him. "That's pretty impressive," he remarked.

"They're handsome birds, one of my favorites," Morty said. "Bright green body with a gray chest, orange beak and deep blue wing tips."

"How come they were being shipped to Idlewild?"

Morty shrugged. "Black market, probably. People like them as pets. They live longer than dogs, fifteen to twenty years, sometimes more. And they're smarter than most dogs too."

"You sure about that?" Stan said, deciding on the silver-dollar pancakes. "I've met a few dogs who are pretty damned smart. Smarter than some people I know. Not mentioning any names."

Morty knew Stan was referring to Big Paulie. He pushed away the menu. He wanted pie, cherry if they had it. "Truth be told, the monk parakeet is overtaking the cockatiel as the favorite bird to teach to talk. You know any dogs who can talk?"

When Shirley came by and took their order, they paused briefly, then picked up where they left off about Quaker parrots. "It will be interesting," Stan admitted, "to see how these guys do in their new home."

"Oh, I think they'll do fine here. Like most of us, they're highly-adaptable creatures."

Shirley brought their food and set it onto their paper placemats. Morty's pie was a generous slice, with a slab of vanilla ice cream on the side. "You looked like you could use some ice cream," Shirley smiled, displaying her ruined front teeth. "No extra charge."

"Thank you very kindly, Ma'am," Morty told her. "And you're right about the ice cream, I could."

Stan dotted his coin-sized pancakes with butter, using three of the tiny waxed paper cups Shirley had provided.

When the butter melted to his liking, he doused the cakes with syrup until they were soggy. "How about some pancakes with that syrup?" Shirley quipped before she left the table.

"She reminds me of somebody," Stan told Morty.

"Yeah," Morty commented. "Every waitress in every greasy spoon diner everywhere."

"No," Stan said. "My ma. My real ma. The one who gave me away." Then Stan proceeded to tell Morty the abbreviated story of his life: his loser father, his fallen dove of a mother who left him on the doorstep of the family of the man who'd left her in the family way, how that family raised Stan as their own and how he'd had no clue of his true heritage until his birth mother lay dying in a hospital a few blocks from where she'd abandoned him.

Morty's mouth hung open slightly as he listened to Stan's story in disbelief. He hadn't touched his pie. "Man, it's like one of those movies about mistaken heritage and all that where the stable boy is really the true prince," Morty babbled.

"I'm no prince," Stan told him.

"That much is true," Morty admitted, but he was still awe-struck. "And I thought colored folks had all the drama."

"Your ice cream's melting," Stan responded.

Morty selected spoon over fork and began shoveling up the pie and ice cream mixture. "How was it growing up with them?" he asked.

"Swell," Stan said to Morty in a quiet voice. "I always felt loved. I always had everything I needed but still, somehow…"

Morty finished the statement for him. "…you always felt 'less than.' Less than everyone else." Stan nodded, spearing a small pancake, chewing it thoughtfully. "Yeah, me too," Morty confessed. "Me too."

Shirley freshened their coffees then disappeared again. "It's funny," Stan told him. "I know lots of people but I don't have many friends."

"Tell me about it," Morty agreed, wiping his mouth with a napkin. "I feel like you're a friend, though. We been through hell and high water together. Even though we don't really know each other, I feel like I can tell you anything."

Stan assented. "Anything and everything."

"You already have," Morty pointed out.

Stan contemplated telling Morty about Wendy, knowing he would understand loving someone who was unattainable, but decided against it. Then Stan realized something. "I don't even know your name. Your real name, that is," Stan told Morty.

Morty laughed. "Sometimes I almost forget it myself because nobody calls me that. But it's Len. Leonard, really. But only my Granny uses it."

"Mind if I do too?"

"I'd like that," Len said. He thought for a moment. "You know, I feel like I got a new lease on life the way this night turned out. Might as well go with a new name. Or my old name with a new twist."

Stan was stuffed to the brim with coin-sized pancakes. "Do you want anything else?" Stan asked him.

"To eat? Nah, I'm good."

Stan leaned across the table. "No, I mean, in life. The future."

"Sure, I do," Len told him. "But I don't have many prospects. There isn't much I can do."

"Sure, there is. My ma likes to say you can do anything you set your mind to."

Len shook his head sadly. "That's funny. Every chance she had, my ma told me, 'Ain't a lot on your horizon, son.' That's before she dumped me on Granny Lulu. And my pa, he used to say, 'Lucky for you God gave you a strong back, boy, because He sure didn't bless you with brains.' Imagine saying that to your kid. Makes you not even want to try," Len sighed.

"Or else, it makes you want to prove them wrong," Stan proposed. "And I know you can. Prove them wrong, I mean. I told you about my brother's place, right?"

"Feel Good Food? Sure. I eat there whenever I'm in the neighborhood. That fellow George sure can cook. Your brother, too." Stan raised an eyebrow. "And you're not so bad yourself," Len added.

"Well, I'll let you in on a little secret," Stan said. "They're set to open a new place in Connecticut. The guy who's going to run it, Bill, well, he seems like a decent sort. And he's going to need some help. Two fellows to help him, in fact."

It took a second for Len to catch on. "Shoot, I ain't never even been to Connecticut."

"I have, a couple of times, just recently. It's pretty nice. I think you'd like it. But there's someone...someone here I'm not sure I want to leave."

"Is it that Betty chippie?"

"Betsy," Stan corrected. "No, someone else. But I'm not sure I can have this other gal. Or that she'd have me."

Len took a thoughtful sip of coffee. "That's what Granny Lulu would call a conundrum."

"A conundrum?"

"A conundrum basically means you're screwed," Len said. "But Granny's a church lady, so she wouldn't put it like that."

Stan sighed heavily. "But anyhow. Back to Feel Good Food. I think George and Tiger will give us a shot. I been talking you up."

Len allowed himself a slight smile. "I thank you for that. But how do you know I'm not a rat bastard? Like Big Paulie, for instance."

Stan shook his head. "I just got a feeling, that's all. I got a feeling you're good people, as my ma would say. Her folks used to stay stuff like that all the time. My grandparents: Mike and Bridget. They died when I was young but I still remember them."

Len nodded thoughtfully. "What would your Ma think of me?" Len wondered.

"Old Rosie? Oh, she'd like you. She'd like you a lot. But she'd try like hell to fatten you up. She'd say, 'Stanley, any friend of yours'... Then she'd sit you at her table and keep the food coming till you were fit to bust."

"So, we're friends, then?" Len ventured.

"Sure, we are, Len. Don't you think so?"

"I know so," Len told him. "But we started out kinda late."

"Not really," Stan said. "Tiger and George met in the Service and look at them. They've got a friend for life."

"Do you think we can be? Friends for life, I mean."

"Why not? So long as you play your cards right."

Both men laughed. This summoned Shirley with her eternally-filled coffee pot. "Warm you up, fellas?" she wondered.

"No, just the check, please," Stan told her.

Though Len protested, Stan paid the bill. "I'll get the next one," Len assured him. He liked the idea that there would be a 'next one,' and many more after that.

As they were leaving, from the corner of his eye, Stan noticed Shirley's eyes widen when she saw that the tip he'd left was more than the meal itself had cost. At first, she gave the impression that she might chase him down and point out the mistake he'd made. But then she realized it wasn't a mistake but a random act of kindness from a young man to an old waitress on a cold, winter's night. Her eyes softened, a brief smile touched her lips, then she disappeared behind the counter.

Although Stan was unfamiliar with the backwoods of Jamaica, Queens, Len knew it like the back of his hand. "Used to live here for a spell when me and Ma were running from a bad boyfriend or two," he explained. "Ma always liked hiding out in Jamaica. Said it reminded her of her family's home down in the Caribbean. In name only, though. I think she spent a few summers there when she was a girl."

The snow had stopped. Just a dusting of an inch or so laced the streets of the industrial area. Though bustling during the day, in the wee hours, Jamaica had an abandoned, haunted feel. Far off in the distance, like the voice of an old friend, Stan heard the clatter of the El. Len did too. "It's the A train in these parts," Len told Stan as they walked toward the sound. "Goes all the way out to the Rockaways."

"Never been," Stan admitted.

"It's a lot like Coney Island," Len explained. "But not. Even has an amusement park…Rockaways' Playland. We should go."

"We will," Stan told him. "What's your favorite ride?"

Without hesitation, Len told him, "The roller coaster. The Atom Smasher." Before Stan could say anything, Len added, "It's not the Cyclone, mind you, but it's still a hell of a ride."

The tracks of the elevated train came into view. The intense cold transformed Stan and Len's words into a fine, white mist in the chilled air. They spoke of many things during their lengthy walk. It wasn't long before Stan brought up his grandparents again but Len didn't mind. This time, Stan mentioned how Poppa spoke bits and pieces of a dozen or so languages, of how Grandma Bridget loved cooking. Stan also told Len how his grandparents passed, peacefully like angels in each other's arms. Of how losing them still hurt, of how it makes him feel both blue and glad to think of them. "The Chinese have a word for it that means 'happy-sad.'" Stan recalled. "*Bei hei gaao jaap.*"

"That's a mouthful," Len said. "But I know the feeling."

Before long, the stairs leading to the Howard Beach station were before them. It was slightly warmer in the waiting area than on the train platform, so they stayed there until the train came. It was late and they were tired, so they sat side by side in contented quietude as the A rumbled from Queens to Brooklyn. Len stepped off at Washington Avenue but not before leaving Stan with explicit instructions on how to transfer for the train lines that would ferry him home.

It was well past two when Stan arrived, safe and sound, but Rose was still awake. She held the careworn copy of St. Jude's prayer gingerly between her fingertips, he the patron saint of impossible causes. Perhaps there was hope for Stanley after all, Rose thought before she drifted off to sleep, relieved. She truly believed that there was hope for everyone, always.

CHAPTER SEVENTEEN

Snow Drift

There was a certain rhythm, a certain poetry to the weeks that led up to Christmas, a predictability that was both comfortable and comforting. Stan reveled in this sweet cadence since he was a little boy and it filled him with a serene joy to see how Chiara Rose reveled in that very same Christmas cadence now.

He observed how she fancied helping: shaping raw ginger cookie dough into a walnut-sized ball, then rolling that ball in a saucer of granulated sugar before flattening it with the bottom of a drinking glass...opening the cans of peeled tomatoes (ten of them!) with the ancient crank-style can opener...gently unpacking and dusting off the tree ornaments that had been Poppa and Grandma Bridget's (which Rose also cherished when she was a girl)...carefully handing the paper decorations to her grandmother so she could make the front windows festive...and reveling in Rose's stories of Christmas past.

Stan had done these same things when he was Chiara's age and the child's father Tiger had done them as well. Stan liked the way history repeated itself in a positive way, repeated itself and improved itself. Each generation was better, wiser, Stan thought. Each did their utmost not to repeat the sins of their fathers (and mothers). Maybe this wasn't true for Stan himself. Maybe this wisdom skipped an age, like insanity. But his niece Chiara was certainly smarter than he was. Smart as a whip, in fact.

Would it be possible for Stan to love his own children more than he loved Chiara? Would he be lucky enough to even have kids? If Stan had that good fortune, he would love his kids deep and serious, with all his heart and soul, just like his Ma, Terry, Angie and all the other Brooklyn roses in his family did, whether or not these children were born to them.

By mid-December, Terry was hugely pregnant and ordered to stay off her feet as much as possible by Doctors Lewis and Schantz, the obstetrician. This troubled Terry, especially around Christmastime, when she wanted to shop and cook and decorate and sit with the others at the kitchen table as they stuffed peppers, minced onions and garlic, and gently ribbed each other as they prepped.

Instead, Terry was relegated to sit on the ottoman with her feet up "like the Queen of Sheba," she complained. But her sister-in-law, mother-in-law, aunts, even her young daughter, had no problem doting on Terry while Tiger worked long hours at Feel Good Food, overseeing the Borough Park branch, stopping in to visit George at the Jersey City outpost and occasionally checking on Bill's progress in Connecticut.

"Maybe we like being your handmaidens," Angela would say when Terry sobbed that she felt (and looked!) like a lump on a log.

"I'm useless," Terry would sniffle.

"Nonsense," Rose would tell her, taking Terry a cup of calming tea. "Remember, you're making a baby. That's a lot of work."

"We all got help when we needed it," Angela reminded Terry. "When David and Beth were born..." and Angie would retell her sister-in-law the story of the twins' premature birth. How Poppa, Wendy and Stan had built a cradle and set it up near the furnace, crafting a life-sized incubator where the babies grew and thrived. How neighbors from far and wide would bring delicacies so Angela would grow strong: Mrs. Wong's ginger-vinegar soup with pig trotter, Sadie Lieberwitz's matzo ball soup with bone-marrow broth, Marianna Acerno's savory, soupy pastina fortified with hearts, kidneys and livers. Terry had heard this tale often but it never ceased to make her feel assured and cheered.

"It takes a village to raise a child," Elaine Thomas would say to Terry, sharing the old African proverb about how it took an entire community for a child to grow strong and true. "To me, that means before *and* after that child is born," Elaine would tag on for good measure.

When he was free from his duties at Feel Good Food, Stan gladly took on looking after Chiara Rose, building a snowman in the front yard or picking her up from school for a surprise trip to the Loew's 46th to see *Operation Petticoat* ("What's a 'petticoat'?" she'd asked. Then, "Why don't women wear petticoats, anymore?" which launched more questions).

One afternoon, Stan and Wendy took the girl sledding at Owl's Head Park on the cusp of Bay Ridge, just as Tiger had done with them. It was bitter cold that day and few others were there. How Stan enjoyed watching Wendy and Chiara speed downhill on the sled, screaming, giddy, their cheeks bright and rosy with frost as they came to an abrupt stop in a snow drift. This rough landing made them laugh even more. Stan felt his heart might overflow as he dislodged his niece and cousin from their icy prison. He loved the young girl something fierce and gave her a hug after he brushed the snow from her coat. "What's that for?" Chiara asked him.

"It's for nothing," he told the child. Chiara took the sled by its rope and began trudging up the hill.

"It's because he loves you," Wendy called after Chiara, smiling.

Stan's feelings for Wendy were so intense at that moment that he almost took her into his arms and kissed her. Almost. But he held back.

"What's wrong?" Wendy asked Stan. "Why are you looking at me like that?"

"Nothing's wrong," he told her. "Everything's right."

"Come on!" Chiara called from halfway up the hill. Stan jogged up after his niece to take a turn down the slope with her. Wendy waited for them below.

From a distance, Wendy studied Stan as he sat at the back of the Yankee Clipper, the cherry-red paint that announced its name faded from so many bottoms brushing against it for so many years. Stan made space for Chiara to sit between his knees, then raised them protectively around her. He let Chiara hold the rope but steered the sled with his feet without the child's knowledge. Instead of a straight downhill run as prudent Wendy had done, Stan zigged and zagged, darting between trees and bushes, much to Chiara Rose's thrill.

Wendy gasped watching them zoom downhill, her eyes swelling with tears of delight. What a fine father this funny, faithful man would be, she thought. What a good combination she and he might make, the perfect blend of practical and reckless, keeping each other honest. Then Wendy pushed the thought from her mind. Stan was her cousin, after all, forbidden. Technically not a blood relative but in many ways, closer than blood. He had been her first friend. Perhaps this was a useful trait in a mate, perhaps not.

When Stan and Chiara made it to the bottom of the hill, he purposely tipped them over to one side so they fell off the sled and into the snow. Chiara shrieked with pleasure, brushing the flakes from her hat. "Again!" she demanded. "But this time, I want to do it alone."

Wendy and Stan looked at each other. What would Terry do? What would Tiger do? He had been the first to let the two cousins go down the exact same hill solo together more than ten years earlier and they lived to tell the tale. "All right," Wendy told Chiara. "But make it a straight run. No monkey business, you little monkey." Chiara promised to be careful and bounded up the hill, dragging the Yankee Clipper behind her.

"What?" Stan asked Wendy. She had been staring at him without realizing it.

"Nothing," Wendy told him. "Nothing at all." Stan took a hunk of snow, quickly fashioned it into a ball and threw it at her. "Hey!" Wendy laughed. "No fair."

"Who said life was fair?" he said.

From the top of the hill, Chiara proclaimed, "Ready!" She belly-flopped onto the sled and charged down the slope, face-first. Steering with her hands, she bolted downhill, stopping at her uncle and cousin's feet.

"Nice one!" Stan told her.

After a few more solo runs, all three were frozen to the bone and the sun was beginning to dip behind the bare maple trees, making it colder. Stan shuttled them off to a nearby soda fountain for hot chocolates. "It's good but not as good as yours," Chiara told him as she sipped.

"That's because of my secret ingredient," Stan winked.

"What is it?" Chiara piped.

"If he told you, it wouldn't be a secret, now, would it?" Wendy said. But Wendy knew the secret ingredient: love. Bridget used to say the same thing to them when they were young.

Sufficiently thawed and done with their warm drinks, they stood to leave. Chiara begged for one more spin on the orange-topped silver stool at the counter and they relented. Stan rested his hand on the base of Wendy's spine, waiting for his niece to finish twirling. Even through the thickness of her jacket, Wendy felt an electric charge run up her spine and penetrate her core. As Stan knelt before Chiara, buttoning up her coat, he didn't seem to notice the effect his touch had on Wendy. But maybe it was better that way, she thought.

Like Thanksgiving, the dance of days leading up to Christmas was perhaps better than the day itself: the wonderful foods fixed, the spirit of affection with which they were created, the visitors who showed up on the doorstep of 1128 Forty-Seventh Street, unannounced but expected. Stan's family officially met Len, sometimes known as "Morty," on Christmas Eve Day. That's when Len stopped by with a rum cake drenched in a rum butter sauce. It was a traditional Jamaican dish his Granny Lulu had taught him to make and now she said he made it better than she did.

In the commotion of preparation, Rose convinced Len to stay for Christmas Eve supper. Granny Lulu was at church for the evening and he would have been alone anyhow. Quickly falling into step, Len helped the men set up the extra table and chairs in the Martino dining room. Tiger had interviewed Len a few weeks earlier and immediately approved. Witnessing firsthand how Len set to action in the dining room solidified Tiger's decision to hire him at the Connecticut eatery; tasting Len's rum cake later that night seconded the motion.

Len had never seen so much food, each dish better than the one before it. He had never felt so welcome at a table that had not been filled with his own family, even though this one included two cops, people he generally avoided like the plague. Len had never sampled Italian delights like *manicotti* and *capocollo* before but he liked them, he liked them a lot, and he liked Stan's family a great deal, too.

As soon as Len set eyes on Wendy and Stan together, he knew Wendy was "the one" Stan had spoken of at the Idlewild Diner. Len knew by the way they looked at each other, by the way Stan's hand brushed hers as he took the *antipasto* platter to set it on the table. 'Even a blind man could see it,' Granny Lulu would have remarked, just like Astrid did.

Before anyone took a scrap of bread, they all joined hands and Tiger said Grace. Len had an inkling that Stan's brother said the same prayer all the time, thanking God they were together and how he hoped they could all be together again next year. There wasn't a dry eye in the house.

"Poppa used to say that prayer at every family supper," Wendy whispered into Len's ear to clue him in. As she did, Wendy's soft, brown hair fell seductively across her brow, brushing his cheek. She smelled like roses, Len couldn't help but notice. He could see why Stan had fallen for a girl like that, even though she was his cousin.

The prayer of thanks completed, the circle of friends and family dropped hands and began to eat with a voracious fervor. *Antipasto*, a swirl of cured meats, sliced cheeses, savory salads, breads and marinated vegetables gave way to an array of seafood: stuffed squid, fried calamari, a delectable, garlicky symphony of octopus, shrimp, lobster and other saltwater delights concocted from Lucy Ucco's recipe (which prompted a heartfelt discussion of what a wonderful person/ schoolteacher Lucy was). There was thick spaghetti slathered with a sweet crab sauce, savory stuffed mushrooms, marinated string beans, lemony broccoli salad and several other dishes Len had never seen before but he tried them anyhow. They were all delicious.

One course slipped effortlessly into the next, the women whisking away platters and dishes like culinary fairies, replacing them with clean plates and more trays of food. The feast would have fed Granny Lulu's whole parish in Kingston (Jamaica, not New York), yet nothing was wasted. There was talk of giving Mrs. Segrell, who was homebound, a care package of leftovers on Christmas morning, and of leaving a satchel on Doctor and Mrs. Lewis front porch. Plus, everyone, including Len would leave laden with leftovers (or "planned overs" as Stan's Granny Bridget used to say).

Had Len eaten enough? Did he need more grated cheese? Could Len possibly bring himself to finish the last baked clam? (A Sheepshead Bay captain on the *Marilyn Jean* had gifted Stan's stepdad Sully with a heaping bagful of fresh cherrystones and Stan's mom Rose had worked magic with them.) Yes, Len could probably squeeze in the last clam.

There was a course to help them digest which involved stalks of fresh fennel, nuts (and an ancient nutcracker which an onyx-eyed imp named Chiara Rose insisted on wielding) plus an assortment of candies. But this wasn't dessert. Oh, no, dessert came next: a selection of home-baked goods made by the women, their neighbors and friends. There was a mountain of Italian wine cookies made with Muscatel and Golden Blossom honey called *struffoli*. (Chiara tried to teach Len how to say "struffoli" and giggled each time his tongue tripped thickly over the "r" and "l." Chiara's pretty, dark-eyed mother, who was largely pregnant, kept reminding the girl to be polite.) There were platters of ginger snaps, lemon-ricotta drops, a flan, and more, but Len's rum cake held the place of honor. Chiara was only permitted a small taste because it was drenched in liquor and she was already tipsy from the *struffoli*, she claimed.

All the while, Len didn't feel like a stranger. He felt welcome, wanted, important. Stan's relatives were genuinely interested in him, his people and where he came from, though not in a nosy, busybody way, but in the spirit of genuine caring.

"What's Kingston like?" (Terry)

"When did your people first come here?" (Tiger)

"When did you learn English?" (Chiara Rose, who discovered that English was Jamaica's official language but that they also spoke Creole or Patois. Len politely told Chiara that he was born in America and learned English just like she did, as a baby. But that he learned Patois very soon after. This seemed to satisfy her.)

"Did you know a Desmond Morton?" (Harry, who informed Len that Desmond had worked with Poppa at the Brooklyn Navy Yard and often graced their table before he passed.)

"How old were you when Granny Lulu taught you to cook?" (Rose)

"How did you and Stanley meet?" (Sully)

This last question made both Stan and Len take pause. They exchanged brief glances before Len commented, "In the neighborhood."

Although Sully let it go, he knew most neighborhood boys from his years of walking the beat. Because of this, Sully knew Len wasn't from anyplace around here, maybe Bushwick but certainly not Borough Park. The old-salt sergeant would resist the urge to run Len's name through the system when Sully next reported for duty at the Sixty-Sixth Precinct. He would have to trust his son's judgement in friends and Tiger's judgement in hiring new employees. Even if this Len fellow had made a few bad choices up to this point—and who hadn't!

Even his own son had—Sully would do his best to stay true to Rose's credo: think the best of people until they prove you wrong. "You're a better man than I am, Gunga Din," Sully would tell his wife whenever she gently reprimanded him for not doing so. But this time, Sully would try. He would try like hell to think the best of Leonard Morton.

When the long, lingering meal was over, Len convinced the men to let him help put away the extra tables and chairs. "It'll go quicker this way," he said. Len was glad they agreed to let him lend a hand instead of treating him like a guest. It felt good to be part of something again, Len thought to himself.

On the count of three, Len lifted a solid wooden table leaf with Stan. The two worked well together in the dining room and they would work well together in the kitchen or in the front of the house, as cooking lingo referred to the eating part of a restaurant.

At almost midnight, Len kicked a snow drift as he stepped down from the Paradiso porch. Stan had said that's what folks still called the place—the Paradiso House—though no true Paradisos lived in it anymore. It had been Poppa's last name, Bridget's married name, their sons' surnames, their daughters' maiden names, so people up and down Forty-Seventh Street would eternally think of it as the Paradiso House, long after the last of the family was gone.

It was good to have continuity, to have something that endured, Len decided. Granny Lulu was Len's homing device, his rock, his family history. Since she'd mostly raised him, she was his constant, even after his fair-weather father was long gone, even when his Ma, who had wafted in and out of his life like fog, passed, Granny Lulu was always there for him. Strong, resolute, a tiny powerhouse who barely stood five-foot tall, with her sturdy set jaw, her short, wiry hair mostly gone white now, and with her love, always with her love.

Len fished a Lucky Strike from his coat pocket, lit it one-handed, striking a match against the box. The next day was Christmas. He'd mentioned at supper that Granny Lulu was too old to cook a big meal these days—"Can't spend too much time standing on her feet," he explained—and that it was only the two of them. Len usually took her out for Chinese food at Lok's down by Grand Army Plaza. It had become their tradition.

"No one should be alone on Christmas Day," Stan's dishy Aunt Jo had told Len. She said that Christmas supper for them was an open-door buffet at their place that lasted all afternoon. She gave Len their address on Fort Hamilton Parkway and urged him to join them—and to bring Granny Lulu, if she could make it up the stairs of the limestone house. "Just one flight," Harry told Len. "Hell, if I can do it, she can," Harry added, gesturing to his false left leg. (Len hadn't noticed until Harry'd pointed it out.)

"And if she can't make it, we can carry her up in a chair," Stan told his friend.

"Just like the Queen of Sheba," Terry smiled.

Heck, maybe Len *would* take his Granny to meet these fine people. She would fit right in, like a hand in a glove, just as he had. She would dig out her church dress, iron it on the kitchen table, which she would neatly drape with a clean towel, all the while complaining about how she couldn't go, but deep down excited to have a new place to go on the day that Christ was born. Then Granny would carefully arrange her church hat on her head, tip it at a jaunty angle, and nod that she was ready to leave. Maybe Len would buy her a gardenia or a violet for her furs as Billie Holiday sang about, though Granny Lulu had no furs, just a thick, dependable cloth coat. No, he would buy his Gran a rose, a perfect white rose to sport in her buttonhole.

Just then, the church bells rang, it seemed across the whole of Brooklyn. The peals from parish upon parish called together, one meshing into the other, a celebratory wall of sound, announcing the birth of a savior, the season of hope.

Above the clamor of bells, Len heard the rumble of the El beckoning him. But instead of taking it, he made a right at the corner, toward St. Catherine of Alexandria Church, where Stan (and all of the Paradiso children) had been baptized, where Stan's parents (and all of the Paradiso sisters) had been married.

Instead of going home, Len made his way to midnight mass at St. Catherine's with all the other sinners. If there was hope for them, there was surely hope for him too.

CHAPTER EIGHTEEN

Kiss Me

Christmas Day was a whirling dervish of gifts, torn wrapping paper, food, blissful faces, laughter, tears, more food, hugs and a few snowflakes topping it all off like vanilla icing. Just enough snow to make it pretty but not enough to make travel treacherous. Granny Lulu said she felt at ease with "those white folks," even though it took some getting used to that they, in fact, were serving her, instead of the other way around. And gladly at that.

Maybe Dr. King down in Memphis was right, Granny Lulu decided. Maybe we *could* all live together as one, as brothers and sisters. She vowed to finally read his *Stride Toward Freedom*, which her grandson Leonard had given to her the Christmas before. The very same book Dr. King had been stabbed in the chest autographing during a signing at Blumstein's department store in Harlem. And she would also read Dr. King's latest, *The Measure of a Man*, which Leonard had given her this Christmas, a slim book of essays based on Dr. King's fiery, yet hopeful sermons.

Her Leonard (Granny Lulu refused to call him "Morty," "Len," or anything else but his Christian name) was a good boy, a good man, if not raggedy around the edges. Lately, he seemed to have more purpose, more drive, and he wasn't hanging about with that tubby Eye-talian good-for-nothing

Paul Something-or-Other. Granny Lulu liked Leonard's new friend, this Stan fellow, and she liked his family, too.

The week between Christmas and New Year's Day was a busy one for all. Stan and Len took a trip to Sherman with Tiger and George to meet with Bill Karpi and get his seal of approval. Bill immediately took to the eager young men and figured he would be ready for them near the start of spring. In the meantime, Len would be put on the payroll and brought up to speed at Feel Good Food's Brooklyn outpost, working side by side with Stan, who was happy to teach him. Len was also open to putting in time at the Jersey City outpost to get a feel for how things were done there too.

During the Christmas break, it took a great effort to keep a child as inquisitive and energetic as Chiara Rose occupied but in a concerted family effort, they managed. Tiger was busy with work duties and Terry was waylaid on the ottoman, nursing her sore body until her time came to give birth. So, Chiara happily split her days between relatives.

She loved going with her Uncle Augie and Aunt Angela to the Loew's 46th—although the double bill of *The Wasp Woman* and *The Tingler* made for a fitful night's sleep. That evening, the girl was consumed with worries that an insect had lodged itself into her brain just as it had with Judith Evelyn in the latter film. Tiger managed to quell his daughter's midnight fears with soothing stories about Cinderella in her beautiful dress.

On her day off from the bank, Wendy took Chiara to the City on the El to see Saks Fifth Avenue's Christmas windows and the decorations around Rockefeller Center. Chiara's favorite among many favorites were the frothy angels with their trumpets leading way to the magnificent towering Christmas tree. Since neither felt like ice skating at the rink below it, they passed the time people watching. They shared a cup of hot cocoa and a slice of pie at the Horn & Hardart, then headed home, Chiara promptly falling asleep with her head on Wendy's shoulder during the train ride. There was only so much excitement a ten-year-old could bear.

At thirteen, Beth and David were old enough to take Chiara sledding but it didn't hold the same reckless abandon as it did with her Uncle Stan. (Nothing did!) Still, the girl was grateful to be out, this time on the slopes of Prospect Park's famed Cherry Hill.

On the long walk back, they passed the endless expanse of Green-Wood Cemetery where Poppa and Grandma Bridget were buried. Chiara and her parents visited their dual grave often, before holidays, especially. It was the only time her father ever seemed sad. Whenever they went, they would leave a pebble on top of her grandparents' headstone. This was a Jewish tradition, Tiger explained, showing that someone had visited, that the deceased were still remembered, still cherished. When the girl asked, "Are we Jewish?" her father responded, "We're a little bit of everything, just like they were."

Trudging beside Green-Wood, when David said that Stan's real father and mother were buried there, Beth gave her brother a hard shove. "What do you mean?" Chiara asked in wonder. She hadn't known.

"Sometimes you can be so stupid," Beth sighed at David, then told her young cousin the condensed version of their Uncle Stan's origin. "I think you're old enough to know," Beth prefaced, "but you've got to promise not to tell anyone we told you."

Chiara nodded gravely, then raised two fingers in a Girl Scout promise (though she wasn't a Scout yet). "I swear," she pledged. The story of Stan being left on the front porch in a cardboard box as a baby was fantastical, like Moses being set adrift in a basket in the bulrushes in *The Ten Commandments*.

With her Grandma Rose, Chiara went to visit Sadie Lieberwitz, who had a grandson Chiara's age. Though Neil was more interested in the comic books he'd gotten for Hanukkah than playing house, Chiara had to admit that Wonder Woman, with her blue-black hair similar to Chiara's own and her magic lasso, were interesting. Could a girl actually be a superhero? Well, Wonder Woman was living proof.

Grandpa Sully took Chiara down to the Six-Six while he submitted paperwork at the precinct. She sensed her grandfather's importance because people saluted him and called him "Sarge," like the fellow in the Beetle Bailey comic strip. However, Chiara had the feeling Grandpa Sully wasn't as silly and laughable as Beetle's "Sarge." Somehow, she knew that her grandfather was good and fair at what he did, whatever that was. She felt proud of her grandpa, proud to be part of him. And not just because the cops fed her Jujubes from the vending machine but because of the kind of man he was.

Aunt Astrid took Chiara Rose for tea and cucumber sandwiches at the Plaza Hotel. At first, the girl was miserable because she had to dress up in her stiff, starchy Christmas dress and wear white gloves, even while she ate those boring sandwiches. Chiara had been forewarned that she had to keep her gloves on all the livelong day. When and only when she assented to this torture was she permitted to go on the adventure with her aunt.

However, once Chiara and Aunt Astrid arrived at the fancy hotel, the girl's misery faded. The Plaza resembled a palace with its tall walls, flags, white limestone bricks, columns and checkerboard sidewalk. There was a golden statue not far from its grand entryway which Chiara wanted to take a closer look at but Aunt Astrid said, "Later," which meant "Never." From a distance, the statue seemed to be a winged lady with a crown of leaves carrying a branch, leading a man on a horse. Why did the men get to ride when the women had to walk? And why on earth did the lady walk when she had wings?

One of the Plaza Hotel's doors magically opened for Aunt Astrid and Chiara as they passed through. The doorman bowed as though they were royalty. All of the helpers wore outfits like lawn jockeys except none of them had dark skin like George or Tyrone. These fellows were so white, they were pink, paler than Aunt Astrid, who put Estée Lauder on her skin to make her appear more fair than she actually was.

Inside, the Plaza was a symphony of golds and blacks and whites. There were marble columns, plants bigger than Chiara herself and a chandelier of cut glass like so many tears, too many to count. A staircase with gilded banisters swept people upstairs but Chiara and her aunt didn't climb them. (Oh, how the girl wanted to slide down one of those golden banisters!) Instead, Aunt Astrid led them to the Palm Court, which actually had palm trees inside, just as the name implied. There were more gilt-topped columns (this place was lousy with columns!) and a complicated cut-out ceiling. The entire room seemed to shimmer.

When the waiter held out her chair, Chiara worried he might pull it from beneath her as Uncle Stan sometimes did as a joke. But Chiara sensed that no shenanigans went on in the Plaza's Palm Court. She shook out her cloth napkin and put it into her lap, just as Aunt Astrid did, then sat arrow-straight in her chair. It concerned Chiara that the chair's upholstered seat was white. 'White isn't the best color for you,' Chiara's mother often told her as she scrubbed out a stain. Chiara decided to order only white things to eat so she wouldn't make a mess. Plain milk, cottage cheese, vanilla ice cream…

In spite of herself, Astrid smiled at her young niece across the table. "You remind me of Eloise," she said.

"Who's this Eloise?" Chiara wondered.

"Just a naughty girl who lived at the hotel's tippy-top floor," Aunt Astrid told her. "Someone wrote a book about her."

"I'm not naughty," Chiara scowled. "Well, maybe a little, but only sometimes."

Astrid smoothed her napkin and rearranged the shiny silverware in her place setting. "There's even a painting. I'll show you later," she offered.

Afternoon tea at the Plaza went on without incident, no spills, no stains. Afterwards, just as she'd promised, Aunt Astrid brought Chiara to the Eloise portrait. Staring at them was a girl with messy blonde hair tied with a red bow, slouchy white knee socks and a round belly under her white shirt and black skirt. A dog on a leash and a turtle were involved as well. "She lived in a pink, pink, pink room…" Aunt Astrid began.

"…at the tippy-top floor," Chiara finished, remembering what her aunt had said earlier.

"On the way home, we'll get the book," Aunt Astrid said. And they did. Only not at the Borough Park branch of the Brooklyn Public Library but at a giant store called F.A.O. Schwartz practically across the street from the Plaza. Maybe Aunt Astrid did love Chiara Rose after all, she concluded, despite her reprimanding and posture-correcting. Maybe this was just the way Aunt Astrid loved, by trying to turn you into a better you.

Chiara's great aunts Camille and Jo loved her in a completely different manner. It was difficult to believe that they were Astrid's sisters, for they, as well as Grandma Rose, loved unabashedly, without apology: wholeheartedly, with hugs and squeezes and Hershey's Kisses and secret smiles (when they thought Chiara wasn't looking) and letting you lick the cake batter from the wooden spoon without once lecturing you about how the salmonella you could get from the raw eggs was a silent killer.

The girl thoroughly enjoyed being in Aunt Jo's warm kitchen smushed between her and Aunt Camille, learning how to make the traditional Italian New Year's lentil soup. They showed her how to dice carrots, chop celery and wash the tiny legumes in a metal colander. Lentils, the child also learned, were believed to ensure prosperity in the coming year. "How come?" Chiara asked.

"They're supposed to look like Roman coins," Aunt Jo said.

Chiara peered into the colander. "I don't see it."

"Me neither," Aunt Camille admitted. "But if it's going to bring good luck and money, I'm all for it."

"Plus, it's delicious," Aunt Jo added.

They minced and stirred, tasted and perfected with a pinch of oregano, a handful of spinach, a dash of salt, a bay leaf, a twist of pepper, then put in more spinach and a can of tomato sauce. Though most families served the soup on New Year's

Day, it was a Paradiso tradition to have it on the Eve, "to get a head start," Poppa used to say. "But I think he just liked the soup and couldn't wait to taste it," Camille said, sadly remembering him.

While the lentil soup finished cooking, Aunt Jo painted her niece's fingernails a seashell pink, promising it would be dry in time to finish off the soup and pack it away. "The soup's even better the next day," Aunt Camille explained. "When all of the flavors have a chance to mingle. But we can each have a cup when it's done, just to taste it."

Although Chiara liked all of these activities, if you asked, her favorite thing to do on her winter vacation from P.S. 131 was absolutely nothing at all. It was heavenly sitting on the sofa beside her mother, watching television shows like *The Many Loves of Dobie Gillis*. It was just the two of them, Chiara and her mom, and she didn't have to share Terry with anybody. They didn't have to do anything, just simply be. Chiara savored the clean, fresh, Noxzema cold cream scent of her mother's skin, her impossibly soft hair against her cheek and her sugary breath, which smelled like the Vienna Fingers they'd dunked in milk earlier.

Chiara and Terry had fallen asleep, curled together on the sofa, when Tiger returned late that evening from Connecticut. His wife and his child looked so peaceful he didn't have the heart to disturb them. Instead, he covered them with one of Grandma Bridget's crocheted afghans, kissed them each on the top of the head and left them there, snuggled on the sofa. In an oddly beautiful way, Tiger felt Bridget's silent presence in the room, in her and Poppa's old apartment, in the very fibers of the blanket his grandmother had so carefully, so lovingly created years earlier.

Almost as many visitors were expected on New Year's Eve as there'd been on Christmas Eve. Throughout the afternoon, the doorbell constantly rang, though the front door was kept unlocked. Ringing the bell simply let the family know of a new arrival. Tiger and Terry's apartment was the hub of activity, just as it had been when Poppa and Bridget had lived there. Neighbors popped by to wish them the best for the coming year and perhaps had a cordial to toast a (hopefully) sweet 1960.

It was Chiara Rose's job to fetch the Borden Dairy milk crate marked "New Year's Decorations" in Grandma Bridget's unfamiliar hand. The crate was covered with an old checkered dishcloth. "Here, let me," Uncle Stan said, taking the box from Chiara at the bottom of the steps. She didn't protest because not only was it heavy but she didn't want to damage the finery inside: noisemakers, tin horns, paper caps and tiaras. "New Year's Eve is my favorite," he told her, mounting the steps quickly.

"Mine too," Chiara said, trailing him. "I get to stay up late. Plus, there's lots of noise. And food."

"No presents, though," he pointed out, setting down the box in a corner of the parlor.

"That's okay," Chiara said.

"You sure?" he pressed. She nodded, then eventually caught on when Stan couldn't hold back his grin. This was her cue to ransack the parlor, peeking behind pillows, even pulling up the corner of the area rug. "There are only three and they're all in this room," he added.

"Only!" Chiara squealed. She unearthed the first present hidden behind the couch cushion: a dime-store bracelet with rosy paste stones. "My birthstone!" she remarked, slipping it onto her wrist.

The second gift was a yellow box hidden under the ottoman. It said "Mr. Potato Head" in red script and contained plastic parts and pushpins.

"You stick them into a potato," Stan explained. Maybe Chiara's mom would let her borrow a potato from the vegetable bin tomorrow.

The third present was a grown-up looking doll named Barbie, also in a box. She had black hair just like Chiara's and wore a zebra striped swimsuit. Barbie was the most popular toy that year and honestly, the girl had been disappointed she hadn't gotten one for Christmas. Little did she know that her uncle had saved Barbie for New Year's, a gift-giving tradition he'd had with the girl as far back as she could remember. Chiara was thrilled with her Barbie and hugged Uncle Stan profusely until he peeled her from his waist.

"You spoil her so," Terry blushed, then kissed Stan on the cheek. "But thank you," she whispered. All the bedrest had reduced the swelling in Terry's ankles and she was permitted to be up and about, just for the holiday, after admitting that she was going stir-crazy.

Chiara decided that she would save playing with Barbie for later. She had more important things to contend with, like the matter of the pots and pans. That was the best part of New Year's Eve: being permitted to bang cookware with wooden spoons at the stroke of midnight. Since most of her mother's Farberware was being used to prepare their meal, Chiara had established the pleasant ritual of going upstairs to Grandma Rose's and asking to borrow her cookware. They thoughtfully selected the proper implements to use—the cheap aluminum pots from John's Bargain Store had a more unique timbre than the white enamel pots with the red handles. Frying pans had a deeper tone than pot covers, for example. Grandma Rose chose the best ones and helped Chiara carry them downstairs, making sure she held onto the banister.

Wendy arrived, fresh from the Dime Savings Bank. She shook off the cold and hung her Kelly-green winter coat on one of the hallway hooks. "Some things never change," she smiled, assisting her aunt and cousin with the pots.

"And that's good," Rose remarked. "You and Stan used to do the very same thing." Wendy kissed her aunt on the cheek.

"Except she always took the best pots," Stan said. Wendy flushed when she saw her cousin and wondered if anyone noticed.

"Because you always dented them," Wendy countered, "so you could only be trusted with one. The beat-up tin pot." To Chiara, she whispered loudly, "Your Uncle Stanley is the most enthusiastic pot-beater there is." Wendy's voice grew more quiet as she put her lips to the girl's ear. "Once, he even broke a wooden spoon," she confided.

Wendy stood to meet Stan's steely gaze. "That spoon was as old as the hills," he said. "Plus, it already had a crack in it." His face was just inches from hers. Wendy studied the slight chip in Stan's front tooth, gotten when he'd fallen from his tricycle at age five. Wendy fought the impulse to kiss Stan's handsome mouth. Instead, she turned away. She was rescued by the call to carry platters of food in from the kitchen.

There was the cavalcade of dishes. The ever-present *antipasto*, the swirl of meats, cheeses, peppers and olives. There was a bowl of fennel, thinly sliced and simply dressed with olive oil, salt and pepper. Julie, their new neighbor across the street, dropped off a plate of her stuffed mushrooms, which nicely complimented the stuffed peppers and stuffed artichokes they served. And lastly, there was the pot of lentil soup, large enough for a soup kitchen. Too heavy to carry the handful of blocks to Tiger and Terry's place, Harry and Jo had driven it over in the Pontiac, held fast on the floor between Jo's feet, its cover secured with masking tape.

Because she had helped her aunts cook the soup, Chiara Rose was given the honor of ladling it out but she had to stand on a chair to do so. Tiger was at her side, steadying his daughter by holding lightly onto her dress sash. Chiara worked slowly and steadily, not spilling a drop, proud to feed the people she loved with something she'd helped make. Terry, now relegated to a cushioned chair, watched happily as Beth and David passed around the bowls Chiara filled with savory soup. They took their places when all were served and after Grace, they all dug in.

Eighteen were wedged around the vast table but somehow it didn't seem full. There was always room for one more, for more than one more, and there was always enough food. They were blessed.

For the past few years, it had become a tradition to watch Guy Lombardo's New Year's Eve program on C.B.S., which included a live segment from Times Square. The music on the program provided satisfactory accompaniment to all of the eating, laughing and cajoling. Gaetano Alberto Lombardo was not an Italian American but a Canadian born in London (Ontario), hence the name of his Royal Canadians band, but Guy was okay in everyone's book. Everyone except Chiara's, who deemed the band "farty," despite the fact that she wasn't allowed to say "farty" at the supper table.

The only thing that saved Chiara from the numbing boredom of Guy's sister Rosemarie singing "Indian Love Call" was the procession of desserts, which she was determined to lead. Felicia had dropped off one of her lovely lemon Bundt cakes dripping with wonderful icing. (Chiara managed to swipe a fingerful of the frosting from the serving plate without anyone noticing.) There was a two-layered icebox cake which Chiara'd made with Grandma Rose, painstakingly lining up the graham crackers between the puddings. To shake things up, they used butterscotch instead of chocolate pudding to complement the vanilla. "One of the secrets to a happy life is to be full of surprises," Grandma Rose had told Chiara.

And that's when Rose first felt it, when she was making the icebox cake with her granddaughter: a profound pain, an ache on the side of her left breast. It happened when she lifted the pot of butterscotch pudding from the burner. She tried to forget the pain and go about her kitchen duties, which she so enjoyed sharing with Chiara. It reminded Rose of the times she spent with her own mother as a young girl, learning the ins and outs of cookery by doing, watching, smelling, stirring and tasting. Rose was glad Chiara showed interest, just as her father Tiger had before her, and look where it had gotten him. It had gotten Tiger into the restaurant business, that's where.

Stan had the foresight to bring a chocolate layer cake from Feel Good Food, which would be closed the following day for New Year's. The cake begged for the vanilla ice cream Wendy tried her hand at making, which complimented the coffee (both American and Cuban-style espresso) and tea they served.

Although everyone had announced at supper how full they were, they still managed a serving or two of dessert. Even Astrid indulged and only remarked once that she was "watching her figure." As usual, her husband Al joked that he would be happy to watch it for her so she could have a slice of cheesecake (baked by their neighbor Mr. Mancini) without worry.

The midnight hour drew closer. Chiara alternated between exhaustion and exuberance. She was sternly warned to calm down by each adult in the room, except Stan and Wendy, who thought Chiara's hyperactivity amusing. "Just wait till you have your own kids," Terry sighed, exasperated by life itself by this time of night. The baby seemed to be beating a bass drum inside her and this was pressing on her last nerve, literally and figuratively.

As Rose reached for the teapot, she felt that stitch in the left side of her breast again. It must have shown in her face because her daughter-in-law wondered, "What?"

"It's nothing," Rose told Terry. "I just moved the wrong way."

Stan and Wendy's fingertips brushed when she gave him her empty cake plate. She licked her lips and glanced away. "What?" Stan wondered.

"It's nothing," Wendy told him.

Five minutes to the hour, Chiara began doling out pots, pans, covers, wooden cooking implements and decorative headwear. At one minute to twelve, all eyes turned to Guy Lombardo on television. At ten seconds till, they counted down with him, making their way, en masse, to the front door. Though it was a frigid night, they crowded onto the porch, clashing cookery, whooping and hollering and crying out.

When the noise subsided, kisses, hugs and handshakes were dispensed. That's when it happened. Without giving it much thought, Wendy took her cousin Stan by the necktie and pulled him toward her. "Kiss me," she said, and pressed her mouth to his. The rest of the family stared in shock. Camille gasped audibly. Chiara shrieked with delight. The only one who didn't seem shocked was Astrid. "Thank God," she said. "That was a long time coming!"

Harry was speechless and red in the face, but did nothing. Of her own accord, his daughter pulled out of her kiss with Stan and shrugged helplessly in explanation. "What's the big deal?" Astrid chided the rest of them.

Camille offered, "Come on, let's all go inside. It's cold out here."

"We'll talk about this later," Jo stammered and no doubt they would.

Everyone went back into the parlor, everyone except Wendy and Stan. "What?" he asked her.

"Nothing," Wendy said. After some thought, she added, "That love is all there is is all we know of love."

"Huh?" Stan pressed.

"Never mind," she told him. "I'll explain later." As they followed the others inside, Wendy added, "You've got a lot of reading to catch up on."

Yes, 1960 would prove to be an interesting year.

CHAPTER NINETEEN

Best of Luck

Rose didn't want to spoil anyone's holiday. That's why she let it go for so long. Then there was Stan and Wendy's New Year's kiss and what came after: the surprise of it all and the joy. Rose surely didn't want to ruin what was blossoming between them. But the ache from the lump in her chest became so intense that she couldn't ignore the slight but gnawing pain, like a stitch in her side, except in her breast, her left breast. She tried to overlook it for more than a month.

One morning in early February, Sully found his wife at the mirror behind their bedroom door. Rose stood in nothing but her slippers and a full slip, her left arm raised above her head and the fingers of her right hand worrying the left side of her chest. Her face wore a look of concern. "Feel this," she said.

Sully felt, his roughened fingertips not seeking pleasure but rooting out something else, something that shouldn't be there. "It feels hard, like a marble," he told her. "What is it? A pimple? A cyst?"

"I don't know," Rose said.

"Well, Dr. Lewis will. Let's get dressed and go across the street," Sully told her. Even though it was before visiting hours, Dr. Lewis saw them anyway. Eva Lewis, his wife, who also served as his nurse and receptionist, called the doctor down from their upstairs apartment to his office on the first floor. Her "Morris, come…" was tinged with urgency. He came as quickly as he could, pulling on his white coat and fastening it on the landing.

"*Nu?*" Dr. Lewis said, struggling with the last buttonhole.

Eva did the belligerent button easily and straightened out the collar of Dr. Lewis' lab coat. "Rose found a lump," she told him.

How often had Rose sat in Dr. Lewis' examination room? It was all so familiar: the cracked leather examination table covered with white paper, the mint green table holding tongue depressors, cotton balls, alcohol, thermometers, the clean, soothing medicinal smell.

Beside the table, Sully was perched on a stool that was much too small for a man his size. Eva stood just beyond her husband in case she was needed. The examination table was propped up so that Rose could sit comfortably. Although she wore just her lace-topped slip, she wasn't embarrassed. Rose felt as ease with each of these people.

Dr. Lewis hovered above Rose, his forehead furrowed with concern as he palpated one breast and then the other. He lingered on the left one, shaking his head, humming to himself, as was his custom. "Raise your right arm above your head," he said. She did. "Now the left," he told her.

Again, Rose did as she was told. "Do you feel it?" she asked. Dr. Lewis nodded. "It could be a cyst, couldn't it?" she said, her voice cracking.

"Cysts and tumors feel similar," Dr. Lewis admitted, "but cysts are usually filled with fluid. This feels hard. Like a mass."

Dr. Lewis eased down the strap of Rose's slip, exposing her left breast. It sagged slightly with the weight of feeding two children, with the weight of life itself. Her skin was unblemished, except for a depression, a dimple on the side, beneath her left armpit. Dr. Lewis observed and touched. Then he said gravely, "I don't like the way this looks. Or feels. You can get dressed now."

When Dr. and Mrs. Lewis left the room, Sully guided Rose's arm through the satin strap of her slip. Then he helped Rose step into her shift. Her hands were shaking too much to zip the house dress herself so Sully did this without her bidding. He was that sort of husband.

They joined Dr. Lewis in his office. The glass top of his desk was cluttered with piles of paper, open books, pencils, packages and the occasional wooden tongue depressor. Yet when Dr. Lewis needed to find something, he usually did so on the first attempt.

On the wall behind him, pressed into a corkboard with pushpins, were photographs of the children he delivered, patients whose lives he saved and laminated prayer cards from the funerals of those he couldn't. All held equal importance to Dr. Lewis.

"So…" he said, scribbling on a prescription pad. "…I'd like you to go see Dr. Seminara." Dr. Lewis looked up. "He's a breast specialist. The best in Brooklyn." He tried handing the paper to Rose but she was too numb to take it. So, Sully grabbed the note, studying it briefly. It held a name, address and telephone number which began Shore Road 5. "Eva is calling him now," Dr. Lewis added. "She'll get you an appointment today, if possible."

"But…" Rose stammered.

Dr. Lewis reached for Rose's hand across his jumbled desk. He covered her trembling fingers with his strong, firm ones. "Rose, this is beyond my area of expertise," he began in a quiet voice. "But I would trust Marco with my Eva, with my Mindy. With you." Rose nodded; she understood. "Dr. Seminara isn't far. In Bay Ridge." Dr. Lewis addressed Sully. "And don't worry, I'm sure he takes the City's health insurance."

"I'm not worried about our insurance," Rose managed to say. "I'm just worried. Period."

"Don't be worried," Dr. Lewis told her. "Just concerned."

Rose's laugh was a short, sharp bark. "Is there a difference?"

"Worry doesn't do anyone any good but concern fixes things," Dr. Lewis explained.

Eva Lewis managed to get an appointment with Dr. Seminara later that day. The Sullivans thanked Eva, who gave Rose a hug. Dr. Lewis shook Rose and Sully's hands and said, "Best of luck" each time.

The moment the doctor's office door closed behind them, Rose made her husband promise, "Don't tell anyone yet. Please."

Although this request startled Sully, he agreed. It was a rare entreaty coming from a woman who garnered such support from her family, from her trio of sisters, especially. Sully was relieved he had put in his retirement papers just after Christmas and that he would be home day and night to support his wife. "It's probably nothing," he said as they crossed the street, his arm around Rose's shoulder to steady her.

"Thank you for saying that," Rose told him. "But I know it's something. I can feel it in my bones."

The past few nights, Rose had been dreaming of her mother. Nothing out of the ordinary, just the two of them at the stove cooking or at the table preparing *lasagna* or stuffed shells. It was amiable and lovely and so real. Then Bridget would flash Rose a look of concern and would be about to speak. That's the point Rose would wake up with a start. This very same dream had come to Rose every evening since New Year's Eve.

In her most recent dream, as Rose and Bridget were rolling the dough for *pignoli* cookies, all Bridget said was, "Go!" Rose knew exactly what her mother was referring to. So, the next day, Rose told Sully about the lump and together, they went to see Dr. Lewis.

The appointment with the specialist wasn't until late in the afternoon, near suppertime. Rose didn't have a mind for much—shopping or housework—and it was a bitterly chilly February day. She didn't want to see the matinee at the Loew's 46th as Sully suggested, although she'd heard good things about *The 30 Foot Bride of Candy Rock*—and who didn't like Lou Costello? Lou could surely take their minds off their worries, Sully said. But Rose declined, despite rave reviews from Chiara a few days earlier. Instead, Rose chose to do something which always brought her solace: she read.

The strong winter sunlight streamed in through the bedroom window, warming Rose's feet, which were already snug in the slippers her grandchildren Beth and David had given her for Christmas. Rose's body was wrapped in the thick terrycloth robe her niece and goddaughter Wendy had gifted her, practically the same blue as the slippers. How Rose loved reading in the armchair Sully insisted they buy—what a splurge, so expensive! They put the chair at the railroad apartment's front window in what had once been Tiger and Angela's room, then Tiger and Stan's room. It still held twin beds, one for Stan and the extra bed for visiting grandchildren or houseguests, but with the addition of a cloth lounger for reading and a small table beside it.

Rose picked up her copy of *Hawaii* which rested on the table propped beside the easy chair. The tome was hefty, almost one thousand pages, a Christmas gift from Astrid, who still inhaled books and prided herself on knowing the latest and greatest releases. Michener's newest coincided with Hawaii's becoming the 50th U.S. State in 1959. The book began with the creation of the Hawaiian Islands from volcanic debris, then described the native people on neighboring Bora Bora and made a neat segue into the Christian missionaries who came to the main island. *Hawaii* started as a slow, plodding read— Rose wasn't a fan of the science stuff—but the story gripped her. She raced through the part about the early Polynesians and couldn't wait to see what happened next.

As she read, Rose no longer thought of the growth in her breast but became immersed in the story of King Tamatoa, his brother Teroro and all the other inhabitants of that enchanting island. She paused to admire *Hawaii's* cover: the name of the State in rainbow letters and a watercolor of a tranquil tropical shoreline which could have been painted by her brother Julius.

Rose smiled when she thought of gentle Julius, who now lived with his wife Lettie in a sprawling house near the beach in Fairfield, Connecticut. (Their boys Carlo and Matthew were now grown men and married to delightful women.) Fairfield was about forty miles from where Feel Good Food would open in Sherman.

Rose rested the open book against her chest. She gazed out the window onto the street. She saw Chiara Rose bound up the front steps, back from P.S. 131 for lunch. She saw Mr. DeMeo walking his sweet terrier Violet, who barked happily at Chiara, wanting a cuddle or a treat. The girl ran down the steps to give Violet a quick head-scratch then was up the steps again. An instant later, Angela came home with a sack of groceries and told her niece to put on her hat or she'd catch her death of cold. Rose smiled at the reassuring ballet of life on Forty-Seventh Street.

"We'll go there if you'd like," Sully said, gesturing to the book. "Hawaii, I mean." Her husband's voice startled Rose out of her thoughts. Sully stood before her with a plate and a cup of tea. On the dish was a grilled cheese sandwich, slightly charred but still edible. The tea steamed, the red rose decorating the paper tab dangling from the bag's string. A staunch Lipton-ite, Rose recently decided to try this brand because she'd always been partial to roses.

"But Hawaii is so far and so dear," Rose sighed.

"But still," Sully told her. "I'd like to see it. And visit Old Mike's ship in Pearl Harbor." Sully was referring to the *Arizona*, the battleship which Rose's father had helped build in the Brooklyn Navy Yard. It was one of many which had been sunk in Pearl Harbor, starting World War II for the U.S. There was talk of making the site into a national memorial.

"I'm afraid that might make me sad," Rose said.

"Me too but it would also make me proud," Sully admitted. He put the mug of tea on the end table and gestured with the plate. "I tried to do it just like Tiger said, spreading the bread with Hellman's instead of butter. It's a little dark but okay, I think."

Rose smiled. "I bet it's delicious. I'm not very hungry, though," she apologized.

"A girl's gotta eat," Sully told her, quoting the line Poppa liked to borrow from *Body and Soul*, one of his favorite movies. Sully placed the plate onto the table beside Rose.

"I'll try," she told him.

The toasted bread was still warm, the cheese still pleasantly gooey. Sully had grated mozzarella, Rose noted, instead of using squares of Land O'Lakes. One bite and she was transported to a place of care and love and warm embraces. When Rose realized that she was surrounded by tenderness and others' fond feelings for her—the book, the slippers, the robe, the sandwich—she smiled on the inside for there was nothing better than being enfolded in love. Rose managed to eat half the sandwich and finish the whole mug of tea. It felt good to be taken care of, Rose thought and turned the page in *Hawaii*.

The afternoon passed slowly, especially with Chiara Rose back in school. No excited footsteps pounding up the stairs to tell her grandmother what her friend Sian had said during recess. No sharing with Rose a new chapter from *Mr. Popper's Penguins*, which had been one of Stan's favorites too. Despite how engrossing *Hawaii* was, as the doctor's visit grew nearer, Rose's thoughts constantly pooled to the grape-sized lump in her left breast. She could even picture it: hard and resistant and angry.

At three, Sully drew Rose a bath, and though she protested at first—"In the middle of the day? What am I? Cleopatra?"—Rose relented. She stripped off her robe and her shift beneath it, slipped out of her underthings, left them on the checkerboard-tiled bathroom floor and submerged herself in the hot water. Sully took her clothes from the tiles and left Rose alone.

Her husband had mindfully added the Avon Royal Pine bath salts her sister Camille had given her on her last birthday, so Rose was surrounded by the scent of a rich, thick woods. It reminded her of Williams Lake, where she and Sully had spent their honeymoon. Could it really have been more than twenty years earlier? Surely, it felt like only a handful, though so much had come to pass since then. Communions, Confirmations, weddings, funerals…. So much had been gained and lost in two decades.

Rose closed her eyes and rested her head against the rim of the old clawfoot tub. Sully had the foresight to place a clean, folded towel on the rim for her to use as a pillow. Patrick Sullivan was a keeper, Rose thought, smiling slightly. She felt the steam teasing the wisps of hair surrounding her face into tiny curls. Her skin dampened in the heat. She sunk her shoulders beneath the waterline. A succession of images rushed into her head that were soon pressed out by others:

> Running a relay race in grade school (and winning!)…
> Proudly pushing Angela (then known as Kewpie) in a
> pram down Thirteenth Avenue…Tiger (then known as
> Anthony Jr.) in his christening gown…The children's
> joyful faces as they sped by on a Coney Island
> carousel…The children's fearful faces as their father
> Tony ranted about his supper being cold…Dancing
> the *tarantella* at Astrid's wedding to Sam at the St.
> George Hotel…Making *spadini* with her mother
> Bridget…Studying the portrait her brother Julius
> painted of Rose as a pensive child for his first Art
> Students League show…The time her brother-in-law
> Harry brought home his patrol partner, a shy rookie
> cop named Patrick Sullivan, whom she had known
> as a boy…Tony punching Rose deep in the gut and
> her falling to the kitchen floor…The incident in the
> coal cellar…Picking up ten-month-old Stanley from
> the cardboard box that had been set on the front porch
> on Christmas Eve 1937… Dancing with Sully at the
> Rex Manor after their wedding…Standing at the foot
> of Denise Walters' hospital bed… The opening day
> of Feel Good Food…Discovering her parents holding
> each other in their bed, as if asleep, but already dead…

Dr. Lewis's fingers palpating Rose's left breast and the concerned expression on his face...

Rose's life passed through her mind in Technicolor, like a movie montage. Except it was real. It was hers. She sunk further into the bathwater, up to her chin, careful not to wet her hair because she'd just washed and set it the night before. Rose's hand strayed to her neck. The skin was slightly loose but not too bad. Her belly was nicely rounded from carrying two children and dusted with fine stretch marks like the footprints of diminutive birds in the snow. The scar from her hysterectomy was barely visible and soft to the touch. Her opaline toenails bobbed up from the water—she'd let Chiara paint them with polish the girl had gotten in her Christmas stocking. The breasts which had nursed Rose's daughter and son, which had comforted countless sad children as they were drawn into her ample chest in hugs. Now, one mound of flesh had recently betrayed her. It bobbed innocently in the water. Rose's right hand absentmindedly wandered to her left breast, where she worried the lump with her fingertips.

There was a quiet knock on the bathroom door. Sully entered, carrying her terrycloth robe. "I warmed it on the radiator," he said, then added more hot water to the bath. Sully knelt beside the tub and took the bar of Ivory soap. He palmed a rough sponge in the other. "Do you actually use this thing?" he wondered.

"As ugly as it looks, it feels nice," Rose told him. "It's called a 'luffa' and it's all the rage in Sweden, Astrid says."

"I know all about luffas," Sully said. He passed the cake of Ivory along Rose's wet shoulders, then chased the sponge after it.

"You don't have to bathe me," Rose told him. "I can wash myself."

"I know you can," he said. "But I want to."

Rose relaxed in the bathwater and succumbed to her husband's touch. "So, tell me what you know about luffas," she sighed.

"For example, do you know that a luffa is a vegetable?" Sully asked after a pause. "It's in the cucumber family."

"No," Rose said. He reached behind her and moved the sponge to the base of her spine then scrubbed.

"Yes," Sully qualified. "They let the sponge ripen on the vine then dry out. The flesh disappears and the only thing left is the skeleton and seeds, which can be shaken out."

Sully moved to Rose's belly, wisely avoiding her breasts. "You're a regular *World Book Encyclopedia*," she admitted.

"That I am," Sully told her with a twinkle in his cobalt eyes. He lifted one of Rose's sturdy legs and then the other, slipping the mound of soap along the curves that were dusted with pale blue and purple veins. Like the map of a familiar land, these streaks were oddly pleasant to Sully for they marked the topography of a place he loved. This place was not perfect (and really, what is perfect?) but it was safe and it was sure and it was his.

Rose gasped when Sully passed the soap between her legs but instead of pushing his hand away, she held it there, surprising even herself. He let the soap fall to the bottom of the tub, still cupping Rose with his palm, pressing hard where she guided him and easing his touch when she edged him away. Finally, Rose's thighs clasped Sully's fingers desperately. Both of her small, white hands covered his large one, her body arching up toward his fingers which sought, searched and then found.

Rose spasmed in the soapy, piney water, now gone cold, smiled briefly, then began sobbing. Sully held her tightly until she finished, until she pushed him away. "Your shirt is wet," Rose told him, standing in the tub, the bathwater streaming from her skin like Sully imagined it would from the body of Botticelli's Venus.

"It will dry," he said, handing her the towel. Rose swaddled herself in warmth and stepped from the bathtub on shaking legs, ready to face whatever lie ahead.

CHAPTER TWENTY

High Hopes

Although Dr. Seminara hardly looked older than Tiger, Rose was confident in his abilities. He had that perfect blend of knowledge and caring which shone in his warm, brown eyes, even behind his thick tortoiseshell spectacles. Dr. Seminara's office was much neater than Dr. Lewis's and the diplomas lining its walls added to Rose's trust in him for they further professed his expertise. Plus, the doctor shared the name of a picturesque town in Italy. Not just Dr. Seminara's name brought Rose a sense of peace but the notion that her parents were watching over her, protecting her, guiding her. She took this as a positive sign.

But perhaps more important than framed papers on walls, his kind eyes or his last name was the impression Rose got from the doctor—a feeling of hope, a sense of safety that this man could—and would—usher Rose from a horribly frightening place to one of security.

They chatted briefly in Italian, Rose and this Dr. Seminara. Sully desperately tried to follow the few words he knew in the language his wife had spoken as a young child then abandoned for English, but he was lost. When Dr. Seminara sat them at his desk, he talked plainly, in jargon-free terms Sully and Rose could understand. He spoke frankly, not to alarm them but to inform them, which the Sullivans greatly appreciated.

In the examination room, Dr. Seminara touched Rose with quick, deft fingers, first her right breast then the left, then under her left armpit. "Did Dr. Lewis tell you that your lymph node was swollen?" he wondered. Rose shook her head 'no.' "Well, it is," he added.

"Is that bad?" Sully wondered.

"It's not good," Dr. Seminara said. "Although it's presenting itself like a malignancy, I don't think it's very advanced."

Once they were back in his office, Dr. Seminara explained that he wanted to do the surgery as soon as possible. Pathology would test the tissue after he performed something called an excision biopsy—meaning, he would remove the lump and the surrounding tissue. Then if the pathology results said it was cancerous, he would remove Rose's breast in what was known as a radical mastectomy. Rose and Sully's faces dropped in terror.

"They've been performing mastectomies since the late 1800s," Dr. Seminara assured them.

"And how long have you been doing them?" Sully challenged.

"A little more than ten years," he disclosed.

"Cutting off my breast…that sounds downright barbaric," Rose said.

"Mastectomies can be," the doctor admitted. "But not the way I do them." Rose shook her head in protest, resisting. "It can save your life," the specialist added.

"Can or will?" Sully asked.

Dr. Seminara paused. "There's no question that a radical mastectomy will improve Rose's survival rate," he said. "Thirty-three percent of the women who've had them live beyond five years."

"Why, that's only a third," Sully gasped.

"And if I do nothing?" Rose asked.

Dr. Seminara sighed heavily in response. "In that case, it's not a question of if but when," he told her.

Rose had never been one to do nothing. She always fought, even at her worst, even when languishing under Tony's thumb, she fought back. Sometimes she even won.

She gained the courage to glance over at Sully. He looked pale, stunned, as though someone had slapped him across the face without warning. Rose couldn't imagine how she herself looked. "What does it entail?" she pressed. "This radical mastectomy?"

"Well, I remove your breast, the lymph nodes and ligaments in the surrounding area," Dr. Seminara listed. "In advanced cases, it's necessary to take the chest muscles as well as part of the ribcage and breastbone…but again, if this does end up being cancer, I don't think it's advanced."

"It sounds…horrible," Rose whispered.

"It can be disfiguring…" the doctor acknowledged.

"But not the way you do it, right?" Sully repeated.

"Right," Dr. Seminara said, adding, "And remember, it can save you."

Rose kneaded her hands in her lap, studied them. "I just don't know…" she said.

"There are special padded brassieres you'd wear afterwards," the doctor told her. "No one would be able to tell."

Rose continued to gaze into her lap. "Except for me. And him," she said quietly, gesturing to her husband.

Sully took Rose's hands in his. "I fell in love with you, Rose Paradiso, not your breasts," he told her. Then, to Dr. Seminara he said, "I don't think we have a choice here. Do you, Rose?" She shook her head.

Dr. Seminara paged through a large, leather appointment book. He suggested the following week. "But Stan and Wendy's birthdays are next week," Rose worried. "And after that, the baby is due. Terry is going to need my help. A new baby is a lot of work, you know. I just…"

Rose's fingers were now tracing the edges of Dr. Seminara's ink blotter. The sound of his voice made her look up, look him in the eye. "You don't understand," he began, as kindly as he could. "Your left breast is trying to kill you."

Sully hugged Rose around the shoulders. "If it does turn out to be cancer, which I'm sorry to say I think it is," Dr. Seminara continued, "I want you both to know that I've had great success with this procedure. Better than the average."

"How much better?" Sully pressed.

"Sixty percent survival rates."

"I like those odds," Sully told him.

They settled on a date two weeks away, the last Monday in February, which also happened to be Leap Year Day. This would give Rose a chance to prepare: to cook (and freeze meals in the Frigidaire's icebox) and clean and get her affairs in order. It would also give her a chance to tell her family and to get her head around what she must do. Rose could celebrate Stan and Wendy's birthdays on the 14th and 15th of the month, bury her sorrows in Russell Stover Valentine's candy and hopefully, get to hold her grandchild, if the baby decided to arrive on time.

Although Dr. Schantz said Terry's baby had assumed a perfect birthing position and that her cervix was softening, the child showed no signs of coming soon. Terry took long, lumbering walks around the block elbow in elbow with Rose and Angela but still nothing, not even a twang of a labor pain. Just the baby happily bouncing in her belly then lulled into a nap by the swaying movement of the stroll, resting heavily on Terry's bladder, or so it seemed.

As Terry's due date came and went, the neighbors were extremely helpful, dropping off foods which, in their respective cultures, were believed to induce labor. From her own kitchen, Rose brought a platter of eggplant *parmigiana* and a salad doused with balsamic vinegar, both said to bring on contractions. Mrs. Wong brought an especially spicy pork-with-pineapples dish which tasted delicious going down but only succeeded in bringing on a fiery bout of heartburn. Chiara Rose brought ropes of black licorice shoelaces from Dora's Luncheonette and Candy Store which she and her mother enjoyed eating simultaneously from different ends, finishing in an anise kiss. Although it was a pleasant pastime, the licorice did not induce labor as the old wives' tales professed. Mrs. Chaudhry from the new curry shop under the El presented Terry with a flavorful butternut squash dish which she thoroughly enjoyed, but it too did not induce labor. Elaine Thomas sent George over with a salad of romaine lettuce, watercress, walnuts and gorgonzola cheese, its dressing delicately laced with castor oil. But still, nothing.

For the first time within memory, Wendy and Stan agreed to share a birthday cake and requested Mrs. DePalma's "Happy Birthday, Anniversary, Wedding Cake," which Rose gladly made, especially since it contained crushed pineapples, which Mrs. Wong still swore brought on labor. All of the sisters, their spouses and children gathered at Rose and Sully's place to celebrate Wendy and Stan's twenty-third birthday.

When Camille laid eyes on Rose the first time since her diagnosis, she collapsed into tears. "Pish posh, shut off the waterworks," Astrid scolded Camille. "Crying's not going to help anyone." Astrid would be reluctant to admit that she herself sobbed in private at the thought of losing her oldest sister, her rock. Of course, Astrid was hesitant to admit that Rose was her rock in the first place, but Rose indeed was; she was everyone's rock and the family matriarch as well.

Jo put up a strong front, but inside was frightened, frightened for all of them. She'd read articles that said breast cancer seemed to be hereditary and therefore, could be passed along by something called a gene to the females in the family. If this were true, what did it mean for Jo's daughter, her nieces, her sisters, and even herself? Why, look at those nice Ingar women, first the oldest daughter Diane then her mother Fortunata. They passed away of breast cancer within a year of each other.

Together, as a family, they decided not to tell Chiara Rose about her grandmother's diagnosis—she was too young to understand the intricacies of cancer and besides, they didn't want her to worry. All the child knew was that Rose was sick and that she needed to have an operation to make her better.

"But she doesn't look sick," Chiara had told Terry from their perch on the sofa the day before the birthday celebration.

"Looks can be deceiving," Terry sighed, annoyed. The baby seemed to be doing backflips within her and she had to use the restroom yet again. Hadn't she just gone?

"Huh?" Chiara said.

Terry tried again. "Sometimes things happen on the inside of us that we can't see," she offered.

"What kind of things?" the girl pressed.

"Chiara Rose…" her mother breathed, an entreaty, a plea. But at age ten, the child didn't understand subtleties. Instead of accepting what she was told, the girl pushed further, harder. Terry didn't know what else to say.

"I'll go ask Nana Rose," Chiara said finally, getting up.

"No!" Terry snapped.

"But she…"

"I said no!" In one swift movement, Terry lurched forward and smacked her daughter across the face. Chiara's hand flew to the spot on her cheek as though she'd been burned. It was the first time her mother had ever hit her, and the last. Chiara ran out of the room as Terry burst into tears, covering her face with trembling palms.

Despite the drama preceding it, Stan and Wendy's birthday itself went off without a hitch. The cake was perfect, sublime. The fresh strawberries, canned cling peaches and crushed pineapple along with the heavy cream and six eggs melded together for culinary perfection. Their relatives were still trying to get accustomed to Wendy and Stan as a couple—as well as the fact that they had agreed on something as substantial as a joint celebratory cake—but the family was learning.

That evening, Rose read at the kitchen table for she didn't want to disturb Sully, who had turned in early. Stan helped himself to another plate of cake. "Share some with me?" he asked, parking himself at the table across from his mother.

Rose put down *Hawaii*. "Sure," she said, though she was full. Stan took a bite of cake, then gave her the fork. It was something they'd done since he was a boy. After Rose's two forkfuls, Stan steadily worked on the rest. This was also something they had done since he was little—the charade that they were sharing food when he ate most of it.

"I've decided," Stan told her. "I'm not going."

"Going where?" Rose asked.

"To Connecticut."

"But your brother needs you," she told him.

"You need me here," Stan said, "to help."

"When do you ever help with anything?" Rose laughed.

Stan's brow instantly crumpled but when he considered what his mother had said, he laughed too. "Yeah, I guess you're right," he admitted.

"Stanley," Rose told him, leaning across the table. "You can help me by helping yourself. This is a wonderful opportunity." Stan still wasn't entirely convinced. "Go!" Rose added. "I'll be fine."

"Will you?" Stan worried.

"Yes," she said. "I promise."

The days crawled by slowly, which was A-Okay with Rose. She savored things both large and small that happened during the days leading up to her surgery. Together, she and Chiara Rose finished reading *Mr. Popper's Penguins*, the worn copy that had been Stan's, not Chiara's classroom copy. The girl rested her head against the left side of Rose's chest as they did.

"Then they solemnly lifted their flippers and waved, as the great ship moved slowly down the river toward the sea. THE END."

"I feel like I want to cry," Chiara told her.

"Then do," Rose said.

"I can't," Chiara whispered. "It's stuck."

"Don't worry. It will get unstuck when it needs to," Rose assured her.

"I don't know if I'm sad about the penguins or sad about the thing in you that we can't see."

"Maybe both," Rose told Chiara, stroking the black-as-coal bangs away from her granddaughter's face. That's when the girl began to cry softly. At first, Rose said nothing. Then she began to sing a song from a movie they had seen the summer before. Rose didn't remember all of the words but just enough of them to make a difference.

> *"Next time you're found, with your chin on the ground*
> *There a lot to be learned, so look around...*
> *But he's got high hopes, he's got high hopes*
> *He's got high apple pie, in the sky hopes*
> *So, any time you're gettin' low*
> *'Stead of lettin' go*
> *Just remember that ant..."*
> Chiara joined in.
> *"Oops, there goes another rubber tree plant..."*

Chiara and Rose were giggling by the time they finished the silly ditty. "I'm going to miss you, Nana Rose," the girl added after they'd caught their breath.

"I'll only be in Maimonides for a week," Rose reminded her. She couldn't get used to United Israel Zion's new name, even though it had been changed a dozen years already. "Maybe we can sneak you in, like the Three Stooges did in *Dizzy Doctors*," Rose suggested. This made the worry lines fade from the child's face.

The night before her surgery, Rose had trouble sleeping. Her parents kept visiting her in dreams: Poppa reading the *Brooklyn Daily Eagle*; Bridget sitting at her Singer sewing machine or else knitting an afghan, always blue; Poppa trying to find his pipe...

Rose's spirit leapt with joy at seeing her parents again then sunk when she realized it was just a dream and that her folks had been dead for more than a decade. That's when she would force herself to wake, her eyes wet.

Were these dreams a good or a bad omen? Should Rose have asked Angela to do the Overlook Prayer for her last night just before sunset when the Prayer's powers are the strongest?

But knowing Angela, she had already done the Prayer of her own accord. Rose also suspected that Angela had taught the invocation to Terry on the Feast of the Epiphany, one of only two dates each year it could be taught to a female family member. Rose would bet her bottom dollar that Terry had whispered the powerful Overlook Prayer to protect Rose as well.

Rose ultimately decided that dreaming of her parents was a good thing, for they had been and done nothing but good every day they walked the earth. After so many years, Rose's heart still ached whenever she thought of Poppa and Bridget. Rose wondered if anyone's heart would ache for her when she was gone. She sure hoped so.

Sully had a light breakfast of tea and toast. Rose made do with a few sips of water for she couldn't eat before the surgery. She'd packed a satchel with nightgowns, slippers and toiletries, which Sully carried down the stairs. Tiger met them at the bottom landing. "Terry doesn't feel well," he explained. "She can't get out of bed, says her back hurts real bad. But she asked me to give you this." Tiger enveloped his mother in a tight embrace and didn't let go until Chiara Rose tugged at them. The girl held her grandmother around the waist with a desperation, as though she thought she might never see her again.

"Do your best in school today and listen to Mrs. McElroy," Rose told her granddaughter. "She's a good egg."

Sully ruffled up Chiara's hair. "And don't ask anyone to marry you today," he warned.

Chiara knew that February 29th was Sadie Hawkins Day, the only day a woman could ask a man to marry her, which she didn't think was fair. "I'll try not to," she promised her grandfather.

Although Sully offered to drive, Rose insisted they walk the few blocks to Maimonides. It was the way she always visited the hospital, except for the time she was rushed there by ambulance. A temperate day, spring seemed to be lurking just around the bend. The snow had almost melted, except for a few stubborn spots in front yards and on shadowy street corners.

Sully and Rose didn't talk much as they headed toward Maimonides. She held fast to his arm as though it were a beefy life preserver. "You're my rock," she told him in a soft voice. "I'm going to need your help, I think."

"You've been there for everyone all of your life," Sully said. "It's time you let us take care of you."

"I'm not sure I know how," Rose confessed.

"We'll show you," he told her.

CHAPTER TWENTY-ONE

Peace

The operating theatre was white, so white it hurt Rose's eyes. When she opened them, Dr. Seminara's kind face replaced the absolute paleness. "I'm so scared," she told him.

"I know you are," he said. "Don't be."

Someone took hold of Rose's arm, slipped a tight cuff around it. Then she felt a pinch. "This is sodium thiopental," the masked anesthesiologist explained. "It will put you right to sleep."

"No more ether?" Rose wondered.

"Ether," the anesthesiologist laughed. "That's ancient history."

Dr. Seminara pulled his mask over his nose and mouth. "They call sodium thiopental 'truth serum,'" the anesthesiologist continued. "Now don't go telling any family secrets."

Rose felt a warm flow into her arm, then a sense of profound peace. "I'll try not to," she said. "But no promises." Dr. Seminara stood beside Rose, holding her hand firmly. Her field of vision flooded with his beneficent face. Seeing her doctor's caring, compassionate eyes above his surgical mask was the last thing Rose remembered before she drifted off to sleep.

A few blocks away, as Terry lumbered from bedroom to kitchen, she felt a warm woosh of fluid. She immediately knew that she hadn't wet herself but that her water had broken. Thankfully, Chiara Rose was already in school and Tiger hadn't yet left for Feel Good Food. He made an effort to stay close to home after Terry's due date passed and was slated to be in the shop's Brooklyn compound until she gave birth.

Very calmly, Tiger dialed his Aunt Jo while Terry changed her sopping bloomers. Jo would alert the rest of the family, most of whom would make a beeline for Maimonides' waiting room. Next, Tiger phoned his mother-in-law. Terry's overnight bag had been packed for weeks. Tiger grabbed it from the corner of their bedroom where it had patiently waited. Pain streaked Terry's face. "You all right?" he asked her.

Terry bit her lower lip. "As all right as I can be," she grimaced. "Is Aunt Jo going to get Chiara from school?" He told her that Aunt Jo would.

Like Rose, Terry insisted on walking. Maimonides was only four blocks and she reasoned that the nurses would urge her to pace the hospital corridors anyway, just as they had when she was in labor with Chiara. But unlike Rose, Terry would return from the hospital with more than she had left with—a babe in arms; her mother-in-law, with less.

At the corner of Twelfth Avenue, Terry felt as though the child might drop out of her and onto the street, so intense was the push from the inside out, from this child so lazy to be born and now, in such a hurry. Terry stopped at the corner, digging her fingernails into Tiger's arm through his winter overcoat. She nodded when she was ready to go on.

Lost in her drug-dream, Rose was young, younger than her granddaughter Chiara was now. It was the time when she had been known as Rosanna or Roe. In the dream, Rose slipped out from beneath the quilt she shared with her sisters, all three of whom still slept blissfully in the oversized bed.

Across the room, Rose's brothers Kelly and Julius occupied one narrow twin bed, their backs to each other, both pushed to opposite edges of the mattress. Julius stirred, sat up, and grabbed his sketch pad and charcoal pencil from the nightstand. He smiled at Rose then put his finger to his lips. "Don't wake them, Roe," he pleaded. "It's the only chance I get to draw in peace. When everyone else is asleep."

Rose crept quietly up to Julius' side of the bed. He made space for her to sit on the corner and slip beneath the covers with him. Rose peered at Julius's pad. It was a half-finished sketch of Kelly, sleeping. "It looks so much like him," she whispered.

"Of course, it does," Julius whispered back, tugging on one of her long braids. Rose left the warmth of the bed and left her brother to draw.

Their mother Bridget sat at the wooden kitchen table, her nut-brown hair pulled into a bun, her skin unwrinkled, her dazzling green eyes unclouded with age. The early morning sunlight streamed in through the wide window, making the air fuzzy from the flour particles that danced in the rays. Bridget was making pasta from scratch. Or "from scraps," as their neighbor Lydia Martinez would say in her broken English.

Six fresh eggs from Miss DeBoer's chickens waited in a striped bowl. The gravy was already simmering on the stove; its wonderful scent was the culprit that had awakened Rose so early. In a small plate on the range top sat an assortment of tiny meatballs, held aside from the gravy meat for Rose's arrival. "You're late," Bridget smiled, fashioning a deep well in the center of the flour with a gentle fist.

Rose shrugged, yawning, and took the dish of meatballs from the stove. She fished a toothpick from the holder, which was shaped like a donkey pulling a cart. Spearing a bite-sized meatball, she fed the first to her mother. Rose fed the second to herself. "Can I help?" she asked Bridget, washing her hands.

Without waiting for a response, Rose pulled a worn wooden chair beside her mother, careful not to make a sound and wake the others because it would spoil the moment, their special morning moment together. Rose selected an egg from the striped bowl. "Careful, Rosanna," Bridget warned. "Remember, no shells."

Rose cracked the egg perfectly on the bowl's edge her first try, then another until all six eggs sat in the well of flour. Bridget measured the olive oil and let Rose add it to the eggs. The girl carefully mixed the three ingredients together with a fork. It had taken Rose quite some time to master incorporating the eggs and oil into the flour. She was getting better at it but wasn't nearly as good as Bridget, who had perfected the delicate wrist-flick gesture. But Rose was learning and each time, she improved at the task.

Her favorite part of the process came next: mixing the dough with her bare hands when it became too thick to work with the fork. When it was all combined, the dough needed to rest beneath a clean dish towel for thirty long minutes.

As they waited for the dough to set, Bridget poured Rose a little cup of coffee. They drank and polished off the rest of the miniature meatballs. "You're getting the hang of this," Bridget told her daughter. "Soon you won't need me."

"I'll always need you," Rose, the child, told her mother.

The back door opened and Poppa entered the kitchen in his stocking feet, remembering to first leave his work boots on the rear porch. With six children and eight mouths to feed, he never refused overtime at the Brooklyn Navy Yard, even if it meant an overnight shift. Poppa kissed Bridget then Rose on the top of their heads. "Boy, I'm bushed," he said.

"So am I," Bridget admitted.

Suddenly, her parents weren't the parents of Rose's youth. Instead, they were gray and plump and stoop-shouldered. Bridget rose wearily from the kitchen table. She and Poppa began to leave together, leaning into each other's bodies for support. A bright, white light beamed from their bedroom. They walked toward it.

When young Rose tried to follow her parents, she found that she couldn't move. Her feet seemed to be caught in a thick molasses. "Momma!" she cried. "Poppa!"

Rose's parents paused and gazed at her sadly. Bridget looked about to cry. She shook her head. "It's not your time, Rosanna," her mother told her. "Not for a long while yet."

"But I need you," Rose sobbed. "I can't do it alone."

"You can and you will," Poppa said gently. "Dear Old Girl taught you well. And besides, you're not alone. You've got a lot of help."

Rose's parents grew smaller and smaller, the bright, white light emanating from their bedchamber engulfing them. It dimmed abruptly, like a candle snuffed out by a sudden breeze. In the shadows, Poppa and Bridget closed the bedroom door, shutting out Rose with a thud. The kitchen faded and Rose stood alone in the blackness.

Far away, someone was calling her. A voice she didn't know, yet this voice seemed to know her. "Mrs. Sullivan... Mrs. Sullivan," the voice said insistently. Then solid hands grasped both shoulders, jostling her. "Mrs. Sullivan, can you hear me?"

Rose opened her eyes. It was all so dreadfully white: walls, sheets, curtains, uniforms. She closed her eyes against the pale but the voice just wouldn't quit, wouldn't let her drift off. "Mrs. Sullivan, I know you can hear me," the voice said. "I need you to wake up."

Whenever Rose tried to open her eyes, they fought to stay closed. Her lids felt incredibly heavy and seemed crusted with a thick pasta dough. Finally, after much struggle, Rose managed to open her eyes. She saw that the voice belonged to a young nurse with honey-blonde hair and sea-green eyes like Rose's mother's. A tag on the front of the nurse's uniform read "Jessica Montemarano, R.N."

"Jessica," Rose drawled. "Did you know that 'Jessica' means 'God watches' in Hebrew?"

"So, I've been told," Nurse Jessica smiled. "You had us worried, Mrs. Sullivan. You didn't seem to want to wake up." She checked Rose's pulse and seemed satisfied.

"I was having the best dream," Rose sighed.

"Well, you can go back to it soon," the nurse assured her. "Do you know where you are?"

Rose glanced around the room. Silver poles holding sacks of liquid. Steel beds. Machines. Women dressed in uniforms with peaked caps. "The hospital," Rose guessed. "United Israel Zion. Only now they call it something else."

"Maimonides," Nurse Jessica suggested.

"That's it," Rose conceded, closing her eyes.

"Before you go, dreamboat, someone wants to see you," the nurse said. Sully's doughy face replaced Nurse Jessica's pretty one. It amazed Rose how she never tired of seeing this hulk of a man's face, even after several decades. It had aged, it had changed, but still, it was a good face.

Sully cradled a bouquet of roses. "I had such a nice dream," she sighed.

"Was I in it?" he wondered.

Rose shook her head. "My parents. My brothers. My sisters." Then Rose remembered, she remembered the surgery. Her right hand strayed to her left side. It felt numb and there was all of this padding. "Did they take it?" Rose asked. "Did they take my breast?"

Sully nodded. "Yes. I'm sorry but yes, they did. It was cancer. But Dr. Seminara said he got it all."

Rose turned her face away from him and cried. Sully let her; he knew that she had to, that she needed to sob for the loss of her breast without him stopping her. He stood patiently by his wife's hospital bed, crying along with her. He waited until she was through before he spoke.

When Rose's tears subsided, Sully gave her a wad of tissues from the box of Kleenex at her bedside. "And there's something else," Sully told her. "You've got a new grandchild."

CHAPTER TWENTY-TWO

Breath of Life

After making them wait so long, Tiger and Terry's child suddenly couldn't wait to be born. They almost didn't make it to the hospital. By the corner of New Utrecht Avenue, Terry regretted that she'd chosen to walk. She felt a sudden pressure then a deepening fear that her baby would fall to the pavement at Fort Hamilton Parkway. That's when she started sobbing. "It's only one more block," Tiger told her.

"I don't think I can make it," she cried.

Tiger swept Terry into his arms and carried her toward the hospital. An ambulance driver parked outside of Maimonides jumped from his rig and helped Tiger the rest of the way. As they eased Terry into a wheelchair and steered her toward the emergency room, Tiger thought he saw Sully and Rose getting into an elevator but he couldn't be sure. Terry was screaming now in a way she hadn't with Chiara Rose. Tiger was afraid something was terribly wrong.

There was no time to take Terry up to Maternity, for her labor pains were spilling one into the other. In the emergency room, the ambulance driver grabbed a blanket to cover her as he spoke to the nurse on duty.

"I thought that was you, Tiger," said a kind voice behind him. Tiger turned. It was his sister Angela's friend Sally Hinton, the same nurse who had helped the twins David and Beth into the world. Sally was on her way to begin her shift in

Maternity. She hadn't yet clocked in but Terry's wails prompted Sally to stop and palpate the laboring woman's stomach. Sally frowned as she peered under Terry's shift, quickly removing the woman's blood-soaked bloomers. "She's crowning," Sally told a pair of nearby orderlies. Tiger looked at Sally, confused. "That means the baby is coming," she told him. "Now!"

Quickly, Sally wheeled Terry to a curtained area off the main corridor. Two burly hospital workers followed. As they lifted Terry from wheelchair to examination table, she let out a bloodcurdling scream. The baby slipped from her body toward the floor. Sally lurched forward like Ernie Banks playing shortstop and caught the child. "It's a boy," she said.

But the newborn wasn't breathing. He was large and fat and perfectly formed but limp and blue. Still wearing her winter jacket, Sally lay the child across his mother's legs and forced her fingers into his mouth, trying to clear any obstruction. Then she put her mouth to his mouth and breathed. And breathed again. Then the most beautiful sound filled the air: the boy's cry.

One floor away, Rose was out of Recovery and in her semiprivate room. She was thankful for Sully's health insurance, which was better than Tony's had been, for the Police Department trumped the Transport Workers Union. When Nurse Jessica put Sully's fading roses into a plastic water jug, they sprung to life, opening their petals as if breathing a grateful sigh of relief. "You gave us quite a scare," Sully told Rose when they were alone. "They thought you'd never wake up."

"My parents," Rose said, trying to piece together the fragments of her dream for Sully's benefit. "I was little. It was simpler then. No breasts…" she admitted sadly. But he didn't seem to understand. "I'm not making sense," she added.

"No, you are," Sully told her, though he didn't fully grasp what she was getting at.

When he finished his surgeries for the day, Dr. Seminara came to Rose's room. His normally sparkling brown eyes looked tired behind his spectacles. He pulled a chair up to Rose's bed and carefully explained to the Sullivans what he had done. "Pathology showed that it was cancer," he admitted, "but it hasn't spread. That's good, very good." The couple nodded expectantly. He continued, "I managed to get it all. We took several lymph nodes under Rose's arm just to be sure. We'll have the detailed pathology report in a few weeks."

Dr. Seminara took a deep breath. "In the coming years, I think radical mastectomies will be obsolete," he explained. "But for now, they're invasive but effective." What followed was a laundry list of what Dr. Seminara had done to Rose's body to save it from itself. "In addition to a dozen lymph nodes, I took the underlying chest muscles and the ligaments in the surrounding area," he said. "Some surgeons also take part of the breastbone and the ribcage…"

"It sounds awful," Sully gasped.

Dr. Seminara confessed, "It can be. I've examined other doctors' patients where you could practically see their hearts pumping under their skin. But I don't take the breastbone or ribs, so you can rest easy."

"What can we expect afterwards?" Sully asked.

"Well, arm weakness, to be sure. Nurse Jessica will show Rose exercises she needs to do to strengthen her left arm," the doctor stressed. "No heavy lifting for at least a month. And you should avoid carrying packages with that arm from now on, Rose. No blood pressure cuff on the left side plus you have to be careful of cuts on your left hand and arm. They can easily get infected because of the lymph nodes I had to take. Other than that, it should be life as usual."

Rose had been studying the wall during Dr. Seminara's instructions but she turned to him now. "Except I have no breast," she said plainly.

"Yes," Dr. Seminara conceded. "Except you have no breast." He went on to describe the special brassieres they made with a slot cut into the cup so something called a breast form could be inserted. Evalena DeMuccio, a whiz at the sewing machine, had already assured Rose that she would mend her brassieres to accommodate padding. In fact, she had already experimented by making cushions from soft cotton batting for Rose to use as inserts, tenderly taking Rose's measurements before the surgery.

When Dr. Seminara called the contraption a prosthesis, Rose took pause. "You mean, a prosthesis like a wooden leg?" she asked, stunned; the mutilation that had been done to Rose was finally sinking in. "Like what Harry has," Rose addressed to Sully.

"Not a prosthesis made of wood or metal but the idea's the same," Dr. Seminara said. "In the 1800s these breast forms were made of rubber. They were extremely heavy. Then, about 1885, a fellow named Charles Morehouse got a patent for one filled with air, so it would be lighter, less cumbersome."

"Like a spare tire?" Sully suggested.

"In a way. But the point is that Morehouse wanted to make women look and feel more like they did before."

"But nothing could ever do that," Rose told her doctor. "Because nothing is like it was before. I could die," she stressed. "This could kill me."

"That's true," Dr. Seminara said patiently. "But instead, I like to think that it could—and will—save your life. It will just be a different life than it was before. Patients have told me that after breast cancer, in some ways, it's a richer, more meaningful life."

Dr. Seminara also told Rose that he'd inserted a drain in her side which Nurse Jessica would empty twice a day and measure the fluid which trickled into it. Rose reached around her body and felt a long tube that disappeared beneath her left arm. The tube led to a bulblike device that looked like a plastic hand grenade.

"The drain's just for a few days," Dr. Seminara assured her. "Until the fluid stops coming." Rose's chest was so padded with gauze that it felt like she still had a breast but the pain told her that she didn't. "Twice daily, the nurses will change your bandages," he continued. "They're pretty bulky now but each day, they'll get smaller."

Rose was staring at the wall again. Dr. Seminara rolled his chair closer to her bed. He rested his hand on the waffle-patterned blanket. Rose clutched the blanket to her chest and faced him. "Rose, I know it will be difficult but it's important for you to look, to look at yourself," he told her. "To accept what happened to you and then move on."

Rose chewed the inside of her cheek. "What if I can't?"

"You will," he assured her. "Patients tell me that some days, they forget."

"Forget what?" Sully asked.

"They forget that they only have one breast," the doctor said.

Rose squeezed his hand. "I hope so."

Sully observed this conversation helplessly, at a loss about what to say or do. "Thank you, doctor," was all he could muster.

Dr. Seminara nodded then pushed himself from the chair. Many days, his work weighed heavily upon his shoulders and this was one of them. He had come to be fond of the Sullivan Family and wished he were having another sort of discussion with them.

After Dr. Seminara left, Rose told Sully that she was tired and that he should go home. He did as she asked. However, after Sully left, Rose couldn't sleep. All she could do was cry quietly. For some reason, cancer she could deal with; the thought of losing her breast, she could not.

Rose was to stay at Maimonides for a week but she hoped it would be less. Two times a day, a nurse (usually Nurse Jessica), drained the odd bulb attached to Rose's chest. Two times a day, the dressings were changed. But during none of those times did Rose dare to look. She studied the side of the woman's face as she cleaned Rose and tended to her wound. Rose made pleasant small talk with the nurse as she went about her duties—asking the nurse about her family, her children, chatting about the weather—but inside, she was gutted. Rose often sent Sully away and she couldn't deal with her sisters visiting her just yet. Rose didn't want to be fussed over, especially by women who still had two breasts and whose bodies hadn't betrayed them with cancer. Maybe someday she could, but not yet.

Tiger came to visit Rose that first night, the day his son Michael Archangel was born. The new father's joy was palatable, almost permeating Rose's sadness, but not quite. When Angela arrived soon after Tiger left, Rose had been asleep and she pretended to stay asleep for a time. When she decided to open her eyes, Angela just looked at her mother, not saying a word. She sat silently beside her, knowing intuitively what her mother needed: to have private time to think it all through. Rose's roommate Bernice Weiss wasn't the talkative type, for which Rose was very grateful.

When the volunteer from the American Cancer Society stopped by, Rose surprised herself by not sending her away. Maybe it was Marjorie's earnest expression or her determined manner which conveyed the thought that she couldn't fathom anyone not wanting to see her. Rose liked the woman immediately. She liked Marjorie's spunk and her frank brown eyes.

After Marjorie identified herself, she pulled up a chair and asked, "Mind if I sit down?" Rose and Marjorie sat and talked for an hour, Marjorie succeeding in coaxing Rose out of bed to venture to the sun-filled solarium at the end of the corridor. She helped Rose into her robe and off they went.

The words came easy in that cheerful, plant-filled space. Rose's doubts and fears bubbled to the surface and into the air: that Dr. Seminara hadn't gotten it all and Rose would die; that Sully wouldn't find Rose attractive anymore; that people would treat her differently; that Rose would see *herself* differently. Like a shirt on a chair that resembled a monster in the dark of night, Marjorie and Rose shed light upon her fears and turned them inside out so that in the brightness of day, these seemingly terrifying things really weren't monstrous after all.

When they were back in Rose's hospital room, Marjorie was so bold as to ask, "Do you want to see it?"

Rose heard herself respond, "Yes, please."

Marjorie drew the curtain around Rose's bed so her roommate Bernice couldn't see, unbuttoned her blouse and removed it. She slipped the strap of her full slip from her right shoulder and pulled a rubber breast form from her brassiere cup. Then Marjorie slithered out of the bra strap on the right side, the side where they'd taken her breast. To Rose's shock, it wasn't horrific; it was merely a flap of skin, a blank space, an absence, not a disfiguring abomination. "I'm lucky," Marjorie told Rose. "They didn't have to take any of my breastbone or part of a rib."

"Dr. Seminara didn't have to take any of mine either," Rose said.

"That's good," Marjorie nodded. "He's an excellent doctor. The best."

"I'm glad he asked you to come," Rose told her.

"He knows I volunteer for the Cancer Society," Marjorie said. "I do this all the time."

"It makes a difference," Rose admitted. "I feel better."

"You'll feel even better as time passes," Marjorie assured her. She began to pull up her brassiere strap but Rose stopped her.

"Would you mind if I…" Suddenly shy, Rose swallowed the words.

"No, I wouldn't mind if you touched it," Marjorie said, pushing her chest forward slightly. "Go ahead." Rose was gentle but still, Marjorie started. "Your hand is cold," she smiled.

"Sorry," Rose said.

The other woman's flesh was warm and soft beneath Rose's fingers. She traced the line of the incision which went from the center of Marjorie's chest to the right side. Rose noticed a small indentation near the middle. "They call that a divot," Marjorie explained. "Like the dent a bad golfer makes on a golf course."

"Does it hurt?" Rose wondered.

"Not anymore. In the beginning it pulls a little, especially as it heals. But actually, it's still kind of numb around the incision, even after six years."

"Thank you," Rose said. "I just wanted to feel what my husband would feel if his fingers brushed against it."

Marjorie clasped Rose's hand, which was still resting on her chest. "It's not so bad, is it?" Marjorie asked.

"No," Rose declared.

"It's better than the alternative," Marjorie told her. "Not being alive, I mean. I've got a lot to live for."

"Me, too," Rose said. "My grandson was just born yesterday."

"*Mazel tov,*" Marjorie told her, beginning to get dressed. "I hope you get to dance at his wedding."

"I hope so, too."

Marjorie buttoned her blouse and tucked it into her smart skirt, which she said she'd gotten on sale at Mays Department Store downtown. "You might find that some of your tops and dresses won't fit the same way," Marjorie said. "But it's a fun excuse to go shopping and find some new clothes that do."

"Thank you," Rose told her. "Really. Thanks a bunch."

"It's the least I can do," Marjorie shrugged. "Six years ago, I was exactly where you are today. I was afraid I wouldn't live six months, but here I am. Somebody, a lady I didn't know named Agnes, came to visit me at the hospital. She gave me hope."

Without asking to, Rose held Marjorie tightly to her bandaged chest. When they pulled apart, their eyes were wet. "I know you don't want to," Marjorie began, "but the next time the nurse changes your dressings, look. I guarantee it won't be as bad as you think."

"I will," Rose promised her.

Just before she left, Marjorie said, "They should have the rest of your pathology results in a few weeks. It will tell whether you need chemotherapy or radiation…"

"Wait, chemo…" Rose stammered.

"It's a lot to take in, I know," Marjorie began. "But my point is, don't. Don't think about anything, don't worry about anything, until it happens. Take it one day, one minute at a time." Rose gazed at Marjorie curiously. "It doesn't make much sense now but…" Marjorie searched for the right words because the right words would make Rose's journey easier. Then Marjorie's face brightened. "I'm Jewish," she began, "but I've heard that Buddhists believe that you should live in the present."

Marjorie straightened her pillbox hat. She wore it better than Senator Kennedy's wife, who had a fondness for them. "Think about it," Marjorie prodded. "The perfect freedom of finding pleasure in everything: in the blue of a winter sky, in the laugh of someone you love, in the softness of your robe. Despite having had cancer, there is still joy."

Rose mused, "I heard a Bible verse once about joy. Something about…" but she couldn't recall the rest.

Marjorie smiled. "I think I know the one. From the Old Testament, my people's book. Psalm 30. It says, 'Weeping may tarry for the night, but joy comes with the morning.' See you in a few days."

Rose contemplated what Marjorie had told her as the woman disappeared in a whoosh of satin and a hint of Chanel No. 5. Rose sat in her hospital bed, thinking, as the nightstand telephone rang, startling her. It was Tiger, telling Rose to look out the window in exactly five minutes. Rose promised him she would.

When five minutes had passed, Rose ambled to her hospital room window, the one facing Forty-Eighth Street. There stood Tiger and Chiara Rose, waving furiously from the sidewalk. When they started doing jumping jacks on the pavement, Rose laughed and opened the window. "Just for a second," she apologized to Bernice. The cold, night breeze flooded in but felt good. It flushed out the medicinal hospital air.

"I miss you, Nana Rose!" Chiara yelled from two stories down.

"I miss her more," Tiger taunted his daughter.

Rose blew them a kiss and closed the window. This motion pulled at her stitches but it was all right; she needed to hear their voices.

The next night, Rose couldn't sleep, even though she'd had several visitors to tire her throughout the day. She sat up in bed, reading by the glow of a nightlight. Halfway through *Hawaii*, Rose heard a muted tumult at the door to her room. Mrs. Weiss had already drifted off to sleep a few feet away, the radio softly humming doo-wop, for Bernice couldn't sleep without pop music in the background. Rose leaned forward to see Tiger and Chiara Rose steering a wheelchair into her room. The chair held Terry and a little bundle. Rose clapped her hands in delight. "But how…"

"This guy has a lot of pull," Tiger whispered, gesturing to Sully, who followed them into Room 207.

"It also helps to know Sally Hinton," Sully conceded. "She's head nurse now in Maternity, you know."

"Sally delivered your grandson," Terry told Rose, gesturing to the swaddled child pressed to her chest. When Terry held the baby forward, Rose eagerly scooped him up into her arms. He felt lighter than air. "Michael Archangel Martino, meet Rosanna Maria Paradiso Martino Sullivan," Terry smiled, pleased to make the introduction.

"Nana Rose," Chiara corrected. "Those are too many names for a baby to remember." Just as she'd been instructed, Chiara had done a wonderful job containing herself, but now she couldn't hold back. She scooted onto the bed beside her brother and grandmother, covering her with kisses. Then Chiara peeled the blanket away from the baby's head so Rose could see him better. Michael's face was a round, pink apple, covered with down, carved with delicate features like a porcelain figurine in Aunt Jo's curio cabinet. "He's like a weensy doll, isn't he?" Chiara observed.

"That he is," Rose admitted. Her heart was full, bursting with love for this beautiful stranger in her arms, for the granddaughter beside her and for all of the people in the room, even softly-snoring Bernice Weiss. Rose guessed what would come next from her granddaughter.

"Was I that cute?" the girl wondered.

"Cuter," Rose told her in a whisper, leaning closer. She smelled the sweet tang of Junior Mints on Chiara's breath, no doubt a bribe from Grandpa Sully to ensure the girl's good behavior. "Only don't ever tell him I said that," Rose added. "It would only hurt his feelings." At this, Chiara beamed. Rose wasn't sure if it was the prospect of hurting her brother's feelings or the thought of being more adorable than he which made the child grin so, but she didn't ask.

Sully fussed with the roses on the night table. He picked off the odd dead petal, then another that had browned around the edges, ready to fall. Sully was glad to have married into such a fine family. He couldn't have loved Rose's children, her grandchildren—*their* children and grandchildren—any more than if they had been his own blood. For to Sully, they were better than blood; they were the family he chose and they chose him in return.

"We would have brought him here sooner but they wanted to make sure Little Mike was up for it," Tiger said.

Terry explained, "The nursery wanted to watch him for twenty-four hours because he wasn't breathing at first. But his Apgar score was great."

"I bet mine was higher," Chiara piped.

"Oh, it was off the charts, honey," Sully told her, although he was fairly certain there wasn't such a thing as an Apgar score ten years prior.

Rose studied her grandson's face. His chin was strong and solid like Tiger's. She touched the dark fluff beneath his cap, which was silkier than silk. "Did you ever feel anything so soft?" Chiara asked, lightly stroking the side of Michael's head.

"No," Rose remarked. Looking at Tiger and Terry, she said, "And I love his name. Poppa would be honored. How I wish you had known them better," she told Terry in particular.

"Anna Pateau introduced us girls to your mom and dad at the Feel Good Food opening," Terry recalled. "I liked them as soon as I met them."

"It seems like worlds away but I remember that day like it was only yesterday," Rose said.

"Me, too," Chiara said.

Rose poked her granddaughter playfully. "Why, you weren't born yet. It was thirteen, going on fourteen years ago."

"See how far we've all come," Sully mused, gesturing to Terry and his grandchildren. "Who knows where we'll be fourteen years from now."

Rose sat propped up in her hospital bed, her newborn grandson cradled in one arm and Chiara's head nestled against her chest, fully present in that perfect moment. She took a breath, a deep, cleansing, lifegiving breath. "Yes," Rose said. "Who knows?"

CHAPTER TWENTY-THREE

Impulse

tan still hadn't visited Rose in the hospital and it had been two days. He'd meant to but for some odd reason, he couldn't get past Maimonides' front door. Too many visits at too young an age when the woman who had given birth to him lay dying on the third-floor women's charity ward? Or just unable and unwilling to see the strong female who had taken him into her home and into her heart as now being sick and broken? Stan couldn't imagine Rose not being part of his life. And he didn't want to. So, he didn't visit her.

The cardboard sign in Feel Good Food's front door was turned to the "Sorry, We're Closed" side but Wendy could see a light shining from the kitchen area. This meant Stan was prepping for the following day—or hiding. Wendy knocked on the glass. She could see the top of Stan's head behind the tall counter. Had he peered up to see who was at the door and then gone back to work? Wendy knocked harder. Stan came, unlatched the door and opened it. "You sure are persistent," he said.

"It's one of my best qualities," Wendy told him. He locked the door behind her. She followed him to the kitchen where he had been chopping carrots, celery and red peppers for the next day's soup.

"Cup of tea?" Stan asked.

"I was hoping for something stronger," Wendy countered.

"George keeps a stash here. For those long, lonely nights. Thinks no one knows about it," Stan told her, rummaging beneath the stainless-steel prep table, behind the industrial-sized cans of stewed tomatoes and chicken broth. "Here it is," he said, coming out with a pint of Four Roses.

"Bourbon's not my drink but it'll do," Wendy conceded. "It's chilly outside." Stan poured a fair amount whiskey into a tea cup. Wendy took a sip, winced. "None for you?"

"I'm working," Stan told her, gesturing with the paring knife to prove his point. "Besides, I'm trying to cut back."

"Since when?"

"Since a few days ago."

"Since Aunt Rose's operation," Wendy said.

"Just a coincidence," Stan responded.

Wendy took another sip of bourbon. She still didn't like the taste but it made her head slightly fuzzy, which she did like. "Have you visited her yet?" Wendy asked, although she already knew that he hadn't.

"I, uh…" Ever since they were children, Stan couldn't lie to Wendy. The few times he'd tried she'd seen through the fib to the truth beneath. "I wouldn't know what to say to her," Stan admitted.

Wendy rested her hand on top of Stan's, on top of the knife as he chopped. He stopped and looked into her eyes. "You don't have to say anything," she told him. "Just go, just be there. That's all we ever have to do: just be there for each other."

"I know," Stan said. Wendy removed her hand from his. Stan continued chopping carrots. "I will."

"You have a new nephew, too," Wendy offered.

"I congratulated Tiger. I'll see Terry when they get home. I just can't seem to get through that hospital's front door."

"I could go with you," she suggested.

"I think I need to go alone. If I go." With the back of the knife, Stan slipped the vegetables off the butcher block and into a large plastic container half-filled with water. He covered it, put it into the refrigerator then wiped down the wood. "Thursday's gumbo day," Stan said, matter-of-factly.

"I remember," Wendy told him. "It's my favorite."

"I remember," Stan told her as he washed the knife. Wendy gave him her empty mug. Stan washed it along with his own, which had held lukewarm tea.

Wendy took the dishcloth from its hook and dried the first cup. Their hands brushed beneath the towel. "What else do you remember?" she asked.

"Everything," Stan said.

"What are we going to do? About us?"

"What do you mean?"

Wendy placed the cup on the shelf, hard. "Sometimes you can be so thick, Stanley Sullivan," she sighed.

"About what?" he said. "It's late and I'm tired."

Wendy put the other cup beside the first, more gently this time. "I think we should get married," Wendy said.

"Do you?" he smiled.

"You aren't making this easy..." Wendy took a breath. "Stanley, will you marry me?" she asked, her voice quavering slightly.

"You're a little late for Sadie Hawkins Day," he told her.

Wendy gave Stan a shove. "Honestly, you're insufferable."

Stan shoved Wendy back. His arm lingered, caught her around her slim waist. "I wanted to be the one to ask you," he said.

"Well, what were you waiting for?"

"The right time."

"Is this it?"

Stan shrugged. "I guess."

"You guess?"

Stan took Wendy in his arms. "Yes," he said.

"Yes, what?"

"Yes, I would be happy to marry you, Wendy O'Leary." They kissed deeply, seriously, until Wendy pulled away, laughing. "What?" Stan asked.

"I still can't get used to kissing you is all," she grinned.

"That could be a problem."

"I mean, I've wanted to kiss you for a long time but you were my cousin, so I forced myself not to think of you that way. Only it didn't work."

Stan untied his apron and hung it on a peg. "We're still cousins, just not blood. And for the record, I tried not to think of you that way either." He fished a ginger snap out of the covered jar and offered it to her, knowing it was Wendy's favorite. She took it greedily and bit. "I'm trying to stay on the straight and narrow," Stan told her. "For you."

"You should do it for you," Wendy said, her mouth full of cookie.

"For me. For us. Same difference," he admitted.

Stan rummaged through the junk drawer on the stainless-steel stand beneath the cash register. It was filled with useless items like the odd paper clip, assorted rubber bands, mismatched nails, a screwdriver and a few toy capsules from the gumball machine on the sidewalk outside the shop. "What on earth are you doing?" Wendy asked.

"You'll see," Stan told her. He examined pod after pod, finally settling on one. He opened the plastic capsule and dumped its contents into his palm. There sat an adjustable ring with a stone of red plastic. He slipped it onto Wendy's finger. "Now it's official," he told her.

"It's beautiful," Wendy gushed. "And it fits perfectly."

Stan slipped on his jacket and wrapped Wendy's scarf around her neck. She'd never taken off her coat. "Plus, it matches your bloodshot eyes," he joked. Then Stan grew serious. "What will our folks say? About us getting married?"

Wendy thought for a moment. "They've loved us forever, together and apart. I imagine they'll be happy, don't you?"

"I think so."

Stan shut the kitchen lights. He and Wendy stood in darkness, save for the warm glow from the streetlamp outside. "When do you want to tie the knot?" Wendy asked him.

"The sooner the better," he said. "Next week?"

"What's the big rush? Going somewhere?"

Unlatching the front door, Stan let Wendy go out first then locked the door behind them. "As a matter of fact, yes. Connecticut."

Wendy slid her gloved hand through his. "Tell me something I don't know," she said just as she had taunted him when they were children. They made their way down Thirteenth Avenue, toward their respective homes.

"I'm going to start working there in a few weeks. Where does that leave us?" Stan worried.

"Exactly where we are."

They walked past Herb's Pickle Place on the corner of Forty-Fifth. Even though the barrels had been hauled inside for the night, the sidewalk still had a distinct garlic and dill aroma. "Which is?" Stan pressed.

"You work in Connecticut. I work here and finish my correspondence course while I plan the wedding. How does the Waldorf-Astoria sound?" Stan's mouth gaped open in shock. Wendy closed it for him with the tip of her sheathed finger. "But seriously," she told him. "I was thinking of maybe having it at Feel Good Food up in Sherman, come spring. Too soon?"

"Not soon enough," Stan told her.

"My mom and the aunties will help me plan it. Do you think Astrid would make my dress?"

"I think you'd have to fight her off not to," Stan laughed. "Do you think my mom will be better by then?"

Wendy squeezed his arm. "I know so. She'll walk you down the aisle, just like she did Tiger. We made such a cute flower girl and ring bearer, didn't we?"

Stan warmed at the memory. "Where will we live?"

"They have Dime Savings Banks in Connecticut," she said. "I could ask for a transfer."

"And there are loads of local papers up there," he told her. "*The News Times, The Fairfield Citizen.*"

"I'll be done with my course come May. Think they'll hire me?"

"Those rags would be stupid not to," Stan said.

"You're only saying that because you love me."

"I do love you, it's true. But you're a hell of a writer."

Wendy shrugged. "Writings's only putting words together," she told him. "Anyone can do it."

"Sure, anyone can write but not like you. You have a knack for putting the right words together. For making people feel. That's pretty special."

"Hmmm," Wendy said. "Sounds kind of like cooking."

"Cooking's easy."

"For you it is, but not for everyone," Wendy told him. "You throw together raw meat, vegetables, spices, light the burner, stir the pot, fuss with it, and it's great. Only for some people, it's a mess. Why is that?"

Stan shook his head. "I have no clue." They were passing Moe's greengrocer shop. Shuttered, it looked like a sorry place but when it was open and its wooden bins were spilling over with fruits and vegetables of every shade, from shining, maroon eggplants to dusky potatoes and gleaming red apples, it pulsed with life and possibility. "Secret ingredient," Stan finally offered.

Wendy raised her eyebrows, questioning him. "Which is?" She knew what his response would be but she just wanted to hear him say it.

"Love," he said. "It's the secret ingredient in everything."

Wendy rolled her eyes. "Spoken like someone who's stupid in love." She realized that she was channeling her father and hoped Stan didn't notice.

"Think about it," he pushed. "It's true."

"You sound like my mother, always full of hope," Wendy told Stan. "Or Grandma Bridget."

"And you sound like…"

She cut him off. "Don't say it!"

A beat cop came toward them, swinging his nightstick. Normally, this would fill Stan's heart with fear but not tonight, not anymore. It was Gary Calabrese, who they had gone to New Utrecht High School with, and was now a rookie cop. "What's shaking, Gary?" Stan asked.

"Not much, thank God," he told them.

"I feel safer knowing you're protecting the streets," Wendy said. Gary made a face as though he didn't believe her but she meant it. He pushed his cap back on his head. Tall and reedy, Gary possessed an empathy and a calm demeanor that were both valuable and powerful in defusing a domestic dispute or a street fight. Besides, he was well-respected on the streets of Borough Park and knew the neighborhood intimately enough to keep the riff-raff in their place.

"Thank your pop for putting in the good word for me," Gary told Wendy. Although Harry had been off the job for many years, he still had pull on the force. Gary had the tact not to request a favor from Sergeant Patrick Sullivan directly— that might have looked bad to his future coworkers—but he knew Harry'd told Sully that Officer Calabrese was a fine fellow and would be an asset to the Six-Six. So, the rookie cop secured a spot in a precinct in his own community.

"I will," Wendy promised. "But you already thanked him with that nice fruit basket. How my mom went on about those pineapples!"

Gary scuffed his boots bashfully. "The least I could do. I would have given him a bottle but I know he don't drink anymore."

"You stay warm," Wendy told him as they passed.

"Work safe," Stan said.

"This place is a lot safer without that clown Big Paulie hanging around," Gary added. His eyes met Stan's. That's when he knew that Gary knew about his involvement with the street tough. Wendy knew too, but then again, Wendy seemed to know everything.

"Safer for you and me, both," Stan admitted to Gary.

A light shone in the storage room of Mr. Hymen's notions shop, which meant he was probably finishing up an order. The front window was dusty and crowded with bolts of cloth of all types: corduroy, satin, cotton batting and denim. Inside, there were boxes of all sizes filled with buttons, zippers, snaps, threads and such. No matter what you sought Mr. Hymen seemed to have it and he knew exactly where it was located in his great mess of a shop, finding it in "a quick minute," as he liked to say.

"Let's go down Forty-Eighth," Stan suggested.

"All right," Wendy agreed. She had a feeling where they were headed and she was glad.

They walked the next few blocks in silence, passing frosty fences, icy front walks and snowed-in gardens. Wendy nudged Stan and gestured to "Mary on the Half Shell" as Poppa used to call a statue of the Blessed Mother decorating a yard. Grandma Bridget always scolded him for being "sacrelig" when he said this but it made Stan and Wendy laugh.

The couple navigated New Utrecht Avenue as it sliced through Forty-Eighth Street on an angle, the El rumbling overhead to the Fort Hamilton Parkway station. Stan stopped at the corner of Forty-Eighth and Fort Hamilton. "This is where I leave you," he told Wendy. "All right?"

"I think I can make the last few blocks alone," she assured him. "Especially knowing Officer Calabrese is walking the beat."

Stan gave Wendy a small smile and took her into his arms. Although their lips had iced in the night air, the inside of their mouths were warm. They shared what Wendy thought of as a "movie star kiss:" the kind of kiss they'd witnessed side by side on the screen in the dark of the Loew's 46th but never dreamed they'd experience with each other.

When they pulled apart Wendy felt lightheaded and Stan was in no condition to visit his mother. But the additional block he had to walk in the March frost would curb his desire and steel his reserve for what he needed to do. Wendy turned up Stan's collar against the cold. Once satisfied, she headed toward Fiftieth Street, looking back once to see Stan hunched against the steady wind, his watch cap-covered head tucked low, his jaw set.

At Maimonides, Stan passed through its double doors without trepidation for the first time in more than ten years. Although it was no longer visiting hours, the staff let him in anyhow. Between the family's connection to Nurse Sally Hinton and Sully's years as a beat cop, they were permitted minor discretions like this. Everyone in Borough Park knew that Stanley was Sully Sullivan's son.

Stan was surprised to see his father's friend Liam still working the hospital's elevator. Liam had been at his post when Stan had gone to visit Denise, his blood mother, all those years ago, and he was there now. It was something of a comfort. "Not sure of the floor," Stan admitted to Liam after a few pleasantries.

"Second floor," Liam said knowingly. "Women's. Make a sharp right after you get out. The nursery's there too, just to the left of the elevator, if you want to pop by and see your nephew." Liam closed the doors and the elevator started going up.

"You seem to know everything," Stan remarked in wonder.

"My wife wouldn't agree, but thanks," Liam cracked. He asked after Sully and the rest of the family, but not Rose because she was in the hospital, so he already surmised she wasn't well. "Cold as a witch's tit outside," Liam added, shuddering. "Can't get the chill out of my bones."

Stan let the bad analogy pass without pressing it; there were details of Rose's condition Liam didn't know so he couldn't be blamed.

Thanking Liam for the ride, Stan made a right but the sound of a lone baby crying drew him left, to the nursery. He easily found the bassinet marked with the card that read "Martino." The child was called Michael Archangel, in honor of their grandfather. It was a good, strong name.

Michael Archangel Martino was bawling his heart out, just like Chiara Rose used to do. The night nurse jostled the bassinet to succor the child. When this didn't work, she lifted the baby out of the bassinet and cradled him in her arms. "Yours?" she mouthed to Stan.

On impulse, he nodded 'yes,' though it wasn't quite true. Then he went to visit his mother.

CHAPTER TWENTY-FOUR

Double Delight

Due to the circumstances of Little Mike's birth, both Dr. Schantz and Dr. Gabbur, the newborn's pediatrician, wanted to ensure that the baby's breathing was steady and strong, and that his mother had a chance to heal, for the tyke had torn her in his rush to be born after his tardiness. Because of this, the doctors arranged it so that mother and son could stay at Maimonides a few extra days, and luckily, the health insurance company concurred. The child had rebounded nicely after Nurse Sally breathed life into his purpling body and no further respiratory difficulties had been encountered during his entire stay at the nursery. In fact, Little Mike had been one of the most enthusiastic wailers in the unit so his doctors were confident his lungs had fully recovered.

It was simply happenstance that Rose was declared ready to leave Maimonides on the same day as her grandson and daughter-in-law. Rose worked hard to strengthen her left arm, diligently tracing her fingertips up the wall in the exercises Marjorie and Nurse Jessica had shown her. This helped Rose's battered muscles recover more quickly after the invasive surgery. Her fingers worked well and her grasp was getting stronger.

After a quick examination, Dr. Seminara said Rose could be discharged whenever she wanted. "Like right now, for instance?" she asked.

"Are you sure?" he countered, explaining, "Some women appreciate an extra few days to rest and be waited on."

"Not me," Rose said. "No offense but the food here is terrible."

Dr. Seminara laughed. "I figure you're a pretty good cook."

"I hold my own," Rose conceded. "Come by for Sunday supper sometime and see," she added.

"I believe I will," Dr. Seminara nodded and headed off to sign Rose's paperwork. But before he did, he assured her, "I'll hold you to Sunday dinner, I mean it."

Sully arrived with Jo in tow soon after he received word that Rose could spring the coop. In her sister's small valise, Jo had packed a simple frock of bright coral and a change of underthings. Sully left the room so Jo could help her sister dress. "I brought a shift with a zip front so you could just step into it," Jo explained. "Plus, the color is so flattering with your complexion. Very cheerful." In truth, Rose was slightly pale but Jo didn't mention this.

"I appreciate it," Rose told her sister. "I always liked this dress and besides, it's not too formfitting. I don't think the drain will show."

Jo eased Rose from her hospital gown into the shift, careful not to disturb the drain and tube that sprung from the incision on Rose's side just below her armpit and above the dressings. The tubing was pinned to an elastic compression corset which covered the gauze wrapping Rose's chest. She leaned heavily on Jo as she stepped into the dress. Jo fastened it to her sister's chin then pulled up Rose's beige wool stockings. Then she attached them to Rose's garters.

"How nice you look," Jo said. "You're right, the drain doesn't show. And you can hardly tell that…" Jo couldn't find the words.

"That I have no breast on the left side?" Rose finished for her. "Jo, it's all right to say it."

"I know," Jo admitted. She forced her voice to sound hopeful. "You've got plenty of padding," she added brightly.

"Dr. Seminara said I'll be able to use a breast form in a few weeks."

"Don't forget those inserts Evalena DeMuccio made for you. I bet you can fasten them into place for the time being."

"That's true," Rose agreed. "Stan visited last night. He told me that he and Wendy…"

"Wendy told me!" Jo gushed. "She's over the moon about it."

"We are too. Imagine, us being in-laws."

Jo laughed. "We already know the family's crazy, so there'll be no surprises, right?"

"But we're a good crazy," Rose said. "How's Harry about all of this? I know Stan has had his problems," she worried.

As she usually did, Jo tried to smooth things over. "Who hasn't had their share of problems, right? Stan seems like he's on a steady path now. Besides, Harry has loved Stan since he was a baby. We all have."

Rose gazed out the hospital window. The sky blazed a bright blue. "How did Sully react about letting me walk home?" she wondered.

"Oh, he grumbled at first like he always does. But it's a lovely day, warmish, in the fifties, so he agreed a walk would probably do you good."

"I could use a bit of a stroll," Rose sighed. "To be honest, I'm a little antsy. I've been cooped up here for almost a week. I'm glad Dr. Seminara is letting me go early."

"And on the same day Terry and Little Mike are getting out," Jo smiled, fetching Rose's winter coat from the wardrobe. "It's a double delight." Jo was especially gentle as she eased her sister's left arm into her wrap, but still, Rose winced. "Easy does it," she told Rose.

"I'll try," she conceded. "It will take some getting used to."

Sully returned, having settled the hospital bill. "You ready?" he asked his wife.

"Am I ever," Rose sighed. Gingerly, she took his arm. Sully carried her satchel.

Jo took the roses from the water pitcher. They were still in fine shape. She took note of their unusual shade: creamy ivory in the center while the edges of the petals were tinged with scarlet. "I've never seen roses quite like this," Jo remarked as they stood by the elevator.

"Neither have I," Sully said. "Eddy down at Shannon's said they were called 'Double Delight.'"

Rose and Jo exchanged knowing glances because Jo had uttered those same words only moments earlier. "I think that's a wonderful name for a flower this pretty," Jo told him as they entered the elevator. Liam took them down to the first floor.

Steady on her feet and only mildly aware of the slight ache on the left side of her chest, Rose positioned herself between Sully and Jo. She held each of their arms, not because she needed the physical support but because she wanted to feel their energy, feel their love flow into her. The warm breeze outside promised of spring. The azure of the sky promised more: constancy, not so much the way things were, but the hope of the way things would be.

Behind the trio, a shrill but happy voice rang out. "Grandma! Grandpa! Aunt Jo!" Chiara Rose was beside them almost as soon as they'd heard her call. Beyond the girl, Tiger and Terry walked. He held their newest child while Terry took tender-footed steps beside her husband. When they reached the others, Tiger held his son toward his mother.

"Are you sure?" Terry asked Rose. "I wouldn't want…"

"If I wasn't sure, I wouldn't take him," Rose said sunnily. "My right arm's strong as ever," she added, cradling her grandson against her.

Little Mike looked so much like Tiger as a newborn, it made Rose's heart ache. The baby also resembled Stan, even though Stan had been so thin and scrawny as a wee one. The similarities between the three were almost unnerving. Chiara Rose, on the other hand, had favored Terry as a baby, just as she did now: dark-haired, dark-eyed, dark-complexioned.

Rose savored the sweet weight of her grandson in her good arm, against the unsullied side of her chest. "It's too nice a day not to walk," Terry said, though she was clearly struggling and in discomfort.

"That's exactly what I said," Rose remarked. "Great minds…"

Terry grinned, though it was more of a grimace. "Baby steps," Tiger reminded his wife.

"That's all I can manage right now," Terry sighed.

"Sometimes that's all we can do…baby steps," Rose conceded. "And that's all right. Because soon we'll be running."

Chiara took this as her cue. She crouched down slightly, ready to bolt in her Mary Janes. "No running," Terry warned her.

"Why?" the girl asked.

Terry couldn't think of a reason, so she told the girl, "Go ahead. But just be careful."

"I will!" Chiara chirped, narrowly missing a white-capped nurse, coming in from her break.

Their tired, worn, working-class neighborhood seemed especially splendid to Rose. She ignored the porches pleading for a coat of paint and focused on the heads of crocuses peeping from front-yard soil. She overlooked the shutters in need of a nail or a screw and admired the magnolia blossoms in Mr. DeMeo's areaway. The forsythia buds were ready to burst and then there were the fragrant dogwoods and the distinct (but not unpleasant) cement fragrance of the Callery pear. And clasped in the crook of Rose's arm was her grandson, a blossoming bud of another sort.

The few blocks went quickly, even at a snail's pace. At the front steps of 1128 Forty-Seventh Street, Rose handed Little Mike to Jo, who passed the flowers to her niece. Rose tightened her grip on Sully's arm and mounted the brick steps, five of them, one by one. Terry did the same, leaning lead-like on Tiger and Chiara Rose, flinching with each step. "Thank God there aren't more," she sighed. Then she asked Rose, "Will you be all right?" because her mother-in-law had an additional flight to climb.

Sully set down the satchel and swept Rose into his arms, just like he had done decades earlier after her previous hospital stay. He was careful to avoid pressing into Rose's left side. She buried his face into Sully's strong, sure chest, reveling in the familiar scent of him. He still used Burma Shave Cream and bay rum cologne, as he always had. "She's light as a feather," Sully proclaimed, echoing the words he'd said all those years ago.

Chiara ran ahead of her grandparents and opened the front door, the inner door, then took the steps two at a time to open the upstairs door to her grandparents' apartment. She waited inside, practically jangling in anticipation, hopping from foot to foot, excited to see Rose's reaction to the construction paper banner she'd colored that read, "Welcome Home, Nana Rose." On the oilcloth-covered kitchen table was a plate of chocolate chip cookies the girl had made with her father. An identical dish was waiting on the table downstairs to welcome Terry and Little Mike, as well as a similar sign.

Rose was pleased with the cookies and the handmade banner but the walk had tired her, having been in bed for the better part of a week. After a quick pot of tea with Sully and Chiara, Rose retired to her reading chair by the front porch window. Her husband had thoughtfully brought in the footstool from the parlor, as if losing a breast would mysteriously make one's legs ache, but Rose appreciated the gesture.

Was it 1934 or 1935 when Rose last had a homecoming like this? No, it was 1936, Rose recalled. The year Tony had died. Tiger had been ten, and Kewpie (now called "Angela") had been sixteen. Rose recalled being bowled over by the kindness of her friends and family, of their visits, their thoughtful gifts and the wonderful dishes they left.

For some reason, Rose remembered something Abraham Lincoln had said, something about "the better angels of our nature." To her, it referred to caring gestures such as this, the inherent niceness that exists within all of us. Rose had been blessed to know these "better angels" all her life, even through the darkest times. These better angels saved her, upheld her, and made all the difference.

Rose's mother Bridget had looked after her following her previous surgery, the emergency hysterectomy. Now it was Angela's turn to care for Rose, just as Rose had cared for her daughter when the twins were born. This is what family did for family. In addition to the attendance of fine doctors and nurses, it was these unselfish acts, these tiny kindnesses, which nurtured you back to health. Physicians might heal your body and cut away the bad parts, but the other individuals helped heal your soul, which was just as important.

Physically, Rose didn't feel as poorly as she had after her hysterectomy. She reasoned that the earlier operation had involved several internal organs while the mastectomy was external, just a gland, really, not even an organ. Yet, losing her breast struck Rose more profoundly than the hysterectomy. It was odd, but she had never given much thought to her breasts before. True, they fed her children, they provided comfort—and surely, they gave and received pleasure (a thought which made her blush)—but Rose didn't realize how her breasts made her feel like a woman until one was gone. She also didn't take into consideration how she used her breasts in everyday life—as a wedge when taking an item out of the pantry, for example, when your hands were full. Breasts were another appendage, in a way, like an arm or a leg, and now one of hers was missing.

In the early hours of her convalescence, Rose didn't have much time to contemplate this oddity, for her thoughts were interrupted by a steady succession of short knocks on the front door downstairs. The neighbors had seen the Sullivan/Martino promenade on their way back from Maimonides and now were showing up with dishes and wishes, first stopping downstairs to bring something for Tiger and Terry's new baby and then softly padding upstairs to check in on Rose. The callers didn't stay more than a few minutes because they didn't want to tire her. Sadie Lieberwitz presented Rose with a jar of homemade borscht and a box of apricot hamantaschen that was still warm. She hugged her old friend carefully, promising to return in a few days for a proper visit. "Maybe even a short walk," Sadie said, "because spring is in the air."

From Mrs. Wong at the Chop Suey Palace was a dish she called "Double Delight." It was a savory beef and chicken stir fry with all sorts of vegetables: broccoli, carrots, pea pods and miniature ears of corn. "Make you strong," Mrs. Wong said before she bowed and left, insisting that Rose keep the pagoda-embossed platter she presented it on.

"What a feast we have!" Rose remarked to Sully, gesturing to the kitchen countertop, which was filled with plates, tins, paper satchels and jars of home-cooked deliciousness. "It's too much for two and we don't want it to spoil." They decided to pool their resources and have supper downstairs with the Martinos. This way they could have a visit as well as clear their larders. It proved to be an excellent idea, for the convalescing women had a chance to socialize but not to the point of exhaustion. The men washed up and the females fussed over Little Mike.

Chiara showed no sign of jealousy; quite the contrary. She immersed herself in the role of older sister with care and pride. It was almost as though she'd had something to do with the boy's creation. Chiara quickly learned how to change diapers and soon performed the task better than her father. It was tough at first, her pea-sized fingertips bearing the prickly spots of contact with diaper pins, but she eventually got the hang of it. Before she wiped the child's bottom, Chiara let the tap water warm as she held the washrag beneath it. "He likes it better," she claimed. "I can tell because he doesn't squiggle." Plus, she could make the boy go from wailing to cooing from one moment to the next.

On the second night, Stan popped in on what had become a traditional convalescent potluck dinner. He bore one of Granny Lulu's famed rum cakes. "The spirits take the pain away," he said to Terry and Rose, just as Granny Lulu had told him to.

Stan pulled up a chair at Tiger and Terry's kitchen table. On the menu that particular evening was Aunt Jo's *lasagna*, sautéed escarole and crusty Italian bread from Regina Bakery. Angela ducked in to check on the ladies en route from the Loew's 46th where Beth, David and Augie were working that night. "It's just like old times," Rose smiled, surrounded by her children and her husband. "Only better," she added, because two of her grandchildren were there too. They convinced Angela to stay for supper rather than eat a bologna sandwich at her place alone.

The women were abuzz about Stan and Wendy's upcoming wedding, brimming with questions. Who would make her dress? (Astrid, it went without saying.) Who would make the headpiece? (Evalena DeMuccio, of course.) Where would they get their wedding rings? (Evvy, their neighbor who worked at Milson's Findings in the Diamond District, would get them wholesale.) Stan said that while Wendy had agreed to wedding bands, she was adamant that she didn't want a "proper" engagement ring other than the candy-machine ring Stan had sealed the deal with.

And finally, came the question of who would be in the wedding party? Stan went down the list of bridesmaids and groomsmen, then stumbled on their choice of flower girl. "We're not sure who to pick?" Stan kidded, scratching his chin in mock deep thought. Then he turned to Chiara, who was visibly vibrating with the prospect of walking down the aisle carrying a basketful of flowers and wearing a pretty dress. "Can you think of anyone, punk?" Stan asked her.

Before Chiara could respond, Tiger said, "Maybe Tootsie down the street. Or that kid who always has the runny nose."

"Mildred?"

"That's the one," Tiger nodded.

"Good idea. I'll ask Old Millie."

Chiara was red-faced by now, ready to explode. "I think that's a terrible idea!" she exclaimed. "Mildred smells like tuna fish."

"I hadn't noticed," Stan told her. The women were doing their best to suppress their laughter.

"Me neither," Tiger chimed in. "I think Mildred's just swell."

"Well, I don't!" Chiara shouted.

"Who would you suggest, Terry?" Stan wondered.

"I haven't the foggiest idea," Terry added. "Mom, do you?" Terry asked Rose.

"Arrrgh," Chiara groaned but everyone ignored her.

"Beth is too old, isn't she, Angela?" Rose queried.

"She is," Angela agreed. "And Wendy said Beth's going to have something special to do. So is David, right?"

"That's right," Stan confirmed.

"Well, who does that leave?" Sully wondered aloud. "We've practically gone through the entire family."

By this point, Chiara was jumping up and down in place with her hand raised, just as she did in school when she knew the answer but Mrs. Curry didn't call on her. "Oooh, oooh," Chiara sighed dramatically, holding her arm aloft.

Everyone at the table looked at her. "Yes?" Stan said.

"Me! Me!" Chiara shouted.

"Me, who?" Stan asked.

"Me," she gasped, exasperated, collapsing onto the table. "I want to be the flower girl."

"You?" Stan asked, incredulous. Chiara nodded furiously. "Why, I hadn't even thought of you. Do you think she can handle it?" Stan prodded the others. Chiara nodded more intensely this time.

"It's a big responsibility," Terry pointed out.

"Plus, she's only ten," Tiger added.

"Ten is plenty old enough," Chiara proclaimed.

"Is it?" Sully wondered. "I'm not so sure about that."

Chiara fell into her Uncle Stan's lap, utterly frustrated. She proceeded to sob loudly, her small body shaking. Stan stroked her hair to console her but it didn't work; Chiara cried harder. "I think we might have gone too far," Rose worried.

"Just a smidge," Tiger conceded.

Stan jostled his niece slightly. "Come on, Chi. We were only joking." Still nothing from the wailing girl in his lap. "You were our first choice, I swear," he told her.

Chiara's head popped up, dry-eyed. "For real?" she squealed. "Pinkie promise?" She raised her littlest finger. Stan hooked hers with his.

"Pinkie promise," he admitted.

"Duped by a ten-year-old," Tiger said.

"I really had you going, didn't I?" Chiara chortled. In the next breath, she listed all the shades of pink she considered acceptable choices for her dress. Cotton candy and Pepto Bismol were at the top of her Hit Parade.

"We'll see," Terry told her, "but maybe a pale pink would be best." Chiara wrinkled her nose but reluctantly agreed; she wouldn't want to outshine the bride in too bright a shade. Little Mike wriggled in Terry's arms, rooting for her breast. She excused herself and retired to the bedroom to feed her son. Dinner continued.

Later that week, Rose was surprised to receive a telephone call from Dr. Seminara, who suggested he stop by the house to remove her stitches and drain rather than her make the trip to his office in Bay Ridge. It would be no trouble, he assured her, because it was on his way home from Maimonides. He expected to finish his rounds by two. Would it be all right to visit her then? Although Rose told Dr. Seminara it would be fine, silently she worried, 'Something is horribly wrong. Something he wants to tell me sooner rather than later.'

But when the doctor arrived a quarter past two, his mood was light and his face looked unburdened. He carried the same black leather satchel Dr. Lewis across the street used for house calls but Dr. Seminara's was newer since he was much younger.

After Rose took the doctor's hat and coat, he accepted a cup of coffee and not one but two almond *biscotti* which had been left by Anne Daurio earlier that day. Rose was concerned that she wasn't sufficiently hospitable to the man considerate enough to make a house call but her worry about what Dr. Seminara might tell her outweighed her hostess sensibilities. He suggested they go to the bedroom so he could work in private. "I wouldn't want your granddaughter to walk in on us in the kitchen," he told her. Then he went to wash his hands.

The setting echoed a visit from Dr. Lewis more two decades earlier when he visited Rose's apartment to remove her hysterectomy stitches. This time, Rose was already prepared, having cleaned off the nightstand so the doctor would have space to work, pulling a kitchen chair to the bedside in advance. She wore a duster with a snap front to give Dr. Seminara easy access. Rose sat on the bed then leaned against the headboard and adjusted the pillows so she was comfortable. "Ready?" he asked. She nodded.

Dr. Seminara's fingers were gentle yet firm as he cut away the bandage across Rose's chest. Despite Marjorie's suggestion, Rose hadn't had the courage to examine her incision but now she did. She gasped audibly and turned away. Black thread neatly held together the jagged surgical scar. It was slightly puffy and there was an indentation near her left armpit. "It will take some getting used to," Dr. Seminara conceded, as he cleansed the area with disinfectant, "but I think you'll heal nicely. You have good, strong Italian skin."

"Thank you," Rose told him.

Before he snipped the first stitch, Dr. Seminara said, "You probably won't feel a thing. You'll be numb for a few months at least." Then he made the first cut, deftly slicing all of the stitches. He collected the bits of black thread onto the gauze he'd removed from Rose's chest then checked the drain. "This is clear as well, so I can take it out now," he told her. "I bet you'll be happy to be rid of it." Rose nodded again. She had been emptying its contents and measuring them dutifully for several days.

When Dr. Seminara removed the drain and its tubing, Rose felt a slight tug, nothing more. He covered the incision with a small bandage then turned as she dressed. "I would put gauze pads in your brassiere for a few days to protect the incision after you remove this bandage tomorrow but it shouldn't ooze much," he explained. "For now, you can put something soft in there to fill out the cup. After you heal, you'll be fitted for a breast form.

I'll give you the name of a place down on Fulton Street where you can go. A nice lady named Thelma will measure you."

Proudly, Rose showed Dr. Seminara the pads Evalena DeMuccio had made for her. He held them in his palm and studied them. "Excellent work," he said. "It's thoughtful of Evalena to do this for you."

"I have very good friends," Rose told him.

"I'll bet you're a very good friend, too," Dr. Seminara smiled, disinfecting the shears with alcohol, then disappearing into the bathroom to wash his hands again. "Oh, I almost forgot," he added when he returned. "Your lab work came back." Rose's face dropped and she held her breath but Dr. Seminara's sure touch on her shoulder reassured her. "The rest of your lymph nodes are clear."

Afraid to react, Rose held her face blank and cautious. "So, what does that mean?"

"It means that you're well, that you're cancer-free," he told her. "You won't need chemotherapy or radiation. You can breathe again."

Not only did Rose breathe but she gave a sob of relief, covering her face with her hands. "Oh, thank you. Thank you, doctor!"

"My pleasure," Dr. Seminara nodded. "I like giving positive news." Rose wiped her eyes. "Not only will you go to your son's wedding in a few months but I have every reason to believe that you will hold his children and God willing…"

Rose stopped him. "One day at a time," she said.

At the apartment door, Rose thanked Dr. Seminara for coming then asked, "What are you doing for Easter?"

"Probably working," he conceded. "I'm on call at the hospital. Luck of the draw."

"I wish you'd come for Easter supper."

"I'd love to but I don't know when I'll get my dinner break," he explained.

"A man's gotta eat," she told him. "Just come when you can. We always have plenty."

"I'm sure you do," he smiled, doffing his hat.

"We'll all be downstairs at my son and daughter-in-law's. Just walk right in."

"I will," he told her. Rose had no doubt that he would come because now, Marco Seminara was part of the family, for he had saved her life.

CHAPTER TWENTY-FIVE

Nice Day

Morty, who was now known as "Len," managed to procure his cousin Boo-Boo's car for his and Stan's Connecticut sojourn. "Doesn't Boo-Boo need it?" Stan worried.

"Not where he's going," Len quipped.

"And where's he going?" Stan asked.

"Upstate," Len told him.

Now, upstate, to any streetwise Brooklynite, meant not the Catskill Game Farm or Niagara Falls, but prison. Most likely Sing Sing, which was in Ossining, New York, about thirty miles north of the City, picturesquely situated on the banks of the Hudson River. "We're lucky they didn't send us up the river ourselves," Stan said.

"I'll say," Len agreed. Every day he and Stan thanked their lucky stars that the Idlewild caper had gone awry and that Big Paulie was out of their respective hair. It was rumored that Morrongiello had disappeared somewhere into the salt marshes of New Jersey, his sizeable tail wedged between his legs in shame. Or maybe he just went back to Bensonhurst. Good riddance to bad rubbish was the general consensus in Borough Park.

Len made a right onto Atlantic Avenue which would eventually lead to the Interboro Parkway with its serpentine twists and turns. Cousin Boo-Boo's Buick Electra handled like a dream, cut the curves as smooth as butter, its purple fins slicing through the air like sleek violet knives. "Boo-Boo sure made a lot of bad choices in life but Old Miranda wasn't one of them," Len said, patting the Electra's dashboard as though it were a sensual Latina's thigh. Boo-Boo liked to give all of his cars women's names and this one was called Miranda.

It was a nice day for a drive, both Len and Stan agreed, a perfect day to start anew.

The sunken highway, flanked by several cemeteries, made its way through East New York, which, despite its name, was still Brooklyn. The Interboro led to the Van Wyck Expressway, which led to the Whitestone Bridge. The mighty Whitestone linked Queens to the Bronx. It was a grand suspension bridge with a twenty-three hundred-foot span that rose one hundred and fifty feet above the mean, high water.

The Electra continued from the Whitestone onto the Hutchinson River Parkway, the factories and tall tenements of the Bronx giving way to greenery and suburban homes. Here, the forsythia popped and the redbud bloomed in all their magenta glory. "You can eat those, you know," Stan told Len, pointing them out. "Redbud."

"Naw," Len said.

"Yes, you can," Stan pushed. "My mom showed me when I was little. And how to get the nectar out of honeysuckles." At his mention of Rose, Stan's heart sunk—her illness, the thought of being so far away from his mother, especially now. But she had urged him to go, to make his mark.

"You're just pulling my leg," Len said.

"I'll show you when we get there. I'll bet Sherman is lousy with redbud. And you can eat the whole flower. Not just suck the nectar like honeysuckles. You can eat the whole shebang."

"What does redbud taste like?"

Stan thought for a moment. "Kind of lemony. But real light and soft. I've heard that some chefs use them as a garnish."

"On what?" Len wondered.

"Salads and cakes and stuff."

"Well, I'll be."

"We'll tell Bill Karpi about them."

Len said, "I bet he already knows. Bill seems like a sharp fellow."

"Real friendly too," Stan agreed. "We're lucky. In lots of ways, we're pretty damned lucky."

"And how," Len agreed.

The original plan was for Len and Stan to stay in Sherman four days each week, working long hours. Then they'd be off the next three days, free to spend that time in Brooklyn with their friends and families before returning to Sherman again for another four-day swing. But until Feel Good Food's grand opening, the Brooklyn contingent planned to work six or seven days a week and stay in Sherman so they could get the place up and running. There was much to be done.

Bill had managed to secure an easygoing, dependable fellow who'd worked with his brother Stew to help when they needed it. Miles had been laid off from Connecticut Light & Power and had hungry mouths to feed. Besides, Bill had a good feeling about him, just as he did about the boys from Brooklyn. Maybe when Feel Good Food was really going, Bill's brother Ron could join them but for now, Bill was confident this setup would work out well.

Although Bill and Joan had offered Stan and Len a well-appointed basement space in their cozy cottage just outside of town, the two single men politely declined. The Karpis were awfully accommodating but the thought of sharing residence with a toddler and a newborn—Joan had given birth to their son Robert a couple of weeks earlier—prompted their decision. If Stan's nephew Little Mike's wailing was any indication of life with a baby, he and Len had made the right choice. To ensure their comfort, Bill found his workers a large room at a local boarding house off Route 37.

When the Electra pulled up in front of Feel Good Food's covered-up storefront, a small welcoming committee awaited—the four Karpis, who had just arrived in their Suburban station wagon. Karen was so excited about the strangers' arrival that she jumped in place. She couldn't wait for them to see the crayoned squiggles she'd colored for each of them in construction paper greeting cards. "Perfect timing," Bill said, extending his hand when Stan and Len stepped out of the car.

Joan's arms were full of brawny baby. "I'd hug you but Robert finally fell asleep," she whispered. The petite blonde was pretty as pie but also looked tired. Dark circles were painted beneath her striking blue eyes.

"The Plymouth puts him to sleep every time," Bill sighed. "Thank God," he added. "Boy, does that kid have a set of lungs on him."

Karen thrust her construction-paper cards at Stan and Len. "Momma help," she said. "I draw."

In return, Stan handed the girl a paper sack of cookies. "This is from George," he told her. "He heard peanut butter chip were your favorite." Karen tore into the sack but not before thanking them after a weighty glance from her mother.

"Just one," Joan warned. "You don't want to spoil your supper."

In a few short weeks, Bill and Miles had worked wonders, transforming an empty box into an inviting eatery. A new floor was laid. Although the stove wasn't hooked up yet, everything else was in place: café tables, chairs, the kitchen setup. Neatly folded on a shelf were the red gingham tablecloths and curtains Joan had made as she waited for her son to be born. The walls were painted a lively red which matched the rig parked in the Sherman Volunteer Fire Department's garage down on Route 39. The scarlet was tempered by white trim, baseboards and chair rail. "Bold color choice," Len remarked.

"Oh, Bill likes bold," Joan commented, gesturing to the turquoise Plymouth parked out front.

"Plus, red's a good-luck color," Bill pointed out.

"That's right," Stan said in disbelief, amazed these country bumpkins also knew. "When I was a kid, the Wongs used to give me red envelopes stuffed with dollars for Chinese

New Year. That's exactly what Mrs. Wong says about the color red."

Where Feel Good Food's Brooklyn outpost sported photographs of the people responsible for the recipes that inspired the dishes the eatery served, Bill decided on a variation on that theme: displaying photos of the owners, managers, workers and their families.

On the wall were Bill and Joan's wedding portrait as well as a posed shot of Tiger, Angela and Stan as youngsters. There was Tiger and George at the Thirteenth Avenue shop's opening day festivities in 1946 as well as George and a corsage-sporting Elaine on their tenth wedding anniversary. The Thomas children lined up with the Martino, Sullivan, Corso and O'Leary children, and next to it, George grinning with his brother-in-law Tyrone. Beside those pictures was a brand-new portrait of Karen Karpi carefully cradling Little Robert in her arms. They hadn't forgotten Miles and his family, nor Len and Granny Lulu. The old blending seamlessly with the new, they had created the kind of warm, welcoming place where you not only wanted to eat a decent meal, but linger a while.

The men worked only a few hours that afternoon, moving boxes, organizing and discussing what had to be done. Bill's brother Stew at C.L.&P. saw to it that Feel Good Food jumped to the head of the queue and had electricity long before they had originally been promised it. Thanks to this, Bill and Miles could work even at night, putting up moldings and painting long after dark. That's how they'd gotten so far ahead of schedule.

In this part of the State, Bill explained, most homes cooked with electricity, something professional chefs distained—the heat distribution wasn't as true or accurate as cooking with gas. Stew saw to it that his friend at Jennings Oil & Propane set up Feel Good Food with an industrial-sized cooking fuel tank outside the premises as well as gave them a fair price for it. Old Man Jennings promised to come by the following day to hook up the hulking Wolf stove that sat dormant in the corner.

Bill gave Stan and Len the rest of the afternoon off to get settled, for they would start in earnest the next morning. "Take a stroll, get a feel for the town while it's still light," Bill suggested. "You can unpack later." Joan promised she would have a proper welcome supper waiting for them at the Karpi Compound the following evening—Bobby had been fussy all day and wouldn't let her put him down.

Both cars drove to the nearby rooming house where Stan and Len would be staying. While his wife and children waited in the car, Bill walked the men up the front steps of Arlene Simpson's yellow clapboard home. Widowed for several decades, Mrs. Simpson rented out rooms to make ends meet. Though she preferred the uncomplicated nature of single women, Mrs. Simpson reluctantly agreed to rent her attic room to the two single gentlemen. But only because Bill Karpi vouched for their character and paid a month's rent in advance. Though she doubted they'd last that long.

"Stanley Sullivan and Leonard Morton," Bill smiled in introduction. Mrs. Simpson's mouth was set in a cold, straight line. She didn't shake their hands but nodded "hello" with a dip of her head, her tightly permed gray poodle curls barely moving. Bill helped the boys move their few bags upstairs as Mrs. Simpson followed in their wake, reciting a litany of "no's" which constituted the house rules.

No pets.
No smoking.
No noise after 10 P.M.
No cooking in your room.
No eating in your room.
No guests of the opposite sex—ever.

Before Bill left Stan and Len at the curb, he reminded them quietly, "Our basement's pretty cozy, just in case."

Then Little Robert started to howl, as if on cue. "We'll give this a shot," Stan said, taking a paper shopping bag out of the Electra's backseat.

"The offer still stands," Bill reminded them before he drove away.

Mrs. Simpson stood on the walkway in her orthopedic shoes, dowdy dress and apron, fists on her hips. "That's a mighty flashy car," she noted.

"Thank you," Len told her before he realized it wasn't a compliment. "It's my cousin Beauregard's. Very dependable and safe."

Noticing the paper grocery sack in Stan's arms, Mrs. Simpson repeated the house's strict no "cooking/no eating" rule. "My mom sent me off with all the fixings for *puttanesca* sauce," Stan explained. "There's plenty for all three of us. I wish you'd let me whip up a batch. Just this once."

"There will be four for supper," Mrs. Simpson barked. "A Miss Larson lives here, too. Corner room, second floor, right across from me."

"There's plenty for Miss Larson as well," Stan promised.

"Supper is served promptly at six," Mrs. Simpson cautioned instead of accepting Stan's kind offer to make dinner.

"Six o'clock it will be," Len assured her.

Not counting restaurants, it appeared as though Arlene Simpson had never had men cook for her before, let alone in her own kitchen. She perched herself on one of her dinette set's chairs, which she'd turned to face the range, and watched them like a hawk.

As Len chopped the onion, expertly denuded and minced the garlic, Mrs. Simpson seemed transfixed. Stan waltzed around her kitchen, seeking out pots and pans, then filled a cauldron with water. She watched in wonder as he reached into the grocery bag and extracted strange and astonishing foods, the likes of which she'd never seen in her sixty some-odd years. I.e., macaroni with a foreign name on its colorful box that was not Mueller's; oil that had a rich, greenish tint and a strong yet inviting odor; olives that were black and crinkled like nanny goat droppings; a head of greens that seemed prehistoric. No, Mrs. Simpson couldn't have been more surprised if Stan had pulled a rabbit out of his porkpie hat.

Len glanced over his shoulder at Mrs. Simpson and smiled. "Trust me, you'll love it," he told her.

Mrs. Simpson turned up her nose skeptically. "I never was one for spice," she informed him.

"It's not spicy, Ma'am," Stan said. "Just delicious."

Mrs. Simpson responded with her customary "Hmmmm" when she strongly doubted something. "And where do your people come from, young man?" she asked, staring straight at Len.

"Brooklyn," he told her.

"But before that," she pressed.

"Here, there and everywhere," Len suggested with a wink. He'd dealt with white folks like Mrs. Simpson before and it never ended well. His skin's pallor often confused people— neither light nor dark, neither white nor brown—and he never knew what to answer. Len was actually born in the wastelands of Flatbush, Brooklyn. Throughout his rough-and-tumble childhood, every few years his mother moved them to an assemblage of less-desirable streets with picturesque names like Saratoga and Malta. Len's life had lacked structure until his Jamaican Granny Lulu took him in. But how could the arc of Len's journey be expressed in a flimsy sentence or two? So, the vague "Here, there and everywhere" seemed to fit.

Mrs. Simpson's face betrayed that she was dissatisfied with Len's response. Her brow creased and her tight-set mouth bowed down slightly. When she opened it to speak, Stan cut her off. "Sicily," he offered. "Len's people are from Sicily."

"Well, where's that?" Mrs. Simpson asked, perplexed.

"The football-shaped island near the boot tip of Italy," Stan said. He turned the burner beneath the water pot to "high." It would take some time for the electric coils beneath it to redden and heat.

"Oh, so Leonard's Eye-talian," Mrs. Simpson huffed. "Why in tarnation didn't he say so?"

"Some folks don't consider Sicily to be part of Italy," Len countered.

"That's right," Stan added. "Italy was a whole bunch of little countries right up until the time of our Civil War. But some people still can't get used to the idea of Italy being its own country."

"Well, I'll be," said Mrs. Simpson.

For a brief moment, Stan felt bad for fibbing and stretching the truth but he'd learned that a white lie was easier for some people to digest than reality. He'd witnessed it firsthand when all of that trouble popped up in Cuba with Battista, and most recently, Castro. Because of this, their neighbor Lydia Martinez discovered it was preferable to say that she was from "the Islands," than from that particular troubled Caribbean isle. Plus, people seemed to be satisfied with her vague response of "the Islands," never asking which specific island she hailed from.

Stan grabbed a saucepan from the side cabinet where Mrs. Simpson told him they were stowed. He opened two cans of Cento tomatoes with the Easy-Crank can opener Mrs. Simpson kept in the junk drawer. She leaned forward with interest as Stan crushed the peeled plum tomatoes into a bowl barehanded. (He'd made sure to thoroughly wash them first.) "I'm Italian too," Stan told Mrs. Simpson. "On my father's side."

Stan's birthright revelation was met with a hearty nod from his landlady. Len, on the other hand, didn't offer any explanation of his heritage. Instead, he silently slid the wooden cutting board on the countertop toward Stan. Piled onto it were neat heaps of onion, garlic and sliced olives. The cutting board, the boys learned, was hewn from a mighty oak tree felled on this very land by Mrs. Simpson's grandfather. He'd made wooden kitchen implements—boards, spoons, candy dishes—from the scraps that were left after he'd crafted furniture. Examples of Grandpa Mikalsen's finery were scattered throughout the woman's home.

Stan figured this would be as good a time as any to get Mrs. Simpson tipsy, so he broke out a bottle of *limoncello*. It had been distilled by his cousin Billie Paradiso in Tucson from lemons grown in her own garden. Each year, Billie shipped several bottles of the homemade booze to the Brooklyn Paradisos. Stan poured a healthy draught into a cordial glass he found mixed among Mrs. Simpson's juice tumblers. He passed the drink to her with a bow.

Mrs. Simpson looked at the *limoncello* suspiciously as she finished her revelation about her furniture-making grandfather. In her next breath, Mrs. Simpson slipped nimbly back into her interrogation of her new tenants. "And your mother, Stanley…where are her people from?" she asked.

"Poland mostly, from what I gather," Stan responded, heating a few tablespoons of olive oil to a gentle simmer. "With a smidge of German and Russian thrown into the mix," he said. "I have what my Grandpa Mike liked to call a 'Heinz 57 lineage,'" Stan added, referring to the vinegary condiment in almost every American's Frigidaire.

Knowing that Mrs. Simpson would soon meet Rose, who Stan considered to be his true mother, he tagged on, "But I was adopted by my Momma Rose when I was just a baby. Hers is the only family I've ever really known." Stan's gaze met Mrs. Simpson's shyly and somehow she knew not to ask any more questions. Instead, she took a sip of *limoncello*.

"I'm not usually one for spirits," she admitted, taking a much bigger second sample. "But this is very nice." Already, their tea-totaling landlady was somewhat sozzled. They could hear it in her voice, which was slightly thickened and blurred.

"Stan's Cousin Billie swears her *limoncello* protects against colds and whatnot," Len added. "So, it has medicinal value."

While Stan lightly browned the onion and garlic, Len tended to the head of broccoli rabe, giving it a healthy rinse under the faucet. He began coarsely chopping it on the cutting board. "What's that?" Mrs. Simpson wondered, aghast.

"In Italy, they call it rapini but here we call it broccoli rabe," Len said.

Mrs. Simpson wrinkled her brow. "Never saw it before in my life."

"It's good," Len said. "Kind of like broccoli and lettuce had a baby...but not." She still looked skeptical. "Don't worry, I think you'll like it," he added.

"It's slightly bitter," Stan explained, slowly adding the hand-crushed tomatoes from the Pyrex bowl into the pot with the olives, garlic and onion. "Like life, my grandfather used to say. But broccoli rabe is delicious. Especially the way Len makes it."

"All I do is follow Grandma Bridget's recipe," Len conceded. "Man, that woman sure could cook," he said, as though he'd known her. Indeed, Len felt as though he had known dear Bridget from the loving way Stan and the rest of the family talked about her.

Next, Len simmered the bright green vegetable in a pot of generously-salted water, which Mrs. Simpson eyed with interest. "Helps get out the acidity," he explained.

With a thick wooden spoon, also fashioned by Granddad Mikalsen, Stan broke apart the bubbling tomatoes into smaller pieces in their pot. "Basil?" he asked.

"Right in the spice rack," Mrs. Simpson told him. "Bottom row." With difficulty, Stan unscrewed the top of the McCormick jar, stuck tight from disuse. "Not my favorite condiment," Mrs. Simpson frowned. "Too minty." By eye, Stan sprinkled about a tablespoon of basil into the sauce pot, then gave it a stir.

Mrs. Simpson's *limoncello* glass was almost empty but she refused another pour, even a light one. "That spaghetti sauce smells heavenly," she said, taking a deep draught of the tomato-scented air.

"Come take a peek," Stan enticed. Mrs. Simpson couldn't resist, rising unsteadily from her chair. Leaning over the pot, she was greeted by a blast of refreshing tanginess. The tomatoes were breaking down into a thick sauce, christened with a golden sheen of olive oil on top and dotted with chopped black olives.

"Oh, my. That looks delicious," Mrs. Simpson sighed.

"Just like Momma Rose's," Len told her, emptying the pot of broccoli rabe into the colander he'd placed in one side of the double sink. "You got a cast iron skillet, Mrs. S.?" he asked.

"Left-hand cabinet, bottom," she told him.

When Len located the skillet, he drizzled the pan with olive oil and turned on the electric burner. The great cauldron of water on the rear of the range had begun to boil furiously, begging for the macaroni. Stan tore open the box of Ronzoni penne and added it to the water.

"That's not elbow macaroni, now, is it?" Mrs. Simpson wondered.

"Is that the only kind you use?" Stan asked. She nodded. "This is just a different shape. Like little pen points, so they call it 'penne.'"

"It means 'pens' in Italian," Len offered.

"Mercy me," she grinned. "You learn something new every day, don't you?" Mrs. Simpson appeared decades younger when she smiled, which wasn't often. Her features were lighter, the lines in her face faded, the hardness in her eyes melted. But just for a moment.

Perhaps Mrs. Simpson's new lodgers would change her dour mood for good—or at least for the next few hours. After all, it wasn't every day a lady had two dashing, young men cook for her. She couldn't remember the last time the old saltbox house's kitchen filled with such unfamiliar but wonderful aromas. Maybe the secret to life was to fill it with the unfamiliar and the wonderful. Maybe not.

"Ten minutes on the penne," Stan said to Len.

"Perfect," Len told him. To the skillet, Len slipped in the garlic Stan had left for him on the board. With a set of tongs he'd fished from the ceramic bucket on the counter, Len added the broccoli rabe in small bunches, moving it around in the pan. "How about a dash of red pepper?" he wondered, looking to Mrs. Simpson for approval.

"I don't like spicy," she reminded him.

"This won't be spicy," he promised. "Just warm and savory,"

"Mr. Simpson, God rest his soul, liked red pepper," she recalled. "Haven't had it since he passed. But I believe I still have a jar of it in the back of the cabinet to your left."

Sure enough, there was. After rustling around on the shelf, Len found the glass cylinder of red pepper flakes. It was hiding behind three canisters of Cream of Tartar and a container of cinnamon sticks that would be perfect for rice pudding.

A petite brunette quietly let herself in the side door. It was almost as though she didn't want to be noticed but the young lady was so attractive that it was difficult for her to disappear into the woodwork. Her curly hair drawn away from her face in a taut ponytail, perhaps to try and detract from her beauty, but this wasn't possible. She was clearly lovely. "Miss Larson!" Mrs. Simpson cried. "In here! We're having a party!"

Miss Larson started slightly and entered the kitchen after she'd hung up her coat in the mudroom. Like the solicitous hostess she was, Mrs. Simpson made introductions all around, adding thoughtful tidbits about each person. The three young folks shook hands, Stan and Len first wiping their damp fingers on a dishtowel.

"Long day?" Len asked Miss Larson, after Mrs. Simpson disclosed that her boarder worked at the Sherman Public Library. Miss Larson certainly looked the part of librarian: voluminous skirt, baggy, partially-untucked blouse, the sort of sensible flats chosen by one who spends most of the day on their feet. But there was something oddly sensuous about this tightly-wound woman.

Miss Larson sighed and finally responded to Len. "Yes," she admitted. "A very long day indeed."

"Sit down. Relax, dear," Mrs. Simpson told her. "The boys are cooking us supper and they have this yummy lemon liqueur." Len put one of Mrs. Simpson's cordial glasses at Miss Larson's elbow. "It's imported," her landlady enticed.

"From Italy?" Miss Larson wondered hopefully.

"Even better," Mrs. Simpson said, clapping. "Arizona."

"I really shouldn't," the younger woman began.

"But you will," Len told her, smiling. He began pouring the golden liquid into the cut-glass cordial cup.

"Just a touch," Miss Larson relented. She tapped Len's shirt cuff when the pour threatened to become too generous.

"Just a smidge more," he suggested.

Miss Larson pulled away her hand. "All right," she conceded. Len filled his landlady's glass as well, with no protests from her this time.

Stan, who'd been silent until now, observed the exchange between these mutual tenants from the vantage point of the kitchen counter. He put a plate on the table between the two women. On a bed of arugula, Stan had artfully arranged pitted green Sicilian olives, roasted red peppers and marble-sized mozzarella balls. Len gave the women forks and placed small dishes in front of them, his fingertips brushing Miss Larson's.

"Oh, I wouldn't want to spoil my appetite," Mrs. Simpson told them.

"Trust me, this only whets the appetite," Len assured her, placing a basket of sliced Italian bread on the kitchen table. "Gets you ready for the feast that's coming."

"It's just a little *antipasto*," Stan explained.

"Anti what, now?" Mrs. Simpson asked.

"*Antipasto*," Stan qualified with a laugh. "It's Latin. Literally means 'before the meal.'"

"Except it's part of the meal," Len said. "Here, like this." He took the heel of the Italian bread and with a fork, layered a roasted pepper with a curl of mozzarella then topped it with an olive. Then he popped the whole thing into his mouth, much to the astonishment of the women.

"Just like that," Stan told them. "But feel free to take human bites," he added as Len chewed. Both Mrs. Simpson and Miss Larson built similar snacks but delicately nibbled at them.

"This is divine," Mrs. Simpson drawled.

"Thank you," Stan said. "My mom made the peppers and Louie down at Bellfiore made the mootz."

"Bellfiore means 'beautiful flower,' doesn't it?" Miss Larson asked.

"Yes, it does," Len told her. Their eyes met, then fluttered away.

With a slotted spoon, Stan fished a piece of penne from the boiling water, blew on it, cut off a corner then tasted it. "Two minutes, maybe three," he announced.

"This is too grand a meal to eat in the kitchen," Mrs. Simpson proclaimed. "Let's you and I set the dining room table," she suggested to Miss Larson. They both drained their cups of *limoncello*.

"Let's," Miss Larson agreed, following her landlady into the dining room. The weary librarian had forgotten how bushed she was and suddenly felt light, airy. Perhaps it was the liqueur or perhaps it was the company.

From a breakfront drawer, Mrs. Simpson took an embroidered tablecloth which had been a wedding gift decades earlier: neat, cross-stitched daisies and roses. After Miss Larson grasped the other end of the cloth, they fanned it out across the table. Matching napkins followed, as well as the fancy dishes: Royal Doulton Old Country Roses. The good silverware still hadn't lost its sheen from the last time Mrs. Simpson had polished it earlier in the year, an ambitious undertaking but well worth the effort. She admired her reflection in a tablespoon then put it into place.

Len had the *limoncello* bottle tucked under one arm and the cordial glasses grasped in his fist. In his other hand, he balanced the *antipasto*. "I'll help, Mr. Morton," Miss Larson offered.

"Only if you call me 'Len,' Miss Larson," he told her, placing everything safely on the dining room table.

"All right, Len," she blushed. "If you promise to call me 'Amy.'"

"I will," he said. "Amy." The name felt good on Len's tongue. So good that he said it again. "It's a deal, Amy." As they returned to the kitchen, he held open the bottom half of the Dutch door so Amy could pass.

"Thank you, Len," she told him, a slight smile on her rosebud lips.

That evening, Amy and Mrs. Simpson learned several things. First, that they did indeed like garlic and that it wasn't spicy when cooked, just incredibly flavorful. They also learned that *puttanesca* originated from the Italian word for "prostitute." (This made them pinken with embarrassment.) And that *puttanesca* sauce earned its name because it had been invented by Neapolitan ladies of the night who found that they could easily whip up a quick batch between clients— its bouquet often lured hungry customers to their door. And lastly, they learned that talking around the dinner table—an act for which both had been severely punished as children— was not only permissible but preferable to silence.

The Italian bread from Regina Bakery in Brooklyn was like no other bread the women had ever tasted—fluffy, not gummy on the inside and crisp, not mushy on the outside. The ladies followed the men's lead and sopped up the extra gravy (not sauce!) with the bread, which was so tasty it didn't require butter. This gravy-mopping gesture was something they would have gotten scolded for at a Presbyterian table but was applauded, even encouraged, at an Italian supper.

Everyone swore they had no room for dessert but when they took a gander at the *cannoli* (also imported from Regina Bakery)—crunchy tubes of deliciousness stuffed with a sweet ricotta filling and dotted with chocolate chips—they changed their tune. Paired with diminutive cups of strong, black coffee brewed in a small aluminum pot called a "moka" (which the boys brought with them as well), *cannoli* were heaven-sent.

As the women washed and then dried the dishes, they worried they wouldn't be able to sleep a wink because of the espresso but in fact, they slept heavily and deeply. Although Stan initially tossed and turned from the excitement of the day and the new, unfamiliar bed, he fell asleep without much trouble.

But Len lay awake for a long while, hands propped beneath his head, watching the branches of the budding spring trees paint shadows on the attic room's walls, trying to imagine how Miss Amy Larson might look leaning across him with her cascades of wavy molasses-shaded hair undone and falling onto his chest.

CHAPTER TWENTY-SIX

Thinking of You

No one in the Paradiso compound realized what a substantial part Stanley was of their lives until he was gone. Although he didn't barrel through a room the way he did as a child, constantly commanding attention, Stan still had a larger-than-life presence as an adult. Rose kept the door to his room closed and didn't even go inside to dust it, for whenever she glanced within, she would be overwhelmed with sadness. The ache in Rose's heart wasn't from the pull of her incision, which was healing nicely; it was from missing Stan. Until the restaurant in Sherman opened, he would be gone, except for a short visit on Easter Sunday.

At first, Wendy relished her time alone. She was free to do what she liked in the spare moments she had—go to the movies with friends, visit museums without her companion complaining that they were bored. In truth, Wendy was free to do as she pleased anyhow but it felt good to know that someone, somewhere cared for her. Wendy was busy—with work, with her class, with wedding plans. But still, Wendy found the time to write Stan letters which she always signed off with, "Thinking of You."

Seventy-seven miles away, Stan sat at a pine desk in the spacious attic room he and Len shared, rolling a pen across the scarred wood surface. "I never know what to say," he confessed to his roommate. Several letters were on the desk beside Stan, written in Wendy's florid handwriting on crisp linen paper, perfumed lightly with Tabu, her signature scent.

"Just tell her what you did," Len suggested. "Tell her you miss her."

Stan truly did miss Wendy but his days were chock-full of duties like getting the kitchen at Feel Good Food in working order, putting the finishing touches on decorating the restaurant, testing out new recipes and perfecting old ones. Scribbling this down on paper to give his fiancée the details of his day was painful for Stan. He'd never liked writing, whereas the words flowed from Wendy's pen almost faster than she could jot them down. In contrast, Stan's letters were full of stops and starts and horrid blotches.

The last time they were in the nearby town of Kent, Len forced Stan to buy a sheaf of fine stationery at House of Books and a real fountain pen. Stan preferred the impermanence of a No. 2 pencil. Plus, he could chew on the eraser, he argued. At the desk in the attic room, Stan's pen was pressed to page, not moving, as though stuck in glue. "Just tell her what you feel," Len sighed.

"On paper?"

"No, by smoke signal," Len said. "Just write like you talk." Then, slightly aggravated, he left Stan alone to groan, sigh, twist his hair into tufts and gnaw on his knuckles.

Too early for Mrs. Simpson to set out breakfast, Len decided to walk down Holiday Point Road toward Candlewood Lake. Although the clapboard houses and white picket fences were so different than the brick tenements and brownstones he was used to in Brooklyn, Len still liked them. The people who lived in these houses were friendly enough, giving a wave or nod as he passed. At this early hour, gardeners were out weeding their flower beds and homeowners were out sweeping their walks. Len's ambiguous skin shade didn't seem to worry them. Was he Italian or from "the Islands?" Was he Greek or from Persia? It didn't seem to matter.

Not a soul dotted the lakefront. It was so beautiful, so serene with a fine mist kissing the shore and the blue of the cloudless sky reflecting Candlewood like a mirror. Though Bill had mentioned how the valley had been flooded by C.L.&P. to create the lake, Len had a hard time imagining chicken coops and garages drowned underwater.

He stood on Candlewood Lake's beach, silently contemplating. Len knew there had to be a lilac bush nearby because he could smell its heady fragrance. Sure enough, Len noticed that the lake's southern shore housed a number of overgrown lilac bushes. Granny Lulu loved lilacs and Len was drawn to them, too.

A figure stepped out of the woods as Len approached the explosion of purple flowers. It was female, shapely, barefoot, with long nut-brown hair that played in the breeze. The woman's back was toward him as she struggled to liberate a cluster of lilacs. "They're early this year," Len said.

The woman gasped, turning quickly. It was Miss Larson. Amy. "You startled me," she laughed. "I thought they caught me. Again."

"Caught you?" Len took out his pocket knife, flicked it open and easily sliced off the pinkish-violet shoot, then another. "Who?"

"The Sherman Police," Amy whispered theatrically. "You just aided and abetted a crime." She took the trimmed lilac branches in her arms. "Apparently, it's against the law to take anything from a public park."

Len assented. "Some rules are made to be broken."

"I like to keep fresh flowers on my desk so everyone can enjoy them," she explained.

"That's awfully thoughtful of you."

Amy shook her head in dissent. "Selfish, mostly. If I were totally honest, I put them out for myself. I wish lilacs bloomed all year round."

"But then they wouldn't be so special."

"I think I'd always appreciate them," she told him. Len and Amy grinned widely at each other, happy, unguarded in the early morning sunlight. But suddenly, Amy realized how she must have appeared to Len: feral, windblown, like an untended garden. She smoothed her hair and pulled it into the elastic band she wore on her wrist. "I bet I look a fright," she apologized. "Like a crazy gypsy woman."

"I think you look great," Len admitted. "Comfortable, free. Though being barefoot in March…"

"It's almost April," she said. "The sun warms the sand so nicely. It feels good against your toes. You should try it."

Len glanced down at Amy's feet, her nails painted a brazen purple, the grayish sand between her toes. "I believe I will," he said, leaning against a picnic table to remove his shoes and socks. Len was relieved there were no holes in his Gold Toes. His left foot and then the right went down onto the hard-packed sand. Len wiggled his toes. The sand felt cool at first, then warmed from within, like flesh. "You're right," he said. "It does feel good."

Amy smiled in approval. "See? I told you." She gazed out onto the lake. "I like to stroll that way, to the cove," she pointed. The beach arced into a sandy crescent, lined with flowering trees and tall pines. The lifeguard's chair sat empty. It wasn't yet swimming season. "Care to join me?" Amy asked.

"I would," Len told her. He picked up his shoes and socks.

"It's okay to leave them. No one will take them," she assured him. "Just put them next to mine." Len placed his footwear neatly beside Amy's under the picnic bench. They could have been the shoes of an old married couple, resting side by side in the mudroom of the cottage they shared.

Amy and Len walked the length of the cove, she naming the types of trees they passed, detailing how Connecticut Light and Power had flooded the valley. Although Len knew the story from Bill, he let Amy retell it. Len liked hearing the excitement in her voice and seeing the way her eyes shone when she recalled going out in a rowboat and spying the rooftops of old farmhouses and barns beneath the lake's surface. "I believe you're pulling my leg, Miss Larson," he told her, though he believed her every word.

"Then you'll just have to come out with me sometime and see for yourself," she challenged him.

"I'd like that," Len said.

They continued walking.

When Amy asked about Len's childhood, he responded, "There isn't much to tell," then proceeded to tell her more than he had told anyone else. Like how he'd moved from decrepit apartment to decrepit apartment with his struggling mother just before the rent was due throughout four of the five boroughs. Len took the care to name them for Amy—the Bronx, Queens, Manhattan, and finally Brooklyn, explaining that they would have gone to Staten Island but there was no bridge connecting it to Brooklyn yet.

In Bushwick, Len was rescued by Granny Lulu (birth name: Lucinda) just before his mother fell ill and died of pneumonia in Kings County Hospital. This had all happened before Len was ten.

Amy listened closely, without judgment, her face changing gradually like the phases of a flesh-and-blood moon, going from amusement to sadness to gladness within a few moments. At one point, she bit her lower lip and looked as though she might cry. That was the first time Len wanted to kiss her but he held back. This surprised him because Len never held back anything, especially where women were concerned. Something within him sensed that this Miss Amy Larson was different, special.

It was a quarter till nine and they needed to get to town. Amy had to open the library by nine and Bill had a mysterious day trip planned for Len and Stan.

As the couple headed back to the beach, it was Amy's turn to do most of the talking. She spoke of aunts with lyrical names like Mavis, Ermaline and Cora married to uncles with equally-colorful names like Eustace, Delbert and Jessup. Raised mostly in Paducah, Kentucky—did Len detect a slight "Bluegrass State" accent?—Amy left not a week after she graduated from Paducah Tilghman High, hopping a bus to New York City, where she quickly realized her mistake.

"So, you already knew the boroughs," Len interrupted. "Why did you let me name them?"

Amy shrugged. "I liked hearing you say them."

"Why did you leave the City?" Len wondered.

Amy continued her tale, recalling how New York was just too big, too fast, too harsh for the likes of her, a country mouse too inexperienced to deal with city-mouse life. After her arrival, Amy took a sequence of unfulfilling jobs, seeking refuge in the worlds she discovered amid the New York Public Library's stacks. She found comfort and solitude beyond the main branch of the Manhattan Library's immense doors which were guarded by two stone lions named Patience and Fortitude.

Some nights Amy tarried at the library until closing time and more often than not, she helped the librarian clear the oak tables of the books littering them. "You have a knack for this work and a love of literature," the librarian noted. No one had ever told Amy she was good at anything. When the kind woman suggested that Amy study to become a librarian herself, suddenly Amy's life fell into place. "I took training classes at night then started looking for a job," Amy told Len. "Katy, the librarian had family in Sherman. They told her of an opening at the local library but she didn't want to leave New York City. I did, though. And here I am."

At the picnic bench, Amy and Len brushed off their feet as best they could. "I like the feeling of sand between my toes during the day because it reminds me of this place," Amy told him. She slipped on a pair of white socks and neatly folded them down like a teenager. Then she stepped into her saddle shoes. The look suited her.

At the corner of Holiday Point Road and Route 37, Len and Amy parted ways. "I'll be fine," Amy assured him. "I do it all the time." They shook hands, though Len wanted to kiss her once more or at least give her a hug. He watched Amy walk down the road, savoring both her firm handshake and the softness of her skin. She turned once to watch him watching her.

Back in Mrs. Simpson's rooming house, Len found Stan just where he had left him, pen poised, paper at his fist but his letter to Wendy completed, no doubt in fits and starts, decorated with cross-outs and smudges but signed off with "Thinking of you" in Stan's chunky script.

"Let's get going," Len told him. "Bill says he has an adventure planned for us today."

"What sort of adventure?" Stan wondered, folding the letter and sealing it into an envelope.

"A field trip," Len told him.

Stan nodded. He scrawled Wendy's address on the front of the envelope. "Think we can swing by the post office first?"

CHAPTER TWENTY-SEVEN

Sunny Sky

I t was a bright, sunny spring day, perfect for a long, leisurely drive.

New Haven, Connecticut wasn't what Stan and Len had expected. They thought it would be like Sherman, only slightly larger. (P.S., it wasn't.) Except for the fact that it was the home of Yale University's Bulldogs, they knew little of the New England town.

Bill made sure to drive past Yale's famous Gothic tower on the way to Wooster Square. "This area is known as New Haven's Little Italy," Bill told them as they rode through the no-nonsense red brick town. "It's not nearly as big as the one in New York City but it holds its own," Bill added. Soon the neighborhood became homier and the signs bearing shop owners' names ended in vowels.

With persistence, Bill had been able to convince a few local wholesalers to supply their wares at a decent price, which, in turn, cut Feel Good Food's bottom line. A number of the Connecticut shops that supplied Danbury could drop off their goods on the way to that town, which was just south of Sherman. This was a lot more reasonable than getting deliveries from Brooklyn or Manhattan companies, many of whom refused to do drop-offs in Connecticut. Whereas, New Haven suppliers could make a neat circuit between Danbury, Waterbury and the other "burys," easily circling back to New

Haven without incurring much expense or tire wear. The deals were as good as sealed but Bill wanted to finalize the agreements in person. "Besides, I think it's important for us to meet our vendors face-to-face," Bill said. "Nothing beats matching a friendly mug to the voice on the telephone. Plus, this way, we get to sample the stuff."

Though many of New Haven's streets seemed run down, closer to Wooster Square, the homes were old and grand, brick (some painted, some not) with impressive porticos supported by columns. At Court Street, Stan noted, "These brownstones are a lot like the ones in Park Slope."

"That's right," Bill told him. "This one reminds me of the music school you showed me on Ninth Street." He gestured to a wide stone structure with a porch in the center. "It's a music school here as well."

A three-story apartment building nearby had several clotheslines that were strung out its rear windows and fastened to a telephone pole in the backyard. "Just like Brooklyn, all right," Len noted.

Bill gestured to a ragged-looking street as they drove past. "Parts of New Haven have seen better days for sure," he admitted. "Interstate 91 chopped the neighborhood in half, and when I-95 came through two years ago, it cut through Sargent's."

"What's Sargent's?" Stan wondered.

"A big hardware company," Bill told them. "Sargent's moved to New Haven from New York City in the 1860s. Back then they made things like cowbells and metal goods. Sarge's even made the hinges for Abraham Lincoln's coffin. Then they became known for their locks. By 1914, Sargent's had 60,000 items listed in their catalog, making them the largest hardware manufacturing company in the United States at the time."

"You sure know a lot about New Haven," Len said.

Bill backed his Suburban into a parking spot on Chapel Street. "I believe in learning as much as I can about the folks I do business with and the place where they live," he told Len.

"We'll drive past Sargent's on the way home so you can have a look-see."

"You mean, Sargent's is still open?" Stan asked.

"Still going strong," Bill nodded. "They had a boom during the War. Even moreso before the Forties. Why, Sargent's actually had boats that went straight from Italy to the New Haven docks. Lots of *paisanos* of yours from the Amalfi Coast and southern Italy came here, Stan."

"Is that so?" Stan said with interest.

Bill nodded. "Let's go," he told them. Bill stepped out of the car and the other two followed suit. This part of New Haven was a miniature version of Manhattan's Little Italy with bakeries, sit-down restaurants and pizzerias, which were known as "apizza" shops here. "Hey, my Grandma Bridget used to say 'apizza,'" Stan recalled fondly. "Now I know why."

"Where did she come from?" Len asked.

"Someplace called Avellino," Stan said. "It's in the south. If Italy's a boot, then Avellino is near where the bootlace would be."

"And your grandpop?"

"Poppa was from San Vincenzo in Calabria, down where the boot would be," Stan recalled. "But they didn't meet in the Old Country. They came to the U.S. as kids and met on the Lower East Side, where they lived. They both went to the Church of the Nativity on Second Avenue and met at nine-o'clock mass."

"That's how lots of people met in those days," Bill said. He pointed to a cream-colored church with a bell tower and a rosette window under which was a cutout for the figure of a saint to be ensconced "on the half-shell," as Poppa used to joke. "Saint Michael," Bill told them. "Watching over Wooster Place."

Len looked around him. Deeper into the neighborhood, more of the storefront signs were in Italian. Most were for establishments that sold fruits and vegetables or else pastry shops and eateries. "What's a *salumeria*?" Len wondered.

"A shop that sells salami and other Italian foods," Stan told him. "See?" In the windows of Carrano's hung ropes of dried sausage, salami, circles of cheese as big as their heads and baskets of Italian bread. "Haven't you been to Little Italy in Manhattan? I mean, being from Sicily and all?" Stan pressed. Len smiled and shook his head. When they filled Bill in on the fib they'd told Mrs. Simpson to ward off her nosiness, he laughed.

The weather that day was so mild that Carrano's door was propped open. The pungent scent of aged cheeses and cured meats tumbled out onto the sidewalk. "Let's go in," Bill suggested. When they did, Frank Carrano greeted them like family, slicing off wedges of provolone and Pecorino Romano for each of them to sample. Next, with his sharp knife, Frank whittled away slices of salami. Each circle of smoked meat tasted so different, some bright with lemon, others sharp with pepper or rich with dried fennel.

Bill left Carrano's with a paper sack full of delicacies and a promise to return plus a handshake agreement from Frank for the best prices in town. They set the bag on the Suburban's rear seat before heading back onto Chapel Street. "That whet my appetite," Stan told them. "How about some apizz?" he suggested, mimicking the way Grandma Bridget used to say it, carelessly dropping the "a."

Len glimpsed down the block. "Which place? Sally's or Pepe's?"

"Why not both?" Bill suggested.

On Wooster Street, Sally's featured pies made in a coal-fired oven that had been blazing since 1938. Sally's only served pizza two ways—plain mozzarella and Italian tomato. The Sherman trio shared a small mootz and washed it down with a glass of Schaefer. The thin-crust pizza was absolute perfection. And "Sally," they learned, wasn't the name of a woman like Stan's Aunt Sally Clare, but a nickname for the owner Salvatore Consiglio.

Frank Pepe Pizzeria Napolitana down the block from Sally's boasted an oven fired with coke (a coal byproduct) and served pies with tomatoes, grated cheese, garlic, olive oil and oregano or with anchovies. In business since 1925, they learned from Frank himself that the nephew who'd originally worked for him broke away to start Sally's, which seemed to be a sore spot with the jovial man, so Bill quickly changed the subject.

After much discussion, Bill, Stan and Len opted for an anchovy pie and a dozen raw—Frank Pepe also served Rhode Island clams. It all went down easy, perhaps tempered by the owner's heavily-accented English. Frank Pepe gladly recounted the story of his immigration to New Haven from Maori at age sixteen. At first, he did factory work but that was interrupted by his service in the First World War. Upon Frank's return with his bride Filomena, also from Maori, he toiled in a succession of establishments—Genneroso Muro's macaroni shop, Tony Apicella's bakery and even had a stint with his own bakery, where Frank delivered bread by cart. His pizzeria was born soon after. "And the rest is *historia*," Frank said.

Back on Wooster Street, Bill, Stan and Len agreed that it was a real tossup as to which pizzeria was better. "But why do we have to choose?" Stan offered.

The dessert selections in New Haven were plentiful. Lucibello's, Libby's or Canestri's? In an area so small, there were at least three pastry shops, possibly more. They sampled *sfogliatella* and *pasticciotti* from each bake shop, breaking away hunks and sharing them between themselves. Bill made sure to get pastries for Joan, Karen, Mrs. Simpson and Amaryllis to sample. ('So *that*'s Amy's real name,' Len thought.)

As Bill and Stan doubled back to pick up more supplies, Len begged off, promising to meet them at a designated spot and help them to the car with the packages. "I saw a shop I'd like to stop at," Len explained. He hoped he could remember where it was.

Down Brown Street, up Fair and finally to Chestnut, Len had almost given up hope but then he spotted the unadorned storefront tucked into Ives Place. "Officina Profumo" was painted in antiquated, flowery script above the doorway. As Len went inside, his arrival was announced by a metal cowbell above the door, no doubt a product of Sargent's.

Len was immediately engulfed by sweetness. Sprigs of dried herbs and flowers hung from the ceiling and glass vials of various sizes lined the dusty shelves. A wizened old woman in a black dress and handknit shawl appeared from behind the counter. Her thinning gray hair was pulled into a tight bun at her neck's nape. "*Si?*" the ancient woman said, and not kindly.

"I'm looking for perfume," Len told her. "For a lady."

"No speaka English," she responded. "*Siciliano?*"

"No speak Italian," Len said slowly. "*Americano.*"

The woman nodded, hugging her shawl close. "*Che tipo?*" she wondered, then listed on her bent fingers, "*Rose? Gardenie?*"

"What kind?" Len guessed.

"*Si,*" she nodded. "Whata kinda?"

"Lilacs," he said emphatically. "*Lilaca?*" he tried.

The woman thought for a moment, not understanding. She shook her head. "Little purple flowers. They grow in bunches," Len tried to explain. He gestured to show the size. "They smell like heaven."

The woman smiled, displaying one crooked front tooth. "Ah, *lilla. Si?*" She pointed to a faded floral print on the wall, beside a sprig of freesia. It depicted clusters of purple lilac flowers. "*Lilla.*"

"*Si, lilla,*" Len told her. He watched with interest as the woman selected one beaker, then another. She added small amounts of the contents into a new glass vessel. A dash of this, a healthy pour of that. The colors of the fluids were all different, some almost black, others pale, nearly transparent. Together they blended to create a light amber shade.

The old crone held the glass to the light then sniffed it with her generous hooked nose. She considered the scent then nodded her approval. Once satisfied, she held the vial beneath Len's nostrils. When he took a whiff, Len's head flooded with soft pink (if the color pink could have a scent!). He detected the essence of odorous petals—roses and freesia, and topping it off, the bright fragrance of lilacs. The scent was neither cloying or overpowering. Instead, it was seductive and subtly commanding, like love itself. "Good," he said. "*Bene.*"

"*Buono*," she corrected. "*Ti piace?*"

Len guessed what this meant. "Yes," he told her. "I like it."

The woman smiled and nodded. Len took out his wallet and fanned a few bills. She pointed to one which didn't seem like nearly enough. "*Por amore, do un buon prezzo.*" Which loosely translated to, "For love, I give a good price." Somehow, Len understood and thanked her.

She fit a cork into the narrow vial to seal it then put the vial into a miniscule drawstring bag of a rough cloth, burlap, perhaps. She tapped Len's chest pocket, signifying that he should keep the satchel close to his heart. "*Se tu per favore?*" she asked.

"*Si*," Len told her, giving her permission to slip the little bag into his breast pocket. With her gnarled fingers, the old woman patted Len's pocket again, for luck or for safe keeping, he wasn't sure.

On the return drive to Sherman, Bill passed Sargent's. He and Stan kept remarking about the strong aroma of flowers that seemed to come and go. "I don't smell anything," Len told them, staring straight ahead at the road. The sun seemed to shine brighter and the sky was an intense shade of blue that Len hadn't noticed before. Perhaps it was the secret he held in his pocket, right near his heart. Perhaps not.

First, they stopped at the shop to put away the supplies they'd bought in New Haven. Then Bill dropped Stan and Len at Mrs. Simpson's. When Stan went to the kitchen to bring their landlady the pastries and other treats, Len took the steps to their attic room two at a time, first pausing to hang the perfume vial in its tiny drawstring bag on Amy Larson's doorknob. In the car on the way home, Len had hastily scribbled on a scrap of paper, "Thinking of you," and slipped the note into the sack with the perfume.

That evening, at supper, when Amy leaned toward Len to pass him the bowl of mashed potatoes, he detected the distinct essence of lilacs and roses.

CHAPTER TWENTY-EIGHT

Carefree Beauty

'She has a kind of carefree beauty,' Jo thought as she watched her daughter step in front of the trifold mirror at Kleinfeld. 'Wendy doesn't have to work on it, she just is. And she doesn't even realize how enchanting she is. But that's how life is when you're twenty-three...' Jo smiled to herself.

Wendy glanced at her mother in the silver glass's reflection, at the faraway look in Jo's eyes. "Are you all right, Ma?" she wondered.

Jo snapped to attention and met her daughter's gaze. "Never better," Jo beamed. She studied the gown Wendy wore. It was weighed down with piles of tulle, had puffy princess sleeves and a high, fussy empire waist. "You look like Cinderella," Jo said.

"Before or after midnight?" Wendy wondered. They laughed together. "I feel like a French poodle in this one."

"Well, I wouldn't exactly say that—you're absolutely beautiful in everything you try on. But maybe this gown just isn't you," Jo conceded.

Rose, Angela, Camille and Astrid were in another section of the bridal shop, flipping through the racked wedding-party dresses. Chiara Rose was off hiding among the skirts of lace and crinoline. Again. The child would tire of the game when no one tried to find her.

Terry was home with Little Mike. Though Wendy had asked her cousin-in-law to be part of the wedding party, Terry politely begged off, saying that she felt like a whale so soon after the baby's birth and besides, who would tend to him during the ceremony? Surely a helpful neighbor would, Wendy suggested, but Terry still demurred. So, Wendy consoled herself with the image of her cousin's beatific, tear-streamed face gazing up at her from the front pew at Holy Trinity, cradling Little Mike in her arms.

As Jo unfastened Wendy's gown, she remembered dressing her daughter as a baby. The toddler's chubby pink back with skin as soft as fallen rose petals had given way to firm, taut flesh, carved as delicately as a museum's marble sculpture. "Are you worried about the money?" Wendy asked in a quiet voice so the salesgirl couldn't hear.

"No," Jo told her. "Like Daddy says, money is no object. You're our only. We want the best for you."

"But I could have worn Angie's wedding dress. Or had Aunt Astrid or Mrs. DeMuccio make my gown," Wendy sighed. "Or bought something off the rack at Bergdorf's with Aunt A's employee discount."

To this, Jo shook her head. "Kleinfeld's is the finest money can buy."

When she'd wed Harry at City Hall, Jo'd worn a smart suit instead of a gown. But the small wedding was perfect, exactly what they'd wanted, especially since money was tight on Harry's patrolman's salary. Plus, he helped support his widowed mother back then. Things were different now. They had savings, rent from their tenants, Harry's pension and his salary from working part-time at Feel Good Food. The O'Learys had built a comfortable life together and it was their wish to send their daughter off to wifedom like Brooklyn royalty.

"I just wish they weren't all so fluffy," Wendy sighed.

The salesgirl's expression sagged as she brought another armful of gowns to Wendy. "Less fluffy," the girl said brightly, making an about-face. "I'll see what I can do."

"I'm an awful lot of trouble, aren't I?" Wendy apologized.

"Not in the least," the salesgirl told her. "You're easy compared to most of them."

"I just don't want to look like a poodle on my wedding day," Wendy explained carefully.

"And you won't," the salesgirl promised, walking away.

She returned with just one gown. It had a satin bodice with cap sleeves of white Venetian lace and a straight skirt that fell to the ankle. "Not fluffy, not puffy, not froufrou, no train, no bustle, no bows," the salesgirl recited. "Just simple and elegant. No nonsense."

Wendy's heart leapt happily when the salesgirl hung the gown beside the mirror. She admired the fabric, which fell in perfect folds like the icing on a cake. She trailed her fingertips along its easy, uncomplicated lines.

"It's lovely," Wendy told her, taking the gown into the dressing room. Jo guided Wendy out of the mountains of tulle she was currently modeling. She carefully stepped out of the dress's crinoline slip which stood stiff and unwieldy. Jo handed the rejected dress to the salesgirl.

Wendy stood there barefoot in the dressing room, expectant, clad in only her nylon slip and stockings. "Well, here goes nothing," she said as Jo zipped her daughter into the narrow gown. It hugged Wendy's body as though it had been created just for her, formfitting yet flowing about her curves like white smoke. "This is it," Wendy told her mother.

"Oh, that's you to a T," Jo agreed.

They ventured out of the dressing room to show the others, who were full of oohs and aahs. Even Astrid had nothing bad to say after she examined the material and tested the strength of the seams. "Norma at Bergdorf couldn't do better," Astrid admitted. "It's perfect."

The salesgirl, whose nametag read "Patsy," leaned in closer. "And you can get it for a steal," she told them. "It's been on the rack a few months and no takers. The gals in Brooklyn don't seem to go for this style, but trust me, it's all the rage in Paris right now." Astrid rolled her eyes at someone using her catchphrase, which she had convinced Chiara Rose she'd invented. "And I have the perfect dresses for the wedding party, too. They echo yours beautifully," Patsy added then scooted off.

Patsy had a talent for giving her customers exactly what they wanted, even if they didn't know what they wanted themselves. She came rushing back with a modest silk sheath of exquisite design that complimented the women's varied physiques from Angela's generous curves to Astrid's sharp edges. As for color, Wendy had the perfect shade in mind. "Pale pink, like an early summer rose," she said. Patsy managed to find the dress in their approximate sizes before moving on to find possibilities for the mothers of the bride and groom, who were easy to fit and to please.

Chiara Rose, of course, wanted a dress with all the bells, buzzers and whistles: tulle like a ballerina skirt with a sash and bow. She pleaded for a bolder shade of pink, to which Wendy agreed, but she drew the line at Pepto Bismol and cotton candy. It wasn't difficult to find a flower girl dress that met the child's approval.

"You came at the perfect time," Patsy told them, writing up the sales receipt. "Late March, right before the busy season. "They don't need many alterations so we'll have them ready in plenty of time for May 14th." Patsy was happy to sell a septet of dresses in the slow, gray days of late winter and also pleased she could offer such an exceptional product at a fair price.

Triumphant and buzzing about the wedding, Jo suggested they head to Hinsch's to celebrate. "Perfect, it's only a couple of blocks," Camille said.

"In these shoes?" Astrid barked, gesturing at her stiletto heels.

"Comfort before beauty," Camille told her, gesturing at her own sensible Cuban heels. When Astrid scowled at her sister's "old lady shoes," Camille said, "I could run for the bus in these if I had to." Then she added thoughtfully, "And at least I don't have a hammertoe."

Camille and Astrid argued politely, just like they had when they were girls, as they walked to Hinsch's Diner, near the corner of Eighty-Sixth Street and Fifth Avenue. They managed to find a booth in the back which could easily accommodate seven.

The youngest Paradiso Sisters continued their argument. That is, until Rose, the eldest, broke it up, just like she did when they were young. "Really! In the grand scheme of things, what difference do your shoes make?" Rose said. "You should both wear the shoes you like...and not complain about it," she added for Astrid's benefit. But Astrid culled an odd brand of joy from complaining—about anything and everything.

Chiara Rose begged for permission to sit on one of Hinsch's silver counter stools topped with green Naugahyde but the aunties wouldn't give in. Rose had to literally peel her granddaughter from a stool, which the girl managed to twirl several times before being extricated. Chiara pledged to behave after they ordered her a chocolate malted in a tall, curved mug with a handle and a red straw. "I'll eat all of my cheeseburger, too," she promised. They knew she wouldn't be able to finish the burger but let her get the milkshake anyhow. It was a special day.

The waitress, whose name was "Peg," aced their confusing drink order: coffee (light and sweet), tea (burning hot), chocolate egg cream, cherry Coke (no ice), and so on. The wedding party was glad they'd been stowed at a rear booth for they were free to chatter like magpies near the busy clatter of the kitchen without fear of disturbing the other diners. The dresses—the fabric, the color, the cut—as well as Wendy's own gown, which was magnificent, were the topic of conversation, as was the price: getting them all at a steal. "How rare is it that the mother of the groom and the mother of the bride are sisters?" Camille chuckled.

The others joined her laughter, all except for Rose, who looked serious. Jo leaned in close. "Don't worry," Jo assured her in a low voice. "You can't tell. The dress hides it. And it's such a gorgeous shade of blue."

Rose stared at Jo in wonder. "How did you know I was worried?"

Jo nudged her. "Because I know my big sister." There was no secret-keeping among the Paradiso Sisters.

"And if it makes you feel any better, you can wear the corsage on the left side," Camille added. "This way you *really* won't be able to tell."

"That's the side you're supposed to wear it on!" Astrid piped, sipping her scalding tea with lemon.

"I know, Maggie," Camille told her. "I was just being silly."

"For you, silly comes naturally," Astrid huffed. Camille bopped her on the head with Hinsch's cumbersome, plastic-coated menu.

"Now you're both being silly," Chiara Rose giggled.

The lunches the Paradiso Party ordered from Peg were as different as they were:

> - plain lettuce with dressing on the side (Astrid).
> - "Who orders lettuce at a luncheonette?" quipped Jo, who had ordered a club sandwich.
> - To which Astrid commented, "You'll never fit into that dress."
> - To which Camille, who'd ordered waffles, said, "You only live once, sis."
> - To which Chiara gasped, "Breakfast for lunch!"
> - To which Wendy pointed out, "You should always order what you like, no matter what time of day it is."

Wendy craved Hinsch's gooey grilled cheese but drew the line at ordering French fries. However, she did indulge in a strawberry shake, despite Aunt A's warning, "A moment on the lips, a forever on the hips."

> - To which Jo commented, "How would you know, A? You don't have any hips."
> - To which Astrid harrumphed and snuck one of

Chiara Rose's French fries when she thought no one was looking.

Like a bumblebee dipping from flower to flower, the conversation buzzed from Easter in a few weeks to the opening of Feel Good Food in Connecticut to the wedding back to Easter. "I bet you miss Uncle Stannie something awful," Chiara said to her cousin.

"I do," Wendy told her. "But he's doing something important. And he writes the sweetest letters."

"You'll have a whole lifetime to share together," Jo, ever the romantic, mooned.

"Yes, plenty of time to get sick and tired of each other," Astrid, who was well into her second husband, pointed out.

Jo clarified, "What I meant was that a few weeks apart is nothing."

"Besides, you know what they say," Camille, the feistiest sister, suggested. "Abstinence makes the heart grow fonder."

The table burst into such enthusiastic laughter that it caused other diners to turn and smile at the boisterous hen party. "They do not say that!" Jo gasped. "And mind your manners," she added, gesturing at Chiara.

"What's abstinence?" the girl wondered, easily managing the tongue-twister of a word.

"Never you mind," Rose told her granddaughter. "It's something your Aunt Cammy knows nothing about." They all cackled even harder.

Although the women claimed they were completely stuffed, they also agreed that it would be a shame if they didn't sample some of Hinsch's famous desserts, so they shared several: a banana split, a dish of rice pudding and slice of chocolate layer cake.

While they were waiting for the sweets to arrive, Jo told Wendy, "I almost forgot. That nice couple upstairs just told us they're moving to Bay Ridge in June. Since they have a baby coming, they'll need a bigger place."

"I'm sure you'll find another tenant real quick," Wendy assured her mother. "It's such a wonderful apartment. The light and…"

"Well, I was thinking you and Stan could move in," Jo said hopefully.

Wendy's face dropped. "Mom, you know Stan's going to be working in Sherman," she said gently. "Indefinitely."

"But it'll just be four days a week once they get the place off the ground, so I thought…"

Tenderly, Wendy touched her mother's arm as it rested on the Formica tabletop. "It's a fine idea but…" The others knew what Jo did not or refused to believe: that Wendy was moving away. The table was silent. Peg soundlessly set the desserts in the middle of the table, along with several long-handled spoons.

"Ma, I found a job," Wendy continued. "At the *News Times*. And not as a secretary, as a junior reporter." Jo's face registered shock. Because her mother didn't respond, Wendy went right on prattling nervously. "I sent the paper a few writing samples. Stories I did for the *Eagle*. Well, believe it or not, they really liked them and…"

A tear splashed onto Jo's green paper placemat. "I…I…" Jo stammered.

"I thought you'd be happy for me," Wendy said. "For us."

"I am," Jo insisted, wiping her eyes. "It's just so sudden."

Astrid plucked the maraschino cherry from the top of the banana split. "Josephine, you've had decades to get used to it," Astrid boomed. "Wendy is twenty-three years old, for God's sake. Why, I left home way before then." Astrid popped the brilliant cherry into her mouth, chewing it viciously.

"That's true," Camille told Astrid, "but we were glad to see you go." Upon hearing this, Astrid almost choked.

Rose jumped right in, trying to patch things up between her sisters. "Camille means, because it was such a great opportunity, you studying at the House of Chanel in gay Paree," she offered.

"I know exactly what she meant," Astrid said.

Jo had recovered enough to tell Wendy, "I'm just surprised is all." She squeezed Wendy's hand affectionately. Now they were both crying. Soon, the most of the table followed suit. Peg noticed and brought more napkins.

"What's wrong?" Chiara asked.

"Nothing," they told her, almost in unison.

"For the love of Pete, Connecticut's not China," Astrid said, blowing her nose like a foghorn.

"But it's not around the corner either," Angela admitted in Jo's defense. They continued eating their dessert, halfheartedly now, all except for Chiara, who had gotten her second wind and was tucking into the rice pudding's topping like a champ.

"You can't just eat the whipped cream," Astrid warned her.

"How come?" the girl wondered. "It's the best part."

"That kid is right," Peg smiled, having just arrived with the check.

The Paradiso women politely wrestled for the scrap of paper; Jo won. "Mother of the bride's honor," she said.

"How about she split it with the mother of the groom?" Rose offered.

"Deal."

"The rest of us will leave the tip," Camille said.

"We will?" Astrid piped.

"Of course, we will," Camille said firmly. "It will be our pleasure."

They left Hinsch's and headed for the corner of Eighty-Sixth and Fifth. In the distance, they saw the B-16 bus chugging up the hill from Fourth Avenue. Rose grabbed Chiara by the wrist as the group sprinted easily across the avenue to the bus stop in front of Woolworth's. Astrid toddled as quickly as she could on her perilous heels. "I told you I could run in these things," Camille ribbed Astrid, fumbling in her purse for change.

"I think I'm getting a shoe bite," her sister sighed.

On the B-16, they all managed to find seats near one another, Chiara climbing onto Rose's lap. Jo gestured to

Woolworth's plate glass front windows as the bus pulled away. "I wanted to pick up a thing or two at the five-and-dime," Jo said, "but the bus got here so fast."

"I'll never shop in F.W. Woolworth again," Wendy told her.

The other women looked at Wendy curiously. "Why not? Their chow mein sandwiches are to die for," Angela said.

"Haven't you heard about what happened at the Woolworth's in Greensboro?"

"South Carolina?" Camille wondered.

"North Carolina," Wendy corrected.

"Honey, that's so far away," Rose told her niece. "Besides, we don't do that kind of thing in Brooklyn."

"What happens there happens here," Wendy said. "If they won't serve colored folks at a 'whites only' counter down South… or just the fact that they *have* a 'white's only' counter down there…it's wrong. I don't want to give Woolworth's my money if they're going to do things like that."

"And what they said to those poor people while they sat at the counter," Rose said. "It's a shame."

"But then everyone started protesting, whites as well as coloreds," Wendy explained. "In just five days, the numbers grew from just four protesters to over fourteen hundred. People started following suit in cities all over the country."

Astrid stood tall in her seat. "I say, hit them where it hurts: in the pocketbook." Everyone, even the bus driver, who was not colored, gawked at Astrid after her remark. Though she had no particular dislike for negroes—Astrid disliked all people exactly the same—she believed that everyone was created equal—regardless of skin color or creed. "I'll shop at Kresge's from now on," she added.

Camille shook her head. "I just don't understand behaving like that to other people. Remember all those wonderful folks Poppa used to bring from the Brooklyn Navy Yard?" she said wistfully. "People from all over the world. Oh, the stories they could tell."

"And the foods they'd bring…delicious dishes from whatever country they happened to be from," Jo recalled.

"It's all about the food for you, isn't it?" Astrid sighed.

As was often the case, her sisters ignored Astrid. "I miss them," Rose said plainly. "Poppa and Momma." Heads nodded in agreement, except for Chiara, who had fallen asleep on her grandmother's lap thanks to the roll and lurch of the B-16.

"How they would have enjoyed this wedding," Jo smiled.

"How surprised they'd be," Camille said. "I only wish they could be here to see it."

"But they are here," Rose told them, wedging her granddaughter's crown beneath her chin so Chiara's head wouldn't loll. "Don't you feel them...Mom and Pop? Why, I feel them all the time. When I'm cooking. When all of us are together. The first time I laid eyes on Little Mike."

Jo agreed. "He does look like Michele Archangelo, doesn't he?"

Before long, the B-16 had made its series of right angles, going up one side of Fort Hamilton Parkway, cutting along Fifty-Sixth Street then going down Thirteenth Avenue toward Prospect Park. The parade of Paradiso Girls, their children and grandchildren exited the bus at the corner of Forty-Seventh Street. Chiara Rose slumped sleepily between her grandmother, aunts and cousin, who said their goodbyes and headed to their respective homes.

As they doubled back to Fort Hamilton Parkway, Jo slipped her arm around her daughter's waist and told her, "Go off and do great things. Do whatever you need to do. Even if it's in Connecticut."

"Thanks, Ma," Wendy said. "I'll always be your little girl. Remember that. Yours and Daddy's."

"No," Jo said with a sad sort of pride. "You don't belong to anyone, never did. You're your own woman, and a fine one at that."

In silence, mother and daughter walked to the limestone house they shared, to the building where Wendy had been brought home from the hospital as a newborn, where Wendy had grown up, where she had grown into a lovely, headstrong, young lady. They would have to find a gentle way to tell Harry that his carefree beauty would soon be gone.

CHAPTER TWENTY-NINE

Remembrance

No matter how many holiday celebrations had been held at the Paradiso family home (which is how Poppa and Bridget's old place would always be known, no matter who happened to live there), each holiday was greeted with excitement and newness. And the unspoken fear that everything wouldn't get done in time. But things did get done. They always did.

Easter 1960 was no different. Having a newborn in the house presented a unique set of challenges but the family took it in stride, either wordlessly grabbing the reins when Little Mike became fussy or handing him off, from one to the other if Terry was occupied and couldn't stop what she was doing. The infant seemed to have no preference for which Paradiso woman held him—unless, of course, he needed to be nursed. Perhaps it was a similar scent to their skin or the silent knowledge that he was loved, cherished, by each of them.

The Martino kitchen was the realm of women, and even if Tiger were there, they would shoo him out of their domain. There was an odd unwritten rule—boys could help (as Tiger and Stan did when they were ten or twelve) but men could not. Perhaps there was something primal, ritualistic, about arranging food for a special gathering. An unspoken decree of females banding together, partnering for one common cause: to feed the people they cared for. It was empowering and nurturing at the same time, a celebration of life and of each other.

Although Easter wasn't surrounded by the same fanfare as Christmas, its preparation was equally as significant. Certain traditional foods—carefully-braided breads studded with pastel-colored hard-boiled eggs, pies filled with rich ricotta cheese and wheat grain—always made an appearance. Certain stories were traditionally retold, if not embellished or else mellowed with time. For instance, Chiara Rose badgered her father to tell the tale of the Easter supper when his father fell face-first into the sweet potatoes. Tiger gladly told it but left out the part about Tony being rip-roaring drunk. "He lost his balance" was Tiger's kindhearted explanation of Tony's graceless nosedive into the yams. Chiara didn't need to know the truth, for really, what purpose would it serve?

A slight chill was in the air that particular Easter morning, but somewhere behind it, the promise of spring. Always the promise of spring.

Stan and Len had driven down from Sherman late the night before, after most of the family had already fallen asleep. All except for Rose, who still was still plowing her way through James Michener's *Hawaii*, this time, at the kitchen table, awaiting her son's arrival.

The next day, while the Martino kitchen downstairs operated in an organized chaos, Stan made his appearance, freshly showered and shaved, dressed nattily in slacks, an Oxford shirt and sweater, sipping a mug of coffee. Seeing him after so many weeks made Wendy's knees weak. "You're a sight for sore eyes," she said. Wendy stopped opening the can of chickpeas for fear that she'd cut herself on its jagged rim.

"You too," Stan told her. They didn't embrace, not in front of a kitchenful of aunties, but their gaze was powerful, electric.

"Why don't you two lovebirds take it outside?" Terry suggested.

"We've got plenty of help," Rose said.

"You sure?" Wendy asked.

"Astrid came early for a change," Camille quipped. "Missed her precious beauty sleep."

"Will wonders never cease," Jo added.

"You two are starting early," Astrid snorted.

"It's never too early," Camille told her, grinning. She bumped Astrid playfully with her hip; Astrid bumped her in return.

Wendy and Stan took this as their cue to leave.

In the vestibule, he eased her into her spring coat, choosing his fiancée's cheerful lavender shell from all of the somber, dark-colored jackets on the hooks. On the front porch, Wendy and Stan embraced, simply held each other, not moving, just breathing. Her skin smelled of roses, he noted. "I didn't realize how much I'd miss you till you were gone," Wendy said.

"We've been together practically every single day since we were babies," Stan told her. They kissed but not for long. On Forty-Seventh Street, someone was always watching— walking their dog or fussing with their garden, even on Easter Sunday. In this case, it was Chiara Rose, who had snuck off to the parlor window to spy on her uncle and cousin. "Come on," Stan told Wendy, taking her hand.

"Where are we going?" she asked.

"For a walk," he said. "I do this every Easter."

Tucked away beside the front steps stood a branch of brilliant yellow flowers. There was a wrapped ball of soil at the end, for planting. "Forsythia?" Wendy ventured.

"Close. *Kerria japonica*," Stan corrected. "Some call it 'Easter rose.'"

"It's very pretty," she told him.

"I thought so too. I got it from Bloomingfields Farm in Sherman before me and Len drove down."

"Where are you going to plant it?" Wendy asked, studying Grandma Bridget's already-bursting front yard.

"I'll show you," Stan told her.

In the spring, Green-Wood Cemetery is as beautiful as any botanical garden. The azalea bushes, many as large as trees, explode with color, ranging from rich fuchsia to blood red, pale pink and the faintest whisper of white. The forsythia, Brooklyn's official flower, come in as thick and insistent as the borough's accent. The cherry blossoms, the magnolias, are so lush, so magnificent that they make the heart both light and heavy simultaneously. Rows of daffodils and tulips stand guard over the crypts and headstones like glossily-robed sentinels.

When the Paradiso children were youngsters, Rose and her siblings would play and run among the graves. These stories were told and retold to Wendy and Stan, then Chiara Rose, so they knew them by heart.

The young couple entered Green-Wood via the rather unceremonious Fourth Avenue gate. Before they passed through the grand Gothic castle's arches which led to the main graveyard near Fifth Avenue, Stan made sure to stop and say hello to Francis, Julia and Carol Browning at their final resting place. Then Wendy and Stan looked diagonally across at the Stylianou clan's monument and moved further down the same row to the Farnes and Valdes Family's headstone. Only after this did Stan and Wendy go through Green-Wood's tall, red sandstone arches which guarded the cemetery's main entrance.

There was a time when Wendy knew more about Green-Wood than just about anything. As a child, she had been macabrely fascinated by its myths: the baby named Adelaide, the dancing couple, the dog Fannie who was buried in a family plot. But Wendy had forgotten much of Green-Wood's lore, replacing this knowledge with tales and fables of other places. However, Stan seemed to have picked up where Wendy left off; he remembered all that she had forgotten.

Stan paused briefly so they could consider the cemetery's splendid entryway from within the graveyard. "Besides the double arch, there are three spires, see?" he pointed out to Wendy.

She liked hearing Stan talk about the place. It slowly sparked her foggy memory. "What's happening in those carvings?" she asked.

"It's a Resurrection theme," Stan said. "And that bell? It rings to announce every funeral procession."

Wendy nodded thoughtfully. Headstones and monuments dotted the hills of Green-Wood as far as the eye could see. "Ask not for whom the bell tolls..." Wendy began, hoping Stan would finish the quote.

"Huh?" he wondered.

"John Donne," she told him.

"John who?" he asked.

Wendy shook her head. "Never mind. You were saying?"

Stan cleared his throat. "I was going to say that this entrance was designed by a guy named Richard Upjohn. The same fellow who did the Grace Church in Brooklyn Heights. It's in the Gothic Greek Revival style."

"Stanley Sullivan, you are full of surprises," Wendy marveled.

Still cradling the spray of Easter rose, Stan took Wendy's arm, leading her along an uphill path. "How so?" he wondered.

"Sometimes you barely know your own name and others you're positively sage-like."

"Poppa told me all about Green-Wood," Stan explained. "We would go on long walks here, just him and me."

A loud squawking interrupted the peacefulness of the cemetery. The couple stopped, turned and followed the noise. It led to the Gothic arch's central tower. They saw flashes of green near the tall spires. "Monk parakeets," Stan told Wendy, smiling. He was glad the parrots from Idlewild had already settled in.

"How in the world did they get to Brooklyn?" she asked. "Aren't they from the tropics?"

"Word on the street is that a crate busted this winter in Idlewild," he said. "But it looks like those parrots are here to stay." He gestured to a large, messy pile of sticks in the tower. "There's their nest."

"How did you know that? About the crate?" Wendy pressed.

Stan shrugged. "I heard some people say some things."

He guided Wendy toward a path on the right. "But Poppa and Bridget's grave is the other way," she told him.

"I want to take you somewhere else first," Stan explained.

"All right," she said.

Their grandparents' final resting place was on a lush hillock beneath a majestic oak but this section was entirely different. The further Stan and Wendy went, the more sparse the trees and other plantings became. He took Wendy further up the bare hill toward Thirty-Sixth Street.

Beyond Green-Wood's black wrought iron fence were the bulky brick outlines of warehouses. As the couple walked further, the Thirty-Eighth Street train yard came into view. The nearest cemetery signpost read Spruce Avenue but Wendy saw no spruce trees, or any trees, in the general vicinity. Out on the street and down the block a was a bar. The faded sign above it read "The Pink Pussycat," but it was boarded up, long closed.

"Come on, it isn't far," Stan said. They trudged up another hill in the dirt where nothing seemed to grow. It was as though even the grass were reluctant to make an appearance. Wendy thought to herself, 'What a sad, lonely place to be buried.' But she said nothing of the sort to Stan.

A small, flat stone marked the location of someone's eternal rest. The slab itself was almost submerged in the soil. Stan drew a fresh, white handkerchief from his pocket, wet a corner with his saliva and began to clean the stone's surface. The black granite gleamed with a fine layer of Stan's spittle. The headstone read:

Anthony Joseph Martino
1896-1936

This was Stan's father. "He worked on the El," Stan told Wendy. "At some point, he took up with the Yellow Queen. Remember her?"

"How could I forget? We were, what, eight or nine when she started following us."

"Eight," Stan said, with emphasis. The Yellow Queen was the nickname he and Wendy had given to the broken women who suddenly began trailing them to and from school. The pair had christened her long before they knew she was the woman who had given birth to Stan.

"I figure she was already pretty sick by then," he added. Stan led Wendy a few paces to a smaller headstone. It read:

Denise Stephanie Walters
1902-1946

Although Wendy had never been to this grave before, she knew at once this was Stan's mother. His birth mother.

Stan lay the Easter rose branch on the ground. He took a switchblade from the pocket of his slacks. Next, he spread out his handkerchief on the dirt and went down on one knee on the hankie, so as not to ruin his new pants. Flicking open the knife's blade, Stan began to dig. "I think I saw a sign that said they don't allow private planting in the cemetery," Wendy told him. Stan's unchanged expression told her that he didn't care.

He made a shallow hole for the *kerria japonica* then put the ball of its root into the hole, patting the soil around the base. The branch stood firmly in the dirt, solid and strong. "Think it will take?" he asked.

"Sure," Wendy said.

"I come here from time to time," he told her.

"I thought you might."

"The Yellow Queen was all alone at the end," Stan said, tinged with a note of sorrow.

"She wasn't alone," his girl assured him, "because she had you."

Wendy wove her arm through Stan's. They stood there silently considering the once-bleak grave, which was now adorned with sunny yellow flowers. "Do you think she'd be proud of me?" he asked his fiancée.

"Of course, she would," Wendy said, almost without thinking. "What's not to be proud of? *Nu?*" she added in Mrs. Lieberwitz's accent, thick with the forests of Eastern Europe.

Stan smiled slightly but didn't laugh. "Let's stop by Poppa and Grandma Bridget's before we go," he said.

Although Green-Wood Cemetery was busy with Easter visitors, few traveled on foot like Wendy and Stan did. It had turned into a lovely morning, made warmer by the sun. The stroll was pleasant, full of brilliant colors and sweet scents. The cherry and pear trees bloomed on the hills surrounding the elder Paradisos' grave, just as they did the morning of Poppa and Grandma Bridget's funeral. Wendy would never forget the feel of the magnolia blossoms beneath her white patent leather shoes that day as their caskets were lowered into the deep double grave.

As headstones went, theirs was beautiful. It was hewn of marble that hailed from Italy, just like the pair of them did. Delicate roses were etched into the stone's top. Beneath Poppa's name and date of birth, it said "A diamond in the rough." (His accomplishments and affiliations were too numerous to mention.) And beneath Bridget's name and birthdate was "A rose among women," for truly she was. Beneath this information, in the center of the stone was the date of their dual death.

One family member had already laid a wreath of fresh flowers on the ground in front of the stone and another had staked an Easter cross decorated with ribbons and palm fronds beside the wreath. "We didn't bring anything for them," Stan lamented.

Wendy thought for a moment. "We brought ourselves. That's the best thing of all."

Then Wendy remembered what their neighbor Ti-Tu had once told her—he had patiently explained that leaving a pebble on a headstone was a Jewish tradition to show that someone had been there. Ti-Tu left a rock whenever he visited his mother, old Bertha Rosenkrantz, at Washington Cemetery on Bay Parkway.

Recalling this, Wendy picked up two small, smooth stones. She gave one to Stan. Together, they each laid the rocks on top of their grandparents' gravestone. Wendy and Stan stood in stillness, praying perhaps, but at the very least, remembering. Remembering the kindnesses, the hugs, the laughter and the sound of their grandparents' voices, always merry, always bright, always filled with love. "I think they'd be happy," Wendy told Stan. "Happy about us."

"I think so too," Stan said. Together they walked away from their grandparents' grave and toward Easter supper.

Absent Friends

There was too much happening for Rose to acknowledge her disappointment that Dr. Seminara hadn't come to Easter dinner. But after the *antipasto*, the *manicotti*, the ham and all the fixings, after the great Capodimonte nut bowl had been set out, retrieved and the used dessert plates were collected from the table, Rose mourned the doctor's absence. She was overcome with a swell of sadness, the way a rogue wave unexpectedly sweeps you under at Coney Island. She kept a plate warming in the oven and had set aside a dish of *antipasto* on Terry's kitchen countertop, just in case Marco showed up.

It was late. The lengthy Easter supper had been finished for at least an hour. Rose's sisters and their families had gone home. Stan and Len were on their way back to Fairfield County. Rose had convinced Terry to go into the bedroom to nurse Little Mike while Rose did a final wipe-down of the kitchen. In Chiara's room, Tiger read *Eloise* to her again. And again.

Rose was carrying the last of the chocolate cake into the kitchen when she heard a voice. "Looks like I missed the party," it said tiredly. Rose turned to see Dr. Seminara in the doorway.

"You're right on time," she told him brightly, though Rose was weary. It had been a long day.

"I remember you said you kept the doors unlocked," the doctor almost apologized, coming into the parlor.

"I'm glad you remembered," Rose said. "And glad you came. Are you hungry, Marco?"

"Starved," Dr. Seminara answered. "This is the first chance I've had to eat all day."

"I figured it might be busy today. Sit, relax. I'll get you a snack."

Dr. Seminara put his medicine bag on the floor and took a seat at the empty table while Rose went into her daughter-in-law's kitchen. She fetched the plate from the oven, first grabbing one of the multicolored potholders Chiara had made on her toy loom. Then Rose took the *antipasto* dish, balanced the bread basket in the crook of her elbow, and brought them to the dining room table.

"That's quite a feast!" Dr. Seminara proclaimed, taking the bread plate from her. Rose set the other two dishes on the table in front of him.

"A little bit of everything," she shrugged. "Nothing special."

"It's all special to me. I haven't had an *antipasto* like this since my mother passed," the doctor said, briefly surveying the contents of the dish. Then he tucked into it.

"Sorry to hear about your mother," Rose told him. "When did you lose her?"

"About twenty years ago," he said between bites. "I was young. Still in med school."

"What was it?" Rose wondered.

"Breast cancer," Dr. Seminara admitted, almost reluctantly. He took the heel of the Italian bread to sop up the roasted pepper juice. "I promised my mother I would do something about it when I became a doctor," he continued. "That's what made me go into this line of medicine. My promise to her." Rose nodded; she was grateful he had. "You've got to give me the recipe for these peppers," he added. "They're manna from heaven."

"I will," Rose said. It was a common request, and the DePalma Family's recipe was so simple anyone could do it. But it did have a secret ingredient: lemon juice instead of vinegar.

Dr. Seminara polished off the *antipasto* in record time. Then he reached for the second plate. It was brimming with *manicotti*, a meatball, a sausage, honey-baked ham, candied sweet potatoes, carrots and green beans, all still piping hot. "This is heaven," he sighed. "Pure heaven."

Rose smiled, inwardly pleased.

As he ate, Dr. Seminara talked about the baby girl named Serena who was born in the vestibule (the mother's fourth, who, like Little Mike, couldn't wait for the maternity ward), the deeply-sliced finger which Dr. Seminara saved from being completely severed, the attempted suicide, handsome Mr. Siederman, in the late stages of pancreatic cancer, at age fifty-nine. "But he went peacefully," Dr. Seminara consoled himself with. "I saw to it that he did."

"One door closes and another opens," Rose offered. "You also helped a baby to be born," she reminded him. Then she asked, "But I thought you were a breast surgeon. How come you were in the Emergency Room?"

"I do a shift there every so often. It keeps me on my toes," Dr. Seminara explained. "Plus, they were shorthanded because of the holiday."

"And Mrs. Seminara doesn't mind?" Rose ventured.

"Unfortunately, she did," he said. "That's why she is no longer Mrs. Seminara. It takes a certain kind of woman to be a doctor's wife. She has to get used to playing second fiddle. She has to realize that sick people come first, come before her. I took an oath before I took my wedding vows."

"Any children?" Rose asked.

His face brightened. "One," he said. "A daughter. Nancy. She's the light of my life."

Tiger came into the dining room, his hair rumpled, as if from sleep. From personal experience, Rose knew that Chiara tried to roughhouse just before bedtime, plagued by a spurt of energy right before tiredness overtook her. Tiger and Dr.

Seminara shook hands. "How's your wife? The baby?" the doctor asked.

"Both fine," Tiger told him, taking a seat across from Dr. Seminara. "Terry's pretty tired, though. Thanks for asking."

Rose went to the kitchen to put on a pot of water for tea. She took out a platter which held the remnants of dessert: a slab of Richard Garcia's cheesecake, a wedge of Nadia Rohrs' decadent, thick-as-fudge chocolate regal, plus the iced, bunny-shaped sugar cookies Terry and Chiara had made. "I'm going to burst," Dr. Seminara complained but didn't refuse the sweets. Tiger took a cookie to accompany the tea.

When Rose returned with the tea tray, the men were discussing Feel Good Food, which Dr. Seminara said was a lunchtime favorite among Maimonides hospital staff. It was quick, cheap and delicious. Dr. Seminara himself was partial to their Italian food but their Southern dishes held a close second. "And then there's the Puerto Rican food," he said.

The eatery had recently been commissioning delicacies like *pasteles* from a local woman and her sister. Milagros Rodriguez and Elise Espinosa were the best *pastele*-makers in neighboring Sunset Park and often sold their wares to area residents. The sisters were more than happy to take on Feel Good Food as a customer.

To the eatery staff, there was nothing better than watching a lace-curtain Irish woman unveil a *pastele* for the first time, unsurely slipping off the kitchen twine, unfolding the parchment paper and finally, opening the banana leaf, furrowing her brow with a shred of doubt, then coaxing a bit of masa-coated pork onto her fork and taking a hesitant taste before she demolished the *pastele* and ordered another. The sisters savored these stories when they dropped off their delicacies.

Pip's teapot sat on the table between the doctor, Rose and her son. Tiger served the steaming liquid as Rose cut thin pieces of each dessert for Dr. Seminara to sample, slipped a cookie onto the plate too. "I hear you'll be the mother of the groom soon," he told Rose.

"Yes," she beamed. "Wendy and Stan decided to tie the knot in Connecticut."

"We're having the reception at our newest Feel Good Food outpost, in Sherman," Tiger said.

"What is that? Your fourth?" Dr. Seminara asked.

"The third," Tiger told him.

"That's more than enough for now," Rose added.

"Sounds like a handful," Dr. Seminara agreed.

Rose had risen before dawn that morning. It had been a full day of Easter egg hunts and woven baskets filled with chocolate, frying *manicotti* shells, mashing sweet potatoes, basting the ham and so on. Now, at eight in the evening, she was pleasantly tired. Tiger was bushed as well, for the baby had him and Terry waking at odd hours. Dr. Seminara himself was battle-weary and bleary-eyed. Though he enjoyed the company, he knew it was time to take his leave.

At the front door, Rose told Dr. Seminara that Sully would be sorry he missed him. "He's driving my old sister-in-law Mary and brother-in-law Tommy back to their rooming house in Sea Gate," Rose explained.

"Please give Sully my regards and thank Terry for her hospitality," Dr. Seminara said. "And thanks to you, too," he called to Tiger, who was clearing the table. "You have a lovely home." Tiger told him that he was very welcome and that he should come back. There was always room for him at their table.

"It was a good Easter," Tiger said to Rose after the doctor had left.

"It's always a good Easter," she smiled. "Except for that one when you were about ten." They laughed together in remembrance of the Sweet Potato Incident, though it hadn't been funny at the time.

"But the years seem to mellow even the bad memories, don't they?" Tiger offered. "And looking back, they don't seem so bad after all."

Rose begged to differ but she didn't breathe a word of dissent to Tiger. Her years with Tony had been difficult, nightmarish, but she was glad that she'd survived, thankful that they'd all survived.

Rose bid her son a good night and made her way upstairs.

CHAPTER THIRTY-ONE

Wedding Bells

"Whose bright idea was it to have your wedding two weeks after the opening?" George asked. He was perspiring heavily as he chopped onions and cussing under his breath as he often did when he was flustered. But like a sudden summer storm, George's wrath soon passed.

Stan felt compelled to answer George's rhetorical question though he knew he wasn't required to do so. "Two weeks and six days to be exact," Stan pointed out. "And as I recall, it was a joint decision."

George glared at Stan.

"Besides, we thought all the kinks would be worked out by then," Stan said. After a beat, he added, "At least most of them." He slipped the pile of minced garlic he'd made toward George, a peace offering of sorts. George swiped it into the pot right after the onions.

Len was determined to stay out of it, quietly deboning chicken thighs to be marinated in a piquant *mojo* sauce. "What do you think, Len?" George posed, dragging him right into the fray.

"I think the opening went off without a hitch," Len told him. "This is the third one. You seem to have it down pat."

And indeed, due to his expertise, George was called to Sherman the week before the new restaurant's unveiling—to lend a hand and offer guidance. Not only was Feel Good Food packed on opening day but every dish came out of the kitchen perfect. By the time they closed their doors, what they thought to be a plentiful supply of food disappeared. It seemed as though all the inhabitants of the "one-horse Yankee town" (as George dubbed it) and the surrounding areas of Danbury, Kent and New Milford, even Wingdale and Pawling, New York, had anxiously anticipated Feel Good Food's ribbon-cutting, and were in attendance.

"It's the most exciting thing that's happened around here since the Sherman Volunteer Fire Department got a new pumper rig," Bill explained.

Two days before Stan's impending wedding bells, George and his crew were prepping what they could after hours, crafting the celebration's *hors d'oeuvres* and storing them in the commercial-grade Frigidaire. They marinated the pork shoulder and chicken, and did whatever else they could do in advance. The following day, the Martinos, Sullivans, O'Learys, Palumbos, Corsos and what-have-yous (with Granny Lulu in tow) would descend upon the colonial Connecticut town, which would never be the same again. The motorcade of cars would carry tins and trays of *lasagna*, meatballs, sausages and other Italian specialties. "Besides, we're just doing the appetizers," Stan reminded George.

"Just!" George echoed. "Just!"

Stan knew that George secretly enjoyed the bustle of the kitchen and sailing through a cooking deadline he deemed unreasonable and unattainable. Especially when this meant making a meal for people he knew—and was quite fond of. Stan planted a fat, juicy kiss on George's cheek just to hear him complain some more. "You know you love it," Stan told George. Then more softly, Stan added, "Thank you."

Although George harrumphed in reply, Stan had worked beside him long enough in the kitchen to know that George's growl translated to "You're welcome."

Bright and early the following day, the Brooklyn convoy was scheduled to begin the slow crawl north and slightly east, the trunks of their Dodges, Fords and Pontiacs jam-packed with garment sacks filled with suits, dresses, gowns, girdles and other unmentionables, shoes, heels, hose and weekend bags. The trays of pastas, meats and whatnot were strategically placed on the floors between feet or else cradled on laps like children. The front and back seats were packed with passengers.

These individuals convened in front of 1128 and 1130 Forty-Seventh Street, the drivers discussing the route, the copilots clutching directions which were carefully scrawled onto sheets of paper. Snacks were assembled and at the ready for the less-than-two-hour drive, and there was a carefully-chosen restroom on the way just in case they needed to stop.

Many of the revelers took the second Friday in May off from work to make Stan and Wendy's wedding a special sort of holiday weekend. Astrid and Al would be riding the train up later that evening, as Old Man Trump (a.k.a. "the rat bastard") refused to let Al take a vacation day.

Six rooms were secured at the Rocky River Inn located in nearby New Milford alongside the rushing waters of the Housatonic River. The wedding guests would bunk there, all except for Granny Lulu. Mrs. Simpson insisted that Len's grandmother stay at her home as a guest, in the frilly room off the parlor she reserved for folks like this. Len tried to beg off, silently concerned about his landlady's possible reaction to the skin color of this proud Jamaican woman, which was several shades darker than his. But Mrs. Simpson pressed and Len relented, hoping for the best.

And speaking of Granny Lulu, Camille and John offered to make a detour to pick up the elderly woman at her doorstep, adamant that the slight diversion was indeed on the way (it was) and no trouble at all (it wasn't). Besides, the thought of this slight but steadfast woman well into her seventies navigating Grand Central Terminal along the Metropolitan-North train line with a suitcase was something they couldn't abide by. In a few short months, Granny Lulu had become part of their extended family along with Len, formerly known as Morty.

Granny waited for the Palumbos on the sidewalk in front of the nicely-kept, four-story blonde brick building where she had a two-bedroom apartment. She wore a prim flower-print dress and a Sunday go-to-meeting hat pinned to her still-thick snowy hair, smiling in anticipation of a weekend away in the country.

John sat in the back so Granny Lulu could stretch out her bum leg in the roomier front seat while Camille drove. Infinitely more patient behind the wheel than her husband, Camille didn't curse like a drunken sailor if someone cut her off. "Last time I went away, it was to my brother Elvin's funeral down in Fayetteville," Granny Lulu confessed as she got into the Palumbo sedan.

"It will be good to take a trip for a happy occasion," Camille told her as they headed toward the Throgs Neck Bridge, which the older woman called "the Frog's Neck." They opted for the more scenic route through Queens and the Bronx rather than taking the Williamsburg Bridge and going through Manhattan. Granny Lulu remarked that she missed Len "like the Dickens" and who didn't love a wedding?

Augie's wood-paneled Country Squire made its way north, filled with lively conversation. The twins were excited about their wedding duties—distributing programs and helping seat the guests. Too old to be flower girl and ring bearer but not old enough to be official members of the wedding party, they knew this was an awesome responsibility. "The bride's side is on the right and the groom side is on the left," David told his sister. "Right?"

"For the millionth time, wrong!" Beth groaned.

David laughed, triumphant. Angela intervened, "He's doing it just to get your goat. You know that, don't you, Elizabeth?"

"But he's so annoying!" Beth sighed, poking her brother. Augie smiled, eager to have a weekend off to spend with his family. The Loew's 46th was in the able hands of Tiger's old pal Jimmy Burns, who often helped out. Augie was thinking of asking Jimmy if he'd sign on as assistant manager if the next few days went smoothly. (The previous fellow in that slot, Larry, hadn't worked out.)

"How many people will be there? Besides all of us?" David asked.

"It's hard to guess," Angela told him. "Ti-Tu and Lily will be coming in from the Island. Tyrone and the rest of the Thomases are driving all the way from Jersey. The wedding was announced Holy Trinity's Banns of Marriage, so you never know who will turn up from the parish."

"There isn't much to do in a little town like Sherman," Augie said thoughtfully.

"And how would you know?" his wife challenged. "You've only been there once, for the opening." Angela added proudly, "Stan says folks have really taken to the place."

"And they've only been open a couple of weeks," Augie said. "That's great news."

"But remember, they've been working on it since the winter. People have been keeping their eye on it. I bet the locals are happy, too. One less vacant storefront is good thing."

"This is true," Augie admitted.

"Plus, my brother has a magnetic personality," Angela added. "I'll bet Stan's made loads of friends in Sherman already."

From the backseat, Beth suddenly piped, "I can't believe we're going to lose Cousin Wendy and Cousin Stan at the same time. That they're both moving all the way up to the boonies."

"They'll do anything to get away from you," David told Beth under his breath. Then, to his parents, "Wendy says it's a big opportunity. For her at the paper and Stan at the restaurant."

"Sherman is not the Arctic Circle," Angela said, trying to console Beth, who was starting to sniffle.

"Don't start blubbering," David warned his sister. "You'll get all blotchy. You don't want that. You'll look like Coleen Gray in *The Leech Woman*." (The sci-fi flick had played the week before at the Loew's 46th and scared the bejesus out of the twins.)

"I swear, you two," Angela began, exasperated. "When you were babies, you couldn't sleep unless you were curled around each other. Now you can barely be civil to one another in a car for two hours."

"But he started it!" Beth screeched.

"No, she did!" David countered. Beth's lower lip quivered and she dug her fists into her eyes to keep from crying.

Already this morning, Beth had flown into hysterics over the hint of a pimple which had started to sprout on her forehead. Angela couldn't take another meltdown. She gently swatted her son's knee from the front seat. "Hey, what's that for?" David asked.

"You know what it's for," Angela told him.

In the rearview mirror, Augie saw his daughter fold her arms over her chest and then saw his son pull a face at his sister. "Don't make me stop this car," Augie warned them. His children retreated to neutral corners of the vehicle and stared out their respective windows. Augie smiled at Angela, content, the back of the Country Squire packed to the gills with the overflow of luggage and garment bags containing all sorts of finery, one of which contained Wendy's crown, dress and veil.

A few cars ahead of Augie's station wagon was Sully's Coronet. Though several years old, it still ran like a charm. Chiara Rose was in the front seat between him and Rose, sleeping on her grandmother's shoulder. Though normally a bundle of energy, the girl was powerless against the motion of a moving car, which instantly lulled her to sleep. Little Mike slumbered peacefully in his mother's arms and Tiger uncharacteristically dozed against Terry. He had been working long hours, shuttling to and from Connecticut in anticipation of the eatery's opening and occasionally pitching in at Jersey City in addition to his duties in Brooklyn. Rose and Terry conversed quietly from front to backseat. "How Momma and Poppa would have loved this wedding," Rose said. "And yours and Tiger's. It's a shame you never really knew them."

"But I feel like I do," Terry conceded. "We live in their old place. We have some of their furniture. I feel their presence all the time."

"Me too," Rose said. "They're constantly making mischief to make sure we don't forget them."

"How so?" Terry wondered.

Rose began, "Well, you might think I'm crazy but sometimes I find the kitchen window open when I know I've closed it. Sometimes the Frigidaire door is open when I'm sure I've closed it too."

"I don't think you're crazy," Terry said. "For us, it's the back door. It's wide open sometimes when I know I locked it."

"That's them," Rose nodded. "I know it's them."

Sully shook his head. "That's pure hogwash. Guinea superstition."

"That's not what you say when Poppa takes your pipe and hides it on you," Rose reminded him.

"Point well taken," Sully admitted. "I do feel them sometimes. Okay, a lot of the time."

Rose turned in her seat and caressed her grandson's cheek. "And in this little guy. I think he favors my father. I hope you don't mind me saying so, dear."

"I don't mind at all," Terry said. "In fact, I love hearing it. And I think he does look like Poppa." The two women clasped hands, front seat to back.

There wasn't much conversation in Harry's Pontiac. The three inhabitants sat in contemplation, each lost in their own thoughts. Sporadically, one would speak but the exchange was brief. Jo gazed out the passenger-side window, watching the landscape morph from city to suburbs to country. From the backseat, Wendy rested a palm on each of her parents' shoulders. "Thank you," she said. "For all of this."

"It's what parents do for their daughters," Harry told her, shrugging off the compliment.

"Not all of them," Wendy said. "I just want you to know that I really appreciate it."

"You're welcome, dear," Jo smiled. "It's our pleasure."

"I know it must be costing you an arm and a leg. The gowns, the…"

"Nonsense," Harry said. "We've been saving up for your wedding day since you were born. A little each week. It will be my honor to walk you down the aisle, Wendy, to give you away…"

"*Give* me away?" Wendy sparred. "Nobody's giving anybody away."

Jo stepped in. "It's just an expression, honey."

"But it's an example of the patriarchy. That women are owned," Wendy pointed out.

Harry changed lanes on the parkway. "Listen, I know that nobody owns you. Or owns any woman. But especially not you. All I mean is that I'm happy to be part of this. Happy you two didn't decide to elope."

Wendy simmered down, doing her best to control her fiery Irish and Italian temper—a sometimes lethal combination of heritage. "I'm glad we didn't either, though the thought did cross our minds," she divulged. "Sometimes a wedding seems like an awful lot of trouble."

"It does but it's worth it," Jo said. "Your dad and I just ran off to City Hall then had Father Dunn do a blessing at St. Catherine's. I'm afraid I broke my mother's heart by not having a true church wedding."

Wendy leaned forward and kissed her mother on the cheek. "I think she forgave you," she told Jo. "Grandma Bridget loved you to pieces. You were a good daughter."

"You are too," Jo admitted, her voice cracking. "And Stanley will make a fine husband."

Harry glanced over at his female passengers, their faces starting to pinken and puff as they held their tears. "Now, don't go bawling on me," he warned. "Or else I'll start too."

The Pontiac was quiet for several miles. They were nearing Pawling, New York, which was only twenty or so miles from Sherman. Harry broke the silence. "Without you two getting emotional, I just want to say that I'm glad Wendy and Stan ended up together," he ventured. "True, he went through a rough patch but who didn't? He turned himself around. Wendy, you and he have been close since you were babies. I think you make a great team. You bring out the best in each other."

The women looked at Harry in surprise, for such a poignant speech was highly uncustomary for a hard-nosed ex-cop like him. Both Jo and Wendy knew Harry was an old softie on the inside and let him speechify without interruption. "I'm glad I'm around to see it, though I'm sorry you'll be moving so far away," Harry said.

"Like Aunt Astrid says, Connecticut's not China," Wendy reminded them. They laughed in spite of themselves. If a few tears slipped out amid the laughter, no one seemed to notice.

So, the Brooklyn caravan made its way to Sherman. The drivers did an excellent job keeping the cars close together so the children could occasionally wave to each other. Just as they'd planned, all four vehicles pulled into a gas station at the crossroads in Patterson, where Route 22 met Route 37. Chiara Rose was doing the "pee-pee dance," so Rose took her inside, warning her not to sit on the service station's toilet seat or else a multitude of horrific diseases would overtake her nether parts. The men stood outside, talking after their gas tanks were filled. Angela took a turn at holding her nephew, falling into the familiar speech pattern of cooing that women are so prone to use with infants, the same, soft lilting voice that females all over the world seemed to practice with babies, no matter their native tongue. The rest stop tableau could have been a boilerplate for a Manet or a Rockwell painting, except it transpired at a rural filling station.

"I read about this place," John said, gesturing to a stucco building next door to the gas station. On the lawn outside were old kids' bikes painted in garish colors and other assorted junk, also vibrantly decorated. A hand-lettered sign with a real hobby horse at the top read "Rosemary's Texas Taco." John continued, "There was an article about this restaurant in the *Daily News*. The owner started with a taco truck in Manhattan and did so well, she opened this place in the 'burbs."

"Let's stop in for a bite," Harry suggested. "Give a local business some business."

"But we've got plenty of snacks in the car," Jo told him.

"I've got to maintain my figure," Harry said, patting his belly. "Come on, just a taste."

The Brooklyn contingent descended upon Rosemary's Texas Taco. Chiara was charmed by the owner, a wiry woman who sported a purple Mohawk haircut and wore her makeup boldly, as though it were warpaint. They pushed tables together and ordered a slew of tacos (the only thing on the menu) and soft drinks, marveling at the eclectic décor while they waited for their food. Granny Lulu refused to order a thing in "that dag-blasted place," not even a cup of water.

Golden garlands were strung from the rafters, as well as fake flowers and stuffed animals. Every inch of Rosemary's Texas Taco was covered by something—discarded baby dolls, pink flamingoes, Christmas lights. Many were in awe of the place while others were in shock. "I've got to talk to Tiger about decorating Feel Good Food like this," Augie said, breaking the silence. "Maybe I'll even redo the Loew's 46th. What do you think?"

The tables exploded in laughter as Rosemary and her helper brought their order. When the group finished their meal, the owner promised to show Chiara something special. The girl ate quickly, savoring each bite. Everyone was pleasantly surprised at the tastiness of the food—uncomplicated Lone Star-State style tacos, no frills. Granny Lulu agreed to take a small taste of Terry's beef concoction and gave it a grudging nod of approval.

Chiara was in heaven when Rosemary led her by the hand to show her the ladies' room. Terry was trepidatious at her child going off to the bathroom with a strange, lilac-maned woman but under all the makeup and hair dye, Rosemary seemed like a fine person.

Texas Taco's restroom was a mermaid's dream, covered in gold spray-painted seashells and ocean creatures, all gilded to gawdy perfection. The sounds of crashing waves completed the picture. Chiara was charmed and washed her hands several times (an act she usually balked at doing even once) because the place was so fascinating. After Chiara's glowing report, each of the women had to see the ladies' loo for themselves. They were equally as impressed, even Granny Lulu.

The cavalcade hit the road, full of talk about Rosemary's Texas Taco. Sucking on the cactus-flavored lollipop Rosemary had given her, Chiara was blissfully silent. Opting for the scenic route, they passed the Quaker Hill Museum in Pawling. They stopped to snap photographs of the odd Victorian stone structure capped with a green witch hat-like steeple. The museum certainly appeared haunted.

In the forty-odd minutes it took to reach Sherman, Wendy fretted each and every mile. Would she make a good wife? Would Stan make a good husband? Would they survive so far from their families? Would she be a good reporter? Would the restaurant continue to do well or would it crash and burn after a few months?

Wendy's parents took note of her pensiveness but they said not a word. Harry studied Wendy's worried reflection in the rearview mirror as he turned onto Route 37. They drove the remainder of the trip in silence, Jo taking Harry's hand on the leather upholstery between them as he gripped the wheel with the other. They smiled in reassurance and love.

The decision had been made for everyone to rendezvous at Feel Good Food rather than go straight to the Rocky River Inn. (How could they not?) Of course, they had made a similar journey for the restaurant's opening two weeks earlier (how could they not?) but they were anxious to see "the boys." Although the eatery was full and a party of three was waiting for a free table, Stan couldn't resist taking a moment to jog outdoors to the parking lot to greet his family. The sight of Stan in his chef's whites and checkered pants took Wendy's breath away. She flew out of the car and into his arms. "I missed you, you knucklehead," she sighed before he kissed her.

"I missed you too, you knucklehead," Stan said.

They quickly moved the food the cars carried into the restaurant's huge, industrial refrigerators, using the back door.

And when the bells of Holy Trinity Church rang a few blocks away, all of Wendy's fears and doubts rang away with them. Announcing neither the hour, the half hour nor a mass, the bells were in honor of the sacrament which would transpire the next day. They were indeed wedding bells.

You see, Father Kiernan was always looking for an excuse to ring Holy Trinity's carillons in celebration. So, when he saw the Brooklyn procession drive past the church, he climbed the bell tower himself to complete the joyous task.

CHAPTER THIRTY-TWO

Just Married

Wendy slept heavily and deeply the night before her wedding. There was so much going on that she was exhausted. From the practice run at Holy Trinity to the rehearsal supper (they went to the French place in town to give the Feel Good Food crew a break) to picking up Astrid and Al at the Pawling train station, they were busy practically every second.

The wedding party occupied several connected rooms at the Rocky River Inn and freely moved between each. This facilitated the men's card-playing, the women chatting and fussing with each other's hair and makeup plus giving the bride-to-be unsolicited marital advice. Rather than go back to the attic room at Mrs. Simpson's, Stan decided to bunk with his parents at the inn so he could spend more time with his family—and Wendy.

She woke long before anyone else, well-rested yet restless with excitement. Dressing silently in slacks and a warm button-down shirt, Wendy went outside and followed the stone-strewn Housatonic River that gave the motel its name, tracking the path of the rushing waters whose soothing voice treated her to such a peaceful sleep the night before. She had only been tracing the arc of the watercourse a few moments when she heard a voice. "Having second thoughts?" it wondered.

Wendy turned. It was Stan, holding two paper cartons: coffee for him, tea for her. Wendy shook her head. "No second thoughts," she assured him. "I can't wait to be your wife."

Although it had been difficult, Wendy and Stan agreed to "save themselves" for their wedding night. This surprised Stan, for he waited for nothing, for no one, as evidenced by his alleyway fumblings with Betsy Mulaney and his brief trysts with others. But Stan didn't want to sneak off with Wendy to a no-tell motel like the Golden Gate Inn in Sheepshead Bay. Why? Because she, and perhaps even he, deserved much better than that. So, they waited.

Wendy accepted Stan's cardboard cup of tea and sipped. It was still warm. She detected the sweetness of honey which her almost-husband knew she preferred to sugar. The syrupy scent rose above the mustiness of the forest floor. "You?" she asked. "Second thoughts?"

Stan shook his head. "But third thoughts. And fourth," he joked.

"Be serious, Stanley!" Wendy demanded.

"I'm never serious," Stan said. "You should know that by now." After another slug of Java, he conceded, "I can't believe this day has finally come." Stan kissed Wendy firmly on the mouth, black coffee melding with honeyed tea. He set both cartons onto the soft earth and stood behind her, cupping Wendy's body against his. They watched the river, listened to its voice. And as they listened, Wendy felt Stan's desire grow against her bottom. Instead of stepping away, she pressed into it, pulled his arms tighter around her in the morning chill. "I want to be a good husband," Stan said.

"I want to be a good wife," Wendy countered.

"Don't worry," he told her. "We'll show each other how."

"I'm not worried," Wendy smiled. "I know we will." She hesitated, "But will we miss our families being way out here?"

"Of course, we will," he said. "Missing people shows you love them."

"But we'll see them. A lot." Stan nodded against the top of Wendy's head, which was nestled beneath his chin. Her hair smelled of the Johnson's Baby Shampoo she still used. He liked that.

"Maybe they'll even let us take a holiday," he proposed. "You know, have everyone over for a family meal at our place."

"Do you think?" she asked hopefully.

Stan nodded again. "Maybe one of the smaller ones, like Palm Sunday. We'll cook together, you and me."

"I'd like that," Wendy told him.

They stood and watched the woods, heard what it had to say. A chipmunk darted on the evergreen-carpeted ground. A brown hare nosed hesitantly from the grasses. Stan told Wendy the names of the birds they heard. The mourning dove's cry, the tufted titmouse who seemed to call "Pe-ter, Pe-ter," the hack of the blue jay. "Bill and Len seem to know them all," Stan admitted. "I'm still learning."

"You'll teach me," Wendy told him. "And our children."

"The woods around our house is lousy with birds," he told her. "You'll see."

When the family had come up for Feel Good Food's opening, Stan took Wendy to see a two-bedroom cottage just off Route 39, near Tollgate Brook. The cottage belonged to a friend of Mrs. Simpson's who had fallen ill and had been recently taken in by her son. The woman, who was named Valerie Watson, was expected to recover but not enough to live on her own. "The family is looking to rent it," Stan told Wendy. "Then possibly sell it."

"Why, I thought I was supposed to move in with you in the attic room at Mrs. Simpson's and Len was going to take the other spare room."

"This will be a lot nicer," Stan offered.

Wendy nodded. "Sometimes things happen for a reason. Serendipity …a happy accident," she explained.

"That too," he said.

Inside, Valerie's cottage was something out of a fairy tale, neat as a pin and completely furnished. The closets were empty of Val's belongings, ready to be filled with theirs. "Oh, it's darling," Wendy exclaimed.

After their brief one-night honeymoon at the Rocky River Inn, this is where Stan and Wendy would spend their days and nights together, where they would begin to build their lives together. It had all fallen into place as it should. The cottage was so close to the shop that Stan could walk to work or Wendy could drop him off before she drove to the *News Times* in Danbury, which was thirty minutes away. But they would have to get a car first. That was their next hurdle.

In the enchanted forest on the morning of their wedding, Wendy told Stan, "I'm glad you didn't sleep in the cottage without me last night."

"I wanted my first night there to be with you," he said. The sun had pulled higher into the sky. They watched it glint through the trees. "I guess we should get going," Stan told her.

Wendy agreed. "They should be up by now. They might think we skipped town."

Stan smiled. They took their cardboard cups of tea and coffee, both cold by now, and walked back to the Rocky River Inn, holding hands, sharing one last kiss as they went.

No one expected the pews of Holy Trinity Church to be so filled with parishioners but it seemed as though the entire community of Sherman and perhaps even New Milford came out to show their solidarity with the town's newest business. Mr. Rizzo, who owned Sherman's gas station (where Bill had previously worked), along with his wife Jo Ann, were in attendance. Ralph Rizzo took pride in boasting that he was indirectly responsible for Feel Good Food settling in Sherman, as well as the wedding being held there. Mrs. Simpson arrived with all her friends in tow, forming an elderly entourage. Old biddies lived and breathed for events like this, for who didn't love young love? Then there was Tracey, the checkout girl at the I.G.A., and her brother Todd. There were even a few men from the volunteer fire department lining the pews.

The Paradiso Family from "The Land of Steady Habits" showed up in full force. This included the bride and groom's Uncle Julius and Aunt Lettie, who were back from traveling the world and were enjoying life in Fairfield, Connecticut less than an hour away. Lettie was gorgeous and gracious in all of her frail Czech beauty, in a china blue dress which matched her eyes. On the arms of their sons Matty and Carlo were their wives Jane and Denise, plus their own sons Jediah, Michael and Christopher. Terry's Aunt Bea and Uncle Nello drove in from Waterbury.

Several friends and neighbors from Forty-Seventh Street gladly made the pleasant Saturday drive up from Brooklyn. As promised, Nunzi and Violetta DeMeo attended, bringing an armload of lilacs and forsythia from their garden to decorate Holy Trinity's altar. For the Connecticut pilgrimage, the branches were laid on a blanket in their backseat as lovingly as one would set down a baby. Kevin Houlihan (a.k.a. "Houlie") from Farrell's and his wife Kaye even showed.

Dr. and Mrs. Lewis came as well. It was one of those rare times the devout Jews had been in a Catholic church. The good doctor was planning to retire soon, and though he and Eva were keen on their native Brooklyn, they were seeking a bucolic country hamlet to settle in their golden years. Eva thought Sherman just might be the place. After all, they already knew people there plus it had the best little eatery which sometimes served Eva's sweet noodle kugel. Though elderly, the Ortez Vegas attended the wedding too, said they wouldn't miss it for the world.

Beth and David had the challenging task of seating guests. It was challenging because when they asked most folks if they were there for the bride or the groom, people—like George, Elaine and their family, for instance—often responded with a jolly, "Both!" Amongst themselves, the twins agreed to disburse the attendees evenly between either section of the oak pews because the "side" debacle was just too confusing otherwise.

The music teacher at the Sherman School, Aldo Bruschi, a tall, dark-haired man with fuzzy knuckles, had been engaged to play Holy Trinity's pipe organ, which he did every Sunday and on occasions such as this. Mrs. Simpson volunteered to sing "Ave Maria" after the exchange of wedding vows, which Stan accepted with trepidation. He'd never heard his aged landlady sing, not even as she puttered around the house. But how could he refuse such an offer?

As it had been prearranged, Len escorted several of the unescorted women down the aisle. First, he showed Granny Lulu to her seat. The old gal was lovely in a mauve frock and matching wide-brim hat. Then Len went to fetch Terry, so pretty in her satin shift, carrying Little Mike. Len deposited them in the front row beside Granny, who gladly took the baby when he started to fuss. Lastly, Len led Amy to her seat, simply radiant in a yellow pencil-cut suit and parson's hat. His breath caught in his throat when she took his arm. He didn't need to tell Granny Lulu that Amy was "the one" for she could see it in his eyes.

Finally, everyone was seated and all was ready. Augie's children took their places beside him in the first pew.

Tiger stood on the altar as Mr. Bruschi began Mendelssohn's "Wedding March." Wendy and Stan's uncles Al and John, looking dapper in their Zeller tuxedos, escorted the couple's aunts (their respective wives). Each man had a sprig of lily of the valley in his lapel while each woman held a single calla lily. Their gowns, in a shade called "blush," were exquisite and each auntie was beautiful in a different way. It took all of their husbands' reserve not to cry.

Angela, the maid of honor, followed the bridesmaids and groomsmen, alone. She looked regal as she strode, smiling widely and filled with joy. Angela's gown was a slightly darker shade of pink than the others.

The wedding guests seemed to hold their breath as Chiara Rose made her way toward the altar, a vision in bright pink. Those familiar with the girl were aware that her conduct could often be erratic but this day she behaved, taking her role as flower girl quite seriously. Chiara scattered just the right amount of rosy petals to her left then to her right with each step. She didn't trip nor skip nor run nor rush. By the time she reached Holy Trinity's altar, one final handful of rose petals remained in the basket. She sprinkled it at her own feet then took her place beside her mother and brother in the front pew. Granny Lulu offered the girl an already-unwrapped Brach's butterscotch candy as a reward for her good behavior.

Stan and Wendy broke with tradition when they chose to have both of their parents escort them to the altar. They had been to a handful of Jewish weddings where this was a common practice and decided they wanted to do this as well. Though Father Kiernan was skeptical at first, he agreed when Wendy told him plainly, "Our parents are equally important to us, Father."

Rose, in a navy-blue gown, looked glorious, ecstatic that the foundling she had welcomed into her life decades earlier would soon be a husband. Sully was strong and stalwart but those who knew him could tell that he was on the verge of tears, for this young child he had taken as his son (and given his name) soon after he had taken Rose as his wife, was getting married, and Sully now had the honor of walking him down the aisle.

Wendy was glad she had her parents, one on either side of her, to support her as they did all of her life, for without them, she surely would have fallen. Her legs trembled beneath the layers of satin and Venetian lace. She was thankful she'd chosen to wear low-heeled pumps, for otherwise, she was certain she would have tripped. In her shaking hands, Wendy held a magnificent bouquet of ruby-red "Just Married" roses.

When Wendy, Harry and Jo came into view, a hush fell across Holy Trinity. The bride was so stunning, she hardly seemed real. Ethereal, like a cloud or a dream that hadn't yet been imagined. With his arm slipped through his daughter's, Harry's limp was barely noticeable. Perhaps because all eyes were focused on the resplendent bride. Perhaps because Harry was supported by the women he loved, Mr. O'Leary appeared a steady ship rocking on a still sea. And Jo reflected the beauty of her daughter, swathed in an emerald gown the shade of shimmering gemstones.

Father Kiernan stood front and center at the altar, a sparse, modern, yet striking structure, made more impressive by the huge vases of lilacs and forsythia, skillfully arranged by Violetta DeMeo. Behind the priest was a wall of hewn river stone. Set into the stone was a stained-glass disk of the Father, Son and Holy Ghost (which could have been fashioned by Picasso). It created the perfect backdrop.

Harry raised the mantilla of lace that covered his daughter's beatific face, kissed her cheek then took his place in the pew, leaving Wendy to climb the altar steps to her husband, alone. "Dearly beloved, we are gathered here..." began Father Kiernan.

Strategically-placed handkerchiefs and Kleenex tissues were used liberally throughout the ceremony. Father Kiernan, who was known for his heartfelt sermons, outdid himself this day. He had taken the liberty of getting to know Stanley for the brief time he'd worked in Sherman and Father K. (as Stan called him) was impressed with the young man's drive and fortitude. Just one conversation with Wendy the evening before and the priest knew she was a fine woman, an asset to any man or any community fortunate enough to have her.

"...but the greatest of these is love," Father Kiernan continued.

When it came time for Wendy and Stan to exchange their wedding vows, they did so in voices that were clear and strong and certain. They had loved each other since they were babies, often sharing the same crib and sleeping in each other's arms. Their marriage was merely an extension, a maturation of this love.

Tiger easily found their rings in his tuxedo pocket. They were simple circles of yellow gold, Wendy's so much more delicate than her intended's. Stan's ring was large enough to pass over his knuckle, a tortured joint which had known cuts from kitchen knives and graters. Tiger did not drop the rings as he had feared, but placed them surely into Father Kiernan's palm.

As Aldo Bruschi began the familiar chords of "Ave Maria," Arlene Simpson joined him in song in a voice that seemed uncharacteristic for such old fussbudget. It was sweet yet not saccharine. It was ardent yet not cold. It caused tears to be welled up in chests, tears that didn't reach the eyes but somehow touched the soul. Wendy and Stan looked at each other in surprise. She squeezed his hand; he squeezed back in the silent language that long married people sometimes have but is rarely seen in newlyweds.

And far off in the shadows in the rear of Holy Trinity Church, Wendy saw an elderly woman standing beside an elderly man, their arms intertwined. The woman wore a dark, simple shift. Her hair, faded to several shades of silver, was wound into a bun that her husband fondly referred to as her "meatball." The man was dressed in a freshly-pressed but careworn three-piece suit. He sported small, round spectacles similar to those President Roosevelt had worn. A pocket watch (a gift upon his retirement from the Brooklyn Navy Yard) gleamed in the dim light. The old couple smiled at the young couple at the altar.

As Mrs. Simpson held the closing note of "Ave Maria" for an impossibly long moment, Wendy tugged upon her new husband's arm, eager to point out the old folks in the back of the church. But by then, it was too late for they were already gone. And besides, it was now time to kiss her husband. When the couple's lips met, the entire church erupted into applause.

For the recessional hymn, Mr. Bruschi chose Handel's "The Arrival of the Queen of Sheba," not well-known but perfect in his eyes for it was jaunty, upbeat and lively, like the coming of a long-awaited spring after an endless, heartless winter. Wendy and Stan led the way, laughing down the aisle. The wedding party spilled into the nave, followed by Chiara Rose, her parents, grandparents and all the rest.

On the steps of Holy Trinity, anyone within firing range was pelted with hunks of rice and the sugar-coated almond candies Italians were partial to hurling at just-married couples. Parked outside the church was a burgundy and cream Chevy no one had seen before. "What's this?" Stan asked his father-in-law over the celebratory din.

"It's yours," Harry said. "We knew you two needed a car to get around in the country…"

"…and to visit us in Brooklyn," Jo added.

"A bunch of us pooled our resources," Harry continued. "Rizzo was on the lookout for something special and this is it. A '55 Bel Air. Not brand new but runs like a top."

"Do you like it?" Jo wondered.

"It's perfect," Wendy told them.

Harry handed Stan the keys. He and Wendy hopped inside the Bel Air. Stan drove as slowly as possible to Feel Good Food, while the guests from Holy Trinity Church followed them on foot.

CHAPTER THIRTY-THREE

Rainbow's End

Stan and Wendy's wedding reception was indeed a grand affair. Not that they served elegant victuals like caviar and lobster but it was "grand" in the sense of being memorable. Guests you would never imagine having a single thing in common chatted away like old friends. For example, Mrs. Simpson and Granny Lulu, Dr. Lewis and Father Kiernan, Rose and Jo Ann Rizzo. The lead question was often "So, how do you know Stan and Wendy?" The conversation took off like blazes from there.

As expected, Terry and Joan Karpi talked about their new babies, comparing boys to girls, discussing fussiness, the quality of diapers and the intricacies of their own daughters as well. Though Karen was much younger than Chiara Rose, the older girl took the younger one under her wing, making sure she had enough to eat, concocting little games to amuse her and telling her stories about Brooklyn and its quirky residents.

The Feel Good Food establishment itself was beautifully appointed and took on a radiance in the late afternoon glow. Although it wasn't yet dark, candles in cut-glass cups glittered from each table. Vases of spring flowers of every variety were placed beside the candles: tulips and crocus along with lilacs and forsythia.

For the café tables, Wendy had chosen linen of blush pink which matched the wedding party's gowns. Astrid gladly whipped up a dozen tablecloths in one evening and was honored Wendy had asked her to do the task. 'History repeats itself,' Astrid thought as she worked at her streamlined mint green portable Singer sewing machine, recalling how she'd also done the table dressings, as well as the curtains, for the shop's Brooklyn outpost. (Elaine Thomas had mirrored Astrid's actions for the New Jersey place.) Bill managed to borrow card tables from Holy Trinity to set up in the garden out back. They were decorated to the nines as well.

Bill's brother Ron and Miles pitched in to finish preparing and serve the food, which was set out in huge trays buffet-style. They'd hired two local boys to clear away plates and utensils, wash them and put them out again. This way, Feel Good Food's owners and managers could enjoy the festivities without lifting a finger to see that they ran smoothly. Ron and his crew made sure of that.

The wedding cake was made by a local lady named Liz, who, along with her husband Karl (and their five children!) ran the Quaker Cove Camp and Retreat on the shores of Candlewood Lake. The camp paid them but a pittance for all of their hard work, so Liz baked cakes on the side, cakes which looked too gorgeous to eat but tasted even better than they looked.

For these particular newlyweds, Liz created a three-tiered masterpiece of ivory frosting with pastel-colored buttercream flowers cascading over the edges, white cake with vanilla and strawberry custard inside. As she crafted her confections, Liz always filled them good wishes and warm thoughts, and especially, with love. This cake was no exception.

The young couple moved from table to table like butterflies in a garden, neglecting no one and making every guest feel important, which they indeed were. Stan and Wendy were overwhelmed by the boxes piling up on the gift table and the long, narrow envelopes accumulating in the traditional satin pouch Wendy carried. "A busta," the old Italians called it. The word "busta" literally translated to "envelope," but the term "a busta" had come to mean "a boost"—meaning that the monetary gift inside the envelope would be a boost to get the young couple off to a strong start.

Unwrapped and propped up on the gift table was a charming landscape painting of a country barn, a weeping willow tree and a trellis of roses. With a glance, Wendy knew this was from Uncle Julius and Aunt Lettie. She smiled about the roses, aware that Uncle Jul included them in the picture because he knew Wendy prized roses, as all Paradiso women did. She and Stan would later learn that to the back of the painting was affixed an envelope filled with a generous amount of cash.

Behind Feel Good Food, the grassy area Joan promised to turn into a proper garden was decorated with great pots of flowers from Bloomingfields Farm: gardenias, hyacinths and daffodils. The card tables were also festooned with Aunt Astrid's fine pink cloths and more candles in their cut-glass holders. The guests chatted amicably as the sun continued its journey west, painting the sky with the most captivating purples and pinks.

In Feel Good Food's garden-to-be, during what is known as "the magic hour" or the "golden hour"—those enchanted few minutes just before sunset when the light is exquisite—Len crossed paths with Amy. Her saffron-shaded suit was especially becoming with her rich complexion and he told her so. "I think it's just the light," Amy demurred, blushing. She never did know how to field a compliment.

"No, it's more than just the light," Len told her.

"It's that special time of day," she stammered. "Some call it the gloaming," she explained. "You know, twilight."

"It's not twilight or the gloaming," Len pressed. "It's you…and that smart suit."

"I thank you very much, kind sir," Amy said with a curtsey. "There's a little shop in New Haven where an old Italian woman will make you anything you want. I fell in love with the fabric and…"

Before that moment, Leonard Morton had never kissed Amaryllis Larson, although he had wanted to several times as they walked the shores of Candlewood Lake or strolled among the tall trees of Cathedral Pines. However, Len kissed her now. Amy's lips were soft and firm as he imagined flower petals would be. She giggled in mid-kiss. "What?" Len asked, inches from her pretty face.

"I was wondering when you would finally do that," Amy sighed. "And wondering what the heck took you so long," she added, raising a perfectly-shaped eyebrow.

Len didn't know what to say. "I wasn't sure what you'd think," he stammered, "considering what I was."

"And what exactly are you, Mr. Leonard Morton?" Amy prodded. Gosh, she was lovely, Len thought, with her large eyes the shade of caramel, her smooth, pearly skin and hair the color of molasses.

"I...I'm...not like you," he faltered.

"Why, aren't you human?" Amy pushed.

"Of course, but..."

"For a second, I thought you came from another planet," she said. "Like *Invasion of the Body Snatchers*."

"I'm human," Len insisted, straightening his necktie. "But my mother was a negro and my father was white."

The other people standing around Len and Amy in the garden fell away. Suddenly dark, suddenly, it was just the two of them, illuminated only by candlelight. Amy took Len's hand. "I thought you knew."

"Knew what?"

"Knew that I was just like you," Amy told him. Len was silent; it couldn't be true. "Like that girl 'Jane' in *Imitation of Life*," Amy explained. "You've seen the picture, right?"

Len nodded. He stared at Amy, dumbfounded. "But your skin, your hair, I...I..."

"I straighten my hair with lye," she continued. "If I don't, it gets as kinky as yours." Amy reached out and caressed the short crop of curls that covered the top of Len's head. He was so happy he thought he might cry, but instead, Len pulled Amy close. Granny Lulu watched through Feel Good Food's window as she spoke with Mrs. Simpson. "But it wouldn't have mattered," Amy told Len. "I would have fallen in love with you anyhow."

He pulled away. "Love?" Len said.

"Love," Amy repeated. "Are you going to run away?" she wondered. "Some men run away when they hear that word."

"Well, I'm not some men," Len told her. He clasped Amy's fingers and said, "There's somebody I want you to meet." They went off to find his grandmother, Len tugging Amy's hand so she'd follow. She did.

George and Elaine Thomas looked out among the varied wedding guests, the number of which seemed to grow. Passersby who may have been walking their dogs or simply out for a spring stroll stopped when they saw the boisterous celebration. Then they came in to wish the newlyweds well and ended up staying for a nosh. They would no doubt become new customers in the coming weeks, especially after sampling the eatery's food.

The Thomases were discussing the success—or failure—of Feel Good Food in such a rural place. When Tiger first proposed opening a suburban outpost, George had his doubts. "It can either fly or fail," George had told his wife in private.

Elaine had worried too. "We know it works in the city but what about with country folks?"

"We'll just have to take that leap of faith," George told his wife with false confidence. In truth, George was worried himself. "We just have to trust Tiger's intuition," he sighed.

To this, Elaine sucked her teeth which she sometimes did instead of saying, "We'll see."

But this day, months after their initial conversation about the proposed restaurant, George and Elaine *had* seen. They had seen that Feel Good Food was embraced by this sleepy Connecticut Yankee town which was ripe for something new. Chamber maids and Chamber of Commerce members, bank employees and supermarket workers alike had given the restaurant their stamp of approval. The two evenings a week Feel Good Food offered supper had proven to be very popular and they were considering the possibility of serving more suppers, perhaps shifting from breakfast and lunch to lunch and dinner. Time would tell.

When Len joined Granny Lulu and Mrs. Simpson's talking circle, Mrs. Simpson seamlessly joined Rose and Sully, requesting Rose's meatball recipe. Len's grandmother, who was initially skeptical of everyone in this odd country bumpkin town, immediately liked Amy. She was honest and strong and funny and serious all at once. And quite attractive.

Upon the asking, Amy gave Granny Lulu the condensed version of what had brought her to "Shady Pines"—the name the elderly woman insisted upon calling Sherman. Granny nodded in approval as Amy talked about how she'd come to love the town. "I see what you mean," Granny Lulu concluded when Amy finished. "It's the kind of place a body can grow a family in, can grow old in." Len silently hoped his grandmother would agree to grow older in Sherman with them.

With sirens and lights blaring, police cars screeched to a halt in front of Feel Good Food but not to curtail the party but to congratulate the couple. The restaurant had quickly become the local cops' favorite place for meal breaks so they knew the staff well. "Best wishes to the new Mr. and Mrs. Sullivan," the sheriff blasted over the bullhorn. The officers were gently coerced into having a piece of wedding cake, then got into their squad cars for they were still on the clock.

Of its own accord, the party eventually disbanded, the revelers leaving first in pairs, then in handfuls. They retired to their homes, to their motel rooms or to their cars to make the drive back to Brooklyn, bolstered by Ron's potent Columbian coffee. Stan and Wendy's relatives piled into their vehicles, enduring the short trip to the Rocky River Inn while the newlyweds lingered awhile, studying the constellations on the clear spring evening.

"Can you believe it, husband?" Wendy asked.

Stan shook his head. "No, wife, I can't," he answered and kissed her. "I'll make a good partner. I promise," he added.

"I know you will," she told him. "You're already pretty swell. But don't let it go to your head."

It was Wendy's turn to drive the Bel Air. She maneuvered confidently along the pitch-black roads, lit only by the car's headlamps, the moon and the stars. Wendy had memorized the way to the hotel and didn't need to ask Stan for directions. He admired his wife's profile, strong and beautiful, in the dashboard light and her smooth hands on the red Bakelite steering wheel. Silently to himself, Stan thought, 'Wife, wife, wife...'

Wendy contemplated her husband, smiled and wondered aloud, "What in the world are you thinking?"

"Nothing," he said, "and everything."

At the door to their room, Stan paused. "What?" Wendy asked, removing her shoes at the doormat. "Did you lose the key?"

Stan's response was scooping Wendy into his arms. "I've got to carry you over the threshold," he explained. As Stan struggled to get the key into the slot, balancing Wendy on one knee, he joked, "Maybe you shouldn't have had that last slice of cake."

Wendy elbowed Stan. "Keep that up and you won't be married for long, buster," she said.

Their accommodations were the closest thing the Rocky River Inn had to a honeymoon suite. It was a spacious, one-roomed cabin set apart from the string of other rooms and overlooked the river. Practically square, at one end was a small sitting room consisting of a loveseat and chair, both covered in the same woodsy fabric. Off to the side was a round bistro-style table and two café chairs. The thick brocade fabric echoed that of the sofa and its mate. At the far end of the room, on a platform, was a king-sized bed with a maroon satin spread upon which were scattered matching tufted pillows. Beyond the bedroom area was the door to a nicely-appointed bathroom with a shower stall, a claw-footed tub, a sink, vanity and commode.

It was the first either had seen of their digs for the night. Harry and Sully had thoughtfully dropped off their satchels of clothing earlier. "Pretty swanky for a one-horse town, huh?" Stan said.

"Not bad," Wendy agreed and jumped onto the bed. Stan followed. They had both waited so long for this moment, what was the bother to wait a bit longer? They spoke in hushed tones as though someone else might hear but there was no one else, just the two of them, finally alone.

Again, Stan and Wendy kissed, this time longer, slower, deeper, for what was the hurry? Twenty-three years old, they had all the time in the world. Or so they thought, as most twenty-three-year-olds do.

Stan ventured beneath the layers of lace and satin, tracing his way up Wendy's stockinged calf to the ticklish back of her knee and just above her garters to her creamy thigh. Stopping at the band of elastic at the crease of her thigh, he slipped down her silky bloomers, then laughed. They were bright red and tarty, so unlike the rest of her outfit.

"Mrs. Wong gave them to me," Wendy explained, balling up the panties in her fist. "Red is a lucky color for the Chinese. Remember? 'Good marriage, many babies,' Mrs. Wong said when I opened the box."

"And you believed her?" Stan asked.

"Come on, they're pretty," she told him. "And they're so soft."

Wendy ran the crimson silk across Stan's cheek. He detected the faint musk of her on the imported cloth. Wendy slipped the underpants across Stan's teeth, grazing his mouth, his lips. No one had to tell Wendy what to do. She needed no book, no manual—though her girlfriends had gotten her a marriage treatise of sorts called *Perfect Wives in Ideal Homes* as a joke. Wendy just instinctively knew how to respond. Her body had craved Stan's for so long that it held all of the answers within. Not even the worldly Betsy Mulaney knew more than Wendy did at that moment.

One instant, Wendy let Stan take her and the next, the tables shifted and he allowed her to be the aggressor. Their bodies fit together perfectly. There was no pain, no blood, just a brief tug of resistance then a letting go, a sigh of flesh and a gasp. There was no shame, no trepidation. They had been accustomed to each other's bodies, with each other's presence for so many years that even these new roles seemed comfortable and right.

So, the push and pull of love began, a brief tumble at first, then more complex unions for longer stretches of time. Wendy and Stan drifted off to sleep tangled in each other's limbs then woke in mid-stroke, as though carrying on from a dream. At times, slumber and wakefulness seemed one in the same, heavy with otherworldliness. They didn't speak often—there was no need to—instead, their gestures, their shudders, their gyrations were the soundless words they used.

Well after dawn, they heard a strange rattling and a soft knock on the door followed by the tap of footsteps moving away. Wendy slipped on the dressing gown from Henrietta's, the shop on Ninth Street where most Brooklyn brides' peignoir sets were purchased. Outside the door stood a tea cart brimming with fresh fruits, muffins, butter and jams plus a pot of tea and a silver thermos of coffee. "Did you order this?" Wendy asked Stan.

He pulled his silk boxers—a gift from his father, who explained, "Every fellow should have a pair of nice drawers for his wedding night"—onto his sore body, shaking his head. "There's a note," Stan told her.

Wendy took the slip of paper and read, "We thought you might need this to keep up your strength." It was unsigned. Wendy promptly blushed; Stan laughed. He could only imagine who sent the note and nourishment. Untroubled, Stan wheeled the tea cart into the room and parked it beside the café table. They ate and drank their fill, ravenous.

After breakfast, Wendy and Stan both squeezed into the shower stall, scrubbing and lathering each other with renewed interest, but quickly, feverishly, because the checkout hour loomed. At any moment, there might be the trepidatious rap on the cabin door from departing relatives.

Dressed, packed and presentable, the couple knocked on their parents' doors before anyone considered summoning the newlyweds. Their cars were packed in no time. "Let's not make a big deal about saying goodbye," Stan announced from the clinches of Rose's bear hug. Pulling away, he looked his mother straight in the eye and added, "Okay?" They agreed. "After all, we'll see you in a few weeks, right?"

"Right," Rose said, managing to keep her tears in check.

"Right," Jo echoed, her lower lip quivering. Overnight, Wendy had gone from being a child, her child, to a wife, Stan's wife.

"Take care of my little girl," Harry told Stan, kindly rather than sounding like a warning.

"Pop!" Wendy piped. "I'm not a girl anymore. I'm a woman. And we'll take care of each other, thanks."

Well before noon, the Brooklyn caravan began its slow journey east, minus Granny Lulu, who had decided to stay in Sherman for a spell. There were hugs, waves, quips and a few false starts before the line of cars veered onto Kent Road, one by one, and faded into the distance. Wendy and Stan watched them go, silently, side by side.

When the vehicles disappeared from sight, they turned to each other. "So," the wife said.

"So," the husband said.

They reached for each other's hand and walked toward where their car was parked. Stan busted out laughing when he caught sight of the Bel Air. Wendy's laughter soon followed. "No wonder they were so quiet," she giggled. Their wedding-gift Chevy was covered with crepe-paper streamers and strung with tin cans, its wide back window filled with soap letters that announced, "JUST MARRIED!"

"Those stinkers," Stan said, shaking his head. He sounded just like Grandma Bridget when one of her yapping Pomeranians got underfoot.

At first, Stan wanted to clean off the back window and remove the dangling cans but Wendy made him leave everything intact. Although Stan feigned annoyance, he was secretly pleased—he would have been disappointed if their family hadn't decorated their car like this.

The newlyweds drove toward Sherman, toward the cottage they had rented which would be their new home, their first home together. It must have rained in the early morning hours because the streets were still damp. The gray clouds were shifting, giving way to a sliver of blue that slowly grew and spread across the sky. Stretching from one corner of the firmament to the other was a faint rainbow. Where the rainbow began and where it ended was anyone's guess.

CODA

The true beauty of roses is that they return each year, no matter what. They challenge wrought iron fences. They stand up to barbed wire. No matter how harsh the winter, no matter how unforgiving the pruning, no matter how dry the summer, roses come back, stronger, more insistent and more lovely than ever each year.

The same could be said of people—each generation is more resilient, each is smarter, each moves further from repeating the mistakes of the previous age. Each is healthier. Each is better.

The "roses" in the Paradiso garden grew more lush and more striking as time progressed. It had been this way for generations. And because of this, there was reason to believe that the garden would continue to thrive long after these individuals were gone.

Some of their stories were passed from mouth to ear. Others were written down. By who? Wendy? Chiara Rose? Someone else? Does it really matter? Were these tales true? Were they fabricated? Is it important? The only thing of significance is that these stories, these people, live on, love on, long after they have become stardust.

And this is what really matters—that we survive in some way, somehow. That we are not forgotten. That our stories, our essence endures, much like the scent of a late Brooklyn rose on a warm, lingering October breeze lives on long after its image has faded. You close your eyes, you breathe deep, and it is there.

Always.

ABOUT THE AUTHOR

Brooklyn born and bred, Catherine Gigante-Brown writes fiction, nonfiction, poetry and plays. Her articles have appeared in publications like *Time Out, New York, Ravishly, Essence* and *Industry*. Her poetry and fiction appear in several anthologies. A handful of her films and theatrical works have been produced. Her first novel, *The El*, was published by Volossal in 2012, and her second, *Different Drummer*, was released in 2015. Her third, *The Bells of Brooklyn*, is a sequel to *The El* and was published in 2017. *Better than Sisters*, a Young Adult/Women's crossover novel, followed in 2019. She is working with a creative team (which includes Volossal's Vinnie Corbo) to bring a musical version of *Different Drummer* to the stage.

Catherine still lives in Brooklyn with her husband and son.

ACKNOWLEDGEMENTS

When I finished writing *The Bells of Brooklyn* and gave it to my publisher, I thought I was finished with that loud, loving, Italian-American family who lived on Forty-Seventh Street in Borough Park. Then Vinnie told me, "You know, people love trilogies…" My first thought was no. No way. I was done. The Paradisos and their kin were put to rest, literally and figuratively. It was time to move on. And yet… here we are.

I chose to begin the story of *Brooklyn Roses* in the year I was born—1959—and to tie up loose ends. To further complicate the business of writing a book, I decided to name every chapter (except for the first and last) for a type of rose. After I wrote of Rose's health struggles, I was diagnosed with a recurrence breast cancer. But like the Paradiso roses, I endure. I finished writing the novel as I recovered from surgery and while on chemotherapy. In so many ways, it was therapeutic for me.

Big thanks go to my husband Peter for standing beside me, still. And to Vinnie Corbo of Volossal for saying "Hell yes" to *The El* almost a decade ago. And to his wife, my friend Jackie, who, once upon a time, hinted that Vinnie would be happy to publish a book of mine that no other publisher wanted. And deep thanks to all of you, who continue to read the books that nobody else wanted.

I would also like to thank my family for always supporting me and being my biggest cheerleaders, especially my sister Liz, for whom the character Beth was named. And I wish to acknowledge faithful readers like Stephanie Simmons, Maria Cornacchio-Kehoe, Valerie Hodgson, Susan D'Alessandro and Theresa Tozzolino, who keep asking for more. Gratitude to my cousin Jediah Cirigliano for letting me use the name of his culinary endeavor, Feel Good Food. A nod also to Dr. Robert Seminara, the kind surgeon who saved my life in 2013 so I could write this book and several others. And many thanks to my friend Chiara D'Agostino, for letting me borrow her lovely, lyrical first name. Long may you shine!